Praise for Gwen Madoc:

'A gritty Welsh saga in the tradition of Meg Hutchinson.'
Middlesborough Evening Gazette

'Compelling tale of passion, betrayal and tragedy . . . Rich characterisation.' *South Wales Evening Post*

'Poignant story . . . indomitable writing talent . . . a fast and exciting style of storytelling . . . Quite simply the greatest.'
North Wales Chronicle

'A wonderfully warm Welsh saga.'
Coventry Evening Telegraph

'This book is compelling reading. Gwen Madoc is to be congratulated on a most enjoyable and very fine piece of literature.' *Bangor Chronicle*

By the same author

Daughter of Shame
By Lies Betrayed
Bad to the Bone

About the author

Gwen Madoc lives in Swansea with her husband, Harry. She worked as a medical secretary and managed a medical clinic before joining the Civil Service. She studied for five years with the Open University. She loves Swansea and its people, and has a keen interest in local history

GWEN MADOC

The Stolen Baby

HODDER

Copyright © 2005 by Gwen Madoc

First published in Great Britain in 2005 by Hodder and Stoughton
First published in paperback in Great Britain in 2005 by Hodder and Stoughton
A division of Hodder Headline

The right of Gwen Madoc to be identified as the Author
of the Work has been asserted by her in accordance
with the Copyright, Designs and Patents Act 1988.

A Hodder paperback

2

A CIP catalogue record for this title
is available from the British Library

ISBN 0 340 83523 0

Typeset in Monotype Plantin Light by
Hewer Text Limited, Edinburgh
Printed and bound by
Mackays of Chatham Ltd, Chatham, Kent

Hodder Headline's policy is to use papers that are natural,
renewable and recyclable products and made from wood
grown in sustainable forests. The logging and manufacturing
processes are expected to conform to the environmental
regulations of the country of origin.

Hodder and Stoughton Ltd
A division of Hodder Headline
338 Euston Road
London NW1 3BH

I

Bronwen Jenkins raced heedlessly down the steep lane leading to Ystrad Farm and the meadows below the Marquis Arms public house, sobbing as she ran, praying she would be in time to stop her father, Big Jim Jenkins, from being injured or even killed.

But what could she do, a mere girl, against a crowd of feverishly excited men gathered there to watch this barbaric fight? They were probably already charged up with blood-lust. She felt sick at the thought.

Granddad Lewis was too old and feeble to intervene. If only her mother was not away in Llanelly at this time, looking after Aunt Sarah. Mam would have got wind of Da's folly before today and put a stop to it.

Bronwen felt a sudden impatience with her father as she ran. He had promised faithfully he would never again risk life and limb in the prize ring no matter how high the purse. But he had broken that promise as soon as Mam's back was turned. Now it was up to Bronwen to prevent a tragedy if she could. But she must!

Clutching at her skirts to raise them above the dusty track churned up by the recent passage of many wheels, she rushed on, only to turn on her ankle, and felt sharp pain shoot up her leg. She cried out at the anguish of it, but would not stop in her flight and stumbled forward. Da needed her.

She could not glimpse the fields ahead because of the thickness of hedges and trees between, but the excited roar of the crowd gathered there told her the fight was already underway, and her heart thudded against her ribs in dread at what she would find.

She emerged from the lane into the big top meadow and lurched to a halt, astonished and aghast at the sight before her. She had thought to see a crowd of men, perhaps twenty, which would have been a strange enough sight in the small village of Cwmrhyddin Cross, but here hundreds were milling about.

And another amazing sight which she had never witnessed before was the scores of vehicles and horses, halted haphazardly around the field. Tradesmen's traps, country gigs, as well as filthy-looking carts, rubbed shafts with fine carriages, barouches and broughams, so that every space of the field's circumference was occupied. Scores of men, of all classes and position, had clambered on top of these vehicles to get a better view, and others had climbed trees nearby. Bronwen stared, bewildered. Men must have come from all over the county, if not the country, to watch the terrible spectacle.

The main focus was the centre of the field, with crowds on foot pressing forward. Their feverish masculine excitement was almost tangible and seemed to thicken the very air about her and Bronwen thought she would choke on it. Suddenly she felt, as a female, she was treading where she had no right to tread, but convention would not stop her, yet she was fearful.

Weaving cautiously around the nearest vehicles Bronwen moved towards the centre throng, the pain in her ankle forgotten. Several men were standing around the edges of the field with slips of paper in their hands talking earnestly with others. Nearby, a man in a dusty top hat was chiding another wearing a labourer's shapeless felt cap.

'Three pennies! A measly three pennies!' he was exclaiming. 'Don't waste my time! The local man is favourite to win. Put a sovereign on him, man, and if you haven't a sovereign, chance a florin. You'll not see another fight like this for many a year.'

With a despondent shrug the labourer moved away, and Bronwen bravely accosted the top-hatted man. 'Where's Big Jim Jenkins?' she demanded, guessing he was a bookmaker. 'Take me to him.'

He leered at her. 'No good plying your trade before the fight ends, my pretty. Afterwards you'll get plenty of takers.' He rubbed his bristled jaw with his thumb. 'Including me. You're a nice bit of skirt, and no mistake.'

Affronted, Bronwen stepped back from him, her face flaming. 'Big Jim is my father,' she cried. 'And you'll answer to him for that insult.'

He grinned. 'Big Jim has got his hands full at the moment,' he said. 'Slasher Tonkin was busting him up good last time I looked.'

Bronwen was appalled. 'You said he was favourite!'

'That's for the punters, you silly wench. Big Jim doesn't stand a chance against the Slasher. Outclassed he is. But these old pugilists never learn.'

Bronwen wrung her hands in distress. 'I must put a stop to it.'

'Only Death, a magistrate or Big Jim's second can stop it now.'

Suddenly there was a great deep-throated roar from the crowds, and the top-hatted man rushed away towards the mobbing men. Bronwen ran after him. She was almost hanging on to his coat tails as he forced his way through the throng, obviously intent on getting to the ringside to see the action.

The foul smells of alcohol, tobacco, sweat and fusty clothing assailed her nostrils as she was pressed on all sides by men's bodies, their shouts and curses almost splitting her eardrums. Arms raised, fists punching the air, eyes gleaming with feverish ferocity they appeared not to notice a mere woman among them, so intent were they on the bloody struggle taking place before their gaze. Steeling herself she clung determinedly to Top-hat's coat, and suddenly, shockingly she was at the ring-side.

The outer perimeter of the ring had been invaded by the inflamed spectators, many of whom were now pressing against the wooden rail surrounding the fighting area. Although the fighters faced each other on a wooden platform raised several inches above the ground, Bronwen could see they had barely sixteen square feet in which to move and avoid each other's blows.

She nearly jumped out of her skin as a whip cracked viciously on the far side of the ring. It cracked again as some man tried in vain to keep order against the mob. A few of the nearest spectators also flinched at the warning and tried to step back, but within a moment they surged forward again, trapped by pressure from behind. Bronwen felt the pressure herself, and had to struggle hard not to be wedged against the platform.

Totally overwhelmed by the deafening noise, the odours and the fierce tension that exuded from the crowding men, she was afraid to look at the fighters, afraid of what she might see.

The gleaming animated faces of those pressing close about her reminded her of the illustrations of demons she had seen in church pamphlets. Hell must be like this, she thought, and recalled the Reverend Isaiah Pugh's dire warnings from the pulpit every Sunday on such evils. If only Da would listen.

Gathering her courage she looked directly up at the fighters. Two men, stripped to the waist, faced each other, their muscled bodies glossy with sweat from their exertions and the hot afternoon sun.

At first Bronwen could not distinguish one from the other. The men stepped cautiously round and about in the ever-decreasing confines of the ring, dodging blows and lashing out with bare knuckles. As they changed position she realised that the smaller of two was her father, Big Jim.

She could not prevent a scream erupting as she caught sight of his poor face. Blood was pouring from his nose, and one brow was also bloody from a terrible gash, the eye completely closed and already swollen. His opponent aimed for the damage time and time again.

'Ho! Ho! The claret's flowing all right,' a man next to her yelled gleefully at no one in particular. 'Who'll give me odds on for the Slasher?'

Bronwen was appalled at his callousness, and deliberately kicked out, catching him on his ankle bone. He yelped and toppled backwards. She did not bother to see whether he had fallen under foot, but allowed the pressure from behind to move her closer the rail.

'Da! Da! Come away home!' she shrieked at her father, but her voice was lost among the din.

She looked around desperately for someone to help her. Top-hat had vanished from sight, but on the other side of the ring, crouching on one knee in a corner she spotted a very familiar face, Lloyd Treharn, the blacksmith's son, her very own sweetheart.

Lloyd was aiding and abetting Da! Bronwen stared at her sweetheart, appalled and hurt. She could not believe that Lloyd of all people was standing by while this terrible punishment was meted out to her father.

Anger flamed in her breast and she began to fight her way around the edge of the ring, kicking at shins and ankles and elbowing her way through the throng. Panting and out of breath she reached the corner where Lloyd knelt.

'Lloyd!'

His gaze was glued on the fight, and he didn't hear her. She tugged at his loose shirt sleeve. 'Lloyd, for pity's sake,' she screeched at him. 'Stop this butchery.'

He turned his head to glance at whoever was bothering him, a look of irritation on his handsome sun-burnished face. When he saw it was Bronwen, he leaped to his feet, his face whitening under his tan.

'Bron! What the devil are *you* doing here? A woman shouldn't witness this. You must go!'

'I'm not leaving without Da,' Bronwen shouted above the noise. 'You must stop the fight, Lloyd. I can't believe you're helping him in this madness.' She shook her head vehemently. 'I'll never forgive you for this. Never!'

'I can't stop it,' he shouted back. 'Big Jim would kill me if I tried. He won't stop until it's over, one way or another. He has his pride.'

Furious, Bronwen began to clamber up onto the platform. There was a bucket of water in the corner, and she made a grab for it. 'I'll stop it myself,' she yelled at him. 'I know what to do. I'll throw in the sponge.'

'Bron! Don't be a little fool!' He tried to push her back down. 'You'll shame us all.'

'Better to be shamed than dead,' Bronwen shouted, struggling in his grasp.

The bucket overturned in the scuffle, water and sponge falling on to the turf out of reach. Bronwen had both feet on the edge of the ring now, and despite struggling against Lloyd's hands pushing at her, managed to wriggle past the wooden rail. But Lloyd immediately grabbed her about the waist again. He was a big strapping lad, and she knew his strength would be too much for her, so she kicked his shin hard. Surprised and in pain he loosened his grip. It was enough for Bronwen to dash forward to the centre of the prize ring.

The boxers were circling each other again, with eyes for no one else but each other and the next punch. Slasher Tonkin's immense back was turned to her as she ran forward, her arms waving desperately to get her father's attention.

'Da! Da! Stop! Don't go on any more.'

Big Jim spotted her with his one good eye and his jaw dropped open with astonishment and dismay.

'Bron!'

He had no time to say another word. Slasher's bare fist smashed into the side of his already wounded head with such force that a new gash opened up and blood spurted out. Bronwen screamed at the terrible sound of bone hitting flesh, and whimpered in terror as Big Jim's knees buckled and he began to sink down. Before he hit the floor, Slasher struck again, a powerful blow to his opponent's unprotected throat, and Big Jim measured his length on the boards of the platform, his face covered in blood.

There were shouts from the mob.

'Foul! Foul!'

'Take him away. He's done!'

Bronwen was grabbed from behind, and unceremoniously pushed to one side. She hardly recognised Lloyd's voice, thick with fury. 'Look what you've done, you stupid girl!'

Appalled, Bronwen could only stand, her hands covering her mouth in horror of what had happened. Had she really been the cause of it?

Slasher Tonkin, built like a mountain, stood with feet astride Big Jim's prone form, staring down at the beaten man.

Then Meurig Caradog, Bronwen's employer at the bakery, and landlord of Ystrad Farm, jumped into the ring, to be greeted with jeers and a chorus of 'Foul!'

Bronwen was astonished to see him here taking part in this terrible spectacle. His wife Mary was supposed to be her mother's longstanding best friend. He must have known of her father's plans and yet, seeing her every day at the bakery, he had said nothing to her. She glowered at him but he ignored her.

As referee, Meurig gestured Slasher to stand back so that Big

Jim's seconds could see to him. Two men moved towards the fallen man, Ben Talbot, the tenant of Ystrad Farm who was also Big Jim's employer, and Tucker the Butcher. The whole village seemed to be here, watching her father's shame and humiliation.

They dragged Big Jim to his corner, and hoisting up his prone form, sat him on Lloyd's knee. A silence had settled over the crowds now as they waited to see if Big Jim would be able to step up to the scratch mark. But there was no more life in him than a rag doll; his body was limp as though boneless while his bloodied and battered head lolled forward on to his chest.

Bronwen caught the scared looks that passed between Ben Talbot and Lloyd, and Billy Tucker shook his head sadly, and with an anguished cry, she turned, pointing an accusing finger at Slasher Tonkin waiting in his corner.

'You murderer!' she screamed at him, her voice ringing in the silence. 'You've killed him! You've killed my Da.'

2

Fletcher Watkins lolled in a chair before the mahogany desk in his brother's over-furnished and over-heated study at the house just outside the village of Roath, nonchalantly flicking dust from his top boots with a fine linen handkerchief.

He suppressed a sigh of irritation at the knowledge that he was in for another boring lecture on propriety, and did not need to look at his brother's expression to confirm it; he could smell Tecwyn's disapproval in the air.

He waited for Tecwyn to begin the tirade, but when the long drawn out silence continued, Fletcher decided to open hostilities himself.

'This is the second time in a month you've summoned me to Brynhyfryd House, Tec,' he began abrasively. 'And I don't like it above half.'

'Nor do I!' Sir Tecwyn Watkins exploded. He waved a sheet of paper in the air. It looked like a tailor's bill. 'Five hundred pounds! You must possess the largest wardrobe in Cardiff. It won't do, Fletch, it won't do at all.'

Fletcher shrugged. 'A gentleman must look the ticket, Tec,' he answered, trying to keep contempt from his voice. 'Surely even you must realise that.' He gave his brother a scornful glance. 'But perhaps you don't, cut off as you are in this rural backwater, away from the hurly-burly of fashionable society.'

'I've never envied the life you lead,' Tecwyn said pithily.

'A pointless and wasteful life to my mind.' He picked up another paper. 'Here's a sample of that waste, a demand for a thousand pounds. A thousand lost on gaming! Damn it, Fletch! This is too much. I've a mind not to pay up.'

'You must. It's a debt of honour,' Fletcher said defensively. 'And my allowance for this month is gone.'

'Honour!' Tecwyn's lips tightened. 'There's no honour in the way you live. Associating with pugilists and other scoundrels of that ilk has coarsened you, Fletch. Fashionable society might find you amusing, but you are no longer fit for decent society. You're on the high road to hell.'

Infuriated, Fletcher leaped to his feet. 'You sanctimonious prig!' he bellowed. 'I don't need or want your approval. How I live is none of your business.'

Tecwyn glared up at him. 'When you drag our family name through the mud it's very much my business,' he said evenly, although Fletcher could see he was barely holding his temper. 'You narrowly escaped conviction and a prison sentence last month for your part in the death of that prize-fighter in the ring.'

'I deny involvement!' Fletcher strode to the fireplace, leaning an elbow on the mantelpiece, feigning indifference.

'You were there all right,' Tecwyn said with certainty.

'Have you had the brass neck to spy on me?' Fletcher demanded huffily, trying to change the direction of the discussion.

'You were in the thick of the disgusting spectacle,' Tecwyn accused. 'Acting as the man's second. You would have gone down, Fletch, and deservedly. It was only my influence kept you from the magistrate.'

Fletcher laughed scornfully. 'What? Do you mean to tell me that Sir Tecwyn Watkins, that pillar of polite society, actually stooped to corrupting authority? You dirtied your hands to protect me? I'm touched, brother.'

'I wasn't protecting you,' Tecwyn retorted harshly. 'I was protecting our good name, which you're so willing to sully.' There was exasperation in his expression, and Fletcher felt the first quiver of uncertainty. 'You would've known the miseries of debtors' prison many times in the past,' Tecwyn went on heavily. 'Had I not intervened and settled matters.'

Fletcher bowed mockingly to cover his growing qualms. 'Thank you, brother. You have your uses, pious prude though you are.'

Tecwyn shook his head. 'It's a blessing in disguise that our sainted mother isn't here to witness your shameless conduct. Her heart would've broken to see the ne'er-do-well you've become.'

Fletcher felt the sting of that barb. 'Don't claim her as your own,' he said savagely. 'She was *my* mother, not yours. You killed *your* mother the day she birthed you.'

Tecwyn's face paled and he looked drawn, and Fletcher was pleased at the pain in his half-brother's face.

'Your mother Blanche was the only mother I ever knew,' Tecwyn said in a strangled voice. 'And I loved and respected her for the generous woman that she was. I named my daughter in her memory.'

'Poor motherless child!' Fletcher scoffed, wanting to hurt Tecwyn further. 'Some might view the loss of your own wife by the same cause as natural justice. You must hate your newborn child for taking your wife's life so soon after marriage.'

'You barbarian!' Tecwyn leaped to his feet and stepped around the desk towards his brother. 'What a monstrous thing to say to any man let alone a brother. I've a mind to knock you down.'

'Have a care, Tec,' Fletcher warned, standing erect and alert. 'I not only patronise the prize ring I also practise the sport myself.'

Tecwyn nodded as though confirming an opinion. 'You've

degenerated into a cold-hearted and callous man, Fletch, and I'm sorry to see it.'

'Save your pity for yourself, Tec,' Fletcher snapped, tiring of the conversation. 'I want none of you, neither your good opinion nor your interference.'

He began to stride towards the door to take his leave. Alexis was waiting for him, and he was already longing for her soft scented body.

'I'm not finished, damn you!' Tecwyn shouted loudly. Fletcher paused, and looked at his brother in mild surprise for Tecwyn very rarely raised his voice.

'I don't wish to hear more.'

'You will hear this,' Tecwyn said firmly. 'I'll not intercede for you again. I demand you change your ways.'

'Demand!' Fletcher was furious. 'You can demand nothing from me. I am my own man.'

'I am glad to hear you say it,' Tecwyn retorted. 'Because from this day forward you'll be responsible for your own debts. I have already issued a notice to that effect in today's *Cardiff Journal*.'

Fletcher started forward taken by surprise. 'The devil you say! You jest surely.'

Without a word Tecwyn turned back to the desk and sat down. 'I'm in no jesting mood. There are changes afoot, Fletch, and you have forced my hand with your reprehensible mode of living.'

'What are you getting at?' Fletcher moved back to the chair before the desk, placing his hands on the back. 'What are you planning, Tec?'

Tecwyn looked at him steadily, and Fletcher did not like the determined expression on his half-brother's face. Tecwyn could not stop his monthly allowance, a condition of their father's will. So what else was he planning?

Tecwyn seemed to read his thoughts. 'Under Father's will I

cannot deprive you of an allowance altogether,' he said, and Fletcher felt his muscles relax in relief. 'You can't deny you have received a very generous allowance since you were eighteen.'

Fletcher gave a derisive snort.

'An income fit for any gentleman to live a comfortable and leisurely life,' Tecwyn persisted. 'But you have squandered it year after year.'

'I need not account myself to you.'

'You need account to someone, and you will if you persist in this loose living.'

'Bah!'

'Your peers decry the prize-ring, and all the criminality that goes with it these days, as do all right-thinking people, from Her Gracious Majesty, Queen Victoria, downwards. Prize fighting is now a despised sport. Your association with it is damaging our proud name in the Principality. I suggest you seek a commission in the army. A friend of mine can arrange it for you, if you so wish.'

'I'll do no such thing!' Fletcher exclaimed heatedly and then hesitated. His brother had not suggested he enter the family business. 'You don't offer me a position I notice,' he said.

Tecwyn looked stern. 'Your dubious reputation bars that. A few years ago it would have been possible. You've sunk too low now, Fletch.'

Fletcher ground his teeth in fury. 'I'll not go quietly into the army just to suit you. I despise the need to earn a living. I was born a gentleman of leisure. It's my God-given right.'

'Then you'll find living difficult from now on,' Tecwyn said, and Fletcher thought he heard irony in his tone. 'From the new year I intend to reduce your allowance by one quarter.'

Fletcher was appalled. 'You can't do that!'

'Father gave me the power to administer your allowance as I saw fit.' He shook his head. 'I can't condone your spendthrift life any longer. When you find gainful employment, and show that you're sincere in mending your ways, I promise to review my decision.'

'But this is outrageous!' Fletcher blustered. 'I have a social position to uphold and . . . commitments.'

'You would do well to rid yourself of these so-called commitments,' Tecwyn said, and the sarcasm was now unmistakable. 'Starting with that notorious adventuress, Mrs Vansier.'

'Leave Alexis out of this,' Fletcher warned.

'Be rid of her, Fletch,' Tecwyn advised. 'Her husband, Vansier the banker, is a powerful man. He could do you and our business great harm if he chose to.'

'So that's it!' Fletcher nodded. 'The damned business again. As you've already made clear, I can never be part of that now, and so I don't give a damn what Vansier does. And as for you, Tecwyn, you can do your worst too.'

'Very well!' Tecwyn leaned back in his chair. 'I know you so well, Fletch. I knew you wouldn't toe the line, to use a term from your own beloved sport. I have taken measures.'

Fletcher felt uneasy at the decided expression that had settled on Tecwyn's face. 'What are you trying to say?'

'I've seen Partridge the lawyer, and have had a new will drawn up. It's all signed and sealed and is kept in his hands for safekeeping.'

'What?'

Tecwyn shook his head again looking saddened. 'Losing my Sarah so soon has made me aware of my own mortality. I must leave the business in competent hands. I won't betray all that Father and I have worked for all these years by letting you remain my heir.' He rose from the chair. 'You'd squander it within a year, and put hundreds out of work in the process.'

'What've you done, Tecwyn?' Fletcher could not keep the tremor from his voice. He had banked on getting the family money at some stage in his life. In fact, he knew he lived mostly on the expectation of that. Heir to the Watkins' coalmines and the immense wealth those mines had accumulated was a passport to any level of society. It *should* be his. He, too, was his father's son.

'My new heir is my newborn daughter, Blanche Sarah Watkins.'

'A two-month old baby and a mere female to boot?' Fletcher was aghast. 'Are you mad, Tecwyn?'

'When I die the estate will be held in trust until she's eighteen, and, of course, will pass to her husband on her marriage.' He smiled. 'I intend to live and see she marries the right kind of man, someone I can trust.'

'But . . . but suppose something should happen to you tomorrow?' Fletcher hissed. 'What of the business then?'

'Should anything happen to me before my daughter reaches maturity, Partridge will administer the estates and appoint any necessary managers.'

'The child might die before you,' Fletcher said anxiously. 'Who will inherit then?'

'Blanche is a healthy infant,' Tecwyn said with confidence. 'I see no reason to fear.'

'Infants die all the time,' Fletcher persisted. 'One sees tiny coffins being paraded on the streets of the town every day.'

'The children of the poor,' Tecwyn said. 'My daughter is of the privileged class. She will be protected from all ills.'

'You're not God, Tecwyn,' Fletcher said sarcastically. 'You can't foresee what He has in mind for your daughter.'

Tecwyn looked thoughtful. 'If my child dies before me, and I don't marry again and produce another heir, then the estates will revert to you, Fletcher. That distresses me, but I see no other course. If the worst should happen I leave it to your conscience not to waste what you inherit.'

Fletcher Watkins rode away from Brynhyfryd House still in shock at his half-brother's pronouncement. A female child was to inherit the Watkins' wealth and estates; unheard of after three generations of male heirs. He felt a rage rise within him at the injustice of it. Tecwyn's decision was unfair and uncalled for.

And what was he to do now? When this got out he would lose face, status and privileges. He would also lose many so-called friends. His heart gave a lurch at his next thought. He might even lose Alexis. He had no illusions about her. He knew what she was, but he could not live without her.

Engulfed in rage, he drove his spurs into his horse's sides unnecessarily, and the creature leaped forward, whinnying in pain. He felt pain, too, he thought savagely. Within the space of a moment as his brother announced his intentions, Fletcher's whole life, his future had changed completely, his expectations dashed. Now in his twenty-fifth year, he had depended on inheriting the Watkins' wealth by the time he was, say forty, still young enough to enjoy all the pleasures a man of quality can expect.

Damn Tecwyn to hell!

He reined in his horse, halting its panicked scamper. What could he do to prevent this catastrophe? Only death would save him. And the child might die yet. And so might Tecwyn. Accidents happened without warning. Children died every day and not only those of the poor.

But such vain hopes would not sustain him. The child might well live and grow to womanhood. With a handsome fortune at her fingertips she would not be short of suitors, and once married every penny would pass completely to her husband and any sons she might have. Then not even death could relieve his fate of ruination.

He could never live the way he wished on three quarters of his present income. He recalled Tecwyn's remarks about debtors' prison and knew them to be true. He had escaped by the skin of his teeth, and like a fool he had taken his brother's benefaction for granted.

Penury and a worse fate stared him in the face. Young as he was, he knew debtors' prison would break him. He had seen it happen to other men. And Alexis would not stand by him. She had other lovers, he knew that, but closed his eyes against the knowledge. He had to if he wanted to keep her, for no one man would monopolise her favours, not without a great incentive. Alexis loved money.

Death *was* the only way out. But not for him. He was young and had too much to live for, provided he had the means to live as he chose. He *must* have the life he deserved, and if someone else must die to fulfil that end, then so be it.

It would be better if the child did die, and then Tecwyn might die, too, of a broken heart.

By the time he reached his lodgings near the castle at the centre of the town, where Alexis waited to pleasure him this night, Fletcher had made up his mind.

The child, Blanche, would die and soon.

3

Fletcher Watkins sat slumped at a table in the far corner of the public bar of The King George, a foul-smelling tavern close to the docks in Tiger Bay. He would not be seen dead in such a place normally but tonight the fetid atmosphere suited his mood. It had been a miserable Christmas time, and the coming New Year promised to be even grimmer. He intended to get very, very drunk, and here, a world away from his own social circle, he could behave as he chose, out of sight of friend or acquaintance.

He gazed around at the pub's seedy clientele, easy women, thieves and pickpockets, the ragbag and dregs of the town. To an onlooker, he reflected with irony, he must seem one of them, clad as he was in rough clothing. And in monetary terms he was at their level, or soon would be, so he had better get used to such haunts.

If Alexis could see him now she would scoff at his weakness. And he did feel weak and helpless. It was one thing to decide Tecwyn's daughter must die. It was entirely another to bring that death about. Try as he might he could not formulate a plan that would achieve the deed without getting caught. He intended to live not swing from the gallows.

At the thought of Alexis he downed half of his drink in a hurry, and coughed as it caught in his throat. Her lovely face had been so hard looking when she had given him her ultimatum. No money – no favours. She would not warm his bed again until he was once more Tecwyn's heir. That had cut deep. He had hoped he meant something more to her than the means of good living. She had raged at him, as though being cut from the will were his fault entirely.

She would not stay another moment she said with a man who could not pay her dressmaker's bills. He had begged her that, even if she would not stay, she would be discreet about his financial problems, but she had readily talked. Now the whole town knew, and if the child did meet a foul end in the future he would be the first to be suspected. He was done for.

'Here, wench!' Fletcher waved an arm at a slovenly girl bringing a tray of tankards to a table nearby. 'Fetch me a bottle of your best whisky and a clean glass.'

She tossed her head. 'Let's see the colour of your money first, mister. Been had like that before, I have.'

'Why, you impertinent drab!' Fletcher shouted. 'I'll see the landlord. Fetch him now.'

'You don't want to be doing that, Mr Watkins,' a gravelly voice said at his elbow. 'That's asking to be slung out onto the street, that is, and with a fresh crack in your cranium, to boot.'

Fletcher whirled in his seat and stared up at a fashionably dressed man he knew only too well and disliked intensely, a gambling acquaintance, Jebediah Crabbe.

'I don't need advice from you, Crabbe,' Fletcher snarled, infuriated to be recognised by such as him. Scheming, bad-tempered and crooked in his dealings, Crabbe was the last person Fletcher wanted to witness his slide into penury.

Crabbe did not reply, but held up a sovereign, smiling at the smirking girl. 'Fetch that bottle like the man said, my pretty peach, and two glasses.'

He flipped the coin at her – it landed in the low neck of her grubby dress, lodging neatly between her breasts. She gave a laugh that was more like the screaming of a cat than human and bounced off.

'I hardly recognised you in them old togs, Mr Watkins,' Crabbe said conversationally.

His pleasant tone roused Fletcher's suspicions that this meeting was not by chance. These were confirmed when Crabbe sat down at the table uninvited and removed his hat to balance it on his knee.

'It doesn't do to wear fine clothes in this part of town,' Fletcher said morosely, wondering what the devil Crabbe wanted with him. 'It invites attack.'

'Very wise, I'm sure,' Crabbe agreed. 'Though I hear you have little worth stealing these days.'

Fletcher scowled at his impertinence. Crabbe, although a taciturn character, was usually deferential with him. 'Mind your manners, Crabbe,' he said shortly. 'I may be tapped at the moment, but I'm still a gentleman.'

'Maybe so, but it's the money that talks, Mr Watkins,' Crabbe said. 'I'm sure that truth is coming home to you now.'

'What the devil are you getting at?' Fletcher did not really need to ask but was irked by the scornful light in Crabbe's eyes.

'A little bird told me you were moving down to Queer Street,' Crabbe answered. 'You have my sympathies, Mr Watkins. An uncomfortable position to be in.'

Fletcher stared at him with open dislike. A biggish man solidly made, Crabbe was no more than two years older than he, yet seemed much more seasoned and weathered. A product of his lowly class, Fletcher concluded sourly, for despite Crabbe's fashionable clothes, his uneducated accent gave him away. But the big man's choice of words made Fletcher uneasy.

'What little bird?' Crabbe's success with the ladies, though mystifying, was legendary, and Fletcher thought suddenly of

Alexis, and jealous anger rose. 'You've been seeing Alexis, damn you!'

'No, no, Mr Watkins,' Crabbe said smoothly. 'I don't have the pleasure of Mrs Vansier's acquaintance, to my deepest regret. A handful, that one.' He winked and leered. 'Two handfuls, eh! She was showing off the handfuls in an opera box at The Adelphi Theatre last night in the company of a prosperous looking gentleman. Very luscious!'

Enraged, Fletcher half rose from his chair, feeling he would choke at the man's coarse joke against Alexis. 'Shut your filthy mouth, Crabbe,' he muttered with difficulty. 'Or I'll shut it for you.'

'Now! Now!' Crabbe's tone changed to harshness immediately. 'That's no way to talk to a friend who's come to get you out of a tight hole.' He tapped his cane lightly on the floor. 'And certainly not with Betsy here.'

Fletcher sat down hurriedly recognising that as a very real threat. Everyone knew Crabbe referred to his cane as Betsy. A prissy name for a deadly weapon, for the cane itself was a sheath for a rapier. Unlike Fletcher, Crabbe had no fear of attack in this squalid part of town, not when he had Betsy with him, and it was said he was not averse to using the rapier to devastating effect on the slightest pretext.

'You're no friend of mine, Crabbe,' Fletcher said sullenly.

'That's where you're wrong, Mr Watkins,' his dangerous companion replied. 'I may be the only friend you have just now.'

'Then God help me!'

'He works in mysterious ways, Mr Watkins. I like to think He sent me to help you.'

Fletcher frowned at the hypocrisy. 'What are you blathering about?'

The girl brought the bottle of whisky and glasses at that moment and dumped them on the table. She reluctantly offered Crabbe the change from the sovereign, but he pushed it back into her hand.

'Keep that, my lovely one,' he said huskily. 'You might earn it later.' He winked at her and squeezed her hand. She giggled and waltzed away, swinging her hips seductively.

Fletcher's lips drew back in disgust. 'How could you contemplate going with a sluttish girl like that?' he asked.

Crabbe chuckled. 'I've no intention of going with her, as you so delicately put it. The last thing I need is a touch of the clap.' He tapped the side of his nose. 'Slut she might be, but it pays to understand women of all classes, Mr Watkins. Women can be very useful,' he said. 'She'll remember me as the generous gent who fancied her and made her feel special.'

'How could she be useful to anyone?' Fletcher was scornful. 'Except flat on her back?'

'Born and bred here, she is, probably,' Crabbe said wisely. 'Knows the place like the back of her hand; nooks, crannies and hiding places the Constables don't know about. Who can tell, one day Betsy may not be able to get me out of a spot of bother. That girl, or another one like her, might be inclined to help save my life.'

'You're an incredibly devious devil all right,' Fletcher said with grudging admiration for the man's resourcefulness. 'How can you help me?'

Crabbe poured a shot of whisky into each glass, and pushed one across the table to Fletcher.

'A couple of nights ago, while in your cups you were indiscreet, Mr Watkins,' he said quietly. 'You wanted a little job done, but you picked the wrong man.'

Fletcher felt a spasm of panic go through him. So Crabbe was out to blackmail him. He deeply regretted his stupid behaviour the evening in question. Yes, he had been drunk, but not so far gone that he did not remember what he had said or let slip about wanting the child Blanche Watkins dead. He had even gone so far as to offer to pay handsomely. Later, he had been fearful the man would tell the authorities, but he had told Crabbe instead, and perhaps that was worse.

'I don't know what you're taking about,' Fletcher declared as casually as he could.

'Don't be shy with a friend, Mr Watkins.' Crabbe's tone was heavy. 'You know full well.'

'You're wasting your time blackmailing me,' Fletcher went on doggedly. 'You said it yourself. I've nothing. I'll probably be in debtors' prison by this time next week.'

'I doubt that, not if you do as I suggest, Mr Watkins. I could make you a rich man.'

'What poppycock!'

'I'm not without funds myself, as you might guess,' Crabbe went on. 'But I don't have the right connections any more, so backers are scarce.' He paused and glanced around to see if anyone were near enough to hear what he had to say next. 'You might know I run a prize-fighting booth down on Trawler Row, adjacent to the Bell and Bucket public house.'

Fletcher nodded. 'I've heard of it. I follow the sport myself.'

'I know you do,' Crabbe said. 'Inclined to heavy wagering, so I've heard, and happy to do a bit of sparring yourself. But it's a risky business these days, what with the magistrates on our backs and the peelers chasing away punters.'

'What has all this to do with me and my desperate situation?'

'I'm after your family name, Mr Watkins, or more precisely the wealth and good name of your brother Sir Tecwyn Watkins. A stanchion of good taste, as I understand, and perhaps the setter of new trends.'

Fletcher laughed aloud. 'If you think to persuade Tecwyn to back your risky enterprise you're in for a rude awakening. Why do you think I was cut off? Tecwyn abhors blood sports of any kind.'

Crabbe shook his head sadly. 'The old days of royal

patronage are long gone, of course, but some of the rich old guard still like to see a fight in secret.' His lip curled with disdain. 'This prissy young woman who has just come to the throne, looking down her nose at good honest sport. It's killing the game, Mr Watkins.'

Fletcher was losing patience. 'Get to the point, Crabbe.'

Crabbe's eyes narrowed slyly. 'Very well, Mr Watkins. To put it in a nutshell, nothing but a babe stands between you and a handsome fortune, as I understand it.'

Fletcher nodded silently, feeling something clutching at his heart. He did not know whether it was apprehension or hope.

'I'll undertake to remove that obstacle for you,' Crabbe said still keeping his voice low. 'And in return you will use your considerable wealth to support my enterprise. The game needs money to survive, Mr Watkins. Good fighters are developing in America, and I intend to bring some to Wales.' He nodded sagely. 'They'll attract vast crowds like the old days. There's still big money to be made in the prize-fighting ring, Mr Watkins, even with most of the toffs against us.'

Fletcher felt his mouth go dry. 'How will you do it? Kill the child, I mean?'

'You needn't trouble yourself about the details, Mr Watkins,' Crabbe said, tapping the side of his nose. 'Nothing will happen for a month or two. I have to make careful arrangements. Neither of us wants to get caught, now do we?'

'Months?' Fletcher's shoulders drooped. He had been a fool to hope Crabbe had a solution. 'I'll be languishing in debtors' prison long before you do anything. God knows what evil ills a man can catch in such filthy places. I'll be dead myself.'

Crabbe chuckled. 'I told you I'm a man of means. I'll see that you live well in the meantime.'

Fletcher frowned. 'If you have money, why do you need financial backing?'

'Unlike you Mr Watkins, I'm no spendthrift, and I keep my

gambling within strict limits,' Crabbe said slyly. 'There's money to be made but there's also money to be lost. I bet only on a sure thing, and the wealth of the Watkins family is a certainty.'

'You realise that, even with the . . . er . . . obstacle removed, I'll not inherit anything until my half-brother dies.'

Crabbe was silent, looking at Fletcher keenly. 'I only bet on certainties, Mr Watkins, like I told you,' he said at last. 'And I don't do things by halves.'

Fletcher's jaw dropped open. 'You mean my brother will be . . .'

Crabbe lifted a hand quickly, a scowl darkening his face. 'You have a loose tongue, Mr Watkins,' he said harshly. 'I don't like that. A man who can't be trusted often seals his own doom. Don't talk yourself into an early grave.'

Fletcher glanced around furtively, but there was no one near. 'There's no harm done, Crabbe.'

'No, not now, but I warn you, Mr Watkins, if I am to help you, you must watch your words.'

Fletcher shook his head angrily. 'I'm not a fool, Crabbe. I know what's at stake.'

Crabbe sniffed. 'Very well. Do we have a deal?'

Fletcher hesitated for only a second and then held out his hand only to be met with a low growl of rage from his companion.

'Put your hand away, you dimwit!' Crabbe hissed. 'In a roomful of thieves and miscreants you would have them see us seal a bargain? It would be around the town in no time that something was afoot between us.'

'You go too far, Crabbe,' Fletcher hissed back. 'You should take your own advice, especially when dealing with your betters.'

Crabbe's lip curled, and he looked savage for a moment. 'I should let you rot in debtors' prison, and look elsewhere for funds,' he said harshly.

'Huh! Hard to come by in your game, Crabbe, like you said.'

Crabbe stood up. 'We'll see no more of each other until after both obstacles are out of the way,' he said in a warning voice.

Fletcher looked up at him expectantly.

'Don't worry,' Crabbe responded quickly. 'You'll get your living allowance right away, and handsome it'll be, too.' Crabbe looked scornful. 'Reckon the luscious Mrs Vansier will be back in your bed before midnight.'

With that he turned and strode out of the door to the street. Fletcher jumped up and hurried after him. It was all so vague. He needed to know more details of Crabbe's plans.

The night was very dark and bitterly cold. The only light came from a blazing brazier across the narrow street, where an old woman peddled fresh roasted chestnuts. Crabbe was fast disappearing into the blackness. Fletcher ran after him and grabbed at his arm.

'Wait!'

Startled, Crabbe swung around and raised the cane. He uttered an oath when he saw it was Fletcher. 'You were nearly a dead man then,' he snarled.

'How will you enter my brother's house? Will you abduct the child before . . .?'

'*I'll* do none of these things,' Crabbe said in a low voice. 'Over the next few months I'll be out and about in town, very much in the open. And you must do the same, Mr Watkins.'

'But . . .'

Crabbe gave a grunt of impatience. 'I've already made enquiries of your brother's household and will tell you this. The person who will bring the child away from the house is the one who has every right to do so. Now, let that be enough! Goodnight to you, Mr Watkins. You'll be a rich man in your own right when we meet again.'

Fletcher held on to Crabbe's sleeve, reluctant to let him go. 'Remember, Crabbe,' he hissed urgently. 'It's imperative that the child dies first, otherwise there may be difficulties with my inheriting.'

Roughly, Crabbe dragged Fletcher's hand away from the material of his jacket. 'Maybe you'd prefer to do the job yourself, Mr Watkins?' he said, a sneer in his voice.

Fletcher drew back in alarm that Crabbe was backing out. 'No, no, of course not!'

'Then let me do what I do best without more questions.' Crabbe stepped away. 'Prepare to receive sad news,' he murmured as he went. 'A tragedy is about to overwhelm your family.'

4

Nesta Lewis walked carefully along Merthyr Road towards the centre of the village of Roath, hugging the baby, Blanche, to her breast. She stayed close to the ancient whitewashed wall that ran alongside, fearful of the open ditch on the other, for the rough track, narrow and hardened with frost and black ice, was treacherous underfoot, and one slip could mean disaster for them both.

'See, my lovely girl?' Nesta held the shawled bundle higher as the first cottages came into sight. 'We're almost there, look. We'll see if Mrs Jones the Shop has a pretty scarlet ribbon for that lovely black hair of yours, isn't it?'

Nesta walked past the cottages and the parish church of St Margaret's, past the village green with its one seat made from split logs, and on to the next row of cottage, the first of which was Jones the Shop and post office, the only shop between here and cardiff.

The cottage door stood open as usual even on this cold February morning, and Nesta stepped in to the front room where a narrow wooden counter jostled shelves containing jars of this and that, packets of all colours and mysterious brown paper bags. Nesta always had the urge to rush around tidying things up, but knew better than to show her feelings to the proprietor, a crinkle-faced lady of uncertain age.

'Morning, Mrs Jones,' Nestor said.

'Morning, Miss Lewis,' Mrs Jones replied, shuffling bags, packets and other debris on the counter top, making things even more untidy. 'And how are Sir Tecwyn and Miss Blanche these days?'

'Well,' Nesta said shortly, folding her lips. Nosy old biddy! She did not like discussing her employer with villagers.

Clutching the baby more tightly, she opened her reticule to reach for some coins she had there.

'What've you got in the way of ribbons, Mrs Jones? I want something pretty for Miss Blanche's hair.'

Mrs Jones made a moue as though the request were a nuisance.

'Stock is low,' she said, and glanced at the baby. 'Is it wise to bring a babe of that tender age into a cold February day?'

Nesta was annoyed. 'Miss Blanche is well wrapped up,' she retorted briskly. 'Mollycoddling children never did them any good. Indoors they get one fever after another.'

'Poor motherless child.'

Nesta clenched her teeth to prevent herself saying something she would regret, and then her glance fell on a cardboard box opened and slung to one side. 'Is that a new stock of gloves?'

Mrs Jones sniffed. 'Yes, they came in yesterday.' She seemed reluctant to let Nesta inspect them, but she was determined to buy a pair and took her time choosing. Finally she was satisfied and paid for her purchase.

'I'd get yourself back to Brynhyfryd House as soon as you can before that babe catches pneumonia,' Mrs Jones said slyly. 'What would Sir Tecwyn do then? And you'd be out of employment.'

Nesta did not bother to reply but stuck her nose in the air and lifting her skirts with her free hand turned and marched out of the door. She had worked for Sir Tecwyn for three years and still she was considered an outsider by the villagers. Of course, it was the same in the village of Cwmrhyddin Cross, by

Swansea, where she came from. Outsiders were always under suspicion.

Out on the dirt road again, Nesta could feel Mrs Jones' eyes on her, watching from the cottage window. So, perversely, she turned in the opposite direction to home, determined to sit for a while on the seat on the village green.

It was cold. She was beginning to feel it herself, but Blanche was cosy in her warm clothing and shawl, and was now sleeping peacefully. Give it ten minutes, Nesta thought, and then she would be off back to the house, a mile along the track.

She was about to rise some minutes later when she became aware of someone standing near the other end of the seat and she glanced up in surprise to see a fashionably dressed stranger, carrying a cane. He bowed and doffed his hat.

'Good morning, ma'am. May I sit? I've been walking, and am now most wearied.'

He did not look at all weary, Nesta thought, and appeared young, probably not more than thirty. 'You may have the seat to yourself, sir,' she said primly, consciously trying to correct her accents to speak as her betters did. 'I am just leaving.'

'Oh! Please! Don't let me chase you away,' he said hurriedly. 'I've no wish to intrude. But you make such a wonderful picture – mother and child. Wonderful! Such serenity!'

'I'm not the child's mother!' Nesta exclaimed. 'I'm her nursemaid.'

'Aah! I see. Forgive me. I'm a tender-hearted man, romantic in my outlook, and see beauty and meaning everywhere I gaze.' He bowed and removed his gloves. 'May I sit? My name is Crabbe, ma'am, Jebediah Crabbe, at your service.'

Nesta smiled faintly, unsure. She looked him over. A tall well-built man, who cut a fine figure in his modish clothes. She could tell by the way he spoke that he was not a gentleman by birth. She glanced at his smooth well-kept hands that must never have known toil. The hand that rested lightly on the top

of his cane bore several gold rings. She even thought she saw
the glint of diamond. He was a man of wealth undoubtedly.
Probably one of those industrialists, a businessman like Sir
Tecwyn. She saw no reason to be wary of his motives in
speaking to her, a complete stranger.

'You may sit, sir, for the moment, but I'm returning to my
employer's house soon.'

'And where is that?'

Nesta told him.

'Aah, yes,' he said. 'Sir Tecwyn Watkins. I've heard of that
gentleman. And is he a good employer?'

Nesta fidgeted at the question, and clutched more tightly at
Blanche. 'You must excuse me, sir,' she said evasively, and rose
to her feet. 'It's time I was getting back. The child will need
feeding.'

'Of course!' He took an expensive-looking gold hunter out
of his waistcoat pocket and glanced at it. 'Good gracious! I've
kept you too long. But you have a mile to walk, you say, and on
such dainty feet, too. I can't allow it, no.'

'I beg your pardon, sir!'

'I've a mare and gig tethered near the church,' Jebediah
Crabbe said smoothly, rising to his feet. He towered over her,
but she was reassured by the benevolent expression on his
rather plain features. 'Please let me take you to your employer's
house. After all, it's on my way back to Cardiff.'

Nesta curtsied. Why not? She hoped Mrs Jones was still
watching from the cottage window. Perhaps her stock in the
village would go up being seen in the company of such a
prosperous gentleman.

'Remain here,' Jebediah Crabbe said. 'I'll fetch the gig.'

'No real need,' Nesta said hastily. 'I'll walk along with you to
the church.' It was one thing for Mrs Jones to see her with this
gentleman but entirely another to watch her ride off with him.
Tongues love to wag.

'Roath is a most pretty village,' Jebediah Crabbe remarked as they strolled. 'I'm impressed with it.'

'I find it too quiet, sir,' Nesta said frankly. 'It's no patch on the village where I come from.'

'And where is that?'

For some reason she felt reluctant to say, and made something up on the spur of the moment. 'I was born in Stradey, by Llanelly.'

'You're a long way from home, ma'am. You must miss your family.'

Nesta wetted her lips. She was unwilling to admit her father was no more than a lowly candle-maker even though she loved him dearly. It was not his fault that he had never been able to rise out of poverty. It was easier to tell a white lie.

'I'm an orphan, sir,' she said glibly. 'My father was a prosperous farmer but tragedy reduced our circumstances, and I'm now forced to take employment as a nursemaid.' This was the story she had circulated in the village.

'So you're alone, with no one to care. How very sad,' Jebediah Crabbe said, mournfully. 'I fear I'm in the same position; alone, that is. That I'm wealthier than Croesus is no consolation for loneliness. I'm in dire need of a wife and a family of my own.'

Nesta blinked; surprised that he should speak of such personal matters to her, a stranger.

They reached the gig and Jebediah Crabbe helped her in, his strong hand resting longer than was necessary on her arm. Was he taken with her, she wondered, her heart beginning to flutter? And why not? At nineteen she had the bloom of youth on her. Her features were reasonably fair and her figure slim.

And what of him? Jebediah Crabbe's features might be plain, but there was an air about him that spoke of power and strength. She liked strength in a man. And he was wealthy. He was a good catch and no mistake. She had always thought that if she was fortunate enough to marry well she would be able to help her father; make her parents' lives more comfortable and secure.

Nesta controlled a sigh at the long cherished thought as Jebediah Crabbe flicked the reins and the gig moved off. It was no good hoping for that. He was a stranger in the village, and their meeting was pure chance. She would never see him again.

When they reached the gates of Brynhyfryd House Jebediah Crabbe was most attentive of her. 'Allow me to take the child from you as you alight,' he suggested, holding out his arms.

'Thank you kindly, sir, but I can manage,' Nesta replied politely.

Blanche was her responsibility and she was reluctant to let anyone else have a part in her welfare, with the exception of the child's father.

Jebediah Crabbe offered his hand as they parted, and to her surprise squeezed her own in a most intimate way, and Nesta could not prevent a blush coming to her cheeks.

'Thank you, again, sir, for your kindness,' she said, abashed. 'Have a safe journey back to Cardiff.'

'Why, thank you ma'am,' he said. 'I'm much cheered after being in your company.' After a further bow he climbed back into the gig, flicked the reins and was off.

Nesta stood for a moment on the track, the cold air biting into her cheeks, watching him go. Jebediah Crabbe was a lot older than her, but what a splendid husband he would make. Perhaps she should have been a little more coquettish, she thought regretfully, and sighed again.

Stuck out here, in the back of beyond, she had little chance to meet a man who she could consider as a suitable husband. She had seen enough poverty back home as a candle-maker's daughter, so no impoverished farmer or labourer for her. She would rather remain a spinster than be a poor man's wife, old before her time with childbearing and poverty. If she ever married it would be to a man like Jebediah Crabbe, who would provide for her every wish and be generous to her parents. Would she ever meet anyone like him again?

It was the end of February and Nesta was restless, isolated as she was at Brynhyfryd House. No visitors called these days, not even Mr Fletcher Watkins. She had always looked forward to his visits, finding his rakish presence exciting and stimulating; not that he ever noticed her, of course, a mere nursemaid.

Feeling the need to visit the village, if only for something new to relieve the monotony, Nesta set off along the dirt track to Roath one morning. It was her day off yet she would have welcomed Blanche's company, but the child had the snuffles.

As she neared the parish church of St Margaret's she halted, startled to see a gig and horse hitched at the wooden rail which seemed familiar, yet was too smart to belong to a villager.

Was Jebediah Crabbe back in Roath? Nesta dismissed the idea quickly. She had put all thoughts of him firmly out of her mind over the last two weeks; though in idle moments could not help speculating on what might have been.

Feeling suddenly self-conscious, Nesta headed for the cottage post office. As she stepped inside she half expected, even hoped, to see Jebediah's tall figure but, of course, he was not there.

'Morning, Miss Lewis.' Mrs Jones' speculative glance was disconcerting, and Nesta guessed the meeting with Jebediah Crabbe had not gone unnoticed. 'How is everyone up at the House?'

'Miss Blanche has a runny nose,' Nesta replied casually. 'I thought it wise not to bring her today.'

'Ah, yes,' Mrs Jones said, with a faint smile. 'Three's a crowd, isn't it?'

'What do you mean?' Nesta asked tetchily. 'What are you suggesting?'

'I suggest nothing,' Mrs Jones said, her eyes opening wide in innocence. 'Babies are an inconvenience on times, especially when they are not one's own.'

Nesta folded her lips and decided not to pursue the matter.

'A pennyworth of boiled sweets please,' She said, offering the coin, and accepting the small brown paper bag, in return, she whirled her skirts and stalked out without another word. She passed the blacksmith's wife on the way, the woman giving her the same sort of speculative glance as that of the post-mistress. Was she the subject of gossip?

Nesta felt uneasy, and loitered on the track for a moment. As an outsider she was used to villagers talking about her behind her back, but this was different. It was as if they were aware of something which she wasn't. It would be best to make her way back immediately.

As she neared the church her heart gave a jolt to see Jebediah Crabbe emerge through the postern gate. She had the impression he had been waiting there for her. He bowed as she approached.

'Miss Lewis, my heart lifts to see you again,' he began. 'I trust you're well? And where's the babe? There's nothing amiss with the child, I hope?'

'Mr Crabbe, sir, I'm surprised to see you here again,' Nesta said. She could not help glancing back towards the post office, hoping this time that they were not observed. 'How long have you been in the village?'

'No more than an hour,' he said. 'I enquired at the post office to learn when you might arrive.'

Nesta was disconcerted. No wonder she had received such strange glances. 'I wish . . .' She was about to say she wished he had not done that, but hesitated. She regretted not being more forthcoming with him on their first encounter. Now fate appeared to be offering her a second chance. She should not ruin it by being churlish. 'I wish I had known,' she went on lamely.

'No matter,' he said cheerfully. 'You're here now. You know the area and perhaps you can be of help to me.'

Nesta was surprised again. 'If I can, sir,'

'I'm thinking of buying property nearby,' he told her. 'A good gentleman's house. Do you know of such a place that might suit me?'

'I can think of no estate for sale, sir,' Nesta said. So, he intended to settle in the region. While the idea was pleasing, she was a little disappointed, and chided herself for thinking for one moment that he had returned solely to renew their acquaintance.

He took her arm. 'Let us sit together in the gig and talk,' he suggested, and helped her climb up. Sitting next to him, Nesta felt self-conscious and unsure.

'As regards property,' she said, 'it would be best to ask Mrs Jones the village postmistress. Nothing of interest escapes her.'

'I prefer to trust your judgement, Miss Lewis,' Jebediah said. 'I'm tired of the hustle and bustle of life in the town. It's time for me to settle, find a wife and raise a family. A man is not complete without a family. Don't you agree?'

'I'm sure you're right, sir,' Nesta said, wondering where this was leading, if anywhere.

'You're young yet,' Jebediah said, surprisingly. 'And if you'll excuse me saying so, quite lovely, Miss Lewis. I'm sure there must be some lucky young man waiting eagerly to make you his wife.'

Nesta could not help blushing. 'I'm not attached, sir,' she murmured, embarrassed at his frank speaking.

'Aah!' He said no more but sounded extremely pleased.

Nesta began to feel uncomfortable again, not knowing what was in his mind and fearful of making a fool of herself. 'I must return to my employer's house now,' she said. 'It was nice meeting you again, sir, and I hope you'll be successful in your search for property.' She rose to alight, but Jebediah held on to her arm.

'Wait!' he said. 'I'll take you there. It will be my pleasure.'

'There's no need, sir,' Nesta said hastily. 'I'm used to walking.'

'I'll not have it,' Jebediah said firmly. 'It's obvious that you are of good family and have been used to better things, ma'am. It saddens me to see you brought low.'

'I'm not ashamed of being a nursemaid, sir,' Nesta said with asperity. 'There are worse fates.'

Like being a poor man's drudge, she thought. She was determined that fate would not be hers.

'Forgive me. I didn't mean to offend,' Jebediah said. 'It's just that, from our first meeting, I could picture you as a wife, surrounded by her children, deserving to live in the lap of luxury. Such will be the fate of my wife, when I find her.'

He flicked the reins and they moved off along the track towards Brynhyfryd House, a mile away. Nesta felt, in his company, it would be the longest mile she had ever known, for his words both excited and confused her. What did he mean by speaking to her in this manner? One moment she was sure he had intentions towards her and the next that he was merely being condescending.

For the rest of the journey Jebediah talked about his business interests, a flourishing sawmill outside of Newport and a factory in Cardiff employing fifty men where furniture was produced. Nesta was impressed.

When they reached the gates of Brynhyfryd House, she was about to rise and descend from the gig when Jebediah put his hand lightly on hers in a most tender way.

'I'm a successful man, Miss Lewis, but it means nothing without a wife to share it.'

Nesta held her breath, her mouth agape, awaiting his next words. Suddenly she was flustered. Was he about to propose and on such short acquaintance? What ought she to answer?

But Jebediah said nothing further and instead alighted from the gig to walk around the horse to her side. Nesta felt vexed at his silence and then angry, convinced he was teasing and trifling with her.

'Why do you speak of these things to me, sir?' she exclaimed sharply. 'I'm virtually a stranger.'

'But I don't think of you as a stranger,' he said quickly, surprise registering on his face. 'It's true that we have spoken twice only, but I've been observing you for some weeks.'

'What?' Nesta was alarmed.

'Please, don't be angry with me,' Jebediah said. 'I glimpsed you one day although you didn't see me. Since that time I've not been able to put your fair face out of my mind. Please forgive me.'

Nesta did not know what to say.

'I see I've shocked you, ma'am, and I'm contrite,' Jebediah went on. 'I beg you don't think ill of me. I'll be in Roath again this time next week. Please honour me with your company, if only for an hour.'

Well, that was plain enough, Nesta thought, with a quiver of excitement. He *was* interested in her after all. She could hardly contain her feelings of elation, but managed to keep a demure expression. He must not think her too easy.

'You honour me, sir,' she returned. 'But I'm not sure that my duties will allow it.' She looked at him pertly through her eyelashes. 'Besides, I don't know whether it would be proper. We haven't been formally introduced.'

'I'm a plain man,' Jebediah said, and she detected an edge to his voice as though he might lose patience. 'In my rational world I see no need for such shallow manners. But if my lack of fancy etiquette offends you, Miss Lewis, we'll say no more, and will not meet again.'

'Oh, no, Mr Crabbe, sir!' Nesta protested quickly, realising she had overstepped the mark. 'You don't offend me in the least. I'm honoured to know you.'

His expression softened. 'I'm so glad of it for I'm sure nothing but pleasure and good fortune will emerge from our . . . acquaintance . . . I hesitate to say friendship.'

Offering his hand, he helped her down from the gig, doffing his hat and bowing in a gentlemanly way. 'We'll meet a week today, then,' he said. 'I pray time passes quickly until I'm in your charming company again.'

It was a Friday night and The King George tavern was lively with its motley customers; even so, Crabbe felt strangely at home. He had paid the landlord for the use of the backroom for an hour or two, no questions asked, and he now sat at the table, pouring a good measure of gin into the glass of the woman sitting opposite him.

'Say when, Lil.'

Fat Lil chuckled deep inside her huge bosom, making the rolls of blubber under her chin quiver and ripple like a rip tide. 'Don't know the word, Jeb,' she said. 'Pour up!'

Crabbe obliged until her glass was brimming, and then he looked at the man sitting next to her. 'Same for you, Mangler?'

'Aye! Fill it up.' Mangler Harris pushed his glass forward with a huge hand. 'I've got a thirst on me like the Severn Bore.'

Mangler was a huge man altogether, though none of it was fat, but all muscle. He was deadly in the prize-ring and had earned his epithet.

'What are we celebrating?' Fat Lil asked as she sipped the gin, the glass lost in her bloated hand, the fingers of which reminded Crabbe of half a pound of best pork sausage.

'Celebration comes later,' Crabbe answered. 'When my little scheme bears fruit as it surely will do.' He did not pour himself a drink. Feeling at home was one thing, but he had made too many enemies hereabouts, and it needed a clear mind to stay alive in this locality. 'You both will help me,' he went on.

Neither protested or asked questions, as he knew they wouldn't. Fat Lil and Mangler were the only people in the world he trusted enough to take into his confidence in a trick like this. They knew better than to betray him. They remained loyal mainly because he knew too much about both of them; enough to see them swing from the gallows, but also all three had known a profitable association for many years.

'Who do we have to do in?' Mangler asked with a wide grin.

Crabbe smiled in response. Mangler liked nothing better than helping someone, anyone, shuffle off this mortal coil, but he would need to be patient for his pleasures.

'That also comes later,' Crabbe said firmly. 'First, I want you to find a house to rent, a big one, in a good locality but isolated. Move in and set up house, but expect visitors in time, a young woman and an infant.'

'*Duw, Duw!* You're not turning religious, are you Jeb?' Fat Lil asked with a chuckle. 'Taking in waifs and strays.'

'You know me, Lil,' Crabbe said. 'Always big hearted.'

'Oh, I know you all right, you young devil,' she said. 'And there'll be more than a penny piece in it, I'll be bound.'

'Much more.' Crabbe nodded. 'And now for the details . . .'

His words were interrupted by the door swinging open suddenly, and the landlord stood there looking harassed.

Crabbe bellowed an oath. 'I said no interruptions! Get out!'

'It's this cove, out by here,' the landlord said sweating visibly. 'Demanding to have words with you, he is, Mr Crabbe . . .'

At that moment the landlord was pushed roughly aside and Fletcher Watkins strode arrogantly into the room.

'Crabbe! I want to know what game you're playing.'

Fat Lil rose hastily to her feet, spilling her gin. Mangler rose, too, taking an aggressive step forward, but Crabbe, remaining seated, held up a warning hand.

'Leave it be, Mangler!' he said in a low voice, then looking at the landlord still hovering, 'Get out and shut the door!'

The man went quickly, closing the door behind him. There was silence for a moment. Fletcher Watkins was staring at Fat Lil, as well he might. At six feet in height, she was a mountain of dimpled and cascading white flesh, all of it draped in a shapeless low cut red brocade gown.

Crabbe watched as Fletcher's astonished gaze went to Mangler Harris, who, standing poised on the balls of his feet, was glaring at him evilly, waiting for him to make a wrong move.

'Have you lost your senses?' Crabbe began. 'I've warned you about your careless behaviour before, Mr Watkins. Do you want to see us all hanged?'

Fletcher jerked his head. 'Who are these . . . people? I need to speak to you in private, Crabbe.'

'Then speak away!' Crabbe retorted. 'These are my friends and associates. We're just about to discuss the abduction . . .'

'Wait!' Fletcher interrupted quickly, flinging an apprehensive glance at their companions. 'Tell them to leave first.'

'They're part of my scheme,' Crabbe said. 'It can't be done without them.'

'Then wait until I've gone before discussing details. I've no wish to know what you intend,' Fletcher said his voice less certain. 'I thought our agreement was confidential.'

'It was until you barged in just a minute ago,' Crabbe retorted. 'I intended to keep your identity a secret, yes, even from them. But now they know who you are,' He laughed. 'I don't doubt they'll need paying in future to keep quiet.'

Consternation crossed Fletcher's face. 'I can't pay if I've no money of my own,' he said. 'When can I expect to inherit? It's been months . . .'

'Don't complain,' Crabbe growled. 'You're living like a prince on *my* money, I remind you. You and that Mrs Vansier are acquiring more debts then even I could imagine. It's well for you that Sir Tecwyn is monumentally wealthy.'

'Is that a threat?' Fletcher snapped.

'Take it as you will,' Crabbe snarled back, and Mangler took one step closer. 'These matters can't be rushed, not if we all want to escape the gallows, and if we three must take the drop, so will you, Mr Watkins, I promise you.'

There was silence for a moment, while Fletcher stared around at the others. A fine sweat had broken out on his top lip, and Crabbe was pleased to see it. Fletcher Watkins was as much his creature as these two were, although he did not know it yet, but he would in time.

'The child will be in my custody soon, and you'll get what's due to you,' Crabbe went on in milder tones. 'Now let that be enough, Mr Watkins. And I bid you goodnight. Watch as you go. There are many footpads abroad tonight. I don't want anything to happen to you – not until I get a handsome return on my investment.'

Without another word, Fletcher turned on his heel and slammed out of the door.

'He's a hazard to us,' Mangler growled. 'Do we need him?'

'Until we get our hands on Sir Tecwyn's fortune,' Crabbe said. 'Now listen to what I intend. I'll have the child's nursemaid in my pocket soon, and the child with her. I'll set a little trap for the fair Miss Lewis.' He laughed. 'Already she's panting for my proposal of marriage.'

'Why do we need to rent a house?' Fat Lil asked, her chins quivering. 'It's dangerous Jeb. It means lawyers and signing papers, matters that can be traced back to us, perhaps.'

'Everything will be done in Fletcher Watkins's name,' Crabbe said. 'He wants me to dispose of his niece, and I will, but not until after I prise a ransom from the child's father. This is an opportunity too golden to be missed.'

Fat Lil looked doubtful, and Crabbe was impatient with her.

'We need a safe place to keep the girl and child until after the ransom is paid,' he said. 'Then we'll dispose of them both. That's a job for you, Mangler.'

Mangler grinned and rubbed his huge hands together.

'I don't like it, Jeb,' Fat Lil said.

'The maid is an orphan. She won't be missed by anyone and, if we do this right, she'll be blamed for the abduction.'

'But a child . . .'

Crabbe's fist crashed down on the table. 'It's all or nothing, Lil. You're in or you're a dead woman. What's it to be?'

5

Spring was late in arriving; the morning air still had the chill of winter in it. Nesta sat with Jebediah in the gig outside the church as usual. She did not mind what the villagers thought now. She was being courted by a very eligible and substantial gentleman, and she did not care who knew it.

It was nearing the end of April, yet he had not yet asked the vital question. But at least they were now on first name terms, which was progress, she supposed. She had made up her mind to accept him when he did finally ask for her hand, and she hoped today would be the day.

Nesta fidgeted a little, sending him covert sideways glances. He sat very upright, both hands resting on the top of his cane. It was a little worrying that he had not invited her to his home, but she had come to realise over the weeks since their first meeting in February that Jebediah Crabbe was a man not to be hurried, and it would be unseemly, of course, to hurry the courtship. Still, she was anxious. She could not let this chance of a good marriage slip through her fingers. It would mean so much for her family.

'Do you know much about the Americas, Nesta, my dear?' he asked suddenly.

Startled out of her reverie, Nesta admitted she knew nothing.

'Aah! Then it'll be a journey of discovery for you, dearest, an adventure,' he said jovially. 'Great opportunities are there for a capable man like myself, with a talent for making money, especially when he has a good wife at his side.'

'You're going abroad?' Nesta felt a twinge of panic and knew that it echoed in her voice. Would he never ask her? Had she been making a fool of herself, imagining an attachment when there was none?

He turned to her, beaming. 'Shall you not like it, my dear, living abroad?'

Nesta felt breathless, smiling uncertainly. Should she give him a little push? 'I'm sure I'll find it wonderful with you, Jebediah.' She smiled coyly and fluttered her lashes. He reached over and took her hand in his, and Nesta held her breath, waiting.

'Yes, a man could double his fortune in America, live like royalty in the grandest of houses,' said Jebediah. 'A flock of servants at your beck and call, Nesta dear. And the travel we would do, Paris, Rome.'

'Oh! Rome!' Nesta clapped her gloved hands together in excitement. 'I've always wished to see Rome.'

'And you shall, my dear, you shall.' He took the gold hunter out of his waistcoat pocket and glanced at it. 'Time passes, I regret to say,' Jebediah said. 'We must part, but not for long.'

'Must we?'

'Aah! You feel as I do, I can see,' Jebediah said wistfully. 'It must be for now. But take heart, my dearest one.' He lifted her hand to his lips and imparted the briefest kiss. 'Next time we meet I'll have a very important question to ask you; a question that will affect the rest of our lives.'

'Oh, Jebediah,' Nesta answered breathlessly. 'Ask your question now, do!'

He hesitated, and then patted her hand. 'Be patient a little longer, dear one. I await news of great good fortune which will add to my wealth considerably. When we meet this time next week be prepared to change your life for ever.'

The month of May came in glowing like a beautiful woman, and Nesta felt some of that radiance must be in her own face as she went to meet Jebediah. All doubt was gone. He had made his intentions very clear. Today he would ask her to be his wife; her whole position in the social world would change. He might even have a ring for her hand.

She was a little late, which she decided was the proper thing, not to be thought over eager, and so was disconcerted to find no horse and gig outside the church. She strolled further into the village as far as the post office. The unexpected warmth of the day had brought people, mostly children, out onto the village green. There seemed to be more activity than usual at the post office and Nesta felt conspicuous as she stood uncertainly on the dusty track.

She had never known Jebediah to be late. He was always waiting for her, dependable and steadfast. Had something happened to him? Nesta twisted the cord of her reticule more tightly around her wrist. Oh! Had fate played a trick on her; snatching away her one chance at the last moment?

The blacksmith's wife and Mrs Jones came out onto the front step of the post office, their heads together, and Nesta felt her face flame in consternation. They were laughing at her! How dare they? Common countrywomen, with hardly a decent bonnet between them.

Twitching her skirts Nesta turned on her heels and with head held high marched back towards the church. She would hide out of sight in the shelter of the postern gate, she decided. Jebediah would arrive soon.

She had no way of measuring the passage of time, except to watch the sun move slowly across the skies. It was a lovely day. One could feel summer hovering, waiting to make an entrance.

Nesta sighed deeply and painfully. Just the kind of day to receive and accept a proposal of marriage.

When the sun was in mid heaven she knew it was useless to wait any longer, and, with a little jolt, realised she had no way of contacting him, knew absolutely nothing about him, apart from what he had told her. She did not even know in what direction he lived, except that his business interests were in Cardiff. The town was not all that far away on horseback, but it might as well be John o'Groats as far as she was concerned. All she could do was wait until he made contact, if he ever did.

Nesta trudged back to Brynhyfryd House with a dark shadow hanging over her. Another week to wait before her fortunes changed. Luckily, not being on friendly terms with other servants at the house, she had not shared confidences. No one knew of her expectations. In one way that was harder. She had no one to talk to, no one to reassure her.

When she reached the gates of the house, Nesta threw back her shoulders and held her head high. This was a passing disappointment. Something untoward had happened to keep him from her. Jebediah would be there the following week, full of apologies and explanations. She had waited months, she could wait another week.

In the days that followed, Nesta found the tedium of her existence at Brynhyfryd House ever more irksome after months of planning and dreaming of her new life with Jebediah. At the end of the longest seven days she had ever known, she had to stop herself from running all the way to their usual meeting place outside the church the following week. Purpose-fully late, she halted when the gates of St Margaret's came into sight further along the track. There was no familiar gig, no horse, and no sign of Jebediah Crabbe.

Stifling a moan of disappointment, and with a handkerchief pressed to her lips, Nesta turned on her heels and returned the

way she had come. What a fool she had been to be taken in by
him. He had trifled with her, although, she was thankful to
remember she had done nothing shameful, nothing to damage
her reputation, and nothing was really lost, she reminded
herself miserably. She still had her position in Sir Tecwyn's
household, and no one was aware of her folly.

It was early the following week that a letter arrived for her at
Brynhyfryd House, Nesta knew, even before opening it, that it
was from Jebediah, for no one else knew of her whereabouts,
not even her parents.

Rushing to the privacy of her room to read it, she surveyed
the contents with utter dismay. He had suffered a setback in
business and had lost most of his fortune. Knuckles pressed to
her lips in distress and keen disappointment, Nesta read on.

> *I am distraught, my dearest Nesta. What must you think*
> *of me, having promised you so much? I must tell you my*
> *heart is broken at the knowledge that I cannot keep my word.*
> *I am determined to try my luck in America. I have made one*
> *fortune. I can make another. If only you would trust me*
> *enough to share my dreams. If you will, meet me at the usual*
> *place and time. I pray you do.*
>
> *Your devoted servant, Jebediah Crabbe.*

Nesta sat on the bed, the letter pressed again her breast, her
heart thumping wildly. He had not deserted her after all, and
what he had promised was still there if only she had the courage
to take a chance. But he was no longer a rich man, and she had
sworn she would never tolerate marriage in poverty.

She looked around her room, the lonely room she had
occupied for the last three years. She was very fond of her
charge, the child, Blanche, and Sir Tecwyn was not a bad
employer. He was a fair and reasonable man, and had never

given her one cause for concern, but she was tired of the boredom of living in isolation, tired of being merely a nurse-maid. So much more beckoned now that she had met Jebediah. She had thought she was about to move on, and now this!

She glanced at his letter again, hoping to see further than his words. He was no ordinary man, she was certain of that. She felt power in him and much confidence. He might be brought low at the moment, but undoubtedly Jebediah Crabbe would triumph again, and she could share that triumph, if only she had faith.

I was never meant for poverty and deserve the best from life, Nesta thought resolutely. I deserve everything Jebediah has promised and more besides. She glanced around her room again. What had she to lose? She would go with him to America and leave all this servitude behind for ever. Perhaps, in time, her parents could join her there, and live out their lives in comfort.

Jebediah came along the track to meet her, hands outstretched to grasp hers. She expected to see him a changed man, but he appeared as well-dressed and as prosperous as before. He hides his misfortune well, she thought with admiration.

'My dearest Nesta,' he said. His eyes looked misty and she thought she heard a catch in his voice as though he might break down. 'I knew in my heart you would come to me in my hour of need,' he went on. 'I promise you, I mean to build myself up again.' He squeezed her hand. 'But I doubt I can do so without you at my side, Nesta.'

'Oh, Jebediah!' She could hardly believe she had not lost him. 'I'm sorry for your losses. Is it very bad?'

His head was bowed and his shoulders hunched. 'It's a severe body blow,' he admitted, his expression woeful. 'But what distresses me most is the starving children.'

Nesta was startled. 'Children!'

'My faithful employees are now destitute, their children without a crust,' he explained. 'It breaks my heart to think of them cold and hungry. I must find a way to help them.' He shook his head solemnly. 'I'll go to any lengths to do so, beg, borrow or . . . yes, even steal if need be.'

Nesta was shocked at the seriousness of his tone. 'But it's not your fault, Jebediah,' she protested. 'Although it's a tribute to your generous heart to feel as you do.'

'That's true,' he agreed sadly. 'I was given bad advice as regards stocks and bonds. I've lost considerably in the crash, but my employees have lost everything, even their homes. They're on the streets with nothing in their stomachs. And the little ones . . .'

He turned his head away suddenly as though ashamed that she should see him affected, and led her towards the gig. Nesta put a comforting hand on his arm as they walked.

'You're a good man, Jebediah,' she said as he helped her in. 'Not many employers would give one thought to the poverty-stricken.'

He seemed to brighten as he boarded to sit beside her. 'I've booked passage for us on a ship bound for the Americas,' he confided. 'We leave in the middle of next week. Can you be ready, my dearest?'

Nesta turned to him, staring open-mouthed. 'Next week?' Eager as she was for a change of fortune, she had not reckoned on such a sudden departure. What would Sir Tecwyn say to this?

'The captain has the power to marry people on the high seas,' Jebediah said quickly. 'Man and wife before we reach New York.'

'How wonderful!'

'I've such plans, my Nesta,' Jebediah said. 'I've promised you a life of luxury as my wife and I'll see to it that you live as a queen for the rest of your days. I'll work day and night for you.'

Nesta felt her cheeks flush with pleasure at such outspoken devotion. 'Jebediah, I'm quite overcome.' She looked coyly at him from under her lashes. 'And in return I'll be a good wife, loyal and supportive in all things.'

Jebediah smiled broadly and patted her hand. 'What wonders lie before us as man and wife, Nesta, my dear,' he said. 'Think of it. The best of everything. We'll make our home in Boston, among the cream of American society. I'll buy you elegant clothes, and you'll rub shoulders with the wives of magnates and millionaires. They'll be our friends and the doors of their palatial homes will be open to us.'

Nesta clasped her hands before her joyfully. She would start packing her belongings as soon as she returned to Brynhyfryd House, and would write a letter to her parents telling them of her good fortune and the plans she had for their future. Of course, Sir Tecwyn must be told immediately of her imminent departure. She could hardly wait to begin her new life. It was more than she had ever dreamed possible.

'When will you come for me?' she asked eagerly. 'What day? I must know all the details so as to be prepared. I'm sure it must be a long journey to America.'

Jebediah stared at her for a moment in silence, and then his face crumpled in distress. Were those tears running down his cheeks? Nesta was alarmed. 'What is it, Jebediah, dear?'

'These things can't be, Nesta,' he said, a sob in his voice. 'We can't go to America. Although our fortunes would be assured there, I can't run away from my responsibilities. No, we must stay here and help the starving children, even though we'll be poor ourselves. You will stand by me, even in poverty, Nesta. I know you will.'

'What?' Nesta started forward in her seat. 'Stay here in poverty? Jebediah, what are you talking about?'

'We must postpone our voyage,' he said glumly. 'For some

time, or at least until I can find the money to help my old employees. My conscience will not let me desert them.'

Nesta felt a spark of annoyance at this obstacle suddenly set in the path of her new life, and she almost spoke without thinking, but managed to curb her tongue.

'Of course we must help the children, Jebediah,' she said carefully, struggling to blunt the sharpness of her tone. 'But would it not be prudent to leave as planned. Once you've recovered your fortune you could send funds to your workers.'

'But that would be too late to save the little ones,' he said tremulously, and shook his head. 'Unless I can lay my hands on a considerable sum of money quickly, we must put all thoughts of America out of our heads, dear Nesta, right out of our heads.'

Nesta held on to her temper with difficulty. There must be some other way. She had set her heart on a new life in the New World. 'But surely Jebediah, you have friends who would lend you the money?'

He shook his head again. 'Business associates say I've been too generous with wages over the years,' he replied sadly. 'They refused to help.'

Nesta sat back in her seat, a wave of bitter disappointment sweeping over her. One moment she had had everything in the world in her grasp and the next it was gone.

'What are we to do?'

'Sir Tecwyn is a rich man,' Jebediah said. 'It's possible the money could come from him.'

Astounded, Nesta turned to stare at him. 'I could never ask him for money,' she declared emphatically. 'I'm merely the nursemaid to his child, a servant. It's unthinkable.'

'I wasn't planning on asking him, exactly,' Jebediah said smoothly. 'He's an extremely wealthy man, and would not miss the odd trinket or two, something valuable enough to raise a tidy sum for a very worthy cause.'

Nesta gaped in shock at the notion. 'Jebediah! What are you thinking?'

'I'm thinking of America, my dear,' he said mournfully. 'The wonderful life we might have had together, and how fine and elegant you would look among the ladies and gentlemen of Boston.'

'Oh! Don't talk of it!' Nesta cried. 'Our hopes are dashed.'

'Sir Tecwyn has more wealth that he knows what to do with,' Jebediah persisted. 'Surely there's something that might be borrowed for a short while.'

'Borrowed?'

'Oh, my dear Nesta! Forgive me!' he exclaimed in a horrified tone. 'I didn't mean that we should rob Sir Tecwyn, good gracious, no, nothing so underhand. Merely borrow, say a painting, silver candelabra, a valuable ornament.'

'But you intend to sell it,' Nesta said, raising trembling fingers to her lips. 'Isn't that stealing?'

'Only if we don't make restitution, my dear,' Jebediah said calmly. 'Once we've achieved our aim of rescuing the needy and we are settled in Boston, I'd reimburse him in full, with an explanation of our benevolent work.'

Nesta was pensive, thinking of all that she had lost almost in the wink of an eye. It was true that Sir Tecwyn's wealth was legendary, and yet he lived a simple life. That wealth was lying idle while Jebediah could do so much good with it.

'But how will you do it?' she asked him hesitantly. 'Will you come to the house in the dead of night?' The idea of Jebediah creeping about Brynhyfryd House at night was shocking, yet exciting, too.

'Oh, good gracious no, that would be a criminal act,' he said in a scandalised tone. 'No, my dear Nesta, it must be your doing. Find something suitable and bring it to me here.'

'I?' Nesta stared in disbelief. 'Oh, no, Jebediah, I couldn't do that,' she cried, horrified at the notion. 'Sir Tecwyn trusts me, and besides, I'd be blamed. I couldn't face the disgrace.'

Jebediah's shoulders drooped, and he looked glum. 'Then our hopes are dashed forever, my dear,' he said forlornly. 'We can still be married, of course, but quietly and cheaply. It'll be hard at first, money will be short, and we must make many sacrifices. I'll seek low-priced lodgings immediately. Tiger Bay perhaps.'

'Tiger Bay?' Nesta squeaked in disgust. She had never been to Cardiff but had heard of the notorious Tiger Bay, full of rough seafaring men and loose women. 'But surely you still have a house?'

'Auctioned, my dear, to pay my debts. I barely escaped debtors' prison. It might come to that yet if I can't find sufficient funds.'

'Prison? Oh!' Nesta put a hand to her heart, feeling it flutter in panic.

Jebediah sighed heavily. 'To think,' he said slowly, 'Sir Tecwyn has many fine pieces which he never remembers he owns from one year to the next, would never miss. And for the want of a little courage, we could be ensconced in our own mansion in Boston by July.'

'But if you have no money now how could you afford that?' Nesta asked plaintively. 'I don't understand, Jebediah.'

He looked at her, an astonished expression on his face. 'My dear Nesta, didn't you know that in Boston the streets are paved with gold? Everyone's rich.'

'It's too much to ask of me, Jebediah,' Nesta said petulantly. She had not bargained for such a commitment.

'You wouldn't hesitate if you could see their little pinched faces,' he said, a catch in his voice. 'Some are as young as your charge, Miss Blanche.' He paused, looking at her keenly, and Nesta felt her cheeks flush. 'Have I misjudged you, Nesta?' he went on in an intense tone. 'Is your heart not as warm and generous as my own? I could not take less in a wife.'

'I sympathise, of course, I do,' she answered hurriedly, not wanting him to think her hard. She was concerned for any child in need. 'But I'm afraid, Jebediah.'

'There's nothing to fear,' he declared, his voice full of confidence. 'I'll protect you, my dear.' He looked at his pocket watch. 'Now we must part for the moment. I'll meet you again this time tomorrow, when you'll have something for me I'm sure.'

'So soon! But I must have time to think! Besides, I've only one half day off a week.'

'You'll manage to find an excuse to leave the house some- how. Our future depends on it.' He smiled serenely. 'And I know you'll not disappoint the children.'

Nesta was preoccupied for the rest of the day. A little voice of caution warned her to stay away from the village and Jebediah Crabbe. It sounded very much like Meg Lewis's voice. Her mother was always critical of her; suspicious of everything unfamiliar or unconventional, never ventured anything, yet was always complaining bitterly of her lot. Nesta was deter- mined not to be like her and so decided to ignore it.

Besides, she had grown up in the poverty of her father's candle-maker's shop and yearned for the new and exotic life Jebediah had promised. Perhaps he was a little unconventional, but his motives were the best, she was sure of it.

But what could they borrow? It must be something small enough to carry secretly. She must not be seen leaving the house with a suspicious parcel, so it must be something small enough to carry in her reticule.

When Blanche was put to bed, Nesta ventured about the house. There were few servants to encounter, and she knew the housekeeper was entertaining a friend in her small parlour at the back of the house.

Brynhyfryd House had many bedrooms. She knew them

well. Before becoming nursemaid to Blanche she had been a lowly housemaid and assisted the housekeeper with the dusting. She remembered that in one little-used guest room there were two oval miniature paintings displayed on the chest-of-drawers. She had dropped one once while dusting. The housekeeper had reprimanded her sharply, saying the miniatures were by a famous artist and were therefore priceless.

Nesta went along to inspect them again that evening. They were small enough to secrete on her person. But priceless? She was sceptical. If they were so valuable, why would Sir Tecwyn display them here where they were rarely seen?

On impulse Nesta put the paintings in the pocket of her maid's apron. They might just fetch enough to serve Jebediah's urge to feed the hungry, and once that was done they could leave it all behind and begin anew in a new land. Considering it that way, she decided the risk was worthwhile.

Luck was with her the next day when Sir Tecwyn decided suddenly to take his daughter to Newport to visit some distant relatives of his wife. Watching the Watkins' carriage drive away mid morning, Nesta felt a moment's guilt about the paintings hidden in her room but quelled it. Her employer would be reimbursed eventually, she told herself. Everything would be put right. She would have the life she deserved, and Meg and Enoch Lewis would benefit too.

Walking along the track to Roath, Nesta was surprised to find Jebediah and the gig waiting for her half a mile from the village. He helped her into the vehicle and then, to her surprise, urged the horse further along the track and then down a narrow side path out of sight.

Nesta looked around her at the dense undergrowth and closely spaced trees. 'Why are we here, Jebediah?'

'Best not to be seen together,' he said confusing her. 'Now what have you brought me?'

She was uneasy at the strange gleam that came into his eyes as she handed him the paintings.

'Well! What have we here?' He examined them closely and then to her astonishment took out a jeweller's eye piece to inspect the artist's signature. He gave a gasp of satisfaction. 'You've done well, my Nesta,' he said. 'Very well indeed. I couldn't have made a better choice myself.'

'They're not worth anything, I think,' Nesta opined uncertainly, disturbed by his excitement. She was beginning to deeply regret her actions in taking the miniatures.

'Not quite a king's ransom, my dear, but close. Yes, these will certainly do, for a start.'

'What do you mean?' Nesta exclaimed in distress. 'I'll take nothing more from Brynhyfryd House, Jebediah,' she warned sharply. Suddenly she was apprehensive. 'Give them back to me. I must return them immediately. What have you made me do?'

Why had she allowed him to turn her head with his promises of marriage and riches? Nest felt panic rise in her breast, knowing she had been foolish and weak in believing in him. But it was not too late.

She rose and tried to snatch the paintings out of his hand, but he shoved her roughly back into her seat. 'Don't be a foolish girl,' he said sharply. 'Be quiet and listen to me. You will do exactly as I tell you from now on, understand me?'

'Jebediah! What has come over you? I don't understand. You're frightening me.'

'Huh! Frightened? So you should be,' he said with a sneer. 'You common thief!'

'What?'

He held up the miniatures. 'You'll go to prison for taking these, dear Nesta. One word to Sir Tecwyn and you'll be arrested by the authorities. Prison or deportation is certain, but remember, women of your class have been hanged for less.'

'Oh!' Horrified, Nesta's hands flew up to cover her mouth. What was happening? In fright she stared at his sneering expression and saw only a stranger's face. 'Jebediah, why are you saying these things? Why are you treating me like this?' Her spinning mind searched for words to placate him. 'We're to be man and wife soon, remember.'

He gave a snort of derision. 'Jebediah Crabbe marry a mere nursemaid? I think not.' His look was scornful. 'You were so easy to dupe, Nesta. You're no fool, yet your greed and avarice blinded you. I have seen this many times before, even in the canniest.'

'I'm not greedy. It's not true!' Nesta exclaimed hotly, nettled at the jibe. 'And you have no right to say that to me. I only look to better myself and provide for my poor parents as anyone would.'

He laughed. Liar! You have no parents. You told me so yourself. You've fallen into my trap.' His expression hardened; his gaze cold and unfeeling. 'Now you're mine to do with as I will.'

Nesta gasped, giving him a frightened glance. 'What do you mean?'

'I mean you're under my control completely. You'll take one more thing from Sir Tecwyn,' Jebediah said harshly. 'His most prize possession, the child Blanche. You'll fetch her to me tomorrow.'

'I won't do it!' Angry despite her fear, Nesta started up from her seat ready to break free again. 'Let me go! I'm a free woman!'

Jebediah grabbed her arm and roughly forced her back down. 'You can't escape me, Nesta,' he snarled, and she cringed at the ferocity of his tone. 'You're free no longer. You're my creature now, entirely at my mercy.'

'You tricked me, you fiend!' Nesta cried out, struggling in his grasp. 'I'll report you to Sir Tecwyn. He'll know how to deal with the likes of you.'

Jebediah chuckled nastily, holding up the miniatures. 'He'll not take the word of a common thief, I think.' He shook his head. 'I won't hesitate to inform the authorities of your thievery, if you prove difficult.'

'But I meant no harm,' Nesta burst out. 'I thought I was helping the starving children.'

'You thought you were helping yourself,' he sneered. 'To a life of wealth and leisure. You would be immediately condemned.'

'You're twisting my words,' Nesta exclaimed heatedly. 'And I did it because you, my future husband, asked me to. You'd be condemned with me, remember that.'

'I?' He lifted his brows scornfully. 'I've done nothing criminal.' He grinned evilly. 'Have you ever seen a woman hanged, Nesta? I have and I don't recommend it.' His gaze went past her as though remembering. 'As a boy, my father took me to Bristol to see a woman hanged for thieving a loaf of bread,' he went on. 'Thirty minutes she dangled there, choking, until her friends kindly swung on her legs to finish her off.'

'Don't!' Horrified, Nesta put up both hands to cover her face. She felt faint at the images he conjured in her mind. There could be no worse fate. And think of the humiliation for her parents. She had no doubt the shame of it would kill her beloved father.

He chuckled at her distress. 'Yes, it's a long and torturous process, Nesta. It would be such a pity for that pretty neck of yours to be stretched in the same manner.'

'You're a devil not a man!' she cried out.

The paintings were tantalizingly within her reach, and she lunged forward to snatch them from his grasp, but he struck at her with a forceful blow.

'Be still, woman, before I'm forced to do you a mischief!' he growled and Nesta subsided in a heap, staring at him in terror.

She could hardly believe this was happening. Why had she

not seen this side of him before? Why had she not listened to
her mother's voice? Oh, what a careless fool she had been,
allowing herself to be taken in by his lies and false promises.

'Now then,' he went on, his tone still dangerous. 'You'll
bring the child to me here. Also bring a bag with changes of
clothing for both of you.'

'But . . . but why? Why do you need the child? Look,
I'll bring more paintings for you,' she said trying to sound
persuasive. 'Sir Tecwyn has much fine silver. I'll bring you
anything, but not the child.'

Jebediah shook his head. 'It's the child I've wanted all along
and Sir Tecwyn will pay handsomely for her safe return.'

'Abduction for ransom! I want no part of it,' she cried out.
'It's an evil thing you suggest,' She shook her head vehemently.
'Taking the paintings is one thing but abduction . . . no, I
won't do it.'

'I demand you obey me.' A growl sounded deep in his chest.
'You'll fetch her to me, Nesta, or you dangle.' More calmly he
went on: 'You have no option.'

Nesta wrung her hands. 'But Sir Tecwyn will know I had a
hand in it,' she cried. 'I'll never be able to return to Brynhyfryd
House. What will become of me?'

'Don't fret.' He hesitated before going on. 'I guarantee you'll
receive a share of the proceeds from Sir Tecwyn,' he said
smoothly and surprisingly. 'You may travel where you will
after.' His tone grated. 'Either do as I command now or the
alternative is prison and ruin. After that, if you avoid the
gallows, you will end up on the streets, selling your body to
any man for the price of a crust of bread.'

The gallows or the streets! Appalled, Nesta burst into tears,
her hands over her face. This morning she thought she was set
for life, now a terrible fate awaited her. With a howl of misery
and vexation she buried her face in her handkerchief, rocking
back and forth.

'Stop blubbering,' Jebediah grated irritably. 'I've no time for it. I'll expect you and the child at this spot by mid morning tomorrow.'

Nesta stared at him. There was no mercy in his glance and she had no doubt Jebediah would give her up to the authorities without a second thought, so she dare not refuse now. She had got herself into this mess, but there must be a way out.

'But what will you do to her? I'll not have her harmed!'

Sir Tecwyn had trusted her with his precious child, and she would fight for Blanche's life as well as her own if it came to it.

'Have no fear,' Jebediah said. 'Nothing will happen to her. She'll be as safe as you will be. As soon as Sir Tecwyn pays the ransom the child will be returned to him unharmed, and you will be free to go your own way, much the richer.'

Nesta lifted her tear-stained face and regarded him solemnly, her heart filled with deepest doubt. 'You swear, Jebediah?'

He put his hand over his heart. 'I'm a man of my word,' he said.

She continued to stare at him. He had proved himself a liar, so how could she believe the veracity of any word he uttered? But what alternative did she have? None.

It crossed her mind then that Jebediah had set his mind on taking the child for ransom with or without her. Blanche's only hope was for Nesta to do as he insisted. She must appear to go along with the plan and thereby ensure the child's safe return to Sir Tecwyn. She owed them both that.

Afterwards, when Blanche was out of danger, she would take as much money as she could prise out of Jebediah and then return home to her parents in Cwmrhyddin Cross. Her mother might even welcome her when she realised her daughter had money to share. At least she would make sure her parents ended their days in comfort.

6

'I'll take Miss Blanche for a walk in the grounds,' Nesta announced to the housekeeper as she passed through the kitchens to the back entrance after breakfast the following morning. 'She has the sniffles again. The warm air will do her good.'

'Ummph!' The housekeeper's disinterested grunt reassured her that no one was paying much attention.

She had taken the precaution the night before of leaving their outer travelling garments and a canvas bag in the summer house; the bag contained nappies, a change of clothing, as well as a few personal possessions which she could not bear to leave behind. It would be easy enough to slip along a little used path through the surrounding trees to rejoin the wide carriageway near where it led into the road, and so remain well out of sight of the house the entire way.

After preparing them both for travel Nesta sat for a few moments more in the summer house, shaking from head to foot. She could turn back now, she told herself, before any damage was done. She could tell Sir Tecwyn about the ransom plan, and he would have Jebediah Crabbe arrested. But Jebediah would implicate her in a moment, and he had the paintings as proof of her crime. The authorities would never believe the word of a nursemaid against that of a plausible liar. That the gallows awaited her was certain.

No. Jebediah had her as secure as a rabbit in a hutch. As he had so mockingly pointed out, her life was in his hands, so she had little choice but to obey him. But nothing bad would happen to the child, she promised herself, and she was prepared to stake her own life on it.

Wrapping the child securely in a shawl, and grasping the bag, Nesta crept out of the summer house and scurried through the trees. She was already late for her meeting with Jebediah; although she had no doubt that he would wait. The bundle she carried was too precious to him to leave behind.

But what if once he had the child in his possession, he drove her off, leaving her to her fend for herself? She now had nowhere to go and no money. He had promised to see her right, but his promises were like pie crust, made to be broken.

Hurrying along the road towards the village she began to panic that she would not find the side lane where he said he would wait. Then suddenly she realised she had reached it. Her steps faltered as she approached their meeting place, and she clutched the sleeping Blanche protectively to her breast.

There was still time, she told herself, still time to turn and flee. Yet she was convinced now that even if she did turn back today, Jebediah would strike at another time. And if he betrayed her to the authorities for thievery, she would not be free to protect the child, as she had sworn to herself she would. She was Blanche's only hope of survival.

It was not his gig waiting in the lee of the trees, but a large closed carriage and a pair of fine nervous looking horses. There was a crest on the side of the coach but she had no time to examine it. Jebediah appeared suddenly at the horses' heads, his expression wrathful.

'Where the hell have you been, woman?' he demanded to know. 'Each minute we wait could mean discovery. Have I not made it clear what is at stake for you if we are caught?'

'It wasn't easy to get away,' Nesta lied breathlessly.

He jerked open the door of the carriage. 'Well, get in!'

'I'm really to come with you, then?'

'Who'll look after the child if you don't?' he said sharply. 'Not I!'

'Who owns this carriage?' Nesta asked with curiosity.

'Borrowed for the purpose,' he snapped. 'I'm not fool enough to use my own vehicle for this errand.'

'Where's the coachman?' she went on, staving off the moment when she must commit herself by climbing into the coach. 'Is he, too, a helpless victim of your evil schemes?'

'I act as coachman on this occasion,' he said irritably. 'Now enough questions and chatter. Get in the coach. Keep the window drapes drawn,' he went on curtly. 'It's best you keep out of sight.'

Once inside and seated with Blanche cradled in her arms, Nesta had a moment of sheer panic. Jebediah could be planning to take them somewhere to murder them both for all she knew, but then, what profit would there be for him in that?

He was about to close the door.

'Where are we going?' she asked, willing her voice to be steady.

'You needn't concern yourself,' he said offhandedly. 'Rest assured it'll be a safe and secure place.'

For what seemed like an hour the carriage rattled along at high speed as though driven by the Demon Coachman himself. Blanche was now wide awake and screaming as she and Nesta were thrown from side to side as the vehicle jumped and bucked at stones and ruts along the road, and Nesta felt they must be on the road to Hell itself. She cried out to Jebediah several times, but he either did not hear or did not care.

When the road beneath the wheels seemed more level, Nesta settled back in her seat, trying to sooth the fractious child. She guessed, by the sounds outside the carriage, they had reached a fair sized town, probably Cardiff. Surely the journey would end soon? And what awaited them then? she wondered nervously.

The carriage came at a halt at last and Nesta remained seated, with bated breath, waiting for the door to be opened. Blanche still grizzled bitterly and struggled in her arms. And no wonder, Nesta thought. The child must be hungry and she certainly needed changing.

'Go straight into the house,' Jebediah instructed curtly as he jerked the door open. 'I'll take the child.'

'No!' Nesta cringed back. She did not trust him. She would trust no one with her precious charge. 'She remains with me.'

'Very well.'

He took her elbow to hand her down onto a gravelled forecourt of a large house obviously of great age by its appearance. It had a portico over the main entrance and high dark mullioned windows. There were lawns in front and a high wall surrounding it. It felt very secluded, yet reason told her that it could not be too far from the town itself.

'Where are we?'

'No questions,' Jebediah growled. 'The less you know the better. Now step inside quickly. Let us waste no more time. I have arrangements to make.'

As Nesta moved toward the entrance, the door opened and a tall, enormously fat woman stepped out into the porch. She was dressed finely, as a lady of quality might be, but after one look at the folds of fat around her cheeks and the bloated appearance of her features, Nesta realised she was a woman of the lowest caste, and her heart sank in despair.

A giant of a man stepped out behind the woman, and Nesta almost screamed at the coarse, bestial look about his face. He grinned at her insolently, eyeing her up and down in a way that made her blood run cold.

'Mangler, get rid of the carriage,' Jebediah instructed the huge man. 'The river would be the best place. Shoot the horses if you must.'

'Oh! What is this place you have brought us to?' Nesta cried out, appalled that he should speak of shooting the horses so callously.

'Come along, missy,' the fat woman said. 'Get inside where I can keep an eye on you.'

'Inform Cook that a bowl of warm milk sop must be made up immediately for the infant,' Nesta demanded indignantly. 'She's starving.'

'Cook!' The fat woman let out a bellow, the bulges of fat around her body heaving and swelling as she shook with laughter. 'There's no cook here, missy, just me and Mangler.'

Nesta felt the power of sausage-like fingers as the woman took her roughly by the arm, propelling her towards the staircase.

'Upstairs with you,' the woman said. 'I'll make the sop myself and bring it up – when I've got a minute.'

Nesta clung stubbornly to the newel post at the bottom of the stairs with her free hand. She was determined to make a stand although she felt sick with fear. 'Blanche is but seven months old,' she exclaimed angrily. 'What manner of woman are you to deny food to a baby?'

'I got my orders,' the fat woman retorted. 'You stay in the room until . . .'

'Orders? You make this place sound like a prison,' Nesta shrilled. 'I demand to see Jebediah. I'll complain to him.'

'Now look here, missy . . .'

'My name is Nesta Lewis,' she interrupted archly, feeling that assuming a superior air with the woman might conceal her apprehension. 'You may call me Miss Lewis.'

'Hoity-toity!' An angry growl rumbled in the woman's vast expanse of bosom. Nesta ignored it.

'Are you the housekeeper?' she asked tartly, trying not to show how rattled she was.

'Hell's flames!' the woman exploded. 'I'm no housekeeper

I'll have you know. I'm a landlady, I am. Fat Lil Lofton, that's me. Got my own inn, I have, down Tiger Bay way. Just doing Jeb a favour, I am.'

'What kind of a favour?'

Fat Lil's eyes narrowed. 'Too nosy for your own good, you are, missy. Take a warning. Don't rile Jeb. He's dangerous. Understand?'

'Why have we been brought here?' Nesta asked querulously.

At that moment Jebediah Crabbe strode into the hall from the front entrance. He glared at the pair of them standing at the foot of the stairs.

'Why isn't the nursemaid and the brat safely locked up?' he demanded.

'She's demanding food for the babe,' Fat Lil told him, and chuckled. 'Wants to give instruction to the cook, so she does.'

Nesta took the opportunity to snatch her arm from Fat Lil's grasp and rushed across the hall towards Jebediah.

'Blanche is hungry,' she said, looking up at him pleadingly. 'I'll make the sop myself. Let her show me where the kitchen is.'

Jebediah's eyes were hard. 'So, you can cook, can you? Very well, you can earn your keep.' He glanced at the big woman. 'Lil, take her to the kitchen, but keep an eye on her at all times.'

'Is this wise, Jeb?'

'Do you fancy Mangler's cooking?' he asked sarcastically. 'or perhaps you'd like to get your own hands greasy?'

Fat Lil shrugged. 'This is your trick, Jeb,' she said. 'You know best.'

The fat woman lumbered across and grabbed Nesta's arm again, tugging her from the hallway. 'Come on, missy, this way, and no sly tricks.'

The kitchen was huge and surprisingly clean. A fire glowed in the big range grate where an iron kettle was already steaming. Nesta looked around for a safe place to put Blanche while she worked. There was a shallow wicker basket under the table.

Nesta bent and pulled it out. It was a little dusty but nothing more. She wiped the inside round with the hem of her skirts before placing Blanche carefully in it, and put it on the large kitchen table.

'I must have my bag,' she said to Fat Lil. 'Blanche needs a clean nappy.'

Fat Lil's bulbous nose wrinkled. 'Not before time either.' Never taking her glance off Nesta, the fat woman went to the door and called out: 'Mangler! Fetch missy's bag in here.'

A door stood open nearby, obviously leading to the larder, which looked to be well-stocked. A leg of lamb wrapped in muslin hung from a hook in the ceiling, and several loaves were stacked on the marble shelf, each wrapped in a clean linen cloth. A large firestone pot stood on the floor filled with potatoes, damp earth still clinging to them, and two big cabbages whose crisp dark green leaves suggested they had not long been taken from the ground. It looked as though Jebediah expected a lengthy stay.

Nesta brought out one of the loaves, together with a large enamelled jug, sniffing suspiciously at the milk it contained. To her surprise it was fresh.

As she put the jug and loaf on the table, she saw Mangler move to the wicker basket, placing his great hand on it.

'Get away from her!' Nesta screamed in panic and dread, rushing at him. 'Don't you touch her, you monster!'

Fat Lil darted to intercept her before she reached him, grabbing Nesta by the shoulders, holding her as though in a vice, while Mangler bellowed with laughter. Nesta was astonished that a woman of such bulk could move so quickly.

'I could snap the little 'un's neck in a minute,' Mangler mocked. 'Like snapping a twig.'

'Leave her be!' Nesta shouted, struggling desperately in Fat Lil's grasp. 'Take your filthy hands away.'

His face contorted into an even more horrible configuration, and he lunged forward. 'You mouthy wench! It'll give me great pleasure when . . .'

'Mangler!' Fat Lil exclaimed in a warning tone. 'Watch your loose tongue!'

He halted but still looked furious, and Nesta was very much afraid.

'Missy, here, is going to do our cooking for us,' Fat Lil went on in a soothing tone. 'There had better be plenty of it, too. Mangler and me have good appetites, haven't we, Mangler?'

'And we're choosy,' he sneered. 'Your grub had better be tasty.' He grinned mirthlessly. 'I slit the gizzard of the last cook because she put in too much salt.'

He moved away from Blanche's makeshift crib and walked to the other end of the kitchen, where he lowered his immense torso onto a chair. He took a knife from his belt and a piece of wood from his pocket, and began to whittle, grinning all the while at Nesta as though he enjoyed a private joke.

Completely unnerved, Nesta trembled as Fat Lil released her.

'You looking to get your throat slit, or what?' the fat woman hissed in an undertone. 'Get on with your chores, missy, and keep your trap shut.'

Jebediah Crabbe sat in the back room of the King George pub later that afternoon and studied the man sitting opposite him. Chippie Tonkin had been good in the prize ring until he had let the gin and cheap whores get to him. His red blotchy face told of a man already suffering from the clap and the devil knew what else.

'Get there after midnight,' Jebediah instructed. 'The hulla-baloo will have quietened down by then. Let no one see you, other than Sir Tecwyn, understand?'

'What's in it for me?' Chippie said, his bear-like shoulders hunching forward. 'I'm taking a mighty big chance, Jeb. The nabbers might still be hanging around.'

'I think not. They'll be out searching for the nursemaid.

Anyway, you'll get a good cut,' Jebediah answered curtly. It irked him to do business with the man, but he had to trust him – up to a point. Although he knew Chippie no longer had the wits to cheat him. 'You deliver the message, word for word, like I told you. Take this also, and show it to Sir Tecwyn, but not until the second night when he has the money.'

'What is it?'

'The knitted coat the child was wearing when she was taken,' Jebediah said. 'I've splashed it with animal blood. Let him think it's the child's own. He'll be more eager to part with the money if he believes she's hurt and in need of attention by a surgeon.'

Chippie looked dubious. 'But, still, suppose they nab me?' he grumbled. 'I'll be a sitting duck.'

'Sir Tecwyn won't dare do a thing, not while he believes you have his child hidden and hurt. You know what to say.'

Chippie pushed his bulky body up from the chair. 'After I deliver the message, what then?'

'You come back here and wait. And you keep you mouth shut, Chippie. Stay off the gin.' Jebediah grinned menacingly, tapping his cane on the floorboards. 'Or you could wake up to find your throat has been cut.'

'Going back a second time for the loot sounds dangerous to me,' Chippie growled stubbornly. 'I reckon I should be paid double.'

'You'll get everything you deserve, Chippie,' Jebediah said smoothly. And that will be an unmarked grave, he thought to himself smugly. Once the ransom was paid, Chippie was no longer of any use to him, and besides, the poor soak knew too much. If he didn't talk beforehand he would surely talk later, and Jebediah had no intention of ending his own life swinging from a rope.

Nesta cooked the leg of lamb with an assortment of fresh vegetables she found in the larder, and wondered where it had all come from. The stuff looked too fresh to be market produce from the town.

They all sat around the kitchen table. Jebediah had apparently been away from the house most of the day but returned to eat his share of the victuals. Everyone ate well except Nesta. Her stomach rumbled with hunger, but her mouth was so dry with apprehension the food seemed tasteless.

Mangler growled angrily when little Blanche began to cry halfway through the meal. Nesta jumped up quickly to see to her. She had mashed together some carrots, turnip and potato, and adding a little of the rich gravy, fed the child with a teaspoon. It was rough fare for Blanche, but she could not live on sop.

Fat Lil rose from the table. 'That was good grub, missy,' she said approvingly. 'Now hurry and wash up. It's time you were safe in your room.'

Nesta washed the crockery and pans, and having boiled some nappies earlier, put them to dry on the airing rack over the range.

'I need the privy,' she said nervously to Fat Lil later, praying Mangler would not be sent outside with her. The way he kept grinning at her made her believe he would molest her if he could. She doubted the others would attempt to stop him.

'There's a night-stool in your room,' Fat Lil said brusquely. 'Make do with that. But mind you empty it in the morning, though.'

Fat Lil took her and the child to a room on the first floor at the front of the house and ushered Nesta inside.

'We'll be wanting breakfast,' Fat Lil said. 'But not too early, eh?'

She closed the door then, locking it from the outside. Suspecting the key would be left in the lock, Nesta wedged the back of a wooden chair under the doorknob in case Mangler attempted to get in while she was asleep. Only then did she feel safe.

As she laid her head on the pillow, Blanche still in the wicker basket beside her, her thoughts turned to what they had left behind. Brynhyfryd House would now be in turmoil at the child's disappearance. Everyone was probably blaming her. Sir Tecwyn would be distraught, and Nesta was overcome with feelings of guilt at the pain she had caused him. He had lost his wife and now he was losing his child, and her heart ached with remorse at the part she had played in it.

But Jebediah had promised Blanche would be returned to her father once the ransom had been paid. He had proved himself a ruthless man, so could she trust him to keep his word? She was filled with fear at the knowledge that she could not. He had lied to her all along, so he had probably lied about that, too.

She must find a way to leave this house, and make her way back to Sir Tecwyn. She would confess her foolishness and throw herself on his mercy. Perhaps if she restored his daughter to him, he would forgive her and keep her from prison.

She slept fitfully after that decision, waking once or twice in the night when Blanche whimpered. The house was silent, so silent she wondered if she and the child were alone.

Chippie Tonkin tethered the horse Jebediah Crabbe had loaned him for the journey some distance away along the track, and crept through the darkness into the shrubbery around Brynhyfryd House, waiting, making sure there were no watchmen or beadles about.

The moon was riding high now, and he judged it was time he made his move. The house was in darkness except for light issuing from behind partially drawn drapes at french windows on the ground floor. He moved forward cautiously and examined the window catch by moonlight. Taking a knife from his belt he gently and silently worked the blade into the space between the doors, and after a moment felt the latch give.

Quietly, he eased the door open, slipped inside and shielding himself from view with the drapes, peered into the room.

Lamplight showed a man seated at a desk, his head in his hands. Chippie could hear sobbing, and his lips curled with disdain. There was nothing to fear here. He still had the light step of a boxer and was in the room and standing at the desk before the man was aware of his presence.

'Don't call out, or make any sound,' Chippie said in a low voice. 'I've got my knife here. I could slit your throat in a second.'

Startled, the man leaped to his feet, starting back and the chair tipped over with a crash.

'Bloody hell!' Chippie exclaimed, jumping himself at the noise. 'You'll wake the dead!'

'Who are you?' the man gasped. 'What do you want?' He paused, and his tone changed. 'Are you the scoundrel who took my daughter?'

'Keep quiet, and listen to me,' Chippie answered. 'I've got the brat, and well hidden, too. She'll never be found, and only I know where she is.'

'Have you harmed her?' Sir Tecwyn started forward. 'I'll kill you!'

Chippie raised the knife. 'Steady on!' he snarled. 'Quieten down. This is my call, your highness,' he sneered.

He had no time for the gentry. They had used him to make money in the ring, but had left him to lie in the gutter when he could fight no longer. He eyed the man before him. This one was tall but he had no real muscle on him. He could break the back of this one and no trouble.

'Where is she? Where's my Blanche?'

'All in good time,' Chippie said. 'First we do the deal.'

'Deal? What're you talking about?'

'I want money,' Chippie said. He repeated the sum Jebediah Crabbe had told him to ask for. 'And I want it by tomorrow night.'

Sir Tecwyn gasped. 'But it'll take a while to get that much money together,' he said. 'You must give me more time.'

'More time to get the constables on my back, you mean,' Chippie said with a contemptuous grunt. 'You'd better keep them away from me. If I don't return to see to your brat she'll starve to death. You'll never find her in time. She's miles away, underground. Even her skeleton will never be found.'

'Where is Nesta?'

'Who?'

'The nursemaid.'

'Dead.'

'Oh, dear God!'

'Will you pay up, or shall I hop back to Cardiff, and leave the brat to the rats underground? They're nasty little buggers. They'll tear her to shreds.'

'I'll have the money for you and I'll pay you double if only you'll make sure my daughter is safe.' Sir Tecwyn stepped forward anxiously. 'Name your price, man,' he went on eagerly. 'I'll gladly give my whole fortune for the safe return of my daughter. She's all I have.'

'A whole fortune?' It passed through Chippie's mind that he might swindle Crabbe in some way. It might be worth the risk for a fortune, but his gin-soaked brain could not think clearly enough to form a plan, and besides Crabbe was too dangerous a man to cross. But he felt a moment's pity for the father before him. 'She'll be returned, never fear,' Chippie said, although he doubted it.

'When?'

'When I'm ready,' Chippie said lamely. 'I'll be back some time tomorrow night, but remember, no nabbers, or the brat perishes.'

7

Nesta slept heavily towards morning, and it was the sound of Blanche crying bitterly, obviously hungry, that woke her. Nesta dressed quickly, and then put a clean nappy on Blanche.

As she looked down on the trusting little face beaming up at her, Nesta felt like crying with regret and remorse. What terrible danger had she brought this innocent child to? And what fate? She should have been strong and let Jebediah do his worst, she thought miserably. She had fallen among thieves and robbers, maybe worse, and whatever happened to Blanche would be her fault.

Feeling her own stomach rumble with hunger she knew she must take a chance on riling Mangler, and bang on the door to be let out. She pulled the chair away and as she grasped the doorknob the door opened. It was unlocked! If Mangler had been there in the night she had not heard him, and was thankful she had had the foresight to use the chair.

Wrapping Blanche in a shawl, Nesta crept down to the kitchen. She had left the pans on the draining board overnight, but now they were all back in place on their hooks on the wall. The crockery too had been replaced on the huge Welsh dresser that stood at the far end of the kitchen. A new fire burned in the range grate, and a stack of freshly chopped kindling lay to one side. Most surprising of all, the nappies had been brought down from the rack, folded neatly, and put on the corner of the table.

Who had done this, Nesta wondered. Not Fat Lil and

certainly not Mangler, who did no more than sit around all day.

Going into the larder to fetch milk and bread Nesta found a large basin filled with brown eggs and a quarter side of bacon hanging from the ceiling hook. They had not been there the night before, she was certain of that.

Fat Lil had been at pains to tell her that the four of them were alone in the house, but someone else was here, some servant who kept well out of sight. But why?

Suddenly she had need of the privy. Unwilling to leave the child alone in the house, she clutched Blanche to her, and taking the wicker basket, too, she approached the back door which had been locked the day before, but now was on the latch. Opening it she found herself in a semi-enclosed courtyard. The house was much larger than she had realised, with wings stretching out on either side. A long high board fence with a gate in the centre stretched between the wings, completing the enclosure. To one side of the gate was a small stone building, which Nesta guessed was the privy.

She hurried there and let herself in. The soil bucket was empty and smelled of creosote as though recently cleaned. Newssheets torn into squares had been threaded with cord and hung on a tail. Nesta marvelled. It was all so civilised.

When she had finished relieving herself, Nesta was reluctant to go back into the house. None of the others were up yet, she felt sure, and now was a good time to spy out the land, see if there was a way of escape. She might never get another chance of freedom like this.

Nesta went to the gate and tried the latch but it was obviously bolted from the other side. She put her eye to a crack between the boards and peered through. Her field of vision was limited, but she appeared to be looking out over an extensive and well-cared-for vegetable garden. It stretched away some distance, and she could see a small orchard at the far end. The garden belonged to the house, she felt certain, and she was also certain now that the gardener, whoever he was, came and went at will through the bolted gate.

As she continued to peer through the crack a dark shadow passed suddenly between her and the view. Someone was there!

'Hello!' Nesta called loudly and urgently. 'Hello! Anyone there?'

But there was only silence.

A door slammed somewhere in the house behind her and Nesta hurried back to the kitchen. She was well on with frying eggs and rashers of bacon before Mangler put in an appearance. He frowned when he saw the back door was on the latch.

'You been outside alone?' he asked gutturally.

'Only to use the privy,' Nesta answered nervously. 'I came straight back inside.'

'How did you get out of your room?'

As if he didn't know, Nesta thought. 'The door was unlocked this morning,' she answered. 'I thought I was expected to get breakfast, so I came down.'

'You watch your step,' he snarled. 'You don't go anywhere unaccompanied, inside or out. Understand?'

Nesta nodded and got on with preparing the food, hoping either Jebediah or Fat Lil would appear. Being alone with this gargoyle of a man was terrifying. She saw evil in his eyes and was more afraid than she had ever been in her life.

The abduction of Blanche Watkins was the talk of the town. Fletcher Watkins heard the news when taking luncheon at his club in Bute Street. As he listened to the gossip around him, he had trouble keeping the jubilation from his face. Several members approached him with words of sorrow and commiseration. He strove to look solemn as they shook his hand.

'Assure Sir Tecwyn our thoughts are with him,' one man said, and Fletcher realised it would be expected of him to visit his brother in his time of trouble.

He set off for Brynhyfryd House immediately after lunch, riding in style in his new carriage and pair provided with Jebediah Crabbe's money. Fletcher smiled. Soon he would not need Crabbe's support. He would be a rich man in his own right, once Crabbe had dealt with Tecwyn. He had no doubt the child was already dead. Within a month at the most he would be installed in Brynhyfryd House, or else he would sell the estate and the coalmines. They would provide another vast fortune in themselves.

He arrived about three o'clock, the housekeeper letting him in with eyes downcast. The house was still, as though in mourning. Fletcher went straight to the study where his half-brother sat, elbows on the desk, and chin in his hands. Fletcher was shocked at Tecwyn's appearance. He looked a broken man. His skin was grey, his shoulders bowed. But he brought this on himself, Fletcher thought morosely, by cutting me out of his will.

He sat down before the desk. 'Tecwyn, I'm sorry for your grief,' he lied easily. 'The members of my club also send their commiserations on your daughter's death. It's a dreadful occurrence.'

At the words Tecwyn looked up quickly. 'Blanche isn't dead,' he said defiantly.

'Oh, come now, Tecwyn,' Fletcher said, trying not to appear impatient. 'You're not a man to allow self-deception in anyone. Blanche has been done away with by that madwoman. Everyone knows the nursemaid must have been insane.'

'It's the nursemaid who's dead, not my Blanche,' Tecwyn said dully. 'I have it on good authority, the abductor himself.'

'*What?*' Fletcher started up from his chair, and then checked himself. 'You've spoken with . . . with . . .'

'I don't know his name, and even if I did I wouldn't tell you. Blanche's life depends on secrecy.'

'I don't understand.'

'He came here after midnight last night,' Tecwyn said. He rubbed a hand over his face and Fletcher could see that his half-brother had not slept since the child had vanished.

'Who came?'

'Her abductor, a great hulking beast, with a reddened diseased face. From the dregs of humanity. He admitted he has my daughter. He demands a ransom for her safe return.'

Fletcher swallowed down his fear. That description did not sound like Jebediah Crabbe nor yet his henchman Mangler Harris, ugly though he was.

'Have you told the authorities of this demand?' Fletcher asked, trying to keep a tremor out of his voice. 'They should be informed. They must apprehend the villain.'

'No! He has the child hidden, alone in a secret place. If he is taken Blanche will die, either from hunger or savaged by rats. Oh, dear God!' Tecwyn leapt from his chair. 'I can't bear it!'

He went to stand in front of the fireplace, placing his arm on the mantelpiece, and laying his head on it. Fletcher stared at him, not knowing what to say, his mind in a whirl. Surely it could not be true. Crabbe had taken the child and had disposed of her. That was their agreement.

Tecwyn lifted his head. 'But I must be patient,' he said at last. 'I've secured the money he demands, and he'll receive it tonight, but not before he's told me where I can find my daughter.'

Fletcher jumped to his feet. 'You must not pay it!' he exclaimed. 'It's a trick, Tecwyn. This man, whoever he is, doesn't have Blanche.'

'Why do you say that?' Tecwyn looked at him keenly. 'Why are you so sure?'

Fletcher was flummoxed for a moment, thinking he had betrayed himself. 'Because of the nursemaid,' he said hastily. 'It was she who took the child, no one else. This man is merely an opportunist. He's heard about the abduction and is trying to prise money out of you. Don't pay him, Tecwyn.'

'I must. I can't take the chance,' Tecwyn said miserably. 'If there is one chance in a million to get Blanche back safe and well I must take it. I'll give every penny I have to that end.'

Fletcher felt anger swell in his chest. Tecwyn was parting with good money for no reason. 'You say he comes here again this night?'

Tecwyn nodded.

'I'll confront him with you, my brother,' Fletcher declared. 'I'll leave now but will return later.'

'Stand at my side if you must, Fletch, but I want no interference,' Tecwyn said hastily. 'I don't know what this man will do if he finds others here. I can't risk losing Blanche.'

'He doesn't have the child, I'm sure of it,' Fletcher persisted. 'Leave him to me. I'll deal with the rascal. And beat him to within an inch of his life. I haven't dabbled in prize-fighting for nothing.'

'No!' Tecwyn said. 'He'll not be harmed. Nothing matters except Blanche. You'll do nothing, Fletch. In fact, I don't want you here.'

'But Tecwyn, you can't let this scoundrel dupe you.'

'Enough!' Tecwyn roared. 'I'll never forgive you if you ruin this one chance of getting my daughter back.'

Fletcher said no more, but hurriedly rode away from his brother's house. Despite what Tecwyn said he would face this unknown man and unmask him for the fraud he was. He would wait in the grounds and waylay him before he gained entrance to Brynhyfryd House. By Heaven! He would take a whip to the cur or else a pistol; yes, kill him if he had to. Blanche Watkins was dead and the sooner Tecwyn faced that fact the better.

Chippie Tonkin was at the bar of the King George when Jebediah Crabbe and Mangler Harris arrived that afternoon. He followed them to the private back room.

'Well?' Jebediah asked curtly. 'I hope you haven't made a mess of the errand I sent you on.'

Chippie grinned. 'The cove in question was no trouble,' he said. 'Crying like a baby he was, and weak as a lamb.'

'Will he pay up?'

'Aye that he will,' Chippie nodded. 'And gladly.'

'It's as well for your sake,' Jebediah rasped. He would be relieved to be rid of this man. 'You know what to do, but next time, arrive an hour earlier than arranged, just to be sure there is no trap set. When you have finished with Sir Tecwyn come to this house.' Jebediah handed Chippie a piece of paper which the man put in his pocket.

'Don't forget,' Jebediah went on harshly. 'I'll expect you there by one o'clock at the latest.' He gave Chippie a hard look. 'Don't try to gyp me, Tonkin,' he cautioned. 'I'll find you and rip out your throat along with your innards. Do you understand me?'

Chippie nodded, and he looked scared. 'Where will I find you, Jeb, in the meantime, if something should go wrong?'

'Nothing had better go wrong, Chippie,' Jebediah snapped. 'But just the same, Mangler and I are off to Bridgend for the rest of the day. Dick Drummond is fighting the American, Tom McMannon at Ffynonne Farm. It'll be the fight of the year. My money is on the Yankee.'

'Your money is safe then,' Chippie opined with a disparaging sniff. 'Drummond is nothing. My youngest brother, Slasher could nail him and Slasher's only fourteen.' He tried to square his shoulders. 'I could see him off in two rounds.'

Jebediah nodded. 'Aye you might have once, before Madam Gin seduced you,' he said mockingly. 'Now you're only fit for running errands.'

Chippie's face suffused once again, but eyeing Jebediah's cane, said nothing.

'Now sling your hook,' Jebediah instructed, 'And keep sober or you won't see your brother get a day older.'

When Chippie had gone, Mangler pulled up a chair and sat. 'How much longer must we put up with that soak?' he growled. 'He could sink us any minute with his loose tongue.'

'You're right,' Jebediah nodded. 'But I think I've put the fear of the devil into him for now. We'll deal with him after he's served his purpose. Chippie will arrive at the house but he'll never leave it alive. I've had three graves dug in the orchard in readiness.'

Mangler's face brightened. 'So it'll be over by this time tomorrow then?' He rubbed his large hands together. 'Leave that uppity nursemaid to me,' he said, with a chortle. 'I'll have some sport with her before I finish her off.'

'Do as you please,' Jebediah said with disinterest. 'But see the baby off first. I can't stand its crying another night.'

Nesta made the late meal as usual but only Fat Lil and she sat down at the table.

'Where's Jebediah and Mangler?' she ventured to ask.

'Never you mind. They won't be back until tomorrow.'

The fat woman gobbled her food as usual with no more to say. Nesta felt relief to know she could sleep without the threat of being molested by Mangler, at least for tonight.

She spied a quart bottle of gin standing on the Welsh dresser. If only Fat Lil would start drinking before she locked them in their room, then they might have a chance to escape.

'Shall I fetch you a glass?' Nesta offered. 'That gin looks inviting.'

Fat Lil frowned. 'You're not getting any,' she snapped, then paused. 'Although it would be better if you were drunk when . . .' She bit her thick lips. 'Whatever happens,' she went on. 'It's none of my doing, mind, although I dare say Jeb knows what he's about.'

Nesta was alarmed by the scared look in the woman's eyes. 'What's he going to do?'

'Best you don't know,' Fat Lil said rising from her chair. 'Then you won't fret.' She stood with her ham-like hands on her bulbous hips. 'You can leave the washing up for once,' she said. 'Up to your room now.'

'But it's not nine o'clock yet,' Nesta protested.

'Never mind that.' Fat Lil glanced over at the gin bottle. 'I'm going to bed myself.'

With drooping shoulders Nesta climbed the stairs, Blanche in her arms, Fat Lil right behind her. She felt sick with dread. Fat Lil would not look her in the eye, and her nervous demeanour suggested she was frightened. And now Nesta was frightened too.

She went meekly into the room, and Fat Lil paused before closing the door. 'Goodbye, missy,' she said. 'I don't think we'll see each other again.'

'What?' Nesta cried out.

But the door was slammed shut and the key turned in the lock.

Nesta sat on the bed, hugging Blanche to her, shaking from head to foot. Mercifully, the child was sleeping peacefully, unaware of impending danger, but Nesta was all too aware. Whatever this abduction was all about, it was obviously coming to an end, and Nesta had the sinking feeling that it would be the end of her and the child, too. She now realised, too late, that Jebediah Crabbe was not a man who would listen to an appeal for mercy. She had already looked into his eyes and seen death there, her death.

She was sleeping fitfully, bad dreams making her twist and turn, yet instinctively aware of the child next to her, when the sound of the door opening roused her quickly.

She sat up with a jerk, expecting to see Fat Lil, but instead the enormous outline of a man was silhouetted in the doorway. Nesta gave a scream, and the figure shuffled further into the room.

Mangler had come back! And he was ready to molest her and maybe worse. 'Stay away,' she cried out desperately. 'Don't come any closer, Mangler. I've a kitchen knife here.'

'It ain't Mangler,' a guttural unfamiliar voice rumbled. ''Tis I, Jack. Black Jack Crow.'

The man lifted high the lantern he was carrying and shuffled awkwardly towards the bed. Nesta let out a whimper of terror, shrinking back against the pillows. What new horror was this?

By the lantern light she saw a huge misshapen figure of a man, with his head twisted to one side and down towards his chest so that he had to look at her from under his eyelids. As he took another step forward she could see that his leg too was twisted at an angle.

'Stay away,' Nesta cried out at this terrible apparition. 'Who are you? What do you want with me?'

'Came to warn you about the graves, I did.'

'Graves?' Nesta lifted a trembling hand to her throat. What did he mean?

'Three deep trenches dug up in the orchard. They be graves all right. I know 'cos I dug them myself.'

'Oh!' Nesta grabbed Blanche into her arms and scrambled off the bed. 'You're the gardener! Don't you threaten us,' she cried out. 'You're not putting us in any grave. I . . . I have a knife, I tell you. I'll use it!'

'Whisht, girl!' he muttered impatiently. 'Or you'll wake Lil from her gin stupor then we will be done for.' He peered at her. 'I see you had the sense not to undress,' he remarked. 'Good. Now get the rest of your things together, and the baby's. We must move quickly and be well away before Jeb returns.'

'Are we to escape?' Nesta was astonished, and then suspicious. This could be some wicked trap to take her off guard.

'Aye, if we can,' he said. 'But don't stand there gawping, girl.'

Gingerly, never taking her gaze from him, Nesta laid Blanche on the bed. The child was now wide awake, and was about to start grizzling.

'She must have some milk,' she said to him, more to postpone leaving the room than anything else.

'Tsk!' He tried to shake his head. 'We don't have time for it.'

'She's hungry.'

'Dang-ding it!' he expostulated. 'We be three dead 'uns if Jeb returns. Oh! Very well. Meet me down in the kitchen as quickly as you can, but silently.'

He turned to the door and shuffled out. Nesta sat on the bed, overcome with relief that he had gone. But the door was now wide open. Should she risk it? Perhaps she could get away.

She flung her cloak around her shoulders and wrapped Blanche in a shawl. She found her reticule and her canvas bag, and stuffed in what clothing she could. She had very little money, but it might be enough to get them back to Brynhyfryd House and safety.

Nesta crept silently into the kitchen. Black Jack was just lifting a saucepan from the embers of the range fire.

' 'Tis warmed,' he said. 'Spoon it to her, but hurry.'

Nesta sat on a chair with Blanche on her lap and spooned the warm milk into her rosebud mouth. Black Jack was restlessly watching, shuffling about the kitchen as though on hot bricks.

'Why are you helping us?' she asked, watching his every move. She saw now that he was a man of dusky skin, with a wide nose and thick lips. In the better light of the big oil lamp he had lit, she also saw that by the smoothness of his face he was not an old man at all as she had supposed.

'Helping myself, I be,' he said. 'I was digging those trenches yesterday, and suddenly it came to me as clear as a bell. I be digging my own grave.'

'What've you to fear from Jebediah Crabbe?' Nesta asked sceptically. 'You're his servant.'

'I be caretaker of this house, and when it be rented I be rented with it,' said Black Jack. 'Jebediah Crabbe and I be well known to each other. And Mangler and I are old enemies, too.' He spread his arms wide. 'It was he that crippled me in the ring years ago. I've not forgotten or forgiven. One day he'll pay.'

'But why do you fear for your life?'

'I know too much.' He pointed to Blanche enjoying the milk. 'She be the abducted child, Blanche Watkins,' he said. 'The newssheets be full of her murder . . . and yours.'

'But we are not murdered!' Nesta cried out. So that was what everyone thought. Well, she would soon put things right when she returned to Roath.

'But you will be murdered if we don't shift,' Black Jack said impatiently. He grabbed hold of her canvas bag. 'That be enough milk for the babe,' he said. 'We must be away.'

On impulse Nesta pushed the spoon into her reticule, and hurriedly bundled Blanche in the shawl again. 'Where are we going?' she asked breathlessly. 'No coaches will be leaving Cardiff at this time of night.'

'We go to a safe place I know of,' he said. 'It's nothing fancy, but it's clean and the landlady is respectable.' He gave a mirthless laugh. 'Jeb will never think to look for us among honest folk.'

Nesta thought about her shortage of money. Did she have enough for lodging and the coach fare back to Roath? She doubted it. An idea occurred to her.

'Tell me, Mr Crow, have you seen a pair of miniature paintings about the house? Jebediah stole them. They rightfully belong to Miss Blanche here. Help me find them.'

'There's no time, woman, I tell you,' he said angrily. 'Our lives are hanging by a thread.'

'Where does he sleep?' she demanded to know. The

paintings were valuable, and she was in no doubt he would keep them close by him.

Leaving Blanche in her wicker basket in the kitchen, Nesta followed the awkwardly-moving man back upstairs, while he grumbled and cursed under his breath, but she realised she was no longer in fear of him. Black Jack Crow was as terrified of Jebediah as she was.

He opened a door at the top of the stairs, and Nesta stepped into a large bedroom. She hurried to the tall chest, pulled out the drawers one by one and rummaged through them.

'Search the bedding!' she told him. 'The wardrobe, too.'

A few minutes passed and then Black Jack said. 'Do these be them?' He held up the pair of paintings, and Nesta rushed eagerly forward and took them from him. Without these paintings, Jebediah had no proof against her.

'Oh, thank goodness,' she said. 'Now let us go from this terrible place.'

They hurried down the short drive to the gates, Nesta clutching Blanche to her, the paintings in her reticule, while Black Jack carried her canvas bag. She saw that he had nothing of his own with him. While he was not ragged, his clothes were old and much worn. How would he manage to live, she wondered, now that he had left his caretaking work. He was hardly fit for heavy manual labour.

They were on the outskirts of the town and as they walked, dwellings became more numerous. After half an hour or so, when her feet began to ache and Blanche was becoming heavier by the minute, Black Jack stopped outside a small cottage.

'This be the place,' he said.

'Who lives here?' Nesta asked nervously.

'Miss Gamble is the tenant. I be doing a bit of gardening for her from time to time.'

He stepped up and knocked the door. It was opened almost immediately as though someone had been waiting up for his knock, and a small woman, her head enclosed in a mop cap, peered at them.

'It be me, Miss Gamble,' Black Jack said in a low voice. 'And I bring others with me.'

'No dogs!' a high-pitched voice shrilled. 'I'll not have those dirty beasts in the house.'

'No dogs,' Black Jack said as soothingly as his gruff voice would allow. 'Only a babe and a girl.'

Thankfully, Nesta stepped into a large room where even at this hour a huge fire burned in the range. The little thin woman in the mop cap fussed around them like a bluebottle. She peered up into Nesta's face.

'A babe,' she said, and in the lamplight Nesta could see suspicion in her gimlet eyes. 'Are you a widow woman?'

'That she be,' Black Jack said hastily. 'Lost at sea her husband be,' he said. 'She be going home to her family.'

The gimlet eyes darted back and fore. 'She isn't in mourning,' the shrill voice pointed out. 'Disrespectful that is.'

'I have only recently been widowed,' Nesta spoke up, the lie dripping effortlessly from her lips. 'And have no money to buy black yet.'

'No money!'

'She has enough for her night's lodgings,' Black Jack cut in quickly. 'Now, Miss Gamble, where can we lay our heads?'

'The girl and babe must share my bed,' Miss Gamble said. 'You must do with the mat in front of the range.'

Nesta was annoyed to hear that. 'Mr Crow is paying for a bed for the night,' she spoke up sharply. Miss Gamble might be respectable, but she wasn't sure the old woman was honest. 'I think you must find him one.'

Miss Gamble muttered under her breath and looked angered at Nesta's interference.

'Oh, very well,' she agreed grudgingly. 'There's a bed in the room over the stable. Now, I'm away to mine for what's left of the night.' She gave Nesta a ferocious stare. 'Don't wake me when you come to bed.'

'We must rise early,' Black Jack told Nesta when Miss Gamble had retired. 'I must find safe hiding in the town and you must get an early coach to wherever you be going.'

'Blanche and I will return to Brynhyfryd House,' Nesta said. 'Her father will be overjoyed to find that she had not been murdered.'

Black Jack's head twisted awkwardly on his shoulders as he tried to shake his head. 'You can't return there,' he said gravely.

'Why ever not?'

She had the paintings back in her possession. They had probably not been missed in the excitement of Blanche's abduction, so it would be simple to replace them. She already had a tale for Sir Tecwyn of being snatched from the grounds of the house. No one could refute her story, except Jebediah, and she hoped she had seen the last of him.

'Because like me, you and the babe must disappear if you want to go on living,' Black Jack said patiently. 'I heard them talking. The child is in someone's way, and that someone paid Jeb Crabbe to murder her. If you return her to her father, the child will surely be murdered at some time. Jebediah Crabbe is not a man to give up on a deal.'

'But Sir Tecwyn should know that his daughter is safe,' Nesta argued.

'She will only be safe as long as everyone, including Jeb Crabbe, believes the child be dead. You yourself be in danger, girl,' he went on. 'Like me, you know too much for Jeb's good. You could put him and others on the gibbet. Believe me, they'll not rest until you're six foot under.'

Nesta put her hand to her mouth. 'Where on earth am I to go with a child?'

'Have you no family, then?'

Nesta turned to stare into the flames of the fire. Go home to

Cwmrhyddin Cross, back to the poverty she had so eagerly escaped three years ago? And how would she explain the baby? She turned back to look at her companion.

'Do you know where I could sell the paintings for a fair price?'

Black Jack rubbed his jaw. 'There be many pawnbrokers in the town,' he said. 'But we can't risk hawking from one to the other.' He hesitated. 'I know a man who'll deal, and no questions asked.' He held out his hand. 'Give me the paintings now, and I'll go and see him. He's used to visitors on such errands at all hours.'

Nesta hesitated. The value of the paintings were all Blanche and she had between them and destitution. How far could she trust Black Jack?

He frowned at her hesitation. 'I won't gyp you, girl,' he said, a note of regret in his voice that she doubted him. 'I may look like a gargoyle and a scallywag, but I have my pride, and I be an honest man.'

While it was obvious there was nothing to fear from him, it did not make him trustworthy. He was in dread of his life and could disappear into the underworld of Cardiff any time he chose, especially when in possession of a sizable sum. But what other choice did she have? Meekly, Nesta handed the paintings to him.

'You go to your bed,' he advised. 'I'll return as soon as I can. I'll have your money for you, or my name's not Black Jack Crow.'

8

The moon's silvery light threw everything into sharp relief, the light reflecting off every leaf and off the bark of birch trees close by where Fletcher Watkins was hidden. He stood in the shadow of the tall gate pillar, his pistol at the ready. He had been hidden since dusk, determined to be settled long before his quarry arrived.

Having thought carefully of what he intended to do he realised a great deal of risk was involved. The man might have companions. Fletcher did not want to be recognised. He had too many connections to the low life of the town. It was enough that he was obliged to Jebediah Crabbe, a man he loathed and despised, he did not want to be the victim of blackmail besides, and so he took the precaution of wearing a hooded cloak and hiding the lower part of his face with a kerchief.

His limbs were becoming stiff with tension and the waiting, when suddenly he heard the familiar sound of a horse's shoe striking a stone and then the soft whinny of the startled animal. There was a jingle of harness and the creak of leather as the rider dismounted not too many yards from where Fletcher was hidden.

After a moment when he guessed the rider was tethering the horse, he heard footsteps approach the gates of the house, boots scuffing along the dirt track that was the road to Roath. Fletcher shrank back further into the shadows of a high hedge and let his quarry pass through the gates. Moonlight showed him a tall bulky figure in rough clothing walking unsteadily towards Brynhyfryd House about a quarter of a mile away, making no attempt at stealth.

Fletcher emerged from his hiding place and moving silently on the balls of his feet like a boxer he approached the man from behind.

'Don't turn around,' Fletcher commanded curtly. 'I have a pistol.'

Startled, the man did that very thing, almost toppling over sideways as he swung his bulk to face Fletcher.

'What the hell . . .?' He peered at Fletcher, obviously disconcerted at his appearance. 'What are you? A highwayman? I'm just a poor workingman, your honour. I've no money.'

'But you have expectations,' Fletcher sneered. 'You're about to take Sir Tecwyn's money.'

The man started. 'How do you know that? Did Jeb Crabbe send you to watch me?'

It was Fletcher's turn to be startled. 'Are you Crabbe's man?' he asked. 'Is he at the back of this?'

'Well you must know that, squire, if Jeb put you up to making sure I don't run off with the loot.'

'Where is the child?'

The man gave a sour laugh. 'I'm Crabbe's lackey not his confidant. I know nothing of the child's whereabouts.'

'Where are you to take the money?'

The man paused a moment. 'You ask too many questions, squire,' he said finally, his tone changing. 'I think I've had enough of you.'

He lunged forward as though to take Fletcher in a bear hug. Without hesitating, Fletcher fired the pistol. At such close range there was no chance of missing vital organs, and with a curious grunt, the man's knees buckled and he fell sideways onto the path. Fletcher stepped back a few paces, caution telling him to wait. When there was no further movement, he approached the body, and with his foot, turned the man over on his back. He was bleeding profusely from a wound high up near the base of his throat. If he wasn't already dead, he soon would be.

Throwing back the cloak's hood, Fletcher knelt down and began to search through the man's pockets; a few coins, a plug of tobacco and a slip of paper. He pushed that into his own waistcoat pocket. Something else was hidden beneath the man's vest. It was a baby's coat and as he held it up in the moonlight Fletcher gasped, seeing the dark stains on it. Blood!

Blanche Watkins *was* dead. Fletcher straightened, feeling deep satisfaction at the knowledge, and stared down at the prone form at his feet. He had no intention of leaving the man there to be found. Tecwyn might suspect he was responsible, and in anger and revenge at the supposed loss of his daughter, might even report him to the magistrate.

He was thankful for the moon's light once again. Leaving the body lying where it had fallen for the moment, he went in search of the man's horse. It was tethered some little distance along the track. Fletcher led it back, and twisting the man's foot securely into the stirrup, led the horse back out through the gates and along the road, dragging the body with it.

He remembered there was a deep water-filled ditch at one point along the track. A body could lie there for years undetected. He led the horse to the spot, and releasing the man's foot, rolled the body to the edge of the ditch. One kick and the corpse went over the edge and splashed into the deep water. He removed the saddle, harness and bit from the animal and threw them in after the body.

Taking off his hat, he struck the horse's rump with it, shouting wildly as he did so. Eyes staring, nostrils flaring, the horse bolted away along the track towards Roath. Fletcher watched it go as it galloped at top speed. It would be many miles away before it slowed down. There was no evidence left that the man had ever been here, and Fletcher felt safe.

He touched his vest pocket and heard the rustle of paper. The moonlight was not bright enough to read by, but he was certain he would soon learn where Jebediah Crabbe could be found.

It was just before midnight when Jebediah and Mangler Harris returned to a house in darkness. No welcoming lamp was lit as Jebediah had expected.

'Lil's as drunk as a parson, I expect,' Mangler opined. 'You shouldn't have left that quart of gin lying around, Jeb.'

'I didn't,' Jebediah said in a lowered tone. 'I thought you'd provided it.'

'Not me!'

A candlestick was kept on the table by the entrance together with a flint. Mangler lit the candle and held it aloft.

'Chippie should be here by now,' he said grimly. 'If he's bilked us he's a dead man.'

Jebediah stood in the centre of the hall. 'Listen!' he said.

For a moment Mangler stood beside him in silence holding the candlestick. 'I can't hear anything.'

'No, that's just the trouble,' Jebediah rasped. 'No baby crying. Something's wrong. I can feel it in my water.'

They took the stairs two at a time, Jebediah in front, going immediately to the room where Nesta and child were imprisoned. He cursed ferociously when he saw that the door was standing open.

'Flown the coop! Where's Lil?'

'Hell's Teeth!' Mangler shouted in fury. 'I told you we should've done for them straight away. It's the long drop for us now.'

'Not if we can find them and kill them.'

Jebediah stormed along the passage to another door and lifting his foot kicked it open. It swung back against the edge of a chest-of-drawers with a resounding crash, splintering one panel, but the noise did not disturb the mountain of flesh lying on the bed. Fat Lil snored on.

Speechless and inert for a moment, Jebediah stared at the recumbent figure, and then with a roar of fury he stepped forward to rain blows down on her body and head, punching and yelling like someone demented. In that moment he was near to killing her, so angered and frustrated was he.

Fat Lil woke up screaming. 'Murder! Murder!'

She tried to squirm away from his pounding fists and as she managed to sit up, he aimed a blow at her head. It sent her toppling off the bed onto the floor, still screaming, while he kicked at her mercilessly.

'You fat drunken sot!' he stormed. 'Where are they? Where have they gone? I'll have your gin-soaked gizzard for this!'

Her bloated face cut and streaming with blood, Lil could only squeal mindlessly in terror and pain.

'She don't know where they are, Jeb,' Mangler said. 'The fat cow slept right through it.'

Jebediah gave one final furious kick at the enormous abdomen and then stepped back, panting.

'We've got to find them. And where's that damned Chippie with the money.'

'Do you think he came here early and took them away?' Mangler asked. 'Trying to cut in on our game?'

'He doesn't have the nerve or the brains,' Jebediah said, wiping his face with a handkerchief. 'Lil must have left the door unlocked, and Nesta took the opportunity to skedaddle.' He strode towards the door. 'She can't have gone far on foot carrying the baby. Come on! We've got to find her if we want to save our necks.'

'What about Lil?'

Jebediah gave a brief glance at the still quivering mass of flesh.

'Leave her,' he said. 'We'll deal with her later. We haven't the time now. We must search the road between here and Cardiff.'

'Perhaps she went out into the country.'

Jebediah shook his head. 'Nesta's no fool. She told me her home is in Llanelly. She'll be looking to get a coach going west as quickly as possible, if she has enough for the fare.'

He paused, a disconcerting thought striking him. No, Nesta was no fool, quite the contrary. She had probably been planning for such an opportunity. And she would need money.

With an oath he grabbed the candlestick from Mangler's fist, and dashed along the passage to his own bedroom, flung open the wardrobe door, and rummaged inside.

'The bitch!' he yelled. 'She's taken the paintings!' He slammed the wardrobe door shut. 'I'll kill her with my bare hands!'

Nesta spent an uncomfortable night beside a snoring Miss Gamble. Blanche slept fitfully too, and grizzled a lot. Nesta crept into the living-room at an early hour and heated some milk on the range for the poor babe, wondering with a despairing heart whether she would ever see Black Jack Crow again.

Dawn was breaking when she heard the front door open and close, and sliding carefully off the bed, a shawl wrapped around her shoulders, she tiptoed along to the living-room. She saw his skewed dark shape outlined by the glowing embers.

'You were a long time,' she murmured resentfully.

'It took longer than I thought,' he said flatly. 'The cove I went to see is in prison. I had to find someone else.'

Nesta felt her throat close in a spasm of fear. 'Did anyone spot you? Were you followed back here?'

'No, I be a careful man,' Black Jack said. 'I did see one of Jeb's horses tethered in the town, near The Prince Llewellyn inn, Duke Street, where coaches leave for West Wales.' He gave a low laugh. 'Jeb be in turmoil, I reckon, what with you slipped from his grasp and the paintings gone too. There'll be no mercy if he catches us.'

'He mustn't!' Nesta gasped with terror at the thought. 'Where's the money for the paintings? Did you get a fair price?'

He held up a wad of bank notes, smiling lopsidedly. She grabbed at it and held it in her hand with a heavy sigh.

'It's all there,' he said as she started to count out the notes.

It was less than she had anticipated, and she stared at his oblique face with narrowed eyes, trying to read his thoughts. It occurred to her that he could still have cheated her. She could not know how much he had received from his contact.

He took a piece of paper from his pocket. 'Do you know your letters?' he asked.

'Of course I do,' she snapped.

'I know you don't trust me,' he said. 'So I be careful to get a signed note from the buyer. He be reluctant to give it,' he went on. 'But I persuaded him.'

Nesta took the paper from him and looked at it. It showed the exact amount she had in her hand. There could still be trickery involved, but now she was inclined to believe him.

'So, Jebediah is watching coach departures,' she said, feeling worried. It was doubtful Miss Gamble would let them stay here much longer, and where else could they hide? 'What am I to do?'

'He can't remain on watch for ever,' Black Jack opined. 'You must bide your time. A change of clothing, perhaps, and you need to buy a wedding ring.'

Nesta was startled. 'A wedding ring?'

'A spinster woman with a baby will draw unwanted curiosity and attention, and surely, wherever you go, your tale must be that you're a widow-woman.'

'Where would I purchase such things?'

'Any pawnbroker will have both, and be eager to sell,' Black Jack said. 'Before I sold the paintings I went into the coach sheds behind The Prince Llewellyn to look at the notices of departure. A coach going west leaves the inn at eight o'clock this morning. There will not be another going that way until past noon. You must try to catch the earlier coach.'

Nesta put her hands to her throat. 'But if they are watching for us . . . ?'

'You must take your best chance. Your lives depend on it.'

'How long do you think the journey will take?' She was filled with foreboding at the thought of it. Even if they did manage to get clear of the town, Jebediah could follow them west. He believed her home was in Llanelly. How she regretted telling that lie.

Black Jack was thoughtful. 'Probably a day and a half or two, depending on the going and stops on the way.' He indicated the money in her hand. 'But you have ample wherewithal to pay for lodgings on the way.'

'Thank you for being so thoughtful,' Nesta said. 'Do you come that way with us?'

He shook his head. 'We part company this hour. I've found a berth, working as assistant to a ship's cook. We sail for the New World at midnight.'

'You can't leave us, Jack!' Nesta exclaimed in fright.

He shook his head. 'I can't help you further. You must go one way, I the other. But I wish you luck.'

He placed some coins on the table nearby. 'That be for Miss Gamble,' he said. 'Give her my thanks.'

'But you didn't sleep in the bed,' Nesta retorted. 'You owe her nothing.'

He smiled faintly. 'She needs to make a living, too,' he said simply, and Nesta felt suddenly ashamed. This poor twisted man had more humanity in him than half a dozen able men.

'Now I be off,' he went on. 'Take care of yourself and the babe,' he said and turned towards the door.

'Wait, Jack!' Nesta exclaimed. She quickly took some of the

bank notes from the wad, and held them out to him. He looked taken aback.

'What be this, girl?'

'Forget the galley work,' Nesta said. 'Buy your passage to the New World. And there'll be some left over to help you make your way. Take it!' she urged when he hesitated. 'You have saved our lives.'

Hesitantly, he did so, giving her a long stare. 'No one has shown me such kindness before,' he said simply. 'And I thank you.'

He shuffled to the door and watching him go, Nesta wanted to cry out again that he must not leave them alone, but she held her peace. He had a very good chance of escaping Jebediah's clutches without a girl and a baby weighing him down. He could help them no further. She must do it alone.

'No sign of them!' Jebediah crashed his fist down on the kitchen table. 'Where are they? Who's hiding them?'

For the first time he felt a twinge of fear but strove to hide it from his companion. It wasn't wise to show weakness in front of a man like Mangler Harris. He could be trusted just as long as he knew Jebediah Crabbe was master and in control.

'The maid didn't turn up at the coach sheds, not while I was there,' Mangler said. 'And the clerk hadn't seen anyone the like of her.'

Jebediah gave him a savage glance. 'Are you sure you didn't slope off sometime for a glass or a wench?'

'What? With my own neck at risk,' Mangler snarled back. 'We're in deep trouble this time, Jeb, and out of pocket. Hell's Teeth. No baby, no Chippie and no Lil.' He blinked several times, the skin around his misshapen skull taut. 'Do you think Lil will gab?'

Jebediah studied Mangler's tight expression, knowing he was afraid, too.

'I think not,' he replied. 'I put the fear of all hell into her last night. She knows next time she crosses me I'll finish her.'

He glanced at the cold range, where yesterday's ashes were still in evidence, and at the dirty crockery, pots and pans piled up in a stone sink nearby.

'Black Jack has bolted, too, by the look of it,' he went on morosely. 'Took fright at the state Lil was in, I shouldn't wonder, and helped her get away. Thought he was in for the same.'

'The snivelling coward. I did for him good,' Mangler sneered.

His snigger, bordering on hysteria, grated on Jebediah's own jangled nerves.

'Never mind Black Jack,' he stormed. 'Find that damned girl and the brat. Get back to the coach station now.'

'But I've had no grub,' Mangler complained. 'Damn Black Jack for scarpering when he's needed here. I'll maim his other leg when I find him.'

Loud hammering at the front door made both men start to their feet.

'The beadles!' Mangler gasped. 'They've got us!'

'Be silent, damn you!' Jebediah commanded, although his own heart was thumping painfully in his chest.

It could not be the law knocking at their door, he reasoned quickly, trying to soothe his racing heart. Nesta was too deeply involved to go running to the authorities. It was she who had abducted the infant and would swing along with them.

'It's not the nabbers,' he asserted more confidently. 'Open the door. It could be Chippie Tonkin at last.'

'Not me, Jeb!' Mangler drew back, his frightened gaze darting to the back door. 'I'm not walking headlong into a trap.'

With an angry grunt, Jebediah strode out into the passage that led to the front of the house. After a moment's hesitation

Mangler was at his heels. If it was the magistrate at the door, Jebediah speculated, then they would have to bluff their way out of it. There was nothing in the house now that would betray that the girl and child had ever been there.

Jebediah jerked open the front door, still half expecting to see figures in top hats and blue belted coats, and so he started in astonishment to see the man standing in the porch. 'Watkins! What the infernal blazes are you doing here?'

Fletcher Watkins pushed his unbuttoned top coat to one side, and Jebediah saw a pistol wedged in his belt. 'We have unfinished business, Crabbe,' he said harshly. 'And I demand an explanation.'

Watkins barged forward attempting to push his way in. With an angry growl Mangler stepped towards him, his fist raised. Watkins immediately put his hand to his belt.

'Keep that ape-man away from me,' he rasped. 'Or by God, I'll empty my pistol into him.'

'Easy, Mangler,' Jebediah said, relieved that it was not the authorities at the door. 'Let Mr Watkins come in.'

Jebediah led the way back to the kitchen at the back of the house. Fletcher Watkins stared around him with a wrinkled nose, and, despite their situation, Jebediah was amused at the disgust on his face.

'Well, Mr Watkins, to what do we owe the pleasure of your company?' he asked. He was puzzled and worried that their whereabouts were known. He wondered if Lil had been speaking out of turn after all.

He indicted the pistol in Watkins' belt. 'You come well prepared, I see.'

'I am that,' Fletcher Watkins said with a bitter laugh. 'Now that I realise the treacherous men I deal with.'

Mangler growled again, but Jebediah lifted a hand for silence. 'You had better explain yourself, Mr Watkins.'

'It's you that owes me an explanation,' Fletcher Watkins

exploded. 'A ransom for a dead child? What game is this you're playing?'

Jebediah eyed him closely. 'From where did you learn of the ransom?'

'From my brother, where else?' Fletcher Watkins answered. 'A ransom was not in our deal. You'd have taken the money, ransom enough for a king to boot, and kept it, without a word of it to me. That's my money, or will be soon.'

Jebediah strolled towards the table on which his cane lay. 'And how did you know where to find us?' he asked casually. Chippie's failure to turn up with the money, under dire threat, was perhaps about to be explained.

Fletcher Watkins reached into the pocket of his waistcoat. 'I took this from the body of your man,' he said airily. 'Before I pitched him into a ditch.' He held out a slip of paper.

Jebediah recognised it immediately and a new wave of rage engulfed him. 'Chippie Tonkin is dead?' he asked, feeling his neckerchief tighten as his throat swelled. 'Then *you* must have my money?'

'Your man never collected it,' Fletcher Watkins said triumphantly. 'I shot him dead first.'

'You murdered him?' Mangler snarled.

'He attacked me,' Fletcher Watkins said defensively. 'I did no more than defend myself. And, he was on nefarious business.'

Jebediah felt his wrath overtake him. 'You interfering swine!' he exploded. 'You've robbed me, and you'll regret it.'

A red mist suddenly clouded his vision at the realisation that his carefully laid plans had been thwarted once again. He snatched up his cane from the table, and in a second withdrew the fine rapier from its sheath. Grasping the man's right arm to prevent him reaching his pistol, he lunged at Fletcher Watkins, forcing him back against the wall, the rapier's point at the man's throat, already drawing blood.

'No man, or woman for that matter, cheats me of what is mine and lives to tell the tale,' Jebediah snarled. 'I already have a grave awaiting you in the orchard.'

'Wait! Hold up, Jeb!' Mangler exclaimed, attempting to stay his arm. 'If you kill him now we can say fare-thee-well to the loot. Think of our losses already.'

Jebediah was incensed. 'What do I care for that? He has cheated me.'

'And he'll repay handsomely, Jeb,' Mangler went on. 'But let's not throw it all away. Chippie is no loss. We were going to kill him anyway.'

Jebediah stared into Watkins' sweating face, seeing abject fear in his eyes. Mangler was right. Too much had been put into this enterprise to end it all now. Fletcher Watkins would pay dearly, and Betsy might still have her fun yet.

He stepped away from the quaking man, taking the blade from his throat. Watkins staggered sideways, looking limp with relief. He lifted a handkerchief to his bleeding throat.

'I'm the one being cheated,' Watkins said weakly.

'Say no more, fool!' Mangler warned.

Jebediah glared at the wounded man. 'You're a lucky fellow, Fletcher Watkins,' he said harshly. 'But watch yourself, for your luck may run out.'

One day he would kill him when he had drained him dry of all he possessed, even that fine house that belonged now to Sir Tecwyn.

'Until then,' he went on. 'You'll pay through the nose when you inherit, believe me.'

'Yes, but when will that be?' Watkins was recovering his composure, and staggered to a kitchen chair to sit down heavily. 'Blanche Watkins is dead. When will you send my brother to join his daughter?'

Jebediah's eyes narrowed suspiciously. 'How do you know the child is dead?'

Watkins withdrew something from between his waistcoat and shirt. It was a bloodied baby's coat. 'This is my evidence,' he said smugly.

Mangler burst out laughing. 'That's no more than . . .'

'Quiet!' Jebediah cut him short, flashing him a warning glance. He turned to Watkins. 'Yes, the child is safely dead, Mr Watkins, the corpse taken by the river Taff, and the nursemaid along with her,' he went on. 'Your brother's days are numbered.'

Nesta paid Miss Gamble for her night's lodging, and began to gather her belongings, her reticule and canvas bag, although there was now very little to carry as the last nappy had been used that morning. She would leave the wicker basket. It had served its purpose and would be no more than a hindrance on her journey.

Miss Gamble stood by watching her. 'You'd find it easier to manage if you used your head and carried the baby Welsh fashion,' she opined.

Flustered, Nesta was annoyed at her disparaging tone. 'I know a little more about the care of babies than a spinster like you, I think,' she snapped.

'Well, you think wrong,' the little woman snapped back. 'My mother had a baby every two years like clockwork,' she went on. 'I was barely fourteen when she upped and died in child-birth, leaving me to be mother, and often father, too, to my seven brothers and sisters.' She sniffed loudly. 'Oh, yes, I know all about babies.'

Nesta felt chastened. 'I'm sorry I offended you, Miss Gamble.'

'You best be moving to catch that coach. They don't wait for nobody.'

Nesta took her leave, and walking in the direction pointed out by Miss Gamble began the long trek to the town of

Cardiff. It was still early, and she kept up a steady pace, trying to push out of her mind the many fears, doubts and worries which crowded in on her. She thought she knew how the fox must fear being chased by the savage hounds. Savage hounds were after her in the shape of Jebediah Crabbe and Mangler Harris, and they would show as much mercy as mad dogs.

The road began to get busier as she walked, with carriages and gigs passing her, throwing up clouds of dust from the track, and there were people on foot like herself. When she reached the town she realised it was market day. She glimpsed the mighty edifice of Cardiff castle rising above the roofs and chimneys, and in the far distance, the tall masts and rigging of ships in the dock.

The place was bustling; crowds milling to and fro on the narrow pavement, and she found it hard going with the baby in one arm and her bag and reticule on the other. Two men in rough threadbare clothing jostled her.

'The vessel Barbary Belle is about to dock, so I just heard,' one man said to the other. 'Come on! Labour may be needed to unload the cargo. There could be rich pickings.'

They hurried past mindless of her, and Nesta felt her head spin. She must find Duke Street before eight o'clock. As though to spur her on the quarter chimes sounded from a clock tower near by. She had but fifteen minutes to raise her fare and board.

She made for the castle, thrusting her way through the throng as best she could. With so many people about there might be no space left on the coach, and Nesta swallowed a cry of panic at the thought as she hurried along the pavement. Then glancing across the road relief enveloped her as she saw the swinging sign of The Prince Llewellyn inn. She would be in time after all.

She stepped into the road and almost under the wheels of a

passing coal dray, receiving a shouted oath from the driver. That made her jump back quickly, and as she did so she spotted a familiar figure lounging against the wall opposite, avidly watching the comings and goings of people through a tall arch which must lead to the coach departure sheds at the rear of the inn.

Mangler Harris!

Terrified, Nesta shrank back in to the crowd. Had he seen her? She whirled and ran blindly away, not know which way she went, expecting to feel his great hands on her shoulders at any moment.

She ran and ran, sobbing, jostled on all sides, while Blanche in her arms, sensing her panic, wailed loudly. After ten minutes, when Nesta had not been captured, she paused, panting for breath. She had escaped him! They were still free!

Her elation died suddenly. Yes, they were free but her escape route was cut off. What could she do now? She must wait until midday, she decided, and try again. If that failed, she had no alternative but to return to Miss Gamble, but would they find any kind of welcome with her?

Blanche was grizzling and fractious. Poor babe, Nesta thought, her heart full of pity. She was hungry and miserable and needed a change of nappy again.

She paused near a shop window to catch her breath and to think what to do next. There were hours to fill yet, and she could not walk about indefinitely. She glanced in at the window and realised it was a pawnbroker's. Black Jack's advice came into her mind. Then she saw something in the window which gave her an idea. There were several linen sheets displayed in a haphazard fashion in front of the window, their folds yellowed and dusty.

One sheet torn up into squares would do for makeshift nappies, Nesta decided, and taking her courage in hand, entered the shop. The bell ringing made her jump, and as if by magic, a thin, stooped little man dressed in a long black coat seemed to pop up before her.

'Yes? What have you got?' he asked snappily. 'No clothing! I'm awash with clothing.'

'I'm not pawning,' Nesta told him airily. 'I'm purchasing, if your price is right.'

'Oh!' A smile, if it could be called that, split his narrow face. 'Come right in, madam. I'm at your disposal.'

Nesta sized him up. He looked a mean little fellow, but she would not part with a penny piece more than she was prepared to pay. And she must not show how desperate she was.

'The linen you have in the window,' she began haughtily. 'I wish to buy one sheet.'

He drew back his chin. 'One sheet? Of what use is one sheet?'

Nesta raised her brows and looked down her nose at him, trying to ignore Blanche's whimpers. 'Do you wish to make a sale or not? There are other pawnbrokers, you know.'

Hastily, he rushed to fetch the sheets from the window and placed them on the counter. She fingered them carefully. They were of the finest linen. Not ideal for nappies, but beggars could not be choosers.

'How much?'

'A shilling.'

'Absurd!' Nesta flung the sheet back on the counter, and jigged the baby up and down, feeling dampness within the shawl, wishing the child would stop crying for just a moment.

'Sixpence,' he said.

Nesta sniffed and glanced around. Perhaps he was more desperate than she was. The place was a mishmash of all kinds of bric-a-brac, and everything dusty and uncared for. Looking more closely at his coat cuffs she saw they were worn and frayed. Business was not good for the little fellow.

'I'll give you thruppence for the sheet. The cleanest one, mind.'

'What?' He looked astounded.

Nesta shrugged. 'Very well.' She picked up the canvas bag from the counter. 'Good day to you.'

'Wait! Wait!' He came around the counter to where she stood. 'Thruppence it is.'

Nesta smiled condescendingly as she picked the cleanest looking sheet and tucked it into the canvas bag. She turned her back to rummage in her reticule for the coins. As she did so, a glass bowl on the counter caught her eye. Inside was a jumble of jewellery, chains, bangles, necklaces, obviously glass, all dull and lacklustre, but amongst it all she spotted a wedding band. Brass or gold, she could not tell, and she had more sense than to ask.

Turning back to him she handed over the three pennies, which he grabbed eagerly, and then she glanced around superciliously.

'You have a great deal of rubbish here,' she remarked, marvelling at her own ingenuity, while he spluttered incoherently. She let her fingers trail in the bowl and then held up one necklace. 'Glass, of course. How much?'

'Er . . . a shil . . . sixpence,'

Nesta let the necklace fall back into the bowl with a tut of disbelief.

'Thruppence?' he suggested hopefully.

She shook her head, and picked up the ring. 'Brass,' she declared disparagingly. 'How vulgar.'

'That's twenty-two carat gold,' he spluttered.

'Nonsense,' Nesta said. 'I can see the verdigris from here.'

'Thruppence?' he squeaked.

Nesta sighed. 'I don't know. They say it's unlucky to wear another woman's wedding ring, even if it's brass.' She glanced at his hopeful narrow face. 'Oh, very well.'

She paid him and put the ring in her reticule feeling extremely pleased with herself. She had no qualms about beating him down in price. Doubtless, he had given next to nothing to the previous owners for their precious possessions. The ring probably was brass anyway. There could be nothing of real value in this fusty shop.

He stood before her rubbing his hands. 'Does madam require anything else?'

Nesta thought of Mangler waiting in the street and how easily he might have recognised her. 'Do you by any chance have an old fashioned poke bonnet?'

He threw up his hands. 'I'm awash with bonnets.' He scurried into the back of the shop and soon returned with an armful of headgear. 'Madam may choose. They are all very good quality.'

Good quality they might have been at one time, but they were also very much out of date. Most were damp stained, but there was one that looked as if it might do. Nesta held it up, but before she could speak, the pawnbroker interrupted:

'Thruppence,' he declared swiftly.

Nesta nodded, and reaching up with her one free hand undid the ribbon under her chin and removed her own hat. 'You may take this as well,' she told him airily, handing it to him. 'I've no further use for it. It's new,' she assured him when he frowned. 'And quite fashionable. It will be snapped up by some discerning lady.'

Nesta donned the bonnet, and the pawnbroker obliged by tying the ribbon under her chin. She left the shop well satisfied. However, there were still some hours to go before she returned to the coaching depot. She had the means now for making the child clean and comfortable, but there was still the matter of sustenance.

Walking on somewhat aimlessly, searching for what she did not know, Nesta came to a square where rows of ramshackle stalls stood in the open air, selling all kinds of goods. It seemed a popular market, for people milled about listening to the stallholders bellowing their slogans.

She needed bread and milk, but also some kind of container to mix them in. Stopping at one stall she saw the ideal thing, a small pudding basin. She fingered it thoughtfully, aware of the stallholder's sharp eyes on her.

'How much?'

'Sixpence.'

Nesta opened her mouth to begin haggling, but one look at the woman's hard features and set mouth told her she would be wasting her time. 'I'll take it,' she said meekly.

She bought a small round loaf at another stall, and a meat pie from a passing street vendor. She had already noticed a dairy on the corner; went in and bought a small measure of milk in the basin, avoiding the curious stare of the dairyman as she did so.

'Is there a park nearby?' she asked him.

He jerked his thumb, and she followed the direction he indicated. Within five minutes she reached a small park, hardly bigger then the square she had just left. She chose a bench close by a hedge, away from public gaze.

She took the ring from her reticule, examined it more closely for a moment, and then slipped it onto the third finger of her left hand. It fitted reasonably well and looked genuine enough. She admired it for a moment more. To the outside world she was now a married woman and a mother. She felt it gave her a new status, but would her family believe her?

With a helpless shrug Nesta attended to the baby's needs. The torn sheet provided quite a few nappies, enough to see her through the next day or so, or at least until she reached her destination, Cwmrhyddin Cross.

She threw the dirty nappy under the hedge, and then mixed the bread and milk, glad she had had the gumption to retain the spoon, and fed the ravenous child.

Poor little mite! Nesta reflected, and felt tears sting her eyes, tears of jagged remorse. Her foolishness alone was responsible for the child's awful plight, wrenched from the loving arms of her father, probably never to see him again.

She pulled herself together, knowing such feelings were of little use to either of them at this desperate moment. She ate the meat pie and drained what was left of the milk.

The sun was rising higher and she realized it was nearing time to go. She must make her way back to the inn as quickly as possible. Blanche was chortling now that she was comfortable and fed. Nesta kissed her tenderly.

'You're my child now,' she told the baby, whose large dark eyes gazed up at her so trustingly. 'And I'll love you and look after you always.' She prayed that she would be given the chance to make amends. 'But we must change your name, my dear little one.' Nesta searched her memory for something resembling the child's real name. 'Oh, yes, of course. From this moment on your name is Bronwen.'

9

Hurrying along the streets towards the castle, Nesta heard a nearby clock tower strike quarter to noon, and her heart jumped into her mouth. She dare not miss this coach, and she prayed Mangler would not still be watching.

On the pavement opposite The Prince Llewellyn, Nesta drew back into the recess of a shop doorway, her gaze raking the crowds that paraded the pavement opposite. She could not stifle a cry of dismay to see that Mangler was still at his post. Shrinking back further, and clutching Bronwen more tightly, she stared across at him, numbed with fear and nauseated with desperation. Would they never escape? Any minute the coach must come rattling out through the arch, taking with it their last hope for survival. What was she to do? She wished with all her heart that Black Jack were here to help.

There was nothing for it but to slip away again, lose herself once more in the crowds, but where was she to go now? She was about to creep gingerly out of her hiding place, when Mangler stirred, pushing himself away from the wall, and stretching. He moved a few steps along the pavement, looking in the direction of the inn's open doorway. He passed his hand over his mouth as though thirsty, and the next moment seemed to make up his mind, for he strode quickly through the doorway and out of sight.

Nesta held her breath. She could not believe luck had turned her way at last. She offered up a prayer of thankfulness, and head down, her face obscured by the bonnet, hurried across the busy street, frantically dodging carriages and carts, closing her ears to the furious oaths and curses flung her way. And then, her heart still in her mouth, she passed through the high archway and found herself in the yard behind the inn, and before her was the coaches' way station.

Porters with loaded handcarts scurried about, shifting luggage to and fro, while people, possibly prospective passengers, milled around or stood talking in groups. Nesta quickly joined their numbers, screening herself from view from the street. Mangler might return at any time. He must not spot her now.

She caught at the sleeve of a passing porter. 'Where do I pay for a seat on the next coach?'

With a distracted frown, he jerked his thumb over his shoulder, and hurried away with his laden cart. She saw a wooden hut against the back wall of the inn, and a cluster of people around it. Hurrying, Nesta joined their group. Seeing a woman carrying a baby one or two men politely stepped aside, and Nesta found herself at the ticket window. The clerk was gazing at her impatiently.

'Yes, well! What is it?'

'Is there a space left on the midday coach leaving for West Wales?'

He pursed his lips, shaking his head. 'No space left inside, missus. You'll have to ride atop.'

Nesta was appalled. 'I can't do that! Can't you see I have a . . . my baby with me? No! No! You must find me room inside.'

He shrugged, not the least concerned. 'It's ride atop or wait until the morning.'

'But I must leave now!' Nesta cried out. 'It's a matter of life and death.'

'Nothing I can do,' the clerk said impatiently. 'Move aside now please,' he went on, motioning her away with a flutter of his ink-stained fingers. 'Others want to travel if you don't.'

'I do beg your pardon for intervening,' a man's voice said over her shoulder. 'May I be of help?'

Nesta whirled around to stare up in fright at the newcomer. A stout elderly man in a cleric's dog collar and dark clothing raised his hat and smiled beningly at her. There was something vaguely familiar about his features, but she was too over-wrought to remember where they had met previously.

'Don't distress yourself, Madam,' he said soothingly. 'I believe I have the solution.'

He peered through the cubby hole at the clerk. 'I am the Reverend Ellis. I have already booked and paid for space inside the coach. This lady will now take it and I will ride on top. Be so good as to take her fare, my man.'

His name was familiar too, and Nesta was puzzled. She watched hopefully as the clerk ran a grubby finger down a written list in front of him and then tapped a name written there. 'Very good, your worship,' he said respectfully, touching his forelock. 'As you wish.'

'Oh, thank you Reverend sir, for your goodness and kind-ness to a widow-woman,' Nesta fibbed effortlessly, overjoyed at this turn of events, and yet felt like bursting into tears of relief, but there was no time for that now. She hastily paid the required sum for the journey to the village of Cwmrhyddin Cross, on the road to Carmarthen, but still did not feel safe from Mangler.

'May I take my place on the coach straight away?' she eagerly asked the clerk.

'No one boards until the driver is in his seat,' the clerk said importantly. 'Which will be any minute now.'

'Come along, Madam, I will help you board,' the Reverend Ellis said, taking the canvas bag from her. 'Let us join the other passengers. There! See! The driver is climbing to his perch.'

They had to wait several more minutes while the foremost passengers fussed over their luggage before taking their seats.

Nesta endeavoured to keep as many people between her and the archway entrance to the street, terrified of being discovered at the last moment. She would not feel safe until settled inside the coach.

'So you journey to Cwmrhyddin Cross,' Reverend Ellis remarked as they stood together waiting. 'I go there myself.' She heard the curiosity in his voice and was immediately wary. 'Have we met before, Madam?'

'I think not, sir.'

Before he could say more it was her turn to board. He helped her in, saw her safely wedged on the seat between two very rotund gentlemen, and handed her the canvas bag. 'May your journey be as comfortable as maybe,' he said.

Nesta felt guilty. 'Will you be safe, sir, riding atop?'

'If God wills it,' was his simple answer.

Nesta was glad of the bulk of the two men on either side of her. At least she would be screened from view as the coach left the inn. She would escape Mangler's clutches yet.

Before she was ready, the coach took a leap forward, rattling alarmingly on the cobbles of the yard. As curious as she was about Mangler's whereabouts, Nesta kept her head down as they passed through the arch. They were away and free!

The ride was smooth enough while they were still in the town but within the hour the going became roughened as the coach and the four horses trotted briskly along lanes and twisting dirt tracks out in the open countryside. She spared a thought for the Reverend Ellis, atop, probably clutching on for dear life. Where had they met before, and need she worry about it? Her mind filled with spinning the tale she would tell her parents to account for her return, especially in possession of a baby, she had no time to ponder further about him. But he too, was making for Cwmrhyddin Cross.

The two men either side of her, farmers by the looks of them, lit pipes without so much as by-your-leave as soon as the coach was on its way, to Nesta's annoyance and that of another woman on the opposite seat, who coughed pointedly and waved a fan energetically before her face. To no avail. The men puffed on. It was becoming stuffy in the confines of the coach, and Nesta was worried for Bronwen.

Her annoyance changed to embarrassment not an hour later when it became obvious to all in the coach that the child's nappy needed changing. There were tuts of disgust from the woman opposite, accompanied by her pained expression. A gaunt-looking man seated nearest the door dropped open the narrow window, which brought some relief, at least from the smoke.

Nesta felt compelled to speak up. 'I can do nothing until we reach the next halt, wherever that is,' she said pithily.

'The Sheep Inn in the village of Cowbridge,' another man opposite volunteered. 'The driver will change horses there. We'll be able to stretch our legs.'

But it was a very long while before the coach began to slow. The stout fellow sitting next to her took a watch out of his waistcoat pocket. 'Three o'clock,' he announced to no one in particular. 'We've made good time.'

The coach pulled into the yard of a fair-sized inn and came to a stop. The door was immediately yanked open by someone outside. A tousle-haired youngster, wearing the leather apron of an ostler peered in at them.

'Twenty minutes,' he chanted nasally. 'Twenty minutes.'

Nesta wasted no time. Spotting a trough and a water pump, she soon set Bronwen free of her nappy, throwing it down behind the trough, and then gently sponged the child's little rump with clean water, dried her carefully and put on her clean nappy. Bronwen waved her arms and legs happily and smacked her rosebud lips. Nesta was hungry herself, but the child must come first. She must devote her life to Bronwen now that she had deprived her of a father's love and care.

Milk, bread and honey were made available, and Bronwen ate her meal noisily and with obvious delight, while Nesta contented herself with bread and cheese. As she sat on the low wall outside the inn, waiting for the driver to mount to his place again, Reverend Ellis came and sat down next to her.

'Space has become available, so I ride inside from here,' he said conversationally.

Nesta was relieved to hear it. 'I can't thank you enough, sir,' she said earnestly. 'I was worried that a man of your years . . .'

She stopped; acutely embarrassed, but the elderly cleric merely chuckled. 'The Lord will take me in His own time.'

Nesta wished that she could be so philosophical, but, she reminded herself, for all his years, the Reverend had not stared death in the face as recently as she had.

They boarded again, Reverend Ellis sitting opposite her. She was glad to find there was more room since one of the stout farmers had quitted the coach. After a while she was conscious the cleric's steady gaze on her. When she ventured to meet his eye, he spoke:

'It's Nesta, I believe, isn't it?'

Nesta almost fell off the seat with astonishment and then a gripping fear. She stared at him, wordlessly; clutching Bronwen closer, panic making her blood run cold. Had she, after all, walked into a trap?

'Yes, yes, it is Nesta, Nesta Lewis,' he went on with conviction. 'Your parents are my parishioners. Don't you recognise me, child?'

Nesta shook her head dumbly.

'I hold the living at St Marks on the Hill, Cwmrhyddin Cross,' he said. 'Why, I remember you as a child. I officiated at your Christening. You left the village to go into service no more than three years ago, if memory serves me.' He paused and stared at her. 'I'm sorry to see you brought to widowhood so young.'

Her memory jogged, Nesta had a vague recollection of him, but very hazy. In those years, the shame of her family's penury had occupied her constantly. She had striven to get away from it, putting many memories out of her mind. Now she was running back with her tail between her legs; no richer but certainly wiser, and it would be best to begin her deception with the Reverend Ellis, for she might need his support when the time came.

She bowed her head and lifted her knuckle to wipe away a non-existent tear from her cheek. 'Oh, yes, sir. Lost at sea my husband was. A ship's captain, going down with his vessel.'

'Oh, dear me!' The Reverend looked genuinely shocked. 'And what was the name of this courageous man?'

Nesta said the first name that came into her head. 'Crow, sir, Captain Jack Crow. I'm the Widow Crow, and this is my daughter, Bronwen.'

'The poor fatherless mite, may the Lord protect her,' Reverend Ellis said mournfully. 'I will pray for you both, my child.'

Nesta was satisfied that he believed her story. Her mother Meg, always her critic, would not be so easily fooled.

They stopped next at the hamlet of Ewenny. It was a quarter past five o'clock, Reverend Ellis told her, and that they could expect to have a meal provided at the Ewenny Arms, for those who could afford it. Nesta hastily assured him that she could.

After taking another opportunity to change nappies, Nesta fed Bronwen on bread soaked in a rich chicken broth, while Nesta dined on cold mutton and potatoes. She sat with the Reverend Ellis, who seemed to have appointed himself her guardian whilst at the inn.

'Your parents must be looking forward to your return,' he said. 'Despite the sad circumstances.'

Nesta shook her head. 'They know nothing of my plight.' He

looked surprised. 'I didn't want to worry them unduly,' she added quickly.

'Quite so.'

Nesta could not stifle a yawn. 'How much longer will the journey take, sir?'

'Barring difficulties on the way, we should reach the village of Pyle about eight o'clock,' he said. 'There we will rest over-night. With an early start we should reach Cwmrhyddin Cross midday tomorrow.'

Midday tomorrow she would have to face her parents, particularly her mother, and lie in her teeth. Her father, Enoch, an easygoing man, with no real ambition to make a better living, could be easily twisted around Nesta's little finger, but Meg Lewis was another matter altogether. Her mother had always been able to see through Nesta's subterfuge since she was a small child, and had never forgiven her for leaving home just when she could have earned some money to help out.

Nesta felt her heart sink. Meg Lewis would be suspicious and not at all pleased that her errant daughter's return meant two extra mouths to feed. There would hardly be a welcome. Her heart raced a little faster, anticipating the skirmish to come.

Fletcher waited in the shadows of the gateway to Brynhyfryd House, but there was no comforting midnight moonlight as there had been on the night he had killed Jebediah Crabbe's lackey, Chippie Tonkin. The men he waited for this night were supposed to be his allies, but he would not turn his back on them for a second or trust them an inch.

He had insisted on being present when Crabbe outlined his plan for the disposal of Tecwyn. So much depended on the plan's success, the rest of his life, in fact, and, risky though it was, he had determined to be present when the deed was done, to prevent any further mistakes.

He heard the approach of a carriage and pair along the road, and stepped out onto the carriageway, making himself visible by holding high a lantern he had brought with him.

The carriage turned in at the gates and then came to an abrupt halt, Mangler at the reins. In a moment Jebediah Crabbe hastily emerged from inside.

'Mr Watkins!' Jebediah's voice was harsh. 'What are you doing here? Do you want to be recognised, man? You should be establishing your presence in the town.'

'Alexis will vouch for me should the need arise,' Fletcher retorted sharply. 'But that shouldn't be necessary. After all, you're here to arrange my brother's suicide from a broken heart, while I'm here to see there are no tricks and that everything goes well.'

'He'll be in the way, Jeb,' Mangler opined with a threatening growl. 'And what's worse, a witness. I don't like it.'

'Who's master here?' Fletcher asked Jebediah with a sneer. 'You or that ape-man?'

'I'm master, Mr Watkins, as well you know,' Jebediah said in a dangerous voice. 'Look on then, if you must, but I'll brook no interference, no second thoughts on your part.'

'I have no love for my brother,' Fletcher snorted derisively. 'The quicker he's dead the better I'll like it.'

'Very well, then,' Jebediah said. 'We walk from here. Move the carriage out of sight, Mangler, and then follow us.'

It was a quarter of a mile to the house. Fletcher and Jebediah strode in silence. Fletcher felt vulnerable, the hairs on the back of his neck rising at the thought of Mangler somewhere in the darkness behind him. Then suddenly Mangler was striding alongside, but that did not make Fletcher any the less uneasy. He was in treacherous, murderous company, and his only friend was the pistol tucked in his belt.

They moved more cautiously once the house was in sight.

'You're certain about the servants?' Jebediah asked in a hushed voice.

'Just the housekeeper, sleeping at the back of the house, and an elderly gardener, living over the stables,' Fletcher murmured. 'Nevertheless, let Tecwyn make no sound.'

'He'll not squawk a note with my hands around his throat,' Mangler chuckled. 'I guarantee it.'

They approached the french windows which Fletcher knew to be those of Tecwyn's study. The faint light of a lamp was just visible through the drapes.

'He is still up!' Fletcher said breathlessly. He had pictured entering his brother's bedroom, catching him asleep and helpless.

'Then we must go carefully,' Jebediah said.

The blade of Mangler's knife was inserted quietly into the space between the doors, the catch lifted noiselessly, and then the door was inched open. There was a deep silence in the room beyond, broken only by the spit of a log from the fireplace and the shifting of settling coals. With the fire built up at this time of night, Tecwyn obviously had no intention of going to his bed.

Jebediah tugged at Fletcher's sleeve and motioned him to enter, gesturing that he and Mangler would remain hidden for the time being. All at once Fletcher felt afraid. He had not bargained on meeting his brother face to face before seeing him die. He hesitated, and Mangler held up the knife before him, a sneering grin seen faintly on his face. Quelling a gasp for air, Fletcher parted the drapes and stepped inside.

Tecwyn was at his desk, hunched over, hands flat on the surface. He was so still that for a moment Fletcher thought that he must be already lifeless. He could not prevent a gasp then, and Tecwyn suddenly leaped to life, swinging round to face him, astonishment on his pale face.

'Fletch! What's the meaning of this untimely intrusion? Why didn't you enter in a civilised manner through the door?'

Conscious of the two men concealed behind the drapes, Fletcher felt his confidence return. 'Because, my dear brother, I didn't wish to be seen by the servants,' he retorted.

'So, you've come to destitution at last,' Tecwyn said, not without satisfaction, Fletcher thought. 'You're evading the authorities, I take it. Well, Fletch, you'll find no hiding place here.'

'On the contrary,' Fletcher snapped, thoroughly nettled. 'I'm about to become a very rich man. I'm here this night to witness your suicide, brother.'

'What?' Tecwyn looked started, and then glanced quickly down at the desk, where, on the blotting pad, a square of chamois leather covered an object. 'Why do you say that?'

'Is it not obvious?' Fletcher said mockingly. 'You're heart-broken at the loss of your wife and daughter. You've nothing more to live for, Tecwyn. Your wealth means nothing to you, while I . . . I deserve the high life it will give me.'

Tecwyn took a step away from the desk, his expression angry. 'Have you gone insane, Fletch? I believe you have. Your debauchery has finally addled your brain.'

'Keep back, Tecwyn,' Fletcher warned. 'I'm not alone.'

With an angry oath, Jebediah flung back the drapes and he and Mangler strode into the room. At the sight of them Tecwyn stepped back hastily.

'Who are these men?' he asked loudly. 'Why have you brought them here?'

'You shouldn't have treated me so shabbily, Tec,' Fletcher said bitterly. 'Cutting me from your will in favour of a mere girl-child was beyond the pale. It's your own fault Blanche is dead. When you signed that new will you also signed her death warrant.'

Tecwyn stared at him, his face suddenly gaunt. 'What are you saying?'

'He's saying nothing, Sir Tecwyn,' Jebediah interjected,

flinging a warning glance at Fletcher. 'Too much has been said already.'

'Not be me,' Fletcher blazed. 'I've a right to own this house, my father's house, and it will be mine now.'

'We waste time,' Jebediah growled. 'This business should've been over minutes ago.'

'I want my brother to know why he's about to die,' Fletcher retorted. 'He made me suffer long enough.'

Tecwyn stared fixedly at him, a great hatred in his expression.

'So you have come to this degradation, party to your own brother's murder, because of greed.' He shook his head. 'I despise you Fletcher. I was right to cut you off.'

He might once have quailed to see such an expression on Tecwyn's face, but now Fletcher felt all-powerful. 'You're a broken man, Tecwyn,' he went on scathingly and with some triumph. 'And will hang yourself from a tree in the grounds. Mangler here will help you.'

'You're mad, Fletch!' Tecwyn said in ringing tones. 'By God! It was you who took my child, wasn't it? You killed her!' He stepped forward, hands outstretched. 'I'll have your eyes for this. I'll have your very life.'

'Remain where you are, Sir Tecwyn,' Jebediah thundered. 'You can't overcome the three of us. Come with us quietly now, and meet your end like a man. If you rouse the housekeeper, we'll kill her also, and anyone else who discovers us.'

Tecwyn looked at Fletcher, his lip curled derisively. 'You've fallen into a cesspit, Fletch, and are as vile as your companions.'

'I've had enough of him,' Mangler burst out. 'It'll give me great pleasure to throttle the wind from his lungs.'

Mangler lunged forward, but in an instant Tecwyn was back at his desk. He flung aside the chamois cloth and snatched up the pistol it had concealed.

'Stand back, you hyena!' he shouted at Mangler, pointing the pistol at him. 'Stand back or I'll shoot you between the eyes.'

Mangler took no heed but charged on, a deep growl of rage in his throat. With only the briefest hesitation, Tecwyn fired point blank.

With a scream, Mangler staggered back, his hand clutching his opposite shoulder. 'I'm done for!'

'Get out of my house, all of you!' Tecwyn shouted. 'That shot will bring the servants. Run while you can before the authorities find you.'

Fletcher stared at his companions. Mangler clung to a chair for support, while Jebediah was staring at Tecwyn as a wolf stares at a lamb, but remaining immobile, and no wonder. Tecwyn was holding one of those brand-new two-shot pistols from America. They were all helpless while Tecwyn held that pistol.

Stunned at the turn of events, Fletcher was suddenly very frightened. 'What do you propose to do, Tec?' he asked querulously. 'You can't give me up. Think of the scandal.'

'I'll cheerfully watch while your neck is stretched for the murder of my child,' Tecwyn said bitterly.

Jebediah made a movement forward, and instantly Tecwyn trained the pistol on him. 'Don't tempt me to use this weapon again,' he said harshly.

Jebediah indicated the wounded Mangler. 'I merely wish to help my man here.'

Tecwyn looked undecided, and Mangler groaned in agony.

'Very well,' he said. 'But carefully.'

Taking swift advantage of his brother's inattention, Fletcher leaped forward attempting to grab at Tecwyn's gun hand. There was a brief struggle for the weapon, the brothers twisting and turning as they fought for possession. A second shot was let off, but went wide.

Then Jebediah lunged forward also, rapier withdrawn from the cane. As Tecwyn's back was towards him, Jebediah ran him through, the fine stiletto entering below the left shoulder blade. With a cry of pain and shock, Tecwyn's body arched forward as Jebediah withdrew the blade.

Holding his breath, Fletcher stepped away, the pistol safely in his grasp as Tecwyn sank to his knees before him. There he swayed for a moment, head raised, blood trickling from his mouth.

He stared up at Fletcher, he eyes already becoming hazy with impending death. 'My curses on you, Fletcher Watkins,' he croaked, blood bubbling in his throat. 'My wealth will taint your life. You will never again know a moment's peace.'

Then suddenly the light left his eyes, and he fell forward onto the carpet. Fletcher was rooted to the spot, his blood running cold as he stared down at his brother's inert body and the growing pool of blood beneath. Those last dying words would be with him for the rest of his life, he knew it. He struggled to pull himself together. Words could not hurt him.

Jebediah hastily wiped the blade on the folds of a nearby green chenille table cloth before thrusting it back into the cane sheath.

'Come on, you fool!' he hissed at Fletcher, grasping his arm roughly. 'It's done. We must get away. Help me with Mangler.'

Fletcher resisted, refusing to budge, suddenly unable to believe Tecwyn was no more; that his brother could not take revenge. 'We must make sure he is dead,' he said uncertainly, still straining against Jebediah's urging. 'He might be faking. He could still betray me.'

'He's dead all right, and we'll be too, if we hang about much longer.' Jebediah paused. 'Listen! Is that a woman's voice calling?'

They hustled Mangler through the French windows and half dragged, half carried him the quarter of a mile to where the carriage was hidden, bundling him unceremoniously inside.

'I'll act as driver,' Jebediah said harshly. 'We must run like the devil was after us. Suicide is one thing, murder is another. There'll be a hue and cry across the length and breadth of the county. And that's your fault, Mr Watkins. Now, get inside with Mangler.'

Fletcher did not like Jebediah's deprecating tone. 'I take no order from you, Crabbe. Besides, my horse is tethered nearby. I can't leave it. It'll be traced to me.'

'Very well,' Jebediah said. 'We'll leave you to your own fate. But understand this, Mr Watkins.' He poked a finger into Fletcher's chest. 'I hold you responsible if this deed is laid at my door. Your feud with your brother may cost us our lives yet.'

'Poor fatherless child,' the Reverend Ellis murmured, shaking his head as he gazed at Nesta, seated opposite, holding Bronwen in her arms.

Nesta's lips tightened. That was the third time he had uttered those words since the coach had left Pyle that morning.

'Bronwen still has me, Reverend,' Nesta said sharply. 'And I'll work my fingers to the bone for her. She'll want for nothing as long as I have breath in my body.'

'My dear child!' The cleric looked startled at her tone. 'I'm sure you will do all you can.'

'I'm not a child, Reverend,' Nesta said firmly. 'I'm a widow-woman and a mother.'

'Of course, of course, but it's not easy for a young widow alone and without means.' He gave a little cough. 'You need to marry again. I seem to remember a young man in the village, Jim Jenkins, who was devoted to you.'

Nesta had not forgotten Big Jim Jenkins even though she had scorned his proposal three years ago. As a lowly farm labourer, his suit was hardly appropriate or welcome, for all his hand-some looks. She also despised his partiality to prize-fighting, considering it lowering and common. Her recent experiences had proved her right. The sport's devotees were unscrupulous and dangerous. Nesta shivered involuntarily. May the Lord protect her from such as they.

'Jim remains unmarried,' Reverend Ellis said gently. 'While he is still a little wild in his ways, the love of a good sensible woman would be the making of him. I have hopes for him.'

Nesta sniffed. 'As I recall, he was never a regular church-goer,' she said. 'And he never will be, Reverend. I don't know why you bother about saving his soul.'

'That's uncharitable, Nesta,' Reverend Ellis remonstrated. 'Jim is as deserving as anyone else.'

Nesta compressed her lips. Her opinion of Big Jim had not changed over the years. She had witnessed how poverty could turn a marriage into a nightmare as with her own parents. As far as the world was concerned she was the widow of a sea captain, which must hold a certain status and respect. No penny-pinching life as a labourer's drudge for her. She would marry, but she would also bide her time until the right man with the right income came along.

IO

It was midday when the coach finally rolled into the yard behind the Marquis Arms at the crossroads at Cwmrhyddin Cross. Here the horses would change again before the coach and remaining passengers continued their run to West Wales. Nesta was so thankful that the long journey was at last over for her and little Bronwen.

Reverend Ellis helped her step down from the coach. 'You must be delighted to be on home ground again,' he said jovially. 'No doubt your mother will be overjoyed to see you and the little one.'

Nesta smiled faintly, but said nothing. She could expect no real welcome from Meg Lewis. They had quarrelled bitterly the day before she left home three years ago; Meg furiously accusing her of selfishness and abandonment; leaving them just when she might bring some earnings into the home. She doubted her mother had forgiven her and perhaps never would.

Nesta swallowed a lump in her throat at the thought. The journey might be over but there was still an ordeal to face; Meg Lewis's wrath, and at the end of it she might yet be homeless.

The cleric collected his bag and walked with her towards the arch leading to the main road that ran though the village. Nesta dragged her feet in dread of the coming confrontation. She needed a buffer; something that would soften the shock of first contact with her mother.

'Sir?' Nesta began, pausing on the cobbles of the yard to gaze up at him earnestly. 'I wonder if you might do one service for me.'

His lined face had a look of concern at her tone. 'Why, of course, child. What is it?'

'Would you come with me this moment to my father's cottage?'

His concern turned to surprise, and Nesta hastened on to explain herself. 'You see, sir, my parents know nothing of my marriage, let alone my child.'

'What?'

'Captain Crow was much older than me, and I was afraid my parents would not approve of the marriage so I never told them of it.'

Reverend Ellis rubbed his chin thoughtfully, looking very serious. 'You married underage without permission? Dear me, how unfortunate.'

'My marriage is quite legal, sir,' Nesta said quickly. 'The joining was performed with all due ceremony.' She swallowed before continuing with her lie. 'By the rector of St Margaret's Church in Roath.' She judged he would take her word for it and not check the records there. Why should he?

'And of what service can I be to you now?' He sounded doubtful.

'You know the truth of it now, sir,' Nesta said persuasively. 'It would be less of a shock to my parents if you were present when I face them.'

The cleric's presence would give a measure of respectability to her situation, a kind of blessing from the Church. Meg Lewis might be impressed by that initially. At least she could not order

Nesta summarily from her door, not with a member of the clergy looking on.

'I hesitate to be involved in what is, after all, a family matter.'

'We are all part of your flock, sir,' Nesta said.

His cheeks reddened, and he gave a little cough. 'Yes, of course, you are right, child. Well, come along. Let us waste no more time.'

Lining the road on either side of the crossroads were stout poll stone houses and tradesmen's shop fronts which over-shadowed more humble cottages. Some of the businesses looked more prosperous than others. The candle-maker's cottage with its workroom at the front, was the least prepossessing. It was flanked on either side by more favourable-looking premises, Caradog the baker and Baxter the haberdasher.

Nesta felt her spirits sink to see how run down her former home was. She had thought that when she did return it would be as the wife of a man of means and thereby end her parents' poverty. More than anything else, she wanted her mother to think well of her. Now, due to circumstances, regrettably of her own making, she would have to make the best of things for Bronwen's sake, that is, if Meg Lewis would let her.

The cottage door was open for business, but Nesta held back, suddenly fearful. Bronwen was starting to fret loudly from hunger and discomfort. At her hesitation Reverend Ellis stepped over the threshold, while Nesta remained outside trying to quieten the baby. 'Whisht! My darling!' she whispered to the child. 'Be a good girl for me at this moment. I want your grandma to love you.'

'Good day to you Reverend. What can I do for you, sir?'

Nesta recognised her father's voice, and wanted to burst into tears, but held on tightly to her emotions. He would never willingly turn her away, but Meg Lewis ruled the home, such as it was.

'Good day to you, Enoch,' Reverend Ellis began. 'Enoch,

my friend, I have a surprise for you. You have a visitor, or rather, two.'

The cleric motioned her to enter, and although Bronwen still whimpered, Nesta stepped forward hesitantly, clutching the child more tightly, willing her to stop crying.

Enoch Lewis gazed at her, smiling faintly, and she realised he had no notion of who she was. Quickly she pulled back the bonnet to reveal her face.

Her father rocked back on his heels, utterly astonished. 'Nesta! Nesta!' He was speechless, staring.

'Hello, Father,' Nesta said hesitantly. 'How are you? It's so good to set eyes on you again.'

'Nesta, my lovely girl! Welcome home.' Enoch sprang to life, hastening towards her from around the counter, arms outstretched and Nesta burst into tears then. 'There, there, my girl, don't cry,' he said, hugging her. 'Oh, there's lovely to see you. I thought I never would again.'

'Oh, Father, I didn't desert you and Mother, not really. I would never do that. I just wanted to better myself so that we could all benefit.'

'Well,' Reverend Ellis chimed in cheerfully. 'A happy reunion. I must be off, then.'

'No, no, sir,' Nesta exclaimed in agitation. 'Please remain until my mother has seen me. I mean . . . please, sir.'

He regarded her solemnly for a moment, a question in his eyes, and Nesta made her expression pleading. She needed the first moments of facing her mother quiet and without enmity, no matter what strife followed later.

'And where is your good wife?' the cleric asked of Enoch.

'She's feeding the chickens in the yard,' Enoch Lewis said. 'I'll call her.'

He dashed away, and Nesta was left standing with Reverend Ellis. He was gazing at her quizzically, obviously wondering why she did not follow into the living quarters, a narrow sitting room and small scullery at the back. After a moment's heavy silence, Nesta knew she must explain with partial honesty.

'The truth is, sir, my mother didn't want me to leave home,' she began. 'And when I persisted, she . . . she banished me, so, you see, sir, I've no right to enter the home unless invited to do so.'

'My dear child,' he said weakly. 'I had no idea.'

At that moment, the curtain across the passage leading to the rear of the cottage was jerked back and Meg Lewis stepped forward. Her face was hard as she took in Nesta, the baby in the shawl, and Reverend Ellis. Nesta could see it took a great effort for her to crack an empty smile for appearance's sake in front of the clergyman.

'Nesta, what a surprise,' she said tightly. 'Reverend Ellis, how good of you to escort my daughter here, as though she had forgotten where we live or did not want to remember.'

Nesta felt her face flame up, ashamed of her mother's bitter tone in front of the clergyman.

'It was not at all like that, Mrs Lewis, I assure you,' Reverend Ellis said quickly. He shifted awkwardly on one foot and then the other and Nesta regretted his embarrassment. 'I was passing this way on an errand to Baxter's.'

'Well, we mustn't keep you, Reverend,' Meg said. 'I'm sure you're eager to be off home yourself.'

Reverend Ellis stepped smartly to the door, his cheeks turning pink. 'Yes, good day to you all. See you in church on Sunday, I am sure.' Then he was gone.

Feeling suddenly bereft, Nesta stared at Meg Lewis's uncompromising expression. She could not remember a time when her mother had shown affection towards her, not even in childhood. Meg had always pined for a son and was dismissive of her daughter. Noting the hostile light glinting in Meg's eyes, Nesta knew her mother had not mellowed in her absence.

'So, you've come home, have you?' Meg sniffed disdainfully.

'And what've you got to say for yourself, you, and this mewling child?'

'Meg!' Enoch protested in his gentle voice. 'Our girl is with us again and let's be thankful for it.'

'Huh! Am I to put out the bunting, then? Am I to kill the fatted calf?'

Nesta folded her lips, holding back tears, willing herself not to cry again in front of her mother, who would take that as weakness. Bronwen was mewling because she was hungry and so was Nesta.

'We've not eaten since seven o'clock this morning, Mother,' she said tentatively. 'Do you think you could find a little sustenance for the child?'

Meg Lewis clamped her fists on her hips. 'Oh, so that's your idea, is it,' she exclaimed. 'You expect to live off us?'

Nesta felt hurt. Her mother's quarrel was with her not Bronwen who was totally innocent of any blame. 'No, Mother,' she said quietly. 'I ask for nothing more than common hospitality.'

'Meg, please!' Enoch said. He came and stood at his wife's side, and touched her forearm tentatively. 'Why must she stand here? She's our flesh and blood, after all.'

'She had little thought for us, did she, three years ago? Off helter-skelter to find her fortune and not a word from her since. God knows where she's been all this time.'

'There was nothing for me here,' Nesta said patiently. 'I left Cwmrhyddin Cross to find work and earn good money, Mother. You and Father would have shared in any good fortune I found.'

'Huh!' Meg tossed her head, looking sceptical. 'Never saw a penny piece from you over the years, though, did we? Left us to starve. That's was how much you cared for your parents.'

'That's unfair, Mother,' Nesta said calmly. 'I didn't find my fortune, and you're not starved, either.' Her nervousness at seeing her mother again was receding, especially in the face of Meg's open hostility. 'I am glad to see how well you both look,' she went on softening the tone of her voice. Despite everthing it was good to see their well remembered faces, even Meg's scowl. 'I have no intention of being a burden on you.'

Nesta's stomach was rumbling and her arms arched from holding an ever restless Bronwen, who let out a loud yell of temper at being neglected.

Meg's unsympathetic gaze went to the infant. 'If you've brought shame and dishonour to this home . . .?'

'I'm a respectable widow-woman,' Nesta interrupted quickly. 'I returned because I've nowhere else to go. If a daughter can't turn to her family when in need, who can she turn to?'

'Meg!' Enoch pleaded. 'We can't keep Nesta and her child standing here like this. It's not right.'

Without a word Meg turned and walked past the curtain towards the living room. With a smile of encouragement, Enoch put his arm gently around Nesta's shoulders.

'Come on girl,' he said kindly. 'You look done in, and there's a pan of freshly made *cawl* on the hob. Your stomach could do with a bowl of that no doubt. No one makes *cawl* like your mother.'

Enoch urged her into the living room at the back of the cottage which Nesta remembered so well. Small and dark, the room had not changed. Two hard wooden chairs were placed before the big range that dominated the room. The feeling she remembered from childhood of being hemmed in, returned. The only welcome was the delicious aroma of the freshly made vegetable stew, the *cawl* that her mother was so famous for.

'Sit down, Nesta. Let me take your bag. You must eat.'

'Thank you, Father,' Nesta said to him, ignoring her mother's compressed lips and folded arms. 'But my child comes first. I'll change her and then perhaps she could have a little bread and some of the vegetable broth.'

'Your father and I have little enough to live on,' Meg said sharply. 'We can feed no more mouths.'

Nesta unwrapped the shawl from around a wriggling Bronwen and began to remove her nappy. 'My husband left us some money to keep us going for a while.'

'This so-called husband of yours, deserted you, did he?'

'No, he did not!' She glanced at her father. 'I need a bowl of warm water and carbolic soap to bathe her, Father, please,' she said.

Meg clicked her tongue with annoyance, while Enoch disappeared into the lean-to to fetch a bowl and some cold water. Nesta put the bowl in the hearth and lifting the iron kettle nearby poured hot water into it. She gently soaped Bronwen's little body all over, and then glanced up defiantly at Meg standing by watching.

'Can I trouble you for a towel, Mother?'

Meg gave an irritated snort, but fetched a clean towel from a cupboard and handed it to her daughter. 'Why did we never hear of this marriage, then, and the birth of your child?'

Nesta gently patted dry Bronwen's tender skin. 'You banished me from my home three years ago, remember, Mother?' she said. 'I didn't believe you were remotely interested in my life after that.'

'You're right! But you scuttled back quick enough,' Meg retorted. 'What happened to your husband? Where is he? He should face his responsibilities.'

Nesta took the last of the linen nappies from the bag and put it on the child.

'I've already told you. I'm a widow.' She took a deep breath before continuing with her tale. She hated deceiving them, especially her father, but she must protect herself and Bronwen. The truth must never come out or she would go to the gallows for sure. 'He was a sea captain, a respectable man, older than me,' she went on. 'His ship was lost in a storm, and he went down with it. He was a courageous and gallant man.'

'Oh, and what was the name of this paragon of virtue?'

Nesta could tell from her mother's tone that she was suspicious of her story. But then, her mother would be suspicious of anything she said. Nesta was never able do right in her mother's eyes.

'Captain Jack Crow.'

'So how did you catch this man's eye?' Meg asked disdainfully. 'Free with your favours, were you?'

'Meg!' Enoch was scandalised. 'How could you say such a thing to our own daughter?'

'Because Nesta always had ideas above her station,' Meg rasped. 'She could have married Big Jim Jenkins if she had wanted to, but oh, no! He wasn't fine enough, a poor farm labourer.'

'Is it a crime for a girl to want to make a good marriage?' Nesta asked. 'As it happens Jack was the nephew of the housekeeper at the house where I worked as a maid,' she said. Lying did not get any easier, she found. 'He was visiting his aunt, and that's how we met. I . . . I was proud to be his wife. I don't regret it even though I'm now a young widow.'

She wondered, in a moment of panic, whether they had heard about the abduction of Sir Tecwyn's daughter, but was then reassured. They could not connect the tragedy at Brynhyfryd House with her for they had no knowledge of where she had resided over the last three years. She was glad now that she had never found the courage to write to her parents. And besides Cwmrhyddin Cross was a sleepy backwater. Where news was concerned Cardiff was as far away as if it were on the other side of the world.

Enoch crumbled bread in a bowl and spooned broth into it. 'Feed this to your little babe,' he said. 'What's her name?'

'Bronwen,' Nesta said, smiling up at him.

His face was thinner and more lined than she remembered, but his grey eyes still shone with love for her. She felt a lump in her throat at the thought of her dissembling. She longed to tell him the truth, feel his comforting arms around her as she had as a child, while he told her everything would be all right.

He deserved better in life and her resolve to find a rich husband had not been entirely selfish. With money she could have helped her dear father escape the drudgery of his life, and perhaps then Meg Lewis would give him some peace.

Nesta spread the shawl on the mat before the fire and laid Bronwen on it. Fed and cleaned, she looked happy, blowing bubbles and kicking her chubby legs.

'Bronwen.' Enoch gazed down at her, looking pleased. 'A lovely name for our lovely grandchild, Meg.'

'Grandchild, indeed!'

Enoch gave Nesta an apologetic glance before putting a bowl of hot *cawl* in front of her. Nesta ate hungrily, dipping chunks of bread into the rich broth.

'How much money did your husband leave you?' Meg asked suddenly.

Nesta noted the tone of her voice, and suspected her mother hoped to benefit from it. But the money was rightfully Bronwen's, her birthright, and must not be spent carelessly.

'Not a great deal,' she said quickly. 'But enough to keep us fed until I can find work.' Or a husband, Nesta thought to herself. She had not given up hope of that yet.

'Oh, and who pray will tend your child all day while you work? Not I?' Meg blurted out nastily.

'I haven't asked you to,' Nesta retorted and then checked herself. To quarrel with her mother was the last thing she wanted just now. 'I was thinking of the young Rafferty girl,

Mary. She must be fourteen now. Mary could look after Bronwen each day.'

'The Raffertys!' Meg looked scandalised. 'A feckless bunch, not to mention criminal. The Rafferty boys are always in trouble with the constable. Thieving gypsies, the lot of them.'

'You're prejudiced because they're Catholics,' Nesta said. 'Such hypocrisy, Mother.'

'Don't you speak to me like that,' Meg shouted. 'You can get out of this house this minute!'

'Now! Now! Meg. Nesta is our daughter. Don't treat her like a stranger,' Enoch pleaded.

'She *is* a stranger,' Meg insisted. 'We've not seen hide nor hair of her for three years. God knows what she's been up to.'

This was too much to bear and Nesta jumped up from the table. 'I've kept myself respectable,' she retorted hotly. 'More than can be said for my cousin, Dorah, who you repeatedly praised to the skies, as I remember. The Reverend Ellis told me she married Geraint Probert pretty quickly, and I can guess why, and his wife hardly buried a year.'

She had felt a moment of resentment when on the journey Reverend Ellis had told her that her cousin Dorah, now properly married, had a three year old son and a baby daughter almost a year old.

'What are you saying?'

'You know full well, Mother,' Nesta chided. 'It's evident that Dorah set her cap at Geraint even before his wife died. The Reverend Ellis told me Auntie Sarah moved to Llanelly to live, and no wonder. She couldn't face Dorah's carryings on no doubt.'

Meg's face suffused with colour, and Nesta felt she had scored a point. Her mother did not like to be reminded that her older sister's daughter might be no better than she should be. Now Dorah was nicely placed as the wife of a well-to-do tenant farmer, the scandal behind her, whilst Nesta must struggle to scratch a living.

'It's wicked of you to rake that up,' Meg said, glowering.

'It's wicked of you to cast aspersions on my character without cause,' Nesta said quickly. 'It's wicked of you to treat me like a stranger. I'm your flesh and blood.'

Meg drew her lips together tightly, but was silent.

'Your old room is still there for you, Nesta, my dear,' Enoch said gently. 'Why don't you go up with the baby and take a nap. You must be weary after your journey.'

'What makes you think I'll let her stay here?' Meg protested loudly. 'I'll say who sleeps under this roof, not you, Enoch Lewis.'

Nesta turned to her mother, a faint smile on her face, knowing Meg's weakness. 'I'm willing to pay rent, Mother, within reason, of course.'

Meg Lewis looked torn for a moment. 'How much?'

'You can't do it, Meg,' Enoch objection. 'It's not right. She's our own child.'

'Keep quiet, Enoch,' Meg commanded. 'This is between Nesta and me. She can't expect to stay here for nothing.'

'Two shillings a week for the use of the room,' Nesta said quickly. 'And I'll buy my own food. I'll not sponge off you, Mother. Unlike Dorah, I have principles.'

She felt a twinge of guilt as she claimed that. After all, losing sight of her principles in the hope of a good marriage had got her into this mess in the first place. Never again would she compromise her integrity. She had Bronwen to think of now. She loved the child so much she would gladly give her life for her, but she hoped it would never come to that.

Meg looked thoughtful. 'Two shilling and sixpence,' she said stubbornly after a pause.

'No, Mother! I'm not the naïve young girl you used to browbeat. It's two shilling or I look elsewhere and make it known how my own mother is willing to exploit my sad situation.'

Meg looked incensed, her lips compressing until they were invisible.

'I'll find work as soon as possible,' Nesta went on. 'Reverend Ellis also told me there are some new gentlemen's houses built on the road to the church. They may need an experienced nursemaid.'

'Huh! Hoity-toity ideas,' Meg exclaimed nastily. 'You'll toil in the workshop alongside your father, candle-making, then you'll not need the services of any Rafferty.'

Nesta fumed at the suggestion. She would never find a suitable husband working in a candle-maker's dingy workshop.

'You'd like to drag me down, wouldn't you, Mother, in punishment for not being a son,' Nesta blurted. 'But I'll not spend my years toiling in a mean lowly trade.' She paused, suddenly realizing she must have hurt her father's feelings. 'I'm sorry, Father. I didn't intend to belittle you or your living. I just want a better life.'

'No one can blame you for that, my dear daughter,' Enoch said, smiling sadly. 'I regret that you're ashamed of me, however.'

'Oh, Father! I'm not ashamed of you.' Nesta went to him, putting her head against his thin chest. 'Forgive me. I'm the one who should be ashamed. You're the best father in the world.'

'There! There!' Enoch patted her arm. 'We might all have done better for ourselves. I'm sure your mother thinks so. After all, she could have married Emlyn Baxter and be the wife of a rich haberdasher today, living in a fine stone house, had she not got on the wrong side of Emlyn's mother.'

'Be silent!' his wife blared loudly her expression enraged. 'I was a fool to marry you, Enoch Lewis, a penniless candle-maker, and I've regretted it every day of our marriage.'

Meg snatched at her shawl and bonnet hanging behind the back door.

'I'll take a week's rent in advance, if you please, Nesta,' she said pithily, holding out her hand. 'And then I can go to Tucker the Butcher for some fresh tripe.'

When her mother had left them alone, Nesta hugged and kissed her father fondly. 'I'm sorry I brought that tirade on you, Father.'

He shook his head. 'I hear that every day, my dear girl. I'm used to it. It's your mother you should pity. She'll never be happy or satisfied.'

Perhaps she should feel pity for Meg Lewis, but she could not feel or give affection where there was none in return. She had felt Meg's disappointment and enmity for her from a young child, and had never forgotten and never forgiven it. She must rely on her mother now for a roof over her head, but as soon as she was able, she would break away; find herself a husband, and perhaps a decent place for Bronwen to grow up safe.

Nesta clasped her hands over her heart. Oh, there must be something better for her out there, otherwise why had she been spared at the evil hands of Jebediah Crabbe?

II

'She has the temerity to call herself a housekeeper. She's insufferable! I demand you get rid of her immediately, Fletcher,' Alexis Vansier exclaimed irately, beating a riding crop against the back of an upholstered chair. 'Her merest glance at me is insolent in the extreme.'

'Alexis, my dearest,' Fletcher Watkins said soothingly, moving quickly to her side. 'I'm sure you imagine any slight. She's a faithful servant and has been with the Watkins family for years.'

She stared up at him haughtily, the perfection of her lovely face heightened by anger. 'I'll not tolerate her presence another day, I tell you, not another hour. Do you hear me?'

Even in this moment of disagreement, Fletcher felt a quiver of desire in his loins. He would always ache for her and was constantly fearful that she would leave him, for he could not face life without her.

'Oh, my sweet . . .' He reached out a hand to touch her golden hair, cascading freely over her shoulders, but she pulled away, her glance scornful.

'Don't assume ownership of me, Fletcher,' she warned, her tone cold. 'There'll be no more caresses or anything else until that woman is gone. Go now and tell her to pack her bags. Mangler can take her into the village within the hour.'

There was derisive laugher from the other man in the room,

and Fletcher turned to him in anger. 'Get out, Crabbe! Your presence is not required either.'

'Come, come, Mr Watkins,' Crabbe responded amicably. 'We're partners now, on equal footing, I think.'

'Damn your eyes, if we are!' Fletcher exploded.

He was now in full possession of Brynhyfryd House and all of Tecwyn's estates, but had not bargained for Crabbe's interminable company in the house; he and that animal, Mangler.

'I say you and your henchman have outstayed your welcome,' he went on tersely. 'I don't remember inviting you here in the first place.'

Crabbe's face darkened. 'I need no invitation to this house, Watkins.' Fletcher noted Crabbe had dropped all pretence at obsequiousness. 'I've risked the gallows for the Watkins fortune, and mean to have my share. You and I are inseparable from now on.' Crabbe paused, and smiled thinly. 'Until the day you die.'

Fletcher felt a quiver pass through him at the hardly veiled threat, but he had been expecting it. 'I best not die too soon, Crabbe,' he said, striving not to let fear weaken his voice. 'I've taken the precaution of lodging a letter with my lawyer, divulging everything, your part and mine. That letter will be opened in the event of my death from whatever apparent cause.'

A sound like thunder rumbled in Crabbe's throat, but he said nothing.

'Furthermore,' Fletcher went on, 'the letter will be opened should someone, anyone, present power of attorney over me.' He did not doubt Crabbe would use any means no matter how barbaric to gain control of his fortune.

Fletcher glanced at Alexis. 'I've also lodged my will, my dear. You will benefit handsomely, very handsomely indeed, if you're still with me on the day I die.'

Alexis' face twisted in fury. 'You promised me an immediate

settlement, unconditionally. You swore. You may not die for another thirty years.' Her face puckered. 'I'll be an old woman then. No man will want me.'

'Oh, I think they will, Mrs Vansier,' Crabbe interposed mockingly. 'When a woman is wealthy, some men will overlook a wrinkled face and an aging body past its prime.'

'Pig!' Alexis blared, turning her back on him.

'So, you've been clever, Watkins,' Crabbe said. He spoke calmly, obviously having regained his temper. 'It appears you'll live after all.' He laughed mirthlessly. 'And we must take great care of you.'

'I'm glad you appreciate the situation,' Fletcher said airily. He felt easier now that his protection was disclosed. 'But, I'm not ungrateful, Crabbe. You may count on me for financial support in your sporting enterprises. There is, after all, a deal of money still to be made in exploiting good fighting men in the ring.'

Crabbe smiled. 'I'm glad we understand each other. We will get along famously, so long as there is no meanness in you where funds are concerned, and that you accept my wisdom in such matters.'

'It's agreed. Now, I'll lend you a carriage to take you and Mangler to Cardiff. I'll contact you when I'm ready.'

'I think not, Watkins.' Crabbe leaned his arm nonchalantly on the mantelpiece. 'This house is large, too large for two people. I'll make my headquarters here, protecting my investment, so to speak. Mangler remains, too.' He looked at Fletcher, his eyes hooded and dangerous. 'I don't trust you, Watkins, and I have no intention of letting you out of my sight.'

'It's out of the question,' Fletcher blustered. Although he could no longer do him physical harm, as a known criminal, Crabbe's presence would be an inconvenience, not to mention an embarrassment in the higher society that Fletcher planned to enter. He was wealthier now than he had ever dreamed possible. Crabbe was the proverbial fly in the ointment and could turn Fletcher's entire future rancid by his presence.

'Incidentally,' Crabbe went on in a dictatorial tone, ignoring Fletcher's objection, 'I support Mrs Vansier's wish to be rid of the housekeeper. You will remember, Watkins, she was here in the house when your brother met his unfortunate end.' His glance was meaningful. 'Her loyalty was to him. Who knows what she heard and saw.'

'It's absurd.'

'Nevertheless,' Crabbe went on, 'I'll engage a much more suitable woman, and a few more servants.'

'You intend to fill my house with your own cronies and creatures,' Fletcher fumed. 'Am I now a prisoner, to be watched day and night? I don't like it and will not tolerate it.'

'Watkins, my dear fellow,' Crabbe said, his smile narrow and insincere. 'You have little choice. I know too much about you. You're as much one of my creatures as Mangler is.' His features hardened. 'I'm master here now.'

Alexis gave a little snigger, her eyes sparkling with undisguised scorn as she looked at Fletcher. He dragged his gaze from hers, feeling a burning heat rise to his face, but swallowed down his humiliation with difficulty. He paused for a moment, glaring at Crabbe with impotent anger, then strode from the room.

Alexis's mocking laughter rang in his ears as he went, and he felt a helplessness seep through him. He had gained the vast Watkins' wealth, but now he was the mere puppet of an evil and dangerous man. He had struck a deal with the Devil, and must pay the price.

His brother's dying words came back to him as they did each night. *My wealth will taint your life. You will never again know a moment's peace.*

'It's almost a month since you came home,' Meg said brusquely to Nesta one morning. 'I see no sign of you finding gainful employment.'

'Nothing suitable has been on offer,' Nesta said as she spooned warm porridge into Bronwen's eager little mouth.

She was putting on a front for her mother's benefit, yet was becoming a little concerned herself. The money she had received for the paintings was disappearing fast, what with rent and food, but she was determined not to take a lowly position. Respectable suitors would not look for a wife among drudges.

'I intend to see Reverend Ellis at the vicarage this morning,' she went on more confidently than she felt. 'He may have connections to a good family.'

'Huh! Your highfaluting ways will be your downfall yet,' Meg said nastily. 'You'll end up in your father's workshop, mark my words.'

'If I have high-flown ways I learned them from you, Mother,' Nesta said. 'You've never been satisfied with the life Father has provided for you, yet he works his fingers to the bone.'

Meg waved the bread knife angrily. 'Don't you criticise me, you disrespectful madam,' she said, raising her voice. 'I'll not take impertinence in my own home.'

Nesta folded her lips stubbornly. She had no intention of apologising for their continued presence. Her mother went out of her way to be disagreeable, and Nesta knew, not without a twinge of pain, that Meg wanted her and Bronwen gone.

Knowing it would be useless asking Meg to mind Bronwen while she went on her errand to the vicarage, Nesta bathed and dressed the child, and set off with her. The church and graveyard of St Marks on the Hill was roughly half a mile from the crossroads. The vicarage, a large well-appointed house with good grounds, lay halfway between.

Nesta had more sense than to apply at the front entrance, so knocked on the back door. It was opened by a small scruffy-looking boy of about twelve.

'Yes, what you want?' he asked gruffly, wiping his nose on his sleeve.

Nesta was taken aback. She had expected to be greeted by the elderly housekeeper whom she had known for years. 'Who are you?'

He sniffed. 'Billy Rafferty, boot boy. What do you want, missus?'

'Where's Mrs Butler?'

'Bad abed,' he said shortly. 'Can't see nobody.'

He began to close the door, but Nesta quickly put her foot over the threshold. 'I'm here to see the vicar,' she said firmly. 'Go and ask him if he'll see me.'

Billy sniffed again and looked perplexed. 'Not allowed in the drawing-room, I'm not.'

'Then send someone else.'

'Nobody else here.'

Who was looking after the vicar and a sick housekeeper? Nesta wondered. She stepped forward into the large kitchen, and stared dismayed at the mess. Dirty pots, pans and crockery were piled in the stone sink and looked as though they had been there for days.

The kitchen range was lifeless of fire, the grey cold ashes still piled in the hearth. The large table, usually scrubbed to within an inch of its life, was stained and scattered with scraps of food and other debris.

'How long has Mrs Butler been laid up?' she asked in concern.

'Couple of days,' Billy said defensively. 'Did my best, I did.'

'Where's Reverend Ellis?'

'In the drawing-room, eating the bread and milk I made him.'

'You're a good boy, Billy,' Nesta said in a placating tone. 'But I must see the vicar.'

Seeking work with a child in one's arms was hardly sensible. She was about to ask him to mind Bronwen for a moment, but one look at his grubby hands decided her against it.

'I'll find the drawing-room and announce myself,' she told him. 'Meanwhile, riddle out those ashes.' She indicated the cold range. 'Chop some firewood and fill all the coal scuttles. After that, go and wash your hands and face.'

Billy appeared relieved that an adult was taking charge, and darted off to do as he was told.

Leaving the kitchen along a narrow dark passage, Nesta pushed open a green baize-covered door and found herself in the large hall, with its chequered black and white tiled floor. The door on the right was partly opened, and Nesta put her head around it.

Reverend Ellis was sitting before a cold grate, a bowl and spoon still in his hands. His shoulders were bowed and suddenly he looked older than his sixty years. A bachelor, used to being waited on hand and foot, he looked lost.

Nesta gave a gentle tap on the door. He looked up quickly, surprise and delight on his lined face.

'Nesta! And the little one! Come in, please do,' he said, beckoning her forward, indicating she should sit. 'Although there is little earthly sustenance at hand to offer you, I'm still well stocked with spiritual food.'

Nesta could not help but smile at his words as she perched self-consciously on the edge of an overstuffed chair. 'Your household appears to be in dire straits, sir,' she ventured to remark. 'I understand Mrs Butler is taken ill.'

He shook his head. 'She's been failing for some time, but would not let me hire more help for her, fearful that I'd pension her off, no doubt.' He shook his head. 'Dr Powell has little hope of her recovery. I'm at my wits' end.'

Nesta wetted her lips nervously. 'You should employ someone else, sir, before the household is in ruins. You need taking care of, if I may be so bold as to say so, Vicar, as does Mrs Butler, by the sound of it.'

'I'm well aware of it,' he said, shaking his head again. 'But I fear offending her. She has been the mainstay of this house for many years.'

'I came to ask if you knew of a suitable position for me in some good household in the district,' Nesta said tentatively. 'But, sir, I think I'm needed here.'

'Mrs Butler . . .'

'Oh, I wouldn't presume to take her place, sir,' Nesta said hastily. 'She can be assured of that. I'm a good cook, if I say so myself, and not afraid of hard work. I would take it upon myself to nurse Mrs Butler, too.' Nesta paused, gathering her courage to make the next suggestion. 'Of course, it would be better if I lived in, sir. That is, if you don't object to a baby in the house.'

'A baby in the house?' Reverend Ellis looked pleasantly surprised at the idea. 'No, no, not at all.' He looked at the cold grate. 'A baby in the house, well, I never.'

'There's one more thing, sir.' Nesta swallowed hard, cautious of being overbearing and demanding. 'I'll need a little help myself, sir. This house is so large, so many rooms.' Nesta gave a polite cough before continuing. 'Might I suggest you also employ a young girl? I was thinking of Billy's sister, Mary.'

Reverend Ellis looked even more surprised. 'Why, yes! What a splendid idea.' His old face looked suddenly hopeful. 'When would you be able to start, do you think?'

Neither had mentioned payment, but Nesta was not unduly concerned. Reverend Ellis was a fair and honourable man. And then there was the living in to consider. She could get away from her mother at last, and to all intents and purposes, be her own mistress in this house.

'Judging by what I've seen in the kitchen, sir, I think I should start right away.'

'Excellent!' His face lit up. 'Provisions are low I suspect,' he said. 'We need meat and other victuals.'

'I'll see to it at once, Mr Ellis, sir,' Nesta said happily, rising from the chair, taking the bowl and spoon from his hand.

'When I return I'll prepare a hot meal for you and Mrs Butler, and then have a word with Mary Rafferty's mother this afternoon.' Neat paused, wondering if she were being too pushy. 'With your permission, of course, sir.'

Reverend Ellis leaned back in his chair, hands clasped across his waistcoat, his face much brighter than when she had entered the room.

'The household is in your hands, Nesta,' he said. 'I trust you implicitly. You must do what you think fit. Oh, and, Mrs Butler usually looked after the household accounts. Perhaps you will be so kind as to do likewise.' He rose. 'Now I must go to my study and ponder on the subject of my next sermon, "Ask and it shall be given unto you".'

Returning from fetching provisions, Nesta went to Mrs Butler's bedroom on the ground floor at the back of the house, only to discover the poor woman in a state. She had not bathed for days, and had been living on bread and milk provided by Billy.

Nesta expected some hostility from the housekeeper, but was glad at the way Mrs Butler welcomed her. 'Oh! Thank the Lord! A woman at last,' the old lady said weakly. 'I'm wretched.'

Hot water was fetched and Nesta gently bathed her from head to foot, combed her hair, plaited it and found a clean nightdress.

'I'm making lamb stew,' Nesta said when she had finished. 'I'm sure you can eat a little.'

'Anything,' Mrs Butler said earnestly. 'Anything, but milk and sop.'

After everyone had been fed, including herself and Bronwen, Nesta set off for the Raffertys' cottage on the west edge of the village. It was late afternoon, and the sun was still warm, but she carried Bronwen Welsh fashion in the shawl.

The Rafferty cottage was run down and even squalid

looking, although Nesta knew Sheila Rafferty, Mary's mother, was a hard-working woman, deserted ten years ago by a worthless husband. Nesta guessed that the wild and reckless older Rafferty boys, Kieran and his younger brother, Donal, caused her much worry and distress, and drained her of much of the money she earned rubbing and scrubbing in the kitchen of the Manse for the large family of Pastor Owen Owens of Chapel Bethel.

The cottage door was open and Nesta knocked tentatively. She could hear movement inside, but no one came out. Nesta knocked again, more loudly and finally a tall woman, careworn and thin, appeared. When she saw Nesta the tension in her shoulders seemed to ease.

'Thinking it was the rent man, I was,' Sheila Rafferty said in her soft brogue. 'There's nothing for him this week.'

Nesta felt pity for the strain on the woman's face. 'I've come with some good news,' she began. 'Reverend Ellis is taking me on to help Mrs Butler. There might be a place for Mary, too. Would you be willing for her to work and live at the vicarage?'

Sheila Rafferty looked astonished. 'Work for my Mary as well as Billy? Oh, the Lord be praised! Come in, Miss Lewis.'

'Crow, my name is now,' Nesta said quickly. 'Mrs Jack Crow. I'm a widow. My husband was a sea captain, lost with his ship.'

She had told this lie so many times of late that she was beginning to believe it herself. But that was no bad thing. The more she believed it the less likely was she to be tripped up in her story.

'Oh, bless you!' Sheila Rafferty said earnestly. 'You're a woman alone, as I am. Come in, come in, Mrs Crow. Mary is in the kitchen with Grandma Rafferty.'

The cottage had just two rooms downstairs, with a small lean-to at the back. Mary was just putting an iron kettle on the hob, swinging it over the hot coals in the range. No matter how hot the weather was outside, a fire must always be in the grate for cooking and to heat water.

'Sit at the table. You'll take a cup of tea with us,' Sheila Rafferty said to Nesta.

'Well,' Nesta said, surprised that they could afford such a luxury. 'That's very kind of you.'

An old woman sat on a wicker chair by the fireside, a woollen shawl around her thin shoulders. Her granddaughter, Mary now sat at her feet. Colm Rafferty had skedaddled but he had left his mother behind for his wife to support. Sheila Rafferty's life was far from easy.

There was little furniture in the room, and Nesta took the only other chair. She smiled at the old woman and nodded. 'Good day to you, Mrs Rafferty.'

Grandma Rafferty stared back at her in silence, her gaunt lined face without expression, but her dark eyes were lively enough, taking in everything of Nesta's appearance. Her stare was so intense Nesta felt discomforted.

'So this is your babbie, then?' Sheila leaned forward, lifting a hand to move the shawl away to reveal Bronwen's face. 'Oh, 'tis the beauty that she is, too,' she said. 'She'll break hearts, so she will.'

'She has already broken a heart,' Grandma Rafferty said suddenly. 'Her father's heart. And he lies now in his cold grave.'

'Whisht, Ma!' Sheila said, giving Nesta an apologetic glance. 'She means no harm, Mrs Crow. I hope you're not offended.'

Nesta managed a strained smile. 'No. She's probably right. The sea is a cold grave.'

'A foul end he met,' Grandma Rafferty went on in a high quivering voice. Abruptly, she jerked forward, dark eyes wide and staring. 'I see the face of the evil one.'

'Ma!' Sheila rushed forward to shake the old woman's arm. 'Whisht! Be quiet. You know Pastor Owens has forbidden it.'

Nesta was confused and did not know whether to go or stay. She had not yet finished her business with Sheila Rafferty, and had set her heart on having Mary with her at the vicarage. As well as being useful with the work, she would be the ideal one to look after Bronwen should Nesta need a few hours of freedom. A woman could not snare a good husband with a baby hanging over her arm.

Sheila turned to her. 'Grandma Rafferty has the second sight,' she explained apologetically. 'She's too outspoken, and Pastor Owens will not allow it. Not Christian, he says. I daren't offend him. Who else in this village will give me work?'

Nesta dragged her gaze away from the old woman's gimlet eyes, which were fixed on her. 'I'll say nothing,' she said. 'Now, about Mary.'

She glanced at the child sitting on the mat, no more than fourteen years old, her prettiness disguised by a shabby dress, which looked like one of her mother's clumsily cut down, and a mass of dark tangled hair. Nesta made a note to do something about the girl's appearance.

'Mary is very willing,' Sheila began eagerly. 'Obedient, and clever, too.'

'What do you think, Mary?' Nesta asked of the child. 'Would you like to come and work at the vicarage? You would have your own room.'

Mary Rafferty jumped up. 'Oh, may I mother? It's better than sleeping here on the mat.'

Sheila glanced at Nesta, her expression ashamed. 'We've only two small beds, you see Mrs Crow,' she said. 'Kieran and Donal take one. Billy and I have the other, while Grandma sleeps in her chair. It breaks my heart that Mary has to sleep on the mat before the range, but those of us who work must have decent rest.'

Nesta was about to point out that the Rafferty boys were renowned in the village for their idleness, but held her tongue.

It was none of her business. She was here to help Mary as well as herself.

'Then it's settled?' Nesta asked and Sheila Rafferty nodded. 'Good. She might as well begin today,' Nesta went on. 'If she'll pack her things, she can come back to the vicarage with me right away.'

'I'm ready now,' Mary said, spreading out her arms. 'I own nothing else.'

'You can take my old black coat hanging behind the door in my bedroom,' Sheila said, her face turning pink. 'You'll maybe need it in the winter.'

Mary's face was beaming as she dashed up the narrow staircase in the corner of the room.

'This is a wonderful thing you are doing for my Mary,' Sheila said. There were tears in her eyes and Nesta was touched. 'God Bless you, Mrs Crow.'

'And be warned!' Grandma Rafferty screeched suddenly, 'When the streets of the village be teaming with paupers and peers of the realm, fine carriages and carts, the evil one will walk amongst them.' She lifted up a hand, pointing a bony finger at Nesta. 'He searches for you with murder in his heart.'

'Heaven preserve us, Ma!' Sheila shouted at the older woman. 'Will you not listen? You'll have me thrown out of my position at the Manse, and where will we be then?'

Nesta stared at the old woman mesmerised with fright. She had no doubt Jebediah Crabbe still searched for her, but he would never find her in this quiet backwater, she reassured herself. The world never came to Cwmrhyddin Cross so the prediction could not come true.

Nesta shuddered as she stood there, desperately wanting to get away from the old woman and her gimlet gaze. 'Is Mary ready?' she asked of Sheila, trying to steady her voice.

The next moment the girl came running into the room, an old coat over her arm. 'I'm ready, Mrs Crow.'

Nesta could not get out of the cottage quick enough. Mercifully Grandma Rafferty had nothing further to say. As they walked back to the vicarage, Nesta could not help probing.

'Your grandmother appears addled in her mind,' she said hopefully to Mary.

'Oh, no, not her,' Mary said with a laugh. 'She's more than twelve spuds to the dozen.'

'But the strange things she was saying . . .'

Mary stopped and turned to her, alarm in her eyes. 'She meant no harm. Please say nothing, Mrs Crow. Ma will lose her job.'

Nesta bit her lip. 'Of course, I'll say nothing, but has any of her predictions come true?'

'Oh, yes, often. In fact she's never wrong,' Mary said brightly. 'That's why Pastor Owens has forbidden her to speak out. She predicted he would break his leg on a ride to Cardiff last year, and it happened! He says she caused it, and is in league with the Devil.' She sighed. 'Poor Grandma.'

12

'You ungrateful wretch!' Meg Lewis shouted, waving a wooden pudding spoon in Nesta's face. 'You begged us for board and now you desert us again.'

'Mr Ellis needs someone to live in,' Nesta protested, disconcerted at her mother's reaction to her news. 'Particularly since Mrs Butler is incapacitated. The place is in an awful state.'

She had thought her mother would be glad to see them both go. Meg was always complaining about Bronwen's crying at night; always mumbling about the number of nappies hanging over the range to air.

'Your place is working by your father's side, learning the candle-making trade. It's the least you can do since we don't have a son.'

'That's hardly *my* fault,' Nesta said. 'You should've tried for more children.'

'Oh! You indecent creature!' Meg threw up her hands in disgust. 'How you can speak of such a thing to your own mother, I don't know. Shame on you!'

'Why are you complaining, Mother?' she asked tiredly as she stuffed the remaining dry nappies into her canvas bag. 'Two less mouths to feed, remember, even though I've paid my own way since we've been here.'

She was taking nothing more than she had brought with her or had purchased since in the village. Her mother had nothing to whine about now.

'I've come to rely on your rent,' Meg answered belligerently. 'At least you should have the decency to see your parents all right for sustenance.'

'I'm a poor widow-woman,' Nesta reminded her. 'With a child to support.' She stared at her mother's hard unsympathetic expression. 'You're a heartless woman, Mother.'

'And you're a thankless daughter.'

Nesta shook her head in disbelief. 'I'm trying to make a better life for myself and my child, but neither Father nor I can do right for doing wrong in your eyes, can we?'

'If you leave now you needn't come back,' Meg said nastily. 'You won't last long in the vicarage, my girl, not if that Mrs Butler has anything to do with it. You may be homeless yet, but don't expect us to take you in again.'

Nesta's heart ached that there was no love for her from the one person who should have loved her unconditionally. Bronwen will never know such pain, Nesta thought. I'll always love and protect her, because I'm the only mother she will ever know.

She went upstairs without another word and carried down the child's cot, made for her by the local carpenter. It would be difficult carrying everything the half mile to the vicarage, and she realised she should have hired a hand cart. But she would not leave the cot behind. Meg was very capable of locking the doors on her, once she had left.

'People will talk,' Meg exclaimed cunningly. 'A young woman and an unmarried man living in the same house together.'

Nesta's mouth dropped open in dismay. 'Mr Ellis is sixty!' she exclaimed. 'You're making mischief where there is none, Mother, and that's wicked.'

Meg tossed her head stubbornly. 'You mark my words.'

'Then I'll find myself a good husband as soon as I can.'

'Huh! Who will have another man's leavings, and with his brat, too.'

'Goodbye, Mother,' Nesta said sadly. 'I don't think I'll be calling here again under the circumstances.'

She regretted that deeply because she loved her father, and he did not deserve to be ignored. And she needed her family, too, but in the face of Meg's bitterness it would be useless to try to patch things up between them. Perhaps, as time went on, Nesta thought hopefully, Meg's attitude might soften. She hoped so because she was already feeling lonely.

Bronwen was lying on a cushion near the range. Nesta picked her up and wrapped them both in the shawl. she managed to grasp her bag and reticule in one hand, and the side of the cot with the other. It was heavy, and it was a struggle, but she would not be beaten.

She glanced at Meg. 'Well, goodbye, Mother.'

Meg twitched her head stubbornly and looked away. With a sigh, Nesta walked out of the cottage. She had hoped to see her father before going, but earlier that morning he had walked into the town of Swansea to fetch supplies for his trade. She made a resolve not to be separated from him. Meg could not stop him from seeing his grandchild, for that was who Bronwen was now.

Outside, Nesta walked gingerly along the narrow strip of flagstones that edged the road. She was a woman alone, as Sheila Rafferty had said, and was vulnerable, but she was determined that that would not be the case for long.

There were quite a few unmarried men in Cwmrhyddin Cross. It was also true that most were no more than farm labourers, but there was one young man who had already caught her eye. Algwyn Caradog was the eldest son of the village's prosperous baker. His father suffered very poor health, and rumour had it that Algwyn would soon inherit the thriving business.

Nesta had observed him closely about the village and in church over the last few weeks. He had good looks and he had money. What more could a woman want in a husband?

Her cousin Dorah had caught a good husband in Geraint Probert, tenant farmer of Ystrad Farm, and she had not been too particular how she went about it, either. If Dorah could do it so could she, Nesta thought determinedly, although she would never stoop as low as Dorah to get what she wanted.

So deep in thought was she that she did not notice the crack in a flagstone underfoot until her heel caught in it, and she almost lost her balance. Dropping the cot, her one thought was for Bronwen. She clutched the child to her as she staggered forward, trying to save herself from falling with her precious burden, when suddenly she was caught by strong arms, and steadied on her feet again.

'Whoa there, missus!' a deep voice said. 'Mind how you go with the little one.'

Gasping with fright and thankfulness, Nesta looked up into the face of her rescuer. 'Thank you, I'm most obliged.'

'No great thing, it isn't,' he said cheerfully. 'Light as a feather, you are.'

Nesta stared and blinked at the man before her, dressed in workingmen's clothes. It had been three years, but she recognised his voice and his handsome face. Big Jim Jenkins! In confusion and discomfort, Nesta brushed at her skirts. With Algwyn Caradog as her goal for a husband, Big Jim was the last man she wished to be reacquainted with. She kept her head bent, eyes downcast.

'Thank you again,' she said shortly, and snatching up the cot turned away, eager to be gone, but he caught at her arm, holding her back.

'It's you, Nesta!' he exclaimed. 'Heard you were back home, I did. Hoping to see you, I was.'

'Jim!' Nesta gave a little laugh, pretending to suddenly recognise him. 'Well, what a surprise.'

Jim paused, looking keenly at the child in her arms. 'Heard

you were married,' he said more quietly. 'Broke my heart that did. I've never stopped loving you, mind, Nesta. I always hoped you'd come home one day, and we could . . .'

'Please, Jim!' Nesta exclaimed hastily, feeling her face heat up with embarrassment. 'I'm recently bereaved. It's not fitting that you should speak of such things.'

'Oh, *Duw annwyl*! I'm sorry, Nesta.' He looked crestfallen. 'I meant no disrespect, like, but I can't help what I feel for you.'

'I know you meant no harm, Jim,' Nesta said reassuringly.

He was a good man, for all his rumbustious ways, but he would never be more than he was today, which was a pity. Big, strong and handsome as he was, he would make any woman a good husband. But she needed more now.

'I'm glad you've come home, Nesta,' Jim went on. 'I've missed you sorely.'

'I'd rather we didn't rake up the past, Jim,' Nesta said quickly. 'You had my answer to your proposal three years ago.' She shook her head. 'My mind hasn't changed.'

It was more important than ever that she marry well for Bronwen's sake. She had a solemn duty to make it up to the child for depriving her of the life of luxury and privilege she would have known as Blanche Watkins. Nesta resolved that providing a good future for Bronwen must be her main purpose in life from now on.

'But you're a widow now,' Jim said eagerly. 'And still so young, too.' He shook his head. 'A lovely girl like you will want a good husband in the years ahead. You need someone strong to take care of you, someone like me.'

'And recently widowed, Jim,' Nesta reminded him again. 'My late husband was a sea captain; a well set-up man with prospects and of good family.'

'You don't look very prosperous, *cariad*, if you don't mind me saying so,' Jim said gently. 'And why isn't his family taking care of your welfare and that of his child, if they are so well off?'

'That's none of your business, Jim Jenkins,' she exclaimed shortly, annoyed at being caught out. 'Now you must excuse me. I have business to see to.'

She turned away hoping he would desist in his questioning. He was the first person to utter those words, but Nesta was well aware that these same questions were being posed in village gossip, and she had no answer for them.

'Allow me, Nesta,' he said, taking the cot from her grasp. 'This is too heavy a burden for you, with the child, too.'

'I can manage, thank you,' she answered. 'Now I must be on my way.'

'I'll walk with you and carry the cot,' he offered eagerly.

'It's not necessary,' Nesta said and tried to take the cot from his hand. It fell on the flagstone again.

'You were always a stubborn strong-headed girl,' he said, his voice growing husky. 'But I love you in spite of it.'

'You must not talk like this, Jim,' Nesta insisted. 'It's disrespectful of me.'

'I mean no harm or disrespect, Nesta,' he said quickly, picking up the cot again. 'I can't help what's in my heart. It's overflowing to set eyes on you again. There's been no other girl for me these three years.'

'I can hardly believe that!'

There were plenty of unmarried girls in the village. She had been sizing them up over the weeks since she had been home, seeing them as rivals for Algwyn Caradog, although at the moment he seemed to have no favourite from what she had observed.

'It's true!'

Nesta turned away without answering and walked on. Passers by were observing them. It would be around the village in no time that she and Jim Jenkins were courting, and she did not want such talk coming to the ears of Algwyn Caradog.

Jim hurried to catch her up, carrying the cot. 'Where are we going?' he asked.

Nesta sighed wearily. There seemed no way to shake him off for the moment. 'To the vicarage,' she said. 'I'm now keeping house for Reverend Ellis, and I'll live in.' She glanced up at him questioningly, remembering her mother's warning of scandal. 'Have you any objections?'

'None,' he said. 'But if you marry me you need never work.'

'Oh! A rich man you are now, is it?' She was annoyed at his persistence. She cast a glance at his clothing. 'Corduroy breeches under leather chaps are the latest in gentleman's attire, I suppose?'

'I've gone up in the world since you left Cwmrhyddin Cross, Nesta,' Jim said proudly. 'I own a fine stone cottage near the Marquis Arms.'

Nesta stopped in her tracks, surprised. 'You own a cottage?'

'Bought last year,' he said nodding and grinning at her. 'That has surprised you, hasn't it? Didn't think I had it in me, did you?'

Nesta stared at him for a moment and then shook her head. 'How could you, a farm labourer, find the money to buy a cottage, Jim Jenkins? I think you're lying, just to impress me.'

'Ask Ben Talbot if you like,' Jim said confidently. 'He was my second up by Shrewsbury last year when I beat One-Eye Parkins in the ring. I made a nice bit of money.'

Nesta felt a shudder go through her to be reminded of the evil men, like Jebediah Crabbe, who, professing to be sportsmen, made profit from the brutality of the prize-ring.

'As you told me years ago, Jim, boxers see little of the prize money at such events. It all goes to the promoters.'

'Aye! That's still true.' Jim nodded. 'But you see Ben, Bleddyn Williams and Peter Glynn – you remember them, don't you – we all pooled our money and bet on me winning, and a grand sum of money we had to share between us, too.'

'And squandered it all, I dare say,' Nesta said confidently, and then walked on.

Jim kept in step beside her. 'I bought the cottage with my share, and don't regret it. I dreamed one day you would return, and now you have. We could make ourselves a cosy home, *cariad*, and bring up our children.'

'There'll be no more of *that* talk,' Nesta said firmly. 'I'll never marry you, Jim Jenkins, stone cottage or no stone cottage. My sights are set much higher.'

She felt a shaft of remorse go through her at the look of pain that crossed his face at her frank words. She did not mean to hurt him, but Bronwen's needs, her future, must come first, and she must keep her goal firmly in mind.

'Thank you for helping me, Jim, but this is where we part,' she went on more gently as they arrive at the entrance to the carriageway to the vicarage. She reached out for the cot.

'I'll carry this to the door,' he said.

'No!'

'I'll not give up, Nesta. You were meant to be my wife. I just know it.'

There was nothing more to say, and Nesta turned from him, lugging the heavy cot as she went down the carriageway to the back door of the vicarage.

She must make a better way in the world than a farm labourer's wife. She had already taken a step up by helping to keep house for Mr Ellis. Mrs Butler was too frail to survive much longer, and then Nesta would have the title of housekeeper. She would be looked up to in the village, and she would do everything to catch Algwyn's eye. Soon, the shame of what she had done in the past would be safely buried.

13

CWMRHYDDIN CROSS, NOVEMBER 1838

A chill morning wind ruffled her skirts as Nesta stepped over the threshold of the dressmaker's cottage and into the narrow passage that led to the back room where Mrs Thomas dealt with her customers.

'Good morning, Mrs Crow,' the dressmaker, plump and middle-aged, bustled forward to meet her. 'Cold one, isn't it? *Duw! Duw!* Dread the winter, I do. The damp gets in my fingers, like. Plays Hamlet with my stitching.'

'Is my new hat ready, Mrs Thomas?' Nesta asked eagerly, pulling off her gloves. 'I'm looking forward to seeing it.'

It was the final addition to her new wardrobe which she hoped would make a favourable impression on Algwyn Caradog. Over the last few months she had managed to purchase a new gown and walking-out coat made by Mrs Thomas, which had given her extra confidence when attending regular Sunday services at St Marks on the Hill to hear her employer preach his sermons. The hat would be the finishing touch.

'Almost ready,' Mrs Thomas said, leading the way into the back room. 'Just a few touches more, like.'

'I want it for next Sunday,' Nesta reminded her. 'I did tell you that didn't I?'

'Oh, it'll be ready, don't you fret,' the older woman assured her hastily. 'So much attention it'll get by the other ladies in the congregation,' Mrs Thomas went on sagely. 'I want it to be just right, you know.'

The obsequious expression on the dressmaker's round face pleased Nesta no end. It was surprising how quickly her standing in the community had changed since taking up the full position of housekeeper to the Reverend Ellis following the death of Mrs Butler in early October.

'I hope it will,' she answered. A lot counted on it. Algwyn was fashionable himself, and she wanted to prove that she, too, had good taste. An asset in a wife.

'Take a seat for a moment, Mrs Crow.' Mrs Thomas almost curtsied. 'I'll fetch the hat for you to see.'

Nesta sat, waiting with anticipation. She had worked hard at making a good impression. It was important in her purpose to see and be seen by the right people, so she was careful to sit in the pews used by the more affluent members of the community, such as the Baxters and the Caradogs. It had worked, too, for she had at last caught the eye of Algwyn Caradog. While it was early days yet, she was convinced she would finally hook him in the face of any competition.

Mrs Thomas came back carrying the hat, followed by her daughter, Ethel, two years younger than Nesta. The girl had a sullen expression on her face, but Nesta pretended not to notice her.

The dressmaker held up the headgear for Nesta to inspect. 'There! Isn't that a beauty, Mrs Crow? Fine workmanship, even if I says so myself.'

'Oh, it is beautiful,' Nesta agreed, delighted. 'You are clever, Mrs Thomas.'

Mrs Thomas simpered at the compliment, holding a hand mirror while Nesta tried on the new creation.

'That'll do very nicely,' she said to the dressmaker. 'But I must have it for Sunday.'

Ethel Thomas gave a sniff. 'It doesn't suit you,' she said

abruptly. 'It's far too good for you. It takes a lady of quality to
wear a hat like that, not a candle-maker's daughter.'

'Ethel!' her mother exclaimed in a shocked voice. 'What're
you doing?'

'Well! Really!' Nesta exclaimed, jumping up thoroughly
insulted.

'Apologise to Mrs Crow at once!' Mrs Thomas demanded,
but Ethel flounced out of the room without another word.

'Oh, Mrs Crow, I'm so sorry,' Mrs Thomas murmured, her
face reddening in consternation. 'I don't know what has got
into that girl of late.'

Nesta knew full well what had sparked Ethel's spite. It was
sour grapes. On Sundays, outside the church, she had watched
Ethel's coy simpering whenever Algwyn Caradog spoke to
her or paid her attention, which was far too often for Nesta's
liking.

'I'll overlook it this time, Mrs Thomas,' Nesta said, feeling
sorry for the dressmaker's embarrassment, despite her annoyance at Ethel's rudeness. 'But I am a very good customer of
yours and don't deserve to be insulted.'

'I'm well aware of it, Mrs Crow,' Mrs Thomas said humbly.
'It won't happen again, I promise you.'

'I hope not, Mrs Thomas.' With that Nesta took her leave,
but no sooner had she stepped outside on to the road than she
was confronted by Ethel, wrapped up in a woollen cape, the
hood pulled up around her head against the cold wind.

'You're wasting your time with Algwyn,' Ethel blurted out,
her gaze hot with dislike. 'He has no interest in the likes of you,
with your penniless family.'

Nesta lifted her chin high and looked down her nose at the
other girl. 'I'll not lower myself to discuss personal matters on
the public road with you, Ethel,' she said decidedly. 'Or anywhere else for that matter.'

Ethel stamped her foot. 'I saw him first!'

'Don't be so childish!' Nesta retorted. 'Algwyn Caradog is his own man. He'll court whom he chooses.'

'He'll not choose you, with a candle-maker for a father,' Ethel sneered. 'Who looks the other way when the collection plate comes around on Sundays.'

Nesta gritted her teeth at the slur on her father, the best of men.

'I least I have a father,' she exclaimed quickly. 'Which is more than you can say. No one has ever seen hide or hair of yours.'

'Ooh!' Ethel clapped a hand over her mouth, her face screwing up as though she would burst into tears. 'How dare you imply that I'm . . . Oh!'

Nesta straightened her shoulders and adjusted her hat. 'You shouldn't bite off more than you can chew, Ethel.'

'I did have a proper father!' Ethel protested 'He died before I was born.' Her face contorted with spite. 'And you're hardly one to talk. We've only your word for it that you were married when you gave birth,' Ethel flared. 'There are those in the village that don't believe it for a minute. Algwyn Caradog for one!'

Nesta swallowed hard, disconcerted for a moment. Was this another sample of Ethel's jealousy or was there a grain of truth in what she asserted?

'You have a vicious tongue, Ethel Thomas,' she said tightly. 'And do you realise jealousy makes you ugly.'

'Oh!' Ethel gave a little squeal of rage but appeared speechless at last.

Nesta swished her skirts and marched off, but the girl's words rang in her mind. Was there talk? And did Algwyn believe it? It might explain the deep speculative looks he gave her whenever they met. She had supposed her widowhood gave her an added attraction for him, knowing that, by some men's standards, a young widow was considered easy meat.

But was she being naïve again, being taken in as she had been with Jebediah Crabbe? Algwyn could well think her easy if he believed she had had a child out of wedlock.

Nesta felt her jaw tighten. Thanks to Jebediah Crabbe, her understanding of some men's duplicity had increased somewhat. She would be as cunning as they were. If Algwyn was paying her attention for what he could get out of her, she would use his appetites against him; play him like a fish on a line, and then reel him in.

'So there you are, my girl,' Mrs Thomas exclaimed angrily as her daughter Ethel came into the back room, throwing off a cape to fling it on a nearby chair. 'What do you mean by insulting a customer? Are you trying to ruin us, or what?'

'Nesta Crow is nobody,' Ethel snapped. She sat down at the table, took up a section of a lady's jacket, and after examining the half-made button hole, began stitching.

'Her money is as good any anyone else's,' Mrs Thomas snapped. 'We've done all right out of Mrs Crow so far, considering. There was that new gown and jacket, the hat, not to mention the various cut-me-downs I've done for that Rafferty girl. All paid for by Mrs Crow.' Mrs Thomas sniffed. 'And there's more to come I daresay, when she marries.'

'Marries?' Ethel stared. 'What have you heard? Who is she marrying?'

'Tsk! I don't know.' Mrs Thomas shrugged her plump shoulders. 'But there are plenty of young bucks around Cwmrhyddin Cross who would be interested in her. She's smart and comely, and has a good position.'

'Well, she can't have Algwyn Caradog!' Ethel stormed, throwing down the material she was working on. 'I've set my heart . . .'

'Set your heart?' Mrs Thomas started, her face turning pale. 'What do you mean, Ethel?' She both hands to her breast.

'What do you mean, tell me.' Suddenly the breath caught in her throat. 'You haven't been a foolish girl with Lucas Caradog's eldest, have you?'

'No, I haven't!' Ethel flushed, and cast down her gaze.

Mrs Thomas recognised that guilty look in her daughter and her heart turned over in horror. 'Oh my God! This is terrible!'

'I tell you, I've done nothing wrong, Mam,' Ethel said, jumping up. 'Just a few kisses, no more than that, but I know Algwyn loves me. He told me so, and I love him.'

'You can't love him,' Mr Thomas blurted. 'Mustn't love him nor he you. Oh, my God! I never dreamed this would happen. I thought Lucas would have told . . .'

Mam, what're you talking about? Why shouldn't I love Algwyn? What could you possibly have against him?'

Mrs Thomas's legs felt suddenly too weak to hold her body upright, and she flopped down on to a chair nearby. How could Lucas let this happen? He had been a widower from the start, so there had been nothing to stop him telling his sons the truth when they came of age. And he had promised her. But instead he had left the burden of their guilt on her shoulders after all.

'Sit down, Ethel,' she said quietly and then swallowed hard, summoning all her courage. She was about to deal her daughter a body blow from which she might take a long time to recover. 'Something important to tell you, I have.'

Ethel sat down slowly, her gaze fixed on her mother's face. 'Mam, what is wrong? What is it? What are you keeping from me?'

'It's about your father,' Mrs Thomas began hesitantly. 'He didn't die.'

'What?'

'He's alive, and living in Cwmrhyddin Cross.'

Ethel jumped up, shaking her head. 'What are you saying?'

'I never wanted you to know, Ethel, my dear,' Mrs Thomas said. Tears were welling up in her eyes, overrunning cheeks.

She brushed them away with trembling fingers. 'His wife had died in childbirth the year before and . . . and I thought he loved me and would marry me.'

'Mam!' Ethel clapped both hands over her ears, and turning on her heel, moved quickly towards the door. 'I don't want to hear it. Don't say any more.'

Mrs Thomas jumped up from the table. 'Wait! You must hear it, Ethel. I can't let you go on believing what you do. It would be a crime, ungodly.'

Ethel turned slowly. 'I'm illegitimate? Is that what you're saying?'

Mrs Thomas nodded dumbly. 'Don't think the worst of me, my girl. I was in love too and expected to be his wife long before you were born.'

'This man betrayed you?'

'Yes.' Mrs Thomas felt again the pain in her heart when he had told her. 'It seems I wasn't good enough to be his wife,' she said shakily, 'Although he married no one else.'

'What has this to do with Algwyn and me?' Ethel asked plaintively. 'It's been a secret all these years. Algwyn . . . no one need ever know.'

'Your father is Lucas Caradog,' Mrs Thomas blurted. 'Algwyn is your half-brother. It would be incest!'

Mrs Thomas watched in dread as Ethel swayed in the doorway, her face ashen. 'Ethel?'

Ethel clung to the door jamb, staring; her gaze cold and empty.

'No! It can't be true,' she whispered in distress.

'I'm sorry, Ethel, my dear, so sorry.'

Ethel lifted her hand, palm outwards towards her mother. 'Don't say another word, Mam,' she croaked. 'Don't speak to me; don't ever speak to me again.'

'Ethel!' Mrs Thomas cried out. 'Please don't turn from me. You're all I have. Everything I do is for you.'

'You've wrecked my life!' Ethel screamed out. 'I'm in love with my own brother. *You* did that!'

'Lucas promised me that this could never happen.' Mrs Thomas rushed forward, arms outstretched to her daughter. 'Ethel, your father promised to tell his boys the truth about you so they'd be warned never to . . .'

'Don't come anywhere near me, Mam,' Ethel said, revulsion on her face. 'I'll never forgive you for this. It's bad enough that I can't have Algwyn, but no self-respecting man would ever want to marry me, an illegitimate girl. I'm ruined!'

Nesta walked hurriedly towards the crossroads, head lowered, deep in thought. She would be disgraced indeed if what Ethel said was right, and people thought her no better than a harlot. There would be no chance of a good marriage then, and that would mean that she had let Bronwen down by not providing the best for her.

Nesta paused for a moment. But it was better by far to be thought a harlot than for people to discover the real truth, the terrible thing she'd done, stealing a baby from its rightful father, for then she would face the rope around her neck, a painful and ignominious death.

Heaven forbid! A shiver went though her at the thought of it. It would be the end for her parents and for Bronwen, too, for who would take care of the poor baby then? If Bronwen escaped Jebediah Crabbe's clutches she must end up in some orphanage, to lead a wretched life. No! Nesta resolved she would go to the ends of the earth to prevent that, do whatever she had to, no matter what the cost to her.

She paused outside her father's shop. She hadn't stepped foot inside since leaving to work for Mr Ellis, although she managed to see her father from time to time in the village, and had begged him to visit her at the vicarage.

If there was talk about her past, Meg Lewis would surely

know about it. There was bound to be acrimony when they came face to face again, but it might be worth the trouble to discover what was being said. Taking courage Nesta stepped over the threshold and into the familiar front room.

Enoch Lewis looked up at her entrance, and then jumped to his feet in excitement. 'Nesta, my dearest girl! There's splendid to see you, and looking so well and smart, too. How are you, *bach*?'

'I'm well, Father,' Nesta said, reaching up to kiss his cheek. 'And how are you?'

'Middling, middling,' he said. He cast a glance towards the back room and Nesta guessed Meg was there, probably listening.

'What can I do for you, Nesta? Come for candles for Mr Ellis, have you?'

'No, Billy sees to all that,' Nesta replied. She wetted her lips nervously. 'Is Mother at home?'

With that Meg Lewis appeared as if by magic from the back room. There was no welcoming smile on her face, and she stared at Nesta coldly. 'What do you want? We've no money to lend you.'

Nesta blinked, disconcerted. 'I'm not after money,' she said quietly. 'I—I just called in to see how you both are.'

Meg Lewis looked sceptical. 'You want something all right,' she said. 'We've seen neither hide nor hair of you for weeks.'

'I didn't think I'd be welcome.'

'You're not!'

'Megan!' Enoch Lewis spoke curtly, and Nesta was surprised at his tone with his wife. 'Nesta is always welcome in my home.'

'You're an old fool!' Meg Lewis retorted sharply. 'Look at her, with her airs and graces. Housekeeper, my foot!'

'I'm a respectable woman,' Nesta declared. If there were any talk about her that remark would draw it out. 'I defy anyone to say otherwise, even you, Mother.'

Meg snorted, but remained silent, and Nesta felt satisfied. It was Ethel Thomas's spiteful jealousy at work, no more.

'Look,' Nesta said, placatingly. 'Why don't you both come to tea with me at the vicarage next Sunday afternoon? I have my own sitting room and Mr Ellis says I may entertain my family from time to time. I'm sure you both want to see how Bronwen is growing.'

'Thank you, Nesta, dear,' Enoch said eagerly. 'Lovely, that'll be. I miss my little granddaughter.'

'Then you'll go alone, Enoch Lewis,' his wife exclaimed. 'I'll not be cajoled by weak tea and stale fruit cake. Our Nesta gives nothing without expecting something back. And besides, that child is no granddaughter of mine.'

Nesta thought she would choke. 'What do you mean?'

'I mean I disown her and I disown you,' Meg spat out the words. 'I hear how you spend plenty of money on gowns and suchlike luxuries, but never a halfpenny do your poor parents see, and us with hardly a crust of bread some days. You don't care if we starve.'

'Meg, you go too far,' Enoch said angrily. 'We had mutton stew yesterday and *cawl* the day before. I've always made sure you're never hungry.'

'And when will you buy me a new gown?' Meg flashed at him. 'I'm in rags, and ashamed to show my face on the street.'

Nesta looked pointedly at Meg's plain calico dress. It wasn't new but hardly ragged, and she was angered at her mother's spite and deliberate exaggeration directed at her father.

He glanced at Nesta with sadness in his eyes. 'I'm sorry for this poor greeting, Nesta. You're in my thoughts and prayers, and I don't expect anything from you.'

'Oh!' Meg stamped her foot. 'You're a hopeless old duffer, and I don't know why I married you.' With those bitter words she turned on her heel and disappeared into the back room again.

Nesta gazed at her father, tears beginning to well in her eyes. He was looking tired and old, his shoulders stooped. He did not deserve such treatment, and she regretted being the cause once again of his humiliation. She had been thinking of giving her parents a portion of her wages, but knew her father was too proud to accept charity, even from her. But when she married Algwyn Caradog it would be different. There would be money to spare then.

Enoch smiled, and she felt he had sensed her thoughts. 'I'll call in to see you next Sunday afternoon, my girl. I want to see Bronwen, too. She'll have forgotten me by now.'

Nesta put a hand on his arm. 'No Father, neither of us could ever forget you. We love you.'

Nesta took her leave, striving not to burst into tears. She stepped out onto the flagstone walkway outside the shop, head down lest any passer-by should see her distress. So absorbed was she that when a man's strong hand gripped her arm, she was startled and almost cried out in terror.

'Nesta, *cariad*, is that any way to greet an old friend? Have you no smile for me?'

Recognising the voice of Big Jim Jenkins, she glanced up, ashamed that he had caught her in a vulnerable moment.

'Good morning, Jim,' she said, and then glanced around to see if they were observed. Ethel's talk of gossip made her feel uneasy. There was no knowing where loose talk would lead. 'I'm afraid I can't stop. Mr Ellis is expecting luncheon soon.'

'I rarely see you these days, Nesta,' Big Jim said persistently, a perplexed expression on his deeply tanned face. 'I want you to see my fine stone cottage down along the Marquis Arms. Come to tea next Sunday.'

Nesta lifted her chin and wetted her lips. 'I don't think that's a good idea, Jim.' He was used to the rough and tumble of life. She could not imagine him behaving in a civilised way, handling fine china cups. 'Besides, I have other plans for Sunday.'

'Even though you'll not marry me,' Jim said, shifting awkwardly on his feet. 'We can still be friends surely?'

'No, Jim, we can't,' Nesta said decidedly. 'As a widow-woman trying to earn a living, I can't afford to be gossiped about.' She gazed up at him, searching his face. 'Have you heard any gossip about me and . . . and my child?'

Big Jim frowned ferociously. 'No, and I'd better not either,' he said with a growl. 'I'll whip any man that besmirches your name, Nesta. You know you mean the world to me . . .'

'Thank you,' Nesta exclaimed hurriedly. 'I know you mean well, Jim, but we move in different circles now. You understand?'

'No, I don't!' he exclaimed loudly, and Nesta cringed in embarrassment.

'Lower your voice, please!'

'What's come over you, Nesta?' Jim asked, staring at her, his face stern. 'Never took you for a snob, I didn't.'

'I'm not a snob,' she said tightly in an undertone. 'I was married to a sea captain. I have my reputation to keep or else I'll likely lose my position as housekeeper at the vicarage.'

'Housekeeper? What's so high and mighty about that?' Big Jim's tone was impatient. 'You rub and scrub on your knees like any cottager's wife, I dare day.'

'No, it's not the same!' Nesta swished her skirts, thoroughly annoyed. 'Besides, I can't afford to associate myself with you, Jim. I have hopes of a suitor, with social position and a good income. You hardly qualify with your rowdy prize-fighting cronies and other dubious company you keep.'

'I'll change, Nesta, I promise you,' Big Jim said eagerly. 'I'll give up the prize-ring, I swear, if you'll marry me.'

'Out of the question!' Nesta exclaimed, staring up at him

defiantly. 'I already have a gentleman paying me court.' It was quite an exaggeration if not an outright lie, she thought, but it might soon be true. 'A much more suitable match, I assure you, than a farm labourer, always on the edge of penury. I have my child's future to think of.'

Big Jim's face suffused with dark colour. 'Who *is* this man?'

Nesta hesitated. It was one thing to tell a vague lie, it was another to name names, and Jim's fierce expression boded ill.

'That's my concern,' Nesta retorted archly.

He stared at her for a moment, and then his expression relaxed and he smiled. 'You're as clever as you're pretty,' he said, the anger gone from his voice. 'Trying to stir me up, you are; make me jealous. There's no such man.'

'There is too!' Nesta protested, angry that he would dismiss her claim so readily. 'Algwyn Caradog, if you must know. We're walking out together.' Algwyn had not asked her yet, but it was merely a matter of time.

'Algwyn Caradog?' Big Jim's eyes narrowed. 'Money he has, yes, and is set to have much more, but a gentleman he's not.' Abruptly, he seized her arm, holding on so tightly his strong fingers dug painfully into her flesh. 'He hasn't laid hands on you, has he? He hasn't taken liberties?'

'Oh! Let go, Jim!' Nesta snatched her arm away, rubbing at the smarting flesh. 'How dare you take liberties yourself, you ruffian!'

'Nesta, I meant no disrespect,' Big Jim said quickly. 'But Algwyn Caradog is not a man to be trusted with any woman, lady or kitchen maid. See no more of him.'

'You take a lot on yourself, dictating to me,' Nesta said. 'I'll walk out with whom I please.' She lifted her chin. 'And I don't believe a word you say about Algwyn. You're jealous.'

'It's true, I tell you,' Big Jim said earnestly. 'Nesta, I beg you, have no more to do with him.'

'Stand aside, Mr Jenkins!' she exclaimed loudly for the

benefit of anyone who might be watching. 'I wish to continue on my way.'

Nesta stepped around his towering figure and marched on, her back and shoulders stiff with anger and humiliation. Their meeting and disagreement could not have gone unnoticed. There would be talk, and she must avoid gossip. Once she was safely married, speculation about her would cease. She would not be out of the shadow of the gallows until then.

14

The psalm ended, and Nesta sat down on the hard polished pew, placed her psalm book on the rack in front of her and arranged her skirts carefully over her knees. The Reverend Ellis began his sermon, but Nesta wasn't listening.

She stared at the back of Algwyn's head as he sat in the pew directly in front of hers; admiring his broad square-set shoulders, relaxed now against the pew's hard back-rest, and the thick mane of dark glossy hair that overlapped his coat collar.

A handsome head, she reflected; a handsome man and well set up in the community. She could not believe the scandalous things Jim Jenkins had said about him. Jim was jealous and that was the sum of it.

Nesta glanced around surreptitiously at the other worshippers in the packed church. She was surprised that Ethel Thomas and her mother were not present. Good! Without that silly girl simpering at him, perhaps he would pay her more attention.

The last hymn was sung, prayers said, and the service being over, the congregation began to leave the church. Nesta remained in her seat until Algwyn was on his feet and already in the aisle and then she stood up and looked directly at him. As she anticipated his glance was on her, and she nodded, smiling. He smiled and nodded in return, his gaze on her intense. Nesta congratulated herself. His interest was caught, and now she must be clever enough to reel him in.

People were milling about in small groups outside the church door, the women probably gossiping about each other, the men talking business, mainly tradesmen and farmers.

Algwyn was standing alone, separated from his father and younger brother. He came slowly forward as she emerged from the church doorway, his hat held against his chest. He was tall and well-made, although not as powerfully built as Jim Jenkins.

'Good morning, Mrs Crow,' he said lightly. 'Might I say that's a very fetching hat you're wearing?'

Nesta smiled, pleased. 'Thank you, sir. It's meant to be.'

'Yes, you have style.' He raised an eyebrow. 'Learned, I dare say, from the gentry you mixed with in Roath and Cardiff.'

Nesta blinked, shaken at the mention of Roath, and felt a tremor of anxiety in her throat. No one, not even, her parents, knew where she had been in service.

'My style is my own, entirely, sir,' she said, careful to control her voice lest she betray her unease. 'How is your father these days?' she went on evasively. 'He leans heavily on his stick.'

Her hands were trembling and she pushed them quickly inside her muff. It was highly unlikely that the news of the kidnapping of the Watkins' child in Roath earlier in the year had reached this quiet backwater. Cwmrhyddin Cross had no newssheet or journal; villagers relied for news of wars or riot on an occasional newspaper being brought in from Swansea. But Algwyn Caradog, always with a sovereign or two in his pocket, moved about the county more freely than most hereabouts. Had he heard something on his travels? Fear suddenly gripped her heart. Had he learned she was the nursemaid in question and was involved? Was he suspicious?

'Perhaps your late husband's family were helpful to you,' he said.

Nesta gave a little nervous laugh. 'You seem unduly interested in my connections, sir.'

'You've become an interesting woman,' Algwyn said, with a smile. 'Do you know, I don't remember you being about the village before you left. How on earth did I overlook a lovely face such as yours?'

Nesta lifted her chin, sensing a lack of respect in his glance, which took in her form from head to foot. She would not take that from any man, no matter how good a catch he was. 'I think you're a little too familiar, sir,' she returned shortly.

'Oh! I do beg your pardon, Mrs Crow,' he said. There was a light edge to his tone as though he were laughing at her. The suggestion of insincerity in his voice set Nesta's teeth on edge.

'Please excuse me, Mr Caradog.' Nesta moved away, head held high. 'My child awaits my return.'

He came after her. 'My dear Mrs Crow, please forgive me if I've offended you in any way. I have my gig here. Let me drive you to the vicarage.'

'Thank you, no. I'll walk,' she said stiffly. 'Besides, your father is hardly fit enough to tramp the half mile to the cross-roads. I suggest you see to his welfare.'

He followed her down the path to the church gates. 'I'm sorry I've made a bad impression,' he said evenly. 'I had hoped we might get to know each other better, much better. I intended to ask you to take a drive with me this afternoon. The country-side is very lovely westward of the village even late in the year.'

Half an hour ago she would have been thrilled at the invitation to go driving with him, but his strange remarks about Roath were upsetting.

'I have duties at the vicarage this afternoon, Mr Caradog. And my parents are to take tea with me later,' she said. 'But thank you.'

Nesta stepped out smartly down the rough track between the graveyard and farm fields which led from the church to the vicarage and on to the crossroads at Cwmrhyddin Cross.

'Wait, Nesta!' he called. 'I beg you to reconsider.'

She stopped and turned to him in surprise at his familiar use of her first name, but tried not to look disturbed. She was

conscious that others of the congregation were passing either
on foot or in vehicles.

'Mr Caradog? What do you mean?'

He leisurely strode towards her . 'We should talk,' he began.
'I've news of the father.'

'News? I don't understand you.'

'News of Sir Tecwyn Watkins.'

Nesta felt suddenly faint, and drew in a deep gulp of air
before putting a gloved hand over her mouth, staring at him.

'I don't know what or whom you mean,' she said at last.

'You've forgotten your late employer?' He shook his head. 'I
hardly think so. Not after what you did to him.'

Nesta was flustered. 'Explain yourself, sir!'

'We can't talk here,' he said in a low voice, glancing about
him. People were watching them and some were smiling
knowingly. 'I'll bring the gig around to the vicarage at three
o'clock.' He smiled, his blue eyes mocking as his gaze swept
over her stunned expression. 'Don't disappoint me, Nesta. It
wouldn't be wise.'

He bowed deeply, purely for the benefit of onlookers, Nesta
was sure, and then putting his hat on, strolled back towards the
church gates where Nesta could see his father and brother
waited for him.

Nesta prepared the midday meal at the vicarage in a daze,
feeling very frightened. If Algwyn Caradog knew the truth
about her why hadn't he spoken up before? What was his
purpose in keeping quiet?

'Oh! Heavens!' Totally disorientated, Nesta lifted a hand to
her forehead as she stood before the big range in the kitchen.
'I forgot to salt the potatoes.'

'It's all right,' Mary Rafferty said. 'Noticed that, I did. I
salted them for you, Nesta. What's the matter? You don't
look well?'

'It's nothing,' Nesta replied quickly. 'Just a headache.' She turned to the girl washing pots at the stone sink. 'Mary, I know it's your afternoon off, but I wonder if you could look after Bronwen for a couple of hours. I have to go out. I'll make it up to you.'

Mary dipped her head and smiled. 'Are you going courting, Nesta? I heard Mr Algwyn Caradog paid you a lot of attention after church this morning.'

Nesta was aghast. 'Where did you hear that?'

'Down Ystrad Farm earlier when I went to fetch fresh milk,' Mary said blandly. 'Dilys, the milkmaid told me. She'd heard Mrs Probert telling the master there that you were angling to make a good catch for yourself.'

Nesta folded her lips with annoyance. Her cousin Dorah Probert had a loose tongue as well as loose morals, it seemed. Yet it would be foolish to deny she was meeting Algwyn. Mary would see his gig when it appeared.

'Mr Caradog has kindly invited me to go for a drive, Mary,' she said, keeping her tone casual, while in fact her nerves were jangled. 'There's nothing to be made of that.'

Mary gave a little giggle and said no more.

Nesta was ready dressed and waiting in the hall when the doorbell rang, but she let Mary answer it. Algwyn Caradog stepped in, removing his hat. Nesta noticed he gave Mary a long puzzled stare, before turning to her as she waited at the foot of the stairs.

'Good afternoon, Mrs Crow,' he began. 'Perhaps you should take a cloak. The wind is a little keen now.'

'Thank you, sir,' Nesta said quietly. There was no suggestion of disrespect in his expression at the moment, but she was certain it had been there earlier and was uneasy.

She turned to the girl standing by, watching them both with undisguised interest. 'Mary, please fetch me a cloak.'

Mary darted away and Nesta noted Algwyn's gaze followed her.

'Pretty little thing. Who is she?' he asked in a puzzled tone. 'I don't remember seeing her about the village before.'

'Mary Rafferty,' Nesta answered.

'Rafferty?' He looked astonished. 'One of the gypsies from the west of the village? She has scrubbed up well.'

Nesta was annoyed at his disparaging tone. 'The Raffertys are not gypsies,' she said sharply.

'Well, judging by the ramshackle hovel they live in, that's exactly what they are. Dirty gypsies! Of no consequence at all.'

'You're forgetting, Mr Caradog,' Nesta said pithily. 'Their ramshackle hovel is owned by Emlyn Baxter, one of the wealthiest tradesmen in the village, even richer than your father. Mr Baxter presses hard for their rent but will do nothing about their appalling living conditions.'

'If they were tenants of mine I would evict them. Thieving bunch,' he said harshly. 'The older boys will hang yet, mark my words.'

Mary returned with a cloak and as she helped place it around Nesta's shoulders, she noted the way Algwyn's gaze lingered on the young girl.

Outside, he helped Nesta into the gig and then boarded himself, flicking the reins and the obedient horse moved off at a brisk walk.

'Where are we going?' she ventured to ask.

'Towards Penllegaer Woods,' he said. 'The trees are still beautiful this time of year.'

'I'm sure we're not abroad this cold afternoon to admire the trees,' Nesta said archly. 'I'm puzzled by your strange remarks earlier, Mr Caradog. What did you mean?'

'We'll discuss that later.' He glanced at her. 'So you're responsible for the extraordinary change in the Rafferty girl. She has turned into quite a beauty under your tutelage, and has probably already attracted a string of interested young bucks, I dare say.'

'She's only fourteen, sir,' Nesta said in a warning tone, not liking the course the conversation was taking. 'Still a child.'

'But she shows much promise,' he went on.

'I think we should turn back, Mr Caradog,' Nesta exclaimed loudly. 'I find I'm in no mood for an afternoon drive after all.'

'You've little choice, Mrs Crow, if that's really your legal name,' he retorted in a hard voice. 'I know all.' He laughed unpleasantly. 'Even more than the authorities, I think.'

'I've no idea what you're talking about.'

He glanced at her scornfully. 'You keep saying that, but you understand me very well, Nesta. May I continue to call you Nesta?' he went on mockingly.

Nesta was silent, her hands clenched tightly inside her muff. She would say nothing further, she decided, for fear of giving anything away. Despite what he said, he could not know it all.

Algwyn chatted amiably about trivial matters as they drove on, but when they were climbing the slope where the track led into Penllegaer Woods, he paused in his talk and was silent for a while. Nesta waited with growing apprehension.

'I don't want to go into the woods,' she said finally, wetting her lips nervously.

'We'll remain on the track, never fear,' he said. 'I've no wish to get lost in this dense undergrowth.'

'It's too cold for me here among the trees.'

He ignored her grumble. 'You and the child arrived in Cwmrhyddin Cross at the beginning of June,' he said. 'I was in Cardiff a week or so after, and the newssheets were full of a distressing story of murder and abduction, complete with all the gory details.'

Nesta swallowed hard, wondering where this was leading. She closed her lips tightly, determined not to be drawn into revealing anything. She would give him no help.

He halted the gig and turned in his seat to look at her. 'In May a dastardly deed was done in the village of Roath. A child was stolen from her father and a ransom demanded.' He lifted an eyebrow sardonically. 'Have you any comment to make, Nesta?'

She looked straight ahead, fear closing her throat so tightly she couldn't have uttered a word had she wished to.

'No matter,' he said lightly when she remained silent. 'It appears that both the child and her unfortunate nursemaid, one by the name of Nesta Lewis, were brutally murdered by the abductors.'

Coldness was numbing her flesh throughout her body, a coldness that was not due to the piercing November wind which periodically sent clouds of dead leaves swirling up into the air. Nesta watched them and felt dead herself.

'Their bodies were never found,' he went on. 'And now we know why. You were in league with them, weren't you? How much did they pay you?'

'How dare you suggest such a thing?' Nesta cried out, thoroughly disconcerted. She would have stepped down from the gig at that moment, but there was nowhere to go, certainly not into these lonely woods.

'Come, now!' he said harshly. 'You must've been in their pay. How else would you've survived?'

'I was abducted along with the child,' Nesta exclaimed. 'They were planning to murder us both, but I managed to escape with the help of . . . a friend.'

He chuckled. 'An unlikely story.'

'It's true!' Nesta said tremulously. 'I swear it!'

'And who was this friend?'

'The gardener at the house where we were imprisoned. His name is Jack Crow.'

He raised his brows in surprise. 'Your husband?'

Nesta sealed her lips, realizing she had admitted too much.

She could already feel the roughness of the hemp around her throat.

'Was he the abductor?' Algwyn demanded. 'Did you plan it together? Did he kill Sir Tecwyn Watkins?'

Nesta put a gloved hand to her mouth, staring at him. 'Sir Tecwyn is dead?'

'He was killed on the last day of May, the day before you arrived in Cwmrhyddin Cross,' Algwyn confirmed. 'According to the newssheet report he was run through from behind, with either a stiletto or a small rapier.'

'Oh! My God!' Nesta buried her face in her muff, horror shaking her body. Jebediah Crabbe had killed Sir Tecwyn. And he would kill her if ever they came face to face.

'If you're innocent of guilt in this, why didn't you return the child to her father?' Algwyn asked. 'The fact that you didn't is enough to hang you.'

Nesta raised her head and stared at him, wondering why he had kept this devastating secret to himself. She felt the need to vindicate her actions.

'Jack . . . Jack Crow discovered that someone, I don't know who, wanted Sir Tecwyn's daughter dead,' she explained. 'He said that if I returned the child to her father further attempts would be made on her life.' Nesta shook her head. 'Don't you see, I couldn't let that happen.'

'Very noble! Or was it to save your own pretty neck? Where's this man Crow now?'

'He's gone to the New World,' Nesta said quietly. 'He fled in fear of his own life after helping me.'

'I believe you know who killed Sir Tecwyn, don't you?'

Nesta swallowed hard, fear, like a plum stone clogged her throat.

'Tell me, Mr Caradog,' she said at last, her voice quavering. 'Are you a follower of the sport of prize-fighting?'

'What a strange question.'

'Answer me.'

'No, Nesta. I prefer the company of women, and do all my wrestling in the depths of a feather mattress.' He leered at her. 'I like my opponent to be soft and yielding.'

Nesta turned her glance away, her cheeks flaming with embarrassment at his vulgarity.

'Then you had better remain ignorant of who murdered Sir Tecwyn,' she said quietly. 'These men are dangerous. I've no doubt they still look for me and the child. They'll kill anyone who learns their secret.'

'I think you'll tell me, eventually,' he said.

His confident tone stung her. 'And what will you do then?' she asked pithily. 'And more to the point, Mr Caradog, why haven't you told the authorities all you know? Surely, it's your civic duty to help bring these murderers to justice.'

'I don't give a fig for justice,' he said. 'I consider only my own pleasures.'

'I don't understand you.'

'Your life is in my hands, Nesta,' he said, amusement in his voice. 'I can send you to the gallows any time I choose. But that would be such a waste.' He tilted his head to study her. 'You have a lovely face, and your body is . . . tempting.'

He put his hand on her knee, and Nesta flinched away. 'How dare you touch me?'

'Nesta, you're mine to do with as I will,' he said blandly. 'I've had to journey to Cardiff to pay for my pleasures in the past. Now you will satisfy my appetites here in Cwmrhyddin Cross.' He moved closer. 'I've a fancy to taste those lips of yours this minute.'

He seized hold of her, and drew her to him, holding her tightly against his chest. Nesta struggled fiercely in his grasp.

'Release me at once, sir,' she gasped out desperately, trying to avoid his mouth searching for hers. 'This is outrageous behaviour.'

'You would do well not to fight me,' he said harshly. 'I'm not a man given to striking women, but you *will* obey me. You're my property, and will grant my every wish from this moment on.'

'Let me go, you scoundrel!' Nesta cried out terrified. Oh, why hadn't she listened to Big Jim's warning?

'I will *have* you,' Algwyn growled, and seizing her face in one hand, brought his mouth down on hers in a savage kiss.

Nesta continued to struggle until his mouth released hers after a long moment, but he did not slacken his grip on her.

'You're a novelty. I believe I like the fight after all,' he said, amusement in his voice. 'Women don't usually resist me.'

'Why would they when you have to pay them?' Nesta gasped out scornfully.

His jaw tightened, and he looked angry. 'The choice is yours, Nesta. Either you come to my bed willingly, or you face dangling from a rope, a public spectacle.'

'That fate sounds inviting at this moment,' Nesta snapped.

'And what of the fate of the child?'

She was stilled. 'What do you mean?'

'When you're exposed, so will the child be,' he said nastily. 'They still seek to end her life, according to you. She'll be returned to what's left of her father's family. But how long will she survive?'

'Oh God!' This is what she had feared all along, and now he had confirmed her fear. Exposure of her wrongdoing would damn Bronwen to death, as sure as the sun will rise tomorrow, Nesta thought wretchedly.

He released her, and sat back. 'Do we have an understanding?'

Nesta withdrew further on the seat from him, yet knowing she must comply, for she had sworn to protect Bronwen at all costs, not only for what she had done but because she loved the child with all her heart. God help her! What else was she to do?

'What of my reputation?' she asked hesitantly, and then gaining some spirit, lifted her chin defiantly. 'Why not marry me?'

He laughed as though genuinely amused. 'What? Marry the candle-maker's daughter when I can take her any time at my pleasure?'

'You demean me, sir!'

'You'll survive,' he said offhandedly.

'Perhaps you prefer the dressmaker's daughter for a bride?' Nesta challenged, anger and humiliation fuelling her spirit. 'Apparently Ethel Thomas is not too lowly for you. Perhaps you'll marry her?'

To her surprise he burst into genuine laughter. 'Ethel Thomas! It would be incest if I did. She is my half-sister, a little indiscretion of my father.'

Nesta was disconcerted and astonished, too. 'But you flirt shamelessly with her,' she said. 'You lead her on. I've seen it for myself.'

'It amuses me,' he admitted carelessly. 'She's unaware of the connection between us, and is so utterly naive.'

Nesta was not particularly fond of Ethel Thomas, but felt sorry for the unsuspecting girl. 'It's very cruel of you,' she said. 'How will she feel when you eventually marry someone else?'

'She's of no consequence. Her feelings don't concern me.' He spoke with such arrogance Nesta was shocked. 'Besides,' he went on. 'I'm not ready for marriage yet, but when I do take a bride she'll have breeding and money behind her.'

'Meanwhile, I'll be ruined,' Nesta retorted angrily.

'I don't intend that people will know of our . . . association,' he said impatiently. 'Our meetings will be clandestine.' He laughed scornfully. 'I've my reputation to think of.' He gazed at her for a brief moment, his expression intense. 'I'll come to your room at the vicarage.'

'No!'

'Yes! You'll leave the back door unlocked for me each night.'

Nesta was appalled. 'Each night?'

'I'll not trouble you every night,' he said coolly. 'But with the back door always open I can come to you whenever the mood takes me.' He smiled coldly. 'You should be flattered. Women tell me I've good looks and charm, and I excel in matters of the bedchamber.'

Nesta turned her gaze away from his leering smile, and thought of Black Jack Crow; his twisted, grotesque body, and knew who was the better man. Algwyn was not fit to wipe Jack's boots.

'It is who a man is inside that matters not his outward appearance,' she said bitterly. 'You, sir, are an empty shell.'

Without warning he struck her viciously across the face. Stunned, Nesta fell back against the seat, dazed for a moment. Recovering, she stared at him in fear, putting a gloved hand to her stinging cheek.

'I'm preserving your freedom solely for my gratification,' he said harshly. 'I'm not interested in your opinions, only your body. And to all intents and purposes, your body belongs to me. Remember that, Nesta.'

15

Nesta glanced at the clock on the mantelpiece. It was gone eleven o'clock, past the time when Algwyn usually arrived. She sighed, feeling relief that she would be spared his attentions tonight. Thank heavens!

The fire in the housekeeper's ground floor sitting room was banked up with small coal in an effort to keep it going through the damp February night. Nesta arranged the fireguard around the grate and was about to extinguish the oil lamp when she heard the sound of the latch being lifted on the back door in the kitchen adjacent to her rooms.

Nesta's heart sank. At this time of night it could be no one but Algwyn, and her frame stiffened with dread and loathing. She hated what he had made her into; an unwilling mistress. He never ceased to remind her that her fate was in his hands.

Within minutes her sitting room door opened and he strode in.

'Why aren't you undressed ready for me?' he asked without preamble, his tone cutting and without any attempt at feeling. 'My visits are not in any way social, so surely you don't still hope for that?'

His insensitive attitude made her jaws clamp together with fury. For the last three months she had endured his visits to her bed, two, sometime three nights a week in fear of his reprisal if she refused. In his lust he was vigorous, but totally callous of her feelings, and she knew she was no more than an unpaid prostitute to him – a body by which to slake his carnal thirst and she hated and despised him for it.

'I hope for nothing, except to be free of your attentions, sir,' Nesta retorted heatedly, thoroughly nettled.

His lips tightened. 'Be careful, Nesta,' he warned in a granite tone. 'I'll take only so much lip from you. Don't presume to be my equal. I could tire of you very quickly and so be careless in my talk. In riling me you have much to lose. So has the child.'

Nesta felt the old familiar fear clutch at her heart. She must endure all for Bronwen's sake.

'I didn't think you'd be here tonight,' she said contritely, conscious that she had been foolishly outspoken. She must not forget he could betray her any time he wanted. 'Don't you usually carouse with your cronies on Saturday?'

He had been drinking. She could smell it on him. He took off his hat and top coat and threw them carelessly onto a nearby chair.

'My needs don't take days of the week into account,' he said curtly. 'I've had drink, now I want a wench.'

Nesta turned her face away in disgust at his vulgarity. 'You make it sound so vile.'

'It's no more than a commercial arrangement between us, Nesta, dear,' he said scathingly. 'You pay me with your body for my silence.' He picked up the lamp and turned to the door. 'It's fortunate that your bedroom is also on the ground floor,' he remarked. 'So convenient for my requirements. Come along now, Nesta. My desire for gratification is pressing. I can wait no longer.'

Nesta swallowed hard. She knew he would be angry. 'I can't tonight. I'm afflicted today by . . . the curse.'

'Damnation!' he exploded and the lamp shook in his hand. He raised an index finger wagging it at her. 'If you're lying to me, Nesta, by God, I'll . . .'

'I'm not lying,' she cried out. 'And what's more I'm thankful for it. I was late and I began to fear . . .'

He set the lamp down on the table and glared at her. 'Why didn't you tell me this had happened earlier today when we ran into each other at the haberdashers?'

'Because you cut me dead,' Nesta exclaimed heatedly. 'You didn't even acknowledge my presence by a glance; the same way that you ignore me in church on Sundays. People notice these things.'

At the beginning of their compulsory association a great shame overwhelmed her, as though everyone knew of her humiliation, and she had to force herself to attend church as usual, so that there would be no talk and speculation.

'No one can know of our arrangement,' he said. 'I've been the soul of discretion. I've my reputation to think of.'

'You're very careful of your own reputation, but what about mine,' Nesta cried out. 'I live in constant dread of discovery. But there's the greater fear that I'll fall with child.'

He stared at her, hostility in his eyes. 'I trust you'll take steps not to, Nesta,' he said heartlessly. 'It would be a very unfortunate circumstance for you, believe me.'

She stared up into his cold gaze. 'What if it were to happen?' she asked, her voice trembling.

He shook his head. 'Then you'd be of no further use to me,' he said arrogantly. 'In fact, you'd be a liability, and I'd have to take measures to have you removed.'

Frightened at his intentions, Nesta put a hand to her throat. 'What do you mean?'

'I'd be compelled to inform the authorities of my suspicions of your involvement in kidnapping and murder. I couldn't afford to have any bastard offspring running around Cwmrhyddin Cross, making demands on me. I'm not such a fool as my father.'

'You're a beast!' she cried out passionately.

His mouth tightened and his eyes narrowed. 'You'll pay for that insult,' he said through clenched teeth. 'The very next time I bed you.'

'You can't humiliate me any more then you have,' Nesta said staunchly.

'Don't you be so sure,' he growled. He reached for his coat and hat. 'When will you be available to me?'

Nesta swallowed. 'In two or three days,' she said in a low voice. 'How long must this go on, Algwyn?' she went on miserably.

'Until I've had all the sport I want from you,' he said in a disparaging tone. His glance ranged her face and body, 'In truth I find you exciting, Nesta, especially when you try to fight me. You stir me like no other woman I've known. Our association may last for years.' His lips stretched in a sneer. 'On the other hand, I may tire of you tomorrow, if another willing wench takes my fancy. Mary Rafferty for instance.'

Nesta compressed her lips. 'She's only just turned fifteen,' she said tensely. 'Not even you would be that low, surely.'

'Mary's comely shape would tempt any man,' he said, an unrestrained expression of licentiousness passing across his face. 'She's turning into a beauty with a passionate nature, too, judging by that wild black hair of hers.'

'She's an innocent child. You will not touch her,' Nesta cried out. 'I forbid it.'

'What did you say?' He looked furious and took a step towards her. Nesta lifted an arm to shield her face, certain he intended to strike her as he had done before. 'I'll not warn you again, Nesta,' he snarled. 'Don't cross me, or you'll be sorry for it; sorry to death.'

With those parting words he swung around and left the room. Nesta remained silent, afraid to utter a word in case she lost control of her feelings and infuriated him further. When she heard the back door being closed, and knew that he was really gone, Nesta sank down on a chair and burst into tears.

If only she had the courage to defy him, but she dared not. This was her punishment for the crime she had committed against Bronwen and Sir Tecwyn, and she must learn to endure it. And more than her own fate depended on her submission to his demands. If Algwyn did ever betray her and she was taken by the authorities, what would become of Bronwen?

Nesta shuddered to think of it. Even if Bronwen survived Jebediah Crabbe's evil purpose, the thought of her growing up lonely and perhaps uncared for in an orphanage or at best in Meg Lewis's loveless household tore at her heart.

In her bed that night she prayed fervently that she would not fall for a child, for that would be the end of everything.

16

Nesta knelt on the mat in her bedroom on the ground floor, her head hanging over a chamber pot as another attack of nausea overwhelmed her, and she retched painfully. At the same time tears welled in her eyes. Her worst fears were confirmed. She had fallen for a child.

The Lord have mercy on her, for Algwyn would have none.

The bout of sickness over for the moment, Nesta sat back on the mat, wiping her face and eyes with a towel. She could hear Mary moving about in the kitchen next door starting the Sunday morning breakfast, and knew she must make an effort to appear normal in front of the girl. No one must know of her predicament, especially not Algwyn. She must find a way to rid herself of this unwanted pregnancy.

Nesta rose to her feet, feeling unsteady. How could she be rid of it? She knew nothing of such things, and could confide in no one. But she must find a way, for her future and Bronwen's, depended on it.

Nesta tied an apron around her waist and composing herself, went into the kitchen. Reverend Ellis expected a full cooked breakfast each morning, Sundays included, but nauseated by the very smell of food cooking as she was these mornings, it was an ordeal she dreaded.

'Good morning, Nesta,' Mary greeted her cheerfully. The young girl glanced sharply in Nesta's direction and she turned her face away quickly, not wanting the girl to spot the telltale signs of early morning sickness. Mary was young but she was no fool.

'Good morning, Mary,' Nesta said, her back turned, fussing with the pan of bacon and eggs frying on the hob. 'Thank you for getting the breakfast going. Did Bronwen wake you in the night?'

'No, she's as good as gold, that one,' said Mary. 'But she's a little monkey, mind. Standing up in her cot she was this morning, trying to climb over the bars.'

'Thank you for taking such good care of Bronwen,' Nesta said gratefully. 'You're such a help to me.' She glanced at the girl, now busy at the stone sink. 'Are you happy here, Mary?' she asked. 'There's nothing . . . no one bothering you, is there? You would tell me, wouldn't you?'

Mary looked up, surprise on her young face. 'I'm very happy, Nesta,' she said. 'I love my family, but it's wonderful living here at the vicarage. It's so grand. I never want to go back to live at my mother's cottage, never.'

'I'm glad you're here, Mary.' The girl was such good company and such a help.

Mary smiled shyly. 'As soon as I've washed up, I'll put on that new gown you gave me for Christmas,' she said. 'It's so lovely, Nesta, I hardly dare wear it, but I will today. This spring sunshine is making me feel so good.'

For a moment Nesta felt envious. She had made so many mistakes since she was Mary's age, ruined her life, in fact. She wished she could go back and begin again.

'You look a picture in that gown, Mary,' Nesta said kindly. 'It suits you so well.'

After breakfast was served to Mr Ellis, and everyone else had eaten, everyone except Nesta, she left Mary clearing up in the kitchen. She knew she could trust the girl to look after Bronwen when she was at the morning service at St Mark's.

*   *   *

The church was packed on this fine April morning. For the first time in months Mrs Thomas, the dressmaker and her daughter Ethel were seated in their usual pew. Ethel held her head bent, and hardly raised it even after prayers. Nesta thought the girl looked pale, and felt sorry for her. It must be an ordeal, thinking everyone knew of her secret origins. The Caradog family had a lot to answer for.

Nesta knew only too well what Ethel was going through. It had been so hard in the beginning to continue to attend church after Algwyn had forced her to submit to his lust. She felt dirty and used, and thought everyone knew of her shame and blamed her.

But it was important to keep up appearances both in church and about the village, and so she compelled herself to act normally, even to fending off occasional advances by Big Jim Jenkins, earnestly asking for her hand in marriage. She could not accept him now even if she wanted to. She was another man's mistress.

But she was beginning to see Jim in a new light of late. Lowly labourer he might be, but he worked hard and seemed steadier in his ways. She could not help comparing his sincerity with Algwyn's debased nature. She suspected that if she confided in Jim about Algwyn's evil use of her he might kill her tormentor. But then the dreadful circumstances would be revealed, and all would be lost.

If Algwyn was aware of Jim's interest he had said nothing. But lately, to Nesta's secret disappointment, Jim seemed to have lost heart and had stopped offering for her.

Coming out of her reverie, Nesta noticed then that Mr Caradog and his younger son, Meurig, were alone in their pew in front of hers. There was no sign of Algwyn, and Nesta felt glad. She could not have borne the sight of him today, knowing what shameful trouble he had brought her.

Perhaps he had gone away for a few days. Nesta hoped so.

She needed time to think about her new situation and how she could deal with it. She certainly would not tell him of her condition. Once he knew the truth, her whole world would come crashing down.

The house was quiet on this Sunday morning. After she had finished all her usual chores Mary settled down to looking after Bronwen. She loved it when everyone had gone off to church and she had the place to herself, except for her young brother Billy, usually to be found cleaning boots or chopping wood in the stables across the cobbled yard.

On such mornings she could pretend she was the mistress of the house, pretend she had important guests coming to drink tea from the finest china. One day, Mary thought, one day it will happen. One day some handsome gentleman will fall in love with her and sweep her off to be his wife in a grand house just like the vicarage.

Feeling very grown up and fashionable in the new gown Nesta had had made for her for Christmas, Mary went into Nesta's sitting room, and sat Bronwen down on the mat in front of the fire place, giving her the little wooden horse on wheels to play with, Bronwen's favourite toy.

'There you are, my little cherub,' Mary said lovingly. 'Play with Horsey.'

'Horsey!' Bronwen said plainly. 'Horsey! Gee-up!'

The child struggled to her feet, and tottered about the room, dragging the toy behind her until it toppled over. 'Horsey fall down, Mary,' Bronwen said earnestly, staggering towards Mary, arms raised, a tear beginning to glisten in her eye. 'Did he break his leggy?'

Mary burst into laughter, gathering the child up. 'Oh, you're so funny, my little chicken. Where do you get such sayings?' she said. 'No, don't cry. Horsey is fine. He's just having a rest. You've worn him out.'

Mary cuddled her tightly. She was a darling child, and Mary loved her as she would her own baby sister.

'I know,' Mary said soothingly. 'Why don't I find you a freshly cooked biscuit and some milk?'

As Mary turned towards the door it opened, startling her, and she called out: 'Billy! What are you doing in here? Get back to the stables where you belong, you bad boy.'

She drew back in astonishment when instead of Billy a tall broad shouldered man entered the room. Recognising him as Mr Algwyn Caradog, she stared at him disconcerted.

'Mr Caradog! No one's at home, sir,' she began. 'Everyone's at church.' Surely he must know that, and she was puzzled at him being here at this time of the morning.

'I'm well aware of it, Mary,' he said, smiling. 'It's you I've come to visit.'

'Me, sir?'

'I think it's time we got to know each other better.'

'I don't understand, sir,' Mary answered. What on earth did he want with her?

'That's a fine gown you're wearing, Mary,' he said. 'May I say it suits your figure very well.' He looked her up and down, and for some reason she felt uncomfortable under his intense scrutiny. 'How old are you?'

'Just turned fifteen, sir,' she answered. Was he about to offer her employment? She was very happy at the vicarage, and would not leave.

'Fifteen?' He raised his brows as though in surprise. 'I'd have thought you older, especially in that gown. I believe you're fibbing.'

'I swear I'm not, sir.' Mary began to feel nervous at the strange pitch in his voice. 'Can I offer you refreshment, sir?' she went on, not knowing what to say next to change the subject. 'Some tea, perhaps? I'm sure Nesta – Mrs Crow would expect me to see to that.'

'Mrs Crow?' He frowned. 'Has she mentioned me?'

Mary shook her head. 'No, sir. But as she's housekeeper, she knows how to entertain guests.'

He laughed out loud. 'Oh, yes. She knows how to entertain guests all right.' He gave her a long look. 'I think you, too, will do very well entertaining me.'

Mary swallowed hard, clutching Bronwen to her, disturbed by the strangeness of the encounter and the way his eyes never ceased to wander over her form.

Bronwen stirred in her arms, raising a hand and saying: 'Milk! Bron want milk, Mary.'

'Put the child down,' Algwyn said. 'There, on the mat, and come with me.'

'I can't leave her alone, sir,' Mary said hesitantly. 'Mrs Crow has left me in charge of her. She may get into mischief or hurt herself.'

'I said, put her down!' His voice was so loud, Bronwen began to grizzle.

Feeling frightened herself, Mary hugged Bronwen even closer. 'I think you should leave, now, sir,' she said unevenly. 'I don't think Mr Ellis would like visitors calling when he's not at home.'

Algwyn looked furious. 'Don't offer me impertinent back-chat, you slut!' he thundered. 'Put that child down now, before I take her from you.'

'Sir, you're frightening us both,' Mary cried, her heart pounding in her breast. 'Please leave.'

Before she could realise his intentions, Algwyn stepped forward, snatched Bronwen from her arms and dumped the child unceremoniously on the mat before the fireplace. Then he grasped Mary's upper arm roughly and began to drag her toward the door.

'You'll learn to do as I say, or you'll be sorry,' he said harshly.

Bronwen began to howl at being treated so roughly, and

Mary tried to snatch her arm away to tend her. As she tugged in his grasp he swung her around to face him and struck savagely her across the face.

'You gypsy whore!' he thundered. 'How dare you defy me?'

Mary screamed in terror, putting a hand to her stinging cheek as Algwyn seized her roughly about the shoulders and forced her through the doorway.

'Come on, my wild beauty,' he said. His voice was quavering with excitement now. 'Let's see what delights you have beneath that cheap gown.'

Mary screamed again, terrified, as he forced her through the doorway to Nesta's bedroom. 'Let me be! Let me go! What are you doing, sir?'

'I'm doing something I've been thinking about for a long time, and I won't wait any longer,' he said thickly. 'And don't pretend you're not as eager as I am. I see it in your eyes, harlot's eyes. I know that look.'

He pushed her towards the bed, and Mary drew back. 'Sir, what do you intend to do to me?'

'Take off that gown,' he instructed curtly. 'And I'll show you.'

Mary tried to shrink away. 'I will not! Don't touch me!'

'Damnation!' he exploded. 'Take it off before I tear it off you.'

'Billy! Help!' Mary screamed at the top of her voice, but before she could cry out again, Algwyn hit her across the face with his open hand.

'Be quiet, damn you!' He was breathing heavily. 'I don't want to ruin that lovely face of yours,' he rasped menacingly. 'But I will if you don't do as I tell you. Now take off your gown.'

Mary shook her head dumbly. She could hardly believe this was happening to her. As she stared up at him dazedly, he reached out with both hands, and grasping the neck of her gown wrenched at it viciously. The material gave way under his assault, and he laughed out loud, as with further tugs, the rent garment fell from her shoulders, leaving her standing in her cotton chemise.

'What have you done?'

'Not enough!' he said with another laugh. 'Not nearly enough. Let's see what you have, my lovely.'

With that he tore at the chemise, ripping it from her quivering form. Mary lifted both hands, trying to cover her nakedness from his eager gaze, now raking her body, almost slavering in his desire.

'Sir, I'm fifteen only,' Mary quavered in abject fright. 'You're doing a bad thing. God will punish you.'

'If there's any punishment to be meted out, I'll do it,' he answered savagely. 'You're too lippy for your own good, you gypsy witch. Now, come here. I intend to have you.'

Abruptly he lunged at her, forcing her backwards onto the bed, throwing himself on top of her. Twisting her head to and fro, and squealing in terror, Mary struggled as best she could under his weight as he tried to bring his mouth down on hers.

'Don't fight me,' he grated. 'Or it'll be the worse for you.'

'Let me be, for pity's sake,' Mary pleaded. 'I'm just a maiden.'

'Then I'll be the first man to take you, and make you into a woman. You should be honoured,' he said, with a coarse laugh. 'You'll enjoy it, my dear, I promise.'

In terror she felt his hand grasp the waist of her bloomers, to yank them down roughly over her hips.

'No! No! Stop!' Mary struggled wildly, fearing what was to happen. Where was Billy? Someone must help her.

'Quiet! Or I'll knock you senseless,' he hissed furiously. He lifted his weight for a moment and then sat astride her, pinning her body to the bed as he loosened his belt and unbuttoned the flies of his fine twill breeches.

'Don't! Have mercy on me, I beseech you, sir.'

Mary turned her face away, closing her eyes tightly. If only someone would save her, and she prayed fervently for deliverance. But suddenly, he was forcing her legs apart with his knees, and then without warning he thrust the lower part of his body down and forward against her tender crotch. Mary felt intense pain shoot through her lower body, and she screamed in agony. Blackness overcame her senses and she knew no more.

17

The congregation was leaving the church, some clustering around outside to gossip. Mrs Thomas and Ethel seemed anxious to be on their way. Nesta quickly followed, making a point of speaking to them, remarking casually on the fine day, and telling Mrs Thomas that she needed a new frock for Bronwen.

'How is the pretty little mite?' Mrs Thomas asked. Nesta could see the woman was struggling to appear natural, but her face was very drawn, and she looked older. Ethel stood by wordless, head down.

'Bronwen is eighteen months now,' Nesta said. 'Into everything, of course, and turning into a little chatterbox.'

'You must bring her in for measurements,' Mrs Thomas said. 'And choose some fabric. I have a lovely length of sprig muslin that might suit her.'

'I'll bring her in tomorrow,' Nesta promised and took her leave of the two.

Walking along the dirt road that led from the church to the village, Nesta glimpsed Big Jim Jenkins, for once dressed smartly in his best Sunday suit. He raised his hat to her, but Nesta turned her face away, unable to look him in the eye, overcome by shame. If Jim knew what she had become he would never look her way again. What honest, decent man would?

Saddened by her thoughts, Nesta pushed open the back door into the big kitchen, walked in.

'I'm back, Mary,' she called. 'Mr Ellis will be along shortly. He's invited guests for luncheon.'

But the kitchen was empty, and Nesta stared around, puzzled. There was no sign of activity. Mary should be busy at this time, cleaning potatoes and washing the cabbage. The joint of meat should have been in the oven an hour ago. Mary knew Mr Ellis liked his midday meal exactly on time, especially with guests coming.

Then Nesta heard Bronwen crying in another room and rushed out into the passage. As she opened her sitting room door, she almost fell over the child squatting just inside the room. Bronwen's little face was puckered and red. Obviously she had been alone and crying for a long time.

Nesta picked her up, speaking soothingly and then hurried to the foot of the back stairs which led to the servants' quarters where Mary slept at the top of the house.

'Mary? Mary, where are you?' she called up loudly. 'Why have you left Bronwen alone? Mary!'

But there was no answer. What had come over the girl? Nesta wondered feeling a little irritated. Had that new gown gone to Mary's head?

She noticed then that her bedroom door was open, when she knew she had closed it before leaving for church. Going into the room, she had a shock. The double bed was all awry, the sheets in a tangle. And then she stared at the rumpled under sheet, at the dark red stain that marred its pristine whiteness.

Blood! What did it mean? Her glance was drawn to the carpet near the bed. Mary's new gown lay there, torn and destroyed, and amongst the destruction was a cotton chemise, rent in half.

Nesta put a hand to her mouth in dismay and consternation. Oh my God! Mary! Someone had ravished Mary. Nesta stood still, numbed at the terrible truth. Who could have done such a depraved and abominable thing?

Immediately Nesta thought of Algwyn Caradog. He had shown too much interest in Mary these last few months, and he had been absent from church. That was a rare occurrence for him on Sunday, for although he was rotten to the core, he set great store in keeping up a respectable appearance.

At the realization, Nesta was filled with great wrath. The beast! Not content with ruining her, he had destroyed a young girl's innocence. He did not deserve to live!

But where was Mary? Suddenly fearing the worst, Nesta dashed up the staircase to the upper floors. She searched high and low but Mary was not in the house.

As she came slowly down the stairs an icy coldness engulfed her. Had Algwyn hurt Mary, silenced her to save himself? He was arrogant enough to think he could get away with it. She must tell someone, but she had no proof it was he who had attacked Mary, and she could not reveal her own intimate knowledge of the man.

Feeling wretched and frightened, Nesta reached the foot of the servants' stairs to find Mr Ellis in the passageway that led to the front of the house. He stared at her, an uncharacteristic look of irritation on his face.

'Nesta, I have been ringing and ringing for you,' he said shortly. 'Mr Baxter and Mr Tucker are come to discuss church matters. They're in the sitting room and will be staying to luncheon. Please bring in some sherry immediately.'

'Sir!' Nesta began, her voice trembling. 'Something terrible has happened to Mary.'

'What?'

'She's been attacked – ravished,' she went on. 'And is nowhere to be found.'

Mr Ellis looked perplexed. 'Nesta, you are letting your imagination run away with you?'

Nesta shook her head vehemently, and moved toward her bedroom door. 'See the evidence, sir, in here.'

Mr Ellis looked taken aback, and hesitated to enter the room. 'Really Nesta! I hardly think . . .'

'Please Mr Ellis, sir!' Nesta exclaimed loudly, in her agitation almost losing her temper with him. 'An abomination has been committed under your roof. You must do something.'

Slowly he followed her into the room. He stared at the soiled bed and at the pile of torn clothing. 'Oh, God preserve us against such wickedness!' he murmured in a weak voice.

'Billy was in the stables all morning,' Nesta said, clutching Bronwen tighter. The thought that the child had been in the house when the vile act was perpetrated filled her with horror and disgust. She could have been harmed, too.

'Billy?'

'He might've seen or heard something,' Nesta prompted impatiently. 'He must be questioned.'

'I must speak with my guests,' Mr Ellis said, looking confused. 'They will know what to do.'

'But, sir . . .!'

He hurried away and Nesta, fuming at the delay in searching for Mary, followed him through to the large hall. He entered a door on the right. In the large dark panelled sitting room two men were standing near the fireplace talking but turned as the vicar and Nesta entered.

'Gentlemen,' Mr Ellis said hesitantly. 'I regret there will be a delay for luncheon.' He turned and stared at Nesta. 'It appears my kitchen maid has met with misadventure.'

'Misadventure!' Nesta cried out irately. 'She has been raped! In this house this morning, while we were all at church. You must find the beast that did it.'

Emlyn Baxter, the most prosperous tradesman in the village, looked down his nose. 'I believe you employ that Rafferty girl from the west side of the village. Rum bunch, the lot of them, no more than gypsies.'

'I don't think . . .' Mr Ellis began.

'The villain will be one of her many followers, no doubt,' Thomas Tucker put in disparagingly. 'A girl of that low class knows many men. No doubt she asked for it.'

'Mary has no followers! She's a good girl,' Nesta blurted out heatedly, thoroughly angry. 'She's only fifteen.'

'Nesta! Please!' Reverend Ellis glanced at her, obviously scandalised at her raised voice directed at his guests.

Nesta collected herself, conscious that she was in danger of losing her position at the vicarage through disrespect of her betters, or those who considered themselves better because they had more than a shilling in their purses.

'They start early, these gypsy girls,' Mr Baxter said knowledgeably, pointedly ignoring her outburst. 'She's off sulking in a corner, somewhere.'

'Well, I think the magistrate should be sent for from Cadle Mill,' Nesta insisted more calmly, lifting her chin in defiance. 'Her young brother was in the grounds this morning. Billy may have seen someone . . . lurking about.'

Mr Baxter took his pocket watch out and glanced at it. 'I fear I can't wait for luncheon, Vicar. I've pressing matters to attend to.'

'As do I,' Mr Tucker said hurriedly. 'We'll have our meeting on church matters another time, Vicar.'

Without another word, both men left the room, followed by Mr Ellis, stammering his apologies. Nesta waited for him in the sitting room. Bronwen was beginning to grizzle, probably hungry. Nesta's stomach was also rumbling, but she could not think of food while Mary's fate was unknown. The poor misused child might be lying dead in a ditch somewhere. She prayed she was mistaken.

Mr Ellis returned and stared at her uncertainly. 'Nesta, I do not know what has come over you.'

'Mr Ellis, don't you understand?' Nesta asked sharply. 'A young innocent girl has been abused and may be lying dead somewhere. You must do something.'

The elderly priest spread his hands haplessly. 'I have no idea . . .'

'We must speak to Billy immediately,' she said vigorously. 'Come along, sir. He's still in the stables, I think.'

The young boy was lovingly brushing down the vicar's ancient horse when they arrived at the stables. He looked up surprised at the sight of them.

'Billy, where's your sister?' Mr Ellis asked abruptly. 'I want to speak with her.'

Billy's glance slid away. 'I dunno, sir.'

'Billy!' Nesta said sharply. 'Do you know what happened here earlier this morning? Did you see anyone – a man at the house? Now, tell the truth, Billy,' she scolded. 'You're not in trouble, but we must know.'

'Well, Mr Algwyn Caradog was here after everyone went to church.'

'What?' Reverend Ellis stared in dismay. 'But that's not possible. He was with his family in church.'

'No, he wasn't,' Nesta said, shaking her head. It was as she suspected. 'Did he go into the house?' she asked of the boy.

'Yes.' Billy nodded.

'How long did he stay?'

Billy shrugged. 'I dunno!' He indicated the horse. 'I was cleaning out old Maisie's stall, and then I had firewood to chop. I did see him leave, though. On foot he was.'

'And Mary?' Nesta asked her heart in her mouth. 'Did you see Mary after he left?'

Billy shuffled his feet uneasily. 'It was later. I saw her leave through the back gate. Her face was all blotchy, like she'd been crying or something. I called out to her to help bring in the firewood, but she said she was going home to Mam.'

Nesta heaved a sigh, and almost burst into tears of relief. The girl was alive, thank God! But what misery she must be in.

'We must go to the Raffertys' cottage immediately, sir,'

Nesta said urgently to the obviously perplexed vicar. 'Mary must tell us who attacked her. The magistrate must be sent for.'

Mr Ellis lifted a hand. 'Wait! Wait! Nesta. I must think this through. I cannot believe this of Algwyn. The boy is lying for some reason.' He gave her a stern look. 'I'm sure Mr Baxter is right. Mary has been encouraging some man, a farm labourer perhaps. She has been carrying on behind my back and in my house. It is outrageous!'

'No!' Nesta shouted, thoroughly angry with him. 'Algwyn Caradog is a philandering monster. Every man, but you, in the village knows it.' She swallowed hard. 'Jim Jenkins took pains to warn me against him when I first came home.'

Mr Ellis shook his head doubtfully. 'This is a serious allegation to make against a prominent villager. His family are among the richest in Cwmrhyddin Cross.'

'He's not above the law, sir,' Nesta said earnestly. 'Nor is he above God's Laws.'

The vicar's shoulders drooped. 'That's true. No man is above God's Laws. Then, come along. We'll go now to see Mrs Rafferty. Billy, you must come with us. Put old Maisie between the shafts again.'

The drive to the Raffertys' cottage was a short one. Bronwen continued to grizzle in Nesta's arms, but she could not think of pausing to see to the child. Mary's need was greater, and she sensed that the situation Algwyn had created in his lust, might be his downfall, and therefore to her advantage, although she was nervous of the outcome.

Heaven only knew what secrets he would reveal when accused. What had she to lose anyway? Once Algwyn learned of her condition he would toss her to the wolves. But if he were discredited beforehand any accusations he made against her would be suspect, especially since he had delayed denouncing her. She could deny everything.

No, she would not let him get away with what he had done to Mary and to her, no matter what the outcome.

Although Billy ran straight through the open doorway into the Raffertys' cottage, she and Mr Ellis held back, while Nesta knocked respectfully. Sheila Rafferty appeared almost immediately. Nesta could see she had been crying, and her heart went out to the older woman.

'We've come to see Mary,' Nesta began nervously, and then hesitated to see hostility in Sheila's eyes. 'How is she?' she forced herself to ask.

'Then you know what happened to her,' Sheila answered. Her tone was sharp as though in accusation. 'She's been cruelly defiled, ruined by a man lower than a common farm animal.'

'May we come inside?' Reverend Ellis asked in the hushed tones he usually kept for prayers. 'We have no wish to make a spectacle on your doorstep.'

Sheila stepped reluctantly aside, and they entered the humble cottage. Ma Rafferty sat in her usual place at the side of the range. She turned her head and spat into the hearth when her glance lighted on the clergyman. Nesta noticed Sheila did not apologise for her mother-in-law's disrespectful behaviour.

'What do you want with Mary?' Sheila asked. 'She's in no fit state to see anyone.' Tears welled in her eyes. 'My girl, my baby, is destroyed by what this man has done to her,' she said tearfully. 'It would be better for her if she were dead.'

'Oh! Don't say that!' Nesta cried out in distress.

'That is an ungodly sentiment, Mrs Rafferty!' Mr Ellis remarked in shocked tones. 'I will pray for you.'

Sheila gave him a scathing glance. 'It would be better if you prayed for damnation for the wretch who wrecked my girl's life.'

There was silence for a moment and then Bronwen began to cry, howling pitifully. Nesta bobbed her up and down trying to sooth her.

'What ails the babe?' Ma Rafferty asked in her dry cracked voice. Nesta had forgotten her, sitting silent in the corner.

'She's hungry,' Nesta said. 'Since discovering Mary's predicament, I've not had time to feed her.'

'Give her to me,' Sheila said practically. 'I've some warm sop already made for Ma. The child can have some of that.'

She ladled some bread and milk into a bowl from a pan on the hob, and set the bowl on the table. Then she took Bronwen from Nesta's arms and sitting down, proceeded to spoon the mixture into the child's eager mouth.

'This is very kind, and I'll repay you,' Nesta said.

'No need.'

Nesta noted she and Mr Ellis were not invited to sit. 'May we see Mary?' she began. 'It's imperative that we discover the man's identity so that the magistrate is informed of his crime.'

'The authorities will do nothing for the likes of us,' Sheila said bitterly. 'The man will get clean away, mark my words.'

'Has Mary identified him?' Mr Ellis ventured to ask. Nesta could see he was very uncomfortable in the face of such open hostility.

'No.'

'Let us speak with her,' Nesta urged. 'No time must be lost. Once we're given his name, Billy can run down to Cadle Mill and fetch the magistrate.'

'He can take my trap,' Mr Ellis offered.

Bronwen had eaten all she wanted and Sheila handed her back to Nesta.

'I'll see if Mary will talk to you,' Sheila said in a low voice. 'But she's so ashamed.'

'But she mustn't be,' Nesta cried out. 'None of it was her fault.'

Sheila hesitated, her expression darkening. 'Can I be sure of that?' she said, raising her voice a little. 'Mary has been living away from home for months now, out of my influence. How can I be sure she hasn't fallen into evil ways?'

Nesta was shocked and also a little nettled. 'You're not blaming her, surely?' she asked. 'I can assure you, Mary is an innocent, and has lived a very chaste life while at the vicarage. Evil has been done to her, but she didn't seek it out, quite the reverse.'

'I don't know what I'll do should there be consequences . . . do you understand me?' Shelia said. 'We couldn't bear the shame, Ma and me. Mary would have to leave us.'

'That's very harsh,' Nesta said soberly. The idea that Mary's family would not stand by her and support her was distressing.

'That's all very well for you to say.' Sheila gave Nesta a hard glance. 'You're not shamed as we are.'

Nesta bit her lip, vexed, but remained silent. Her shame was yet to come if she could not rid herself of the unwanted child that was hid in her belly. She too would be cast out by all who knew her.

Sheila Rafferty moved to the narrow staircase in the corner of the room. 'I'll fetch Mary,' she said.

After a few minutes Sheila returned, accompanied by Mary, wrapped in a Welsh wool blanket. Nesta was shaken by the girl's appearance. She seemed to have lost substance, but that was only an illusion due to her hunched shoulders and crushed expression. She looked pathetic and lost in her wretchedness. Her pretty face was now blotched, her eyes bloated from crying.

Filled with pity, Nesta rushed forward to embrace her. 'Oh! Mary, my dear girl! I'm so sorry.'

Mary's young face contorted and she began to cry again.

'Mary, tell me who has done this terrible thing?' Mr Ellis asked, stepping towards her. The girl shrank away, staring at him fearfully, and the clergyman stepped back confused.

'Mr Ellis, sir,' Nesta said. 'I wonder if you'd be so good as to wait outside. I believe she's fearful of all men now.'

Mr Ellis spluttered incoherently for a moment as though mortally wounded himself. But Nesta held his flustered gaze with a level look, and without more ado he retreated through the cottage door. She wondered momentarily if she had presumed too far, and put her position as housekeeper in danger. But there was a more important matter to deal with now – Algwyn Caradog's public disgrace.

'Now Mary,' Nesta said in a firm voice. 'You must name this man. I believe I know his identity, but I want you to confirm it.'

'You already *know* who's responsible?' Shelia Rafferty burst out angrily. 'If that's true you must have also known that Mary was in danger, but you did nothing!'

'I've a suspicion only,' Nesta lied, realising she had given more away that she intended. 'Going by what Billy has already told us.'

'Mary should have been safe in your care,' Sheila said still wrathful. 'You're equally to blame then, and I can never forgive you, Mrs Crow.'

Nesta could not help realising the accusation was justified. She had known Algwyn was interested in the girl. He had made little secret of it. He was unscrupulous, and looking down on the Raffertys as he did, believed he could do as he pleased with Mary without retribution. She should have taken more care, but how could she have foreseen he would go behind their backs on the Sabbath?

'Tell me his name, Mary,' Nesta urged.

'I'm afraid,' Mary wailed. 'He said he would kill me if I told.'

Nesta was horrified. 'The vile beast!'

'Name him!' Ma Rafferty cried out suddenly from her corner. 'Name him, and his punishment will be swift.'

The old woman was straining forward, staring wildly into space, her knuckles white as her old hands fiercely gripped the arms of her chair; her black eyes bright and intense. 'Speak!

He'll not harm you; he'll harm no one ever again. The fires of Hell will take him.'

'Ma!' Sheila said impatiently. 'Don't distress yourself and us.'

There was the sound of men's angry voices outside amid the Reverend Ellis's gentler tones. Mary glanced towards the door fearfully as her brothers Kieran and Donal entered. They were two big strapping lads and seemed to fill the small living-room. Even on a Sunday and at this time of the day, Nesta could smell drink on them.

'Mam, what's going on?' Kieran demanded to know in rough tones. 'What's the parson doing at our door?'

'Some man has taken your sister's innocence,' Sheila Rafferty cried out. 'She's brought shame to us.'

'What?' Both lads looked at their sister in fury. 'Is this true, Mary?' Kieran asked. 'Have you been whoring?'

'She's in no way to blame for it,' Nesta cried out, indignant that they should so quickly think the worst of their sister. 'She was attacked at the vicarage while we were all in church.' Nesta turned back to the girl. 'Mary, don't you see? You must tell the truth,' she said gently. 'For your own sake. Otherwise people will believe you encouraged it.'

Mary looked up, fear and misery in he eyes, and gave a huge swallow before she answered. 'It was Mr Caradog, Mr Algwyn Caradog from the bakery. I tried to fight him, but he tore off my clothing. He was so strong.' She lifted both her hands to cover her face. 'Oh, God! I wish I were dead.'

'Algwyn Caradog!' Kieran Rafferty repeated in a dangerous voice. 'He'll pay dearly for this.'

'Billy must go and get Mr Griffiths, the magistrate down at Cadle Mill schoolhouse,' Nesta said hurriedly. She did not like the determined looks that passed between the brothers. 'He'll deal with this by the law.'

'The law!' Kieran growled disparagingly. 'The law despises us. We're poor and we're Catholic. We can rot as far as the law is concerned. No, Griffiths the School will do nothing.' He turned to look at his brother Donal. 'We'll deal with this man ourselves.'

'Aye, we will!' Donal agreed gruffly. 'No one lays a hand on our sister and lives to tell the tale.'

'Caradog should be strung up for it,' Kieran said savagely. 'And I have a mind to do it myself now, this minute. Come on, Donal. Let us search for him.'

Sheila gave a little cry of fear as her sons turned to leave, and Nesta could well understand her concern.

'Do nothing hasty,' she blurted out, running after them. 'Think of your poor mother. Enough shame has been piled on your family already without you adding to it by your recklessness.'

Already on the dirt track that led to the village, Kieran swung around to face her. His lips twisted as he glared at her. 'Keep out of this, missus,' he said brusquely. 'It's none of your business.'

The two young men turned and raced towards the crossroads about half a mile away. Sheila stood on the step next to Nesta, wringing her hands. 'The Good God save us!' she cried frantically. 'More mischief will be done today, I know it. What shall I do?'

Mr Ellis stood on the path looking perplexed. Nesta went to him quickly, and took his arm.

'Send Billy in the trap, Mr Ellis, sir,' she urged. 'He must fetch the magistrate as quickly as possible otherwise there may be a tragedy.'

Billy was in the trap, reins in hand in a moment.

'Mind the horse,' Mr Ellis called out, as Billy moved off at a brisk pace. 'Do not over-run her. She's as elderly as I am.'

'Billy will be careful,' Nesta assured the clergyman soothingly. 'We must follow the Rafferty boys as quickly as possible. You must intervene, sir, if they attempt to do anything unlawful.'

Mr Ellis stared at her and Nesta thought she saw panic in his eyes. It would be a brave and strong man who could prevent the Rafferty boys doing anything they wished. But Nesta took his arm determinedly, and hurried him along the track.

Hurrying while carrying Bronwen used up nearly all her strength and so both Nesta and the cleric were out of breath by the time the crossroads came into view at the hub of the village. Hardly anyone was about, and Kieran and Donal were nowhere in sight.

'They may have gone to the bakery,' Mr Ellis suggested.

Nesta shook her head. 'No one will be there on a Sunday. I believe they may have gone directly to Mr Lucas Caradog's house.'

The imposing home of the Caradog family lay at the top of the gentle incline of Ravenhill Road, where it joined Pentre-gethin Road, the ancient highway down to West Wales. This was the route the coaches took on leaving the Marquis Arms after an overnight stop.

'Perhaps we should walk up to Ravenhill, sir,' Nesta suggested. 'Your very presence at the house may have a sobering effect on the Rafferty boys.'

'If you really think so, Nesta.' Clutching at his arm, Nesta could feel reluctance in every step the clergyman took as they made their way past the crossroads and began to climb the hill.

But they had gone very little distance before they saw a man on horseback racing down Ravenhill Road towards them, his coat billowing out behind him like a dark sail. And behind the horse two figures ran helter-skelter, their shouts of anger renting the air. As the horse galloped ever closer, Mr Ellis and Nesta, clutching Bronwen close to her breast with both arms protec- tively, drew back to the shelter of the hedge out of harm's way.

The rider was Algwyn Caradog in a mighty hurry. As he passed, Nesta could see bulging saddle bags fixed across the horse's flanks, and also attached to the saddle in front was another large soft leather bag.

Algwyn raced on towards the crossroads, but at that moment a slow-moving horse pulling a large and heavy brewery dray hove into sight, sauntering right across Algwyn's path.

Nesta gave a little scream, fearing a collision, but he pulled strongly at the reins to avoid it. Nevertheless, his horse swerved and reared in terror, almost unseating him. It took him a few more seconds to get the animal under control, which left enough time for the Rafferty boys to catch up with him. They were on him instantly, strong grasping hands reaching up to pull him from the saddle, while he beat at their upturned faces with his crop.

Cries of pain, curses and threats filled the quiet afternoon air, and people began to appear on the road, curious to know what the commotion was about. Nesta ran forward towards the affray, but Mr Ellis puffing along beside her, grabbed at her arm, holding her back.

'There is nothing you can do, Nesta,' he said urgently. 'Blood has been drawn. No one can stop this now.'

As Nesta watched it seemed that Algwyn would escape, for he momentarily freed himself, urging his horse on, but the Rafferty boys clung on to the bridle, saddle, stirrups, anything they could lay their hands on, and the horse faltered in its gallop, unable to bear the weight of all three men. The pause was enough for the now maddened lads. They laid rough hold on Algwyn, dragging him half out of his seat.

He fought back, digging his spurs into the horse's sides in a desperate attempt to urge the animal forward. The screaming horse, eyes rolling, mouth foaming, in pain and terrified at the shouting and noise, began a frantic side-stepping dance, and then suddenly reared up throwing Algwyn from the saddle. He fell heavily backwards and Nesta saw his head strike the large granite mile stone that had stood for decades at the centre of the crossroads. After that, Algwyn Caradog never moved again.

18

The morning air still felt warm from the day before as it drifted in through the open bedroom window. Nesta splashed her face with water and reached for the towel nearby, dabbing at her skin carefully.

Then she caught sight of her figure in the long dressing mirror; glimpsed the slight rise in her upper abdomen, and cruelly reminded of her desperate situation, her spirits plummeted. It was a constant nagging worry, even in her sleep, and each morning she woke as tired as she had been the night before.

One consolation was that she was no longer a slave to Algwyn's voracious appetites. It might be a sin to think so, but she was almost glad he was dead. Now her guilty secret of Bronwen's abduction was safe.

Yes, she was safe from that, but he had left her with another pressing problem. She smoothed a hand over the imperceptible swelling of her abdomen, and was filled with bitter resentment towards the life that grew within her. She had tried all ways she knew to be rid of it, but the life within clung on with rapaciousness so typical of its father.

If only she were on good terms with her mother, Nesta thought with a deep sigh. She might have confided in Meg to a certain extent, and together they might have found a remedy.

Meetings between them were just a pinch more affable since Nesta had bought a rather nice silk shawl for her mother last

Christmas and a new pipe for her father. He was a regular visitor at the vicarage now on a Sunday, but Meg still refused to come. Dare she risk telling her mother of her condition even now?

No. Meg would cast her off without a second's thought, and her father might even turn against her. She couldn't risk losing his respect. There was no one else she could turn to. Besides, she suspected it was already too late. Any attempt to flush it from her body at this stage would probably result in her own death.

Each morning she tied her corsets as tightly as she could without cutting off her air supply, but soon she would begin to show. No corset would hide her condition then, and her disgrace would be made public. She felt sick at the thought of how she and Bronwen would be treated, for her shame would be heaped on her child's head too. She could not hope to remain in Mr Ellis's employ. She would be homeless, penniless and friendless. She could understand Mary Rafferty's previous sentiments in wishing she was dead.

A tap came at her bedroom door startling her from her depressing thoughts. 'Are you up, Mrs Crow?'

Nesta recognised the voice of Dilys, the kitchen maid taken on by Mr Ellis in place of Mary. Dilys was forward and knowing and set Nesta's teeth on edge. Nesta disliked her even more for the fact that she had once worked for Dorah Probert. She just did not trust the girl.

'I'll be out directly,' Nesta called firmly, hurrying to dress. 'Carry on with Mr Ellis's breakfast, please.'

Dressed neatly in her dark blue housekeeper's gown, her hair covered in a clean white lace mop cap, and a crisp white apron over her frontage, Nesta sallied forth to face the world, wishing she had never returned to Cwmrhyddin Cross.

The breakfast finished, the washing up done, Dilys, fair-haired, buxom and forthright, was in a chatty mood, and no amount of discouragement from Nesta would shut her up.

'Did you hear about the Rafferty boys?' Dilys asked, on her

hands and knees scrubbing the flagstones of the kitchen floor. 'Found guilty of manslaughter they were, and serves them right,' she said nastily. 'Murder I calls it, killing a lovely man like Mr Algwyn Caradog.'

'Oh, so you knew him well, did you?' Nesta asked scathingly.

Dilys sat back on her haunches, and inclined her head coyly. 'Oh, I think I caught his eye all right,' she said smugly. 'Always chucked me under the chin he did whenever he called at Ystrad Farm where I used to work.'

Nesta could not check herself from asking: 'And who was he calling on at the farm, then?'

Dilys hesitated, giving her a sideways glance, and Nesta knew the girl realised she had spoken out of turn.

'Well, as a matter of fact,' Dilys said candidly, 'he used to call on Mrs Probert sometimes.' She paused again, dipping the scrubbing brush into the bucket of water. 'Usually when Mr Probert was away,' she went on, carefully keeping her gaze averted.

Nesta felt as though a bucket of cold water had been thrown over her. Algwyn and her cousin Dorah! Had he told Dorah anything of Nesta's terrible secret and how he had trapped her into bed? Had they laughed at her as they rolled together in the sheets? Nesta had no doubt their relationship had been illicit. Algwyn had had no honour in him.

Nesta felt her legs tremble with a new fear, and clung on to the edge of the stone sink for a moment to steady herself. If Dorah knew, would she tell? She might, out of sheer spite.

There was a tentative knock at the back door. Dilys went on scrubbing, taking no notice. Nesta felt so shaky she could not be sure of crossing the kitchen without staggering.

'Go and answer that, Dilys,' Nest said sharply. 'It's your job. You're getting very slack, my girl.'

Grudgingly, Dilys scrambled to her feet, and wiping her hands on her sacking apron, opened the door.

'What do *you* want?' she asked brusquely of whoever it was outside. 'Get away from here, go on! We don't want the likes of you hanging about this respectable house.'

'Who is it, Dilys?' Nesta called. She did not like the girl's proprietorial attitude. 'I'll decide who's welcome and who's not. Know your place!'

Dilys snorted angrily. 'It's that Rafferty girl,' she snapped. 'The little tart! How she has got the cheek to show her face after what her brothers did, I don't know.'

'Mary!' Nesta rushed forward and pulled the door wider. 'Mary, my poor girl. Come in.' Nesta elbowed Dilys roughly aside, and the maid gave an indignant squeal.

'My mother says I must have nothing to do with her,' Dilys said angrily. 'She's riff-raff, she is.'

'Well, I wonder what your mother would say if I told her what *you* get up to behind the cow sheds,' Nesta asked her. It was a shot in the dark, but she was gratified to see Dilys's face turn bright pink.

'Come in, Mary,' Nesta said kindly, ignoring the maid. 'How are you, my dear girl? It's been months since we saw each other. I didn't call on you because I wasn't sure I'd be welcome.'

Mary stepped over the threshold. Her pretty face was blotched from crying. Even on this hot morning she wore the coat her mother had given her, and carried a bundle done up in an old shawl.

'Oh, Nesta, I'm in such awful trouble,' Mary said. She glanced warily at Dilys, and then folded her lips, looking more upset.

'Dilys, go and empty the chamber pots,' Nesta commanded quickly. 'You should've done that chore before breakfast.'

Dilys's pert features stiffened with resentment. 'Billy should be doing jobs like that,' she said. 'My mother wouldn't like it.'

'Your mother doesn't work here,' Nesta snapped back. 'And you won't be working here much longer if I have any more of your lip. Now, get about your household tasks immediately, miss, or I'll have to speak to Mr Ellis.'

Dilys flounced out of the kitchen without a backward glance. Nesta relieved Mary of her bundle and took her coat from her shoulders.

'Sit by the range, my dear,' Nesta said. 'I'll get you a cup of tea. The Reverend can spare a spoonful. Then you must tell me what the matter is.'

Mary sipped the tea eagerly and then glanced at Nesta, almost shamefaced. 'Have you heard about Kieran and Donal?'

Nesta nodded. 'What's to become of them?'

'The assizes judge said they're to be transported to a penal colony in the Antipodes.' She frowned. 'What does that mean, Nesta?'

Nesta bit her lip. 'I think it means they're to be sent to a prison on the other side of the earth.'

'We'll never see them again!'

'But at least they are to live; they won't hang,' Nesta said trying to comfort the distressed girl. 'Your mother is very upset?'

'And angry with me,' Mary said with a sob. 'She believes it was my fault, and since discovering I'm with child, she's washed her hands of me. She says I'm a disgrace to the family and has thrown me out.' Mary's eyes widened and she looked frightened. 'Nesta I have no where to go, no roof to cover my head. What's to become of me?'

'You do have a roof, here with me,' Nesta said firmly, furious with Sheila Rafferty for her callous treatment of her daughter. She was reminded of her own mother's previous cold attitude.

'But will Mr Ellis allow it?'

'I'll talk him around,' Nesta said confidently, although she wondered how she would persuade the vicar to take in the disgraced girl. 'You're not to worry. Your place is here now. I doubt Mr Ellis will go so far as to pay you a wage, but you may be allowed to work off your keep. You'll have food and shelter, and who knows what the future will bring.'

'Oh, Nesta, I don't know how to thank you.'

'There! There!' Nesta said as the girl began to cry. 'You can have your old room at the top of the house, too. Dilys goes home to her widowed mother each night.'

Mary stopped crying but looked weary. 'Nesta, I'm afraid for the future,' she said. 'At being a despised outcast in my own home village. If there will be no place for me and my child in Cwmrhyddin Cross, where can I go?'

Feeling choked, Nesta could not answer. Wronged by the same man they were both doomed to be pariahs in the community. Nesta put her arm around the girl's shoulders and they remained like that for a few minutes, and then Nesta pulled herself together. There was no point in dwelling on disaster. Anything could happen.

'Fill the stone hot water bottle, and heat a couple of those bricks in the oven to air the bed,' Nesta suggested at last. 'Then go and lie down for an hour while I talk to the vicar.'

Mr Ellis shook his greying head. 'I can't afford a second maid, Nesta,' he said solemnly. 'And – well – what would my parishioners think of my motives?'

'They would see a man doing his Christian duty,' Nesta said. Her heart fluttered as she spoke. One day she would presume too far in her directness with him. 'You know Mary is not to blame for what happened, sir. It's a disgrace that she's being pilloried by the villagers and deserted by her mother. Taking her in would set a good example of Christian charity.'

Mr Ellis rubbed his jaw thoughtfully with a gnarled hand. 'Dear me. What a predicament.'

'Mary will expect no pay, sir, and she will work for her keep.'

'No pay you say? Oh, very well then. She may abide with us. And I'll pray for us all.'

When the front door bell rang one morning a fortnight later Dilys rushed to answer it. She had been quarrelsome and unpleasant at Mary's return, and had taken it upon herself to act as parlourmaid, answering the door and serving tea to visitors. Nesta was prepared to allow it, if it kept Dilys in better temper and made Mary's lot easier to bear.

Nesta went into the hall to see who the visitor was and to take charge if need be. She was in time to see Dilys about to knock on the study door.

'That will be all, Dilys, thank you,' Nesta said firmly. 'You may go about your duties.'

Before flouncing away Dilys sent her a venomous glance but said nothing in front of the visitor, who stood uncertainly, hat in hand in the hallway. Nesta had to gather her composure about her as she recognised him, for it was Algwyn's younger brother, Meurig. He was just a year or two younger than she, and they had been in school together, but now she knew she must treat him with some respect as though he were her better.

'You've called to see the vicar, Mr Caradog?'

'Yes, if he can spare me the time,' the young man answered. He was softly spoken and had none of the arrogance of Algwyn. She had always liked him for his quiet nature.

'I'll see if he's at home, sir,' she answered respectfully and turned toward the study door to knock.

'Just a moment, Nesta.' He reached out a hand to delay her. 'I understand Mr Ellis has taken in the poor girl, Mary Rafferty. I have a feeling that was your doing.'

Nesta immediately stiffened her shoulders and lifted her chin. 'Do you object, Mr Caradog?'

'Not at all.' He shook his head, his dark brown hair falling in his eyes. In stature he was not as tall and well-set-up in build as

Algwyn had been, but she had no doubt he was the better man. 'I want to thank you for your kindness.'

Nesta was flummoxed for a moment. In what way was Mary's comfort a concern to him? she wondered. He felt guilt, possibly, for what Algwyn had done.

'Mary is my friend,' she said simply.

Mr Ellis was at home to Mr Caradog, and after she brought in a tray of fresh coffee, left them to their business. As she closed the door, Nesta was tempted to listen for a few moments, then decided against it. She would not stoop that low.

'Meurig, my dear boy!' Mr Ellis exclaimed as they shook hands before the fireplace with its high dark marble mantelpiece. 'How are you?'

'I'm well, sir,' Meurig answered respectfully. 'And what about yourself?'

Mr Ellis shook his head. 'I find this hot summer very trying.' He ran his finger around the inside of his white dog collar. 'Be seated please. Now, of what service can I be to you?'

Before answering Meurig took a moment to place his hat on the floor beside his chair. Now he was here he did not know how to begin. The vicar might think his purpose very strange or even suspect, but he had thought about it carefully over the last month or two and was convinced it was the right thing to do, under the circumstances.

'As you know, sir, I'm now alone,' he began.

Mr Ellis shook his head again. 'Yes, losing your brother and then your father was a double blow for a boy of your age. It must pain you greatly.'

'I'm nineteen, sir,' Meurig said quickly. 'And know my own mind.'

'Of course, of course, my boy.'

Meurig gave a deep sigh. Having been always in the shadow of either his father or Algwyn, he was too quick to defend himself perhaps, and knew he was being oversensitive. Time would show he was a man in his own right, and would make his own decisions.

'My father's passing was not totally unexpected,' Meurig went on. 'He'd been ailing for some time.' He looked down at his hands clasped together so tightly his knuckles were white, and he forced himself to relax. 'Algwyn's death was too much for him in his weakened state.'

'Yes, a tragedy indeed,' Mr Ellis said. 'Responsibility for the business must weigh heavily on your shoulders.'

'I alone ran the business long before Algwyn died,' Meurig said defensively. 'When my father became ill it was left to me to take charge. Algwyn had other . . . interests.' He heard un-mistakable bitterness in his own voice and tried to curb it. 'I'm not complaining, and I foresee no difficulty in future.'

He had been bitter in the beginning when Algwyn had left the day-to-day running of the bakery to his younger brother, while he pursued his own pleasures.

'It's to your merit,' Mr Ellis agreed in his old fashioned manner. 'In what way can I help?'

Meurig moistened his lips nervously, wondering how his next words would be taken. 'A great evil has been done to Mary Rafferty,' he said carefully. 'I feel it my duty to . . . make recompense.'

'Very admirable,' the clergyman said. 'The poor girl has been disowned by her family in consequence. She'll be in need of some charity.' He shook his head sorrowfully. 'It's a sad case to be sure.'

Meurig sat forward eagerly in his seat. 'I wish you to act as intermediary, sir. I intend to approach Miss Rafferty with an offer of marriage.'

Mr Ellis rose to his feet abruptly, looking utterly astonished. 'My dear boy! This is folly!'

'It's just,' Meurig asserted strongly, rising too. 'Her life has been ruined by my brother. How else will she find a husband and live a decent life? Algwyn not only stole her innocence, he also stole her future.'

'But marriage . . . such a sacrifice for you!' Mr Ellis rocked back on his heels and stared about him perplexed. 'I feel it is unwise. They say she's from gypsy stock and is a Catholic.'

'I care nothing for such talk,' Meurig said sharply. 'She carries my brother's child, a Caradog. That child must take its rightful place in the family.'

Or what was left of it, Meurig thought. With his father and brother gone, and very few relatives, he needed to feel it was worthwhile carrying on with the business. He needed family, and it was right and just that Algwyn's child should be part of it.

Mr Ellis began to pace the room. Meurig watched him apprehensively. His courage had brought him this far in his belief that he must do right by the Rafferty girl. But if the vicar could not or would not help him, did he have the extra courage to follow it through alone?

Mr Ellis turned and looked at him. 'I think it my duty to dissuade you from this course of action,' he said gravely. 'I'm sure it's totally unnecessary, not to say . . . foolhardy.'

'A debt is due . . .'

Mr Ellis lifted a hand. 'I can appreciate that you might feel some degree of guilt for what your brother has done,' he said quickly. 'But marriage outside your class?' He shook his head. 'Why, it would be the ruin of you, my boy.'

Meurig fidgeted. He had not expected the vicar to put up such an argument and be against his plan so thoroughly. 'I can't see it like that, sir,' he said.

'I've seen a sight more of the world than you, Meurig,' said Mr Ellis resolutely if not a little pompously. 'I'm sure a monetary recompense will suffice to put matters right.'

'I hardly think . . .'

Mr Ellis waved a hand. 'Yes, yes, a sum of say, ten guineas

should be sufficient, indeed very handsome. A fortune for the likes of the Raffertys. The lower orders appreciate ready cash more than anything else.'

'Lower orders?' repeated Meurig, his tone sharpening. He stared at the old clergyman, wondering if he had made a mistake in asking his help. 'I'm no more than a tradesman myself,' he went on.

'But you're much more than that, my boy,' Mr Ellis corrected him. 'You're a landowner, and have that fine house at the top of Ravenhill Road. Your station is far above Mary Rafferty. No, the money will satisfy her entirely, more than she expects to get.'

'And what about the child, Algwyn's child,' asked Meurig quickly. 'How will he or she fare in the Raffertys' world? It's not right the child should suffer poverty. Caradog blood runs through its veins.'

Mr Ellis pursed his lips stubbornly, and Meurig could see he remained doubtful of his plan. Obviously the cleric believed he was setting a dangerous precedent. Some unscrupulous gentry had always sought to do as they liked with the so-called lower orders and feel no compunction, but that behaviour did not set well with him, and he would not be part of it, Meurig determined.

'My mind is made up, Mr Ellis, sir,' he said firmly. 'Marriage can be the only compensation.'

'Let me call a meeting of the elder members of the village council,' Mr Ellis suggested quickly. 'Mr Baxter and Mr Tucker can give you their advice.'

'Certainly not!' Meurig straightened his back. 'I came to you, Vicar, in the belief that this matter would remain confidential between us. I've no wish to make a circus out if it.'

'Tut! Tut, my boy!' Mr Ellis sat down again and waved Meurig back into his seat. 'There's no need to disturb yourself. It was merely a suggestion.'

'I'm determined, Mr Ellis, to do this,' said Meurig, setting his jaw firmly. 'I'll not be swayed from it.'

The cleric's expression was sombre. 'There'll be speculation, talk,' he warned. 'The last thing you need, my boy, is another scandal.'

Meurig spread his hands in exasperation. 'How can marriage cause scandal?'

The cleric pursed his lips stubbornly. 'And what does Mary herself say to this proposal?' he asked at last.

Meurig lowered his head. 'I haven't spoken a word to her. She's a complete stranger to me. It seemed hardly fitting . . .' He looked up. 'That's why I needed your help, sir. I had hoped you would arrange a meeting between the girl, her mother and me, with you acting as arbitrator.'

The vicar raised his grey brows sceptically. 'Apart from the imprudent nature of your plan, I doubt the girl will accept you, brother of the very man responsible for her misery.'

'But the arrangement will be to her good,' Meurig argued. 'There will be no cost to her.' He turned his glance away, feeling his face heat up. 'I'll expect no wifely duty from her,' he said awkwardly. 'Except to keep my house and what servants I have in order.'

Mr Ellis sat down again. 'I must tell you frankly, Meurig, I don't like this at all. The sanctity of marriage may be mocked in what you propose. Marriage is designed for the sole purpose of begetting offspring, not to ease a man's conscience.'

Meurig gave the clergyman a steady look, aware of his own youth and inexperience in the matters of the world. 'This would not be the first marriage of convenience you've performed, sir, I'm certain.'

Mr Ellis sighed. 'No indeed. You're right, and your motives are far above most.'

'Then you'll do it, sir?' Meurig asked eagerly. 'You'll be my champion?'

'Oh dear! What a predicament! And I'm fearful of the consequences.'

'Might we begin by speaking with the girl now, Mr Ellis, to sound her out,' Meurig suggested. The sooner things were underway the better, before he lost his courage entirely. 'Nesta, your housekeeper could be at the girl's side to support her. They're friends, I understand.'

'Nesta is her only friend, I think.' He sat for a few minutes more, head lowered as though in profound thought. Meurig sat watching him with impatience. Abruptly the cleric rose and moved to the bell-pull at the side of the fireplace, and then took his seat again. After a few minutes the same maid who had answered the door entered the study. Blonde and pert-faced, she gave Meurig a broad smile and a long look before addressing her employer.

'You rang, Mr Ellis?'

'Er . . . Yes, Dilys. Ask Mrs Crow and Mary Rafferty to come to the study immediately, please.'

'Yes, sir,' Dilys cast a sideways glance at Meurig, fluttering her eyelashes, and he felt his face flush and he looked away.

When she had gone Mr Ellis sighed heavily. 'Dear me! I do hope you'll not live to regret this decision, Meurig. In aligning yourself with the Rafferty family you're bedding with thieves and murders.'

19

Mary began to weep as she and Nesta made their way to Reverend Ellis's study, and Nesta put an arm around the girl to comfort her.

'He wants to put me out!' cried Mary. 'Where will I go? Oh, Nesta, I'm so frightened.'

'I'm sure that is not Mr Ellis's intention,' said Nesta, trying to sound comforting, but she wondered why they had been summoned in so offhand a manner.

Dilys's message from the study and the triumphant look in her eyes as she relayed it had caused Nesta to be filled with concern. Surely Meurig Caradog had not demanded the girl's immediate dismissal? But perhaps he did hold a grudge against the Raffertys for his brother's death. If that was true it would be grossly unfair to take it out on Mary, more sinned against than sinning.

As she knocked on the study door, Nesta set her jaw firmly. She would fight Mary's dismissal with all the influence at her disposal, and give Meurig a piece of her mind as well.

As they entered the room, Meurig stood up respectfully which threw Nesta into more confusion.

'Mary, Nesta, please be seated,' Mr Ellis said indicating some chairs nearby. Nesta noted a strained expression on his lined face, and expected the worst.

'Mr Ellis, sir, I must object,' Nesta began strongly, sending a stinging glance at Meurig. 'Mary has done no wrong. Why is she to be punished?'

Mr Ellis looked startled at her sharp tone, and glanced hesitantly at his visitor who was still on his feet.

'Please sit,' Meurig said calmly. 'I'll explain.'

They both took the seats indicated. Mary sat on the very edge of her chair, and Nesta could see her clasped hands were shaking uncontrollably.

Meurig sat down, looked at them both for a moment and then cleared his throat. 'I think it best, Mr Ellis,' he said a tremor in his voice. 'That you formerly introduce me to Miss Rafferty before we proceed any further.'

Mystified, Nesta watched as introductions were made, although Mary did not raise her head to look at the young man.

'Miss Rafferty,' Meurig began. 'Let me begin by saying how upset and disturbed I am at what has happened to you. My brother did an evil thing, but I'll try to rectify it.'

Mary glanced up, utter astonishment on her young face now so drawn with anxiety, but she remained silent.

'How is that possible?' Nesta blurted in her stead, staring at him accusingly. Did he think he could buy Mary off with a few sovereigns? 'How can you possibly right such a wrong?'

Meurig's hand went to the folds of the cravat at his throat, his fingers pulling at the silk as though it was too tight for him. He looked suddenly nervous and she could see a film of perspiration on his top lip. In that moment he looked much younger than his nineteen years.

'Through marriage,' he said in a voice that shook a little. 'If Miss Rafferty and her family consent, I'll marry her and bring up her child, my brother's child, as my own.'

'What?' Astounded, Nesta sat back in her chair. Next to her, Mary sat bolt upright.

'I feel it my duty to provide for my brother's offspring, and marriage is the most honourable way I know,' Meurig went on hastily, glancing from Mary to Nesta and back again.

Nesta was absolutely dumbfounded. She stared at him, her

mind buzzing. She too had been wronged by Algwyn Caradog but would never be able to admit it. Mary was to be saved it seemed, while she must go on to bear the shame and condemnation that must be heaped on her when the truth could no longer be hidden. It was so grossly unfair!

'This must come as a shock, Miss Rafferty,' Meurig went on. 'But I can assure you I'm sincere. Mr Ellis here will vouch for my veracity.'

'I do vouch for Meurig's veracity,' Mr Ellis said. He looked stern, which was unusual for him, Nesta thought. 'But I have to say that I'm totally against this proposal. I call it folly. I believe it's something you will both regret.'

Mary gave a sob and Meurig opened his mouth to protest, but the cleric held up a hand.

'There is much bad feeling in the village against Mary's family because of Algwyn's death,' Mr Ellis went on. 'I don't believe Mary will be accepted, even as your wife. You may both be shunned by the more influential members of the community, and even by some of the lower orders.'

Nesta saw Meurig's lips tighten. 'The Proberts, the Baxters and the Tuckers are not gentry, sir. They're no more than farmers and tradesmen, like me.'

'They have money and influence,' the clergyman said seriously. 'They could ruin you if they put their minds to it.' He turned to Mary. 'This young man is making a noble gesture, Mary, but I hope you'll have more sense and refuse his offer.'

Mary rose shakily to her feet. 'Mr Caradog's brother ruined me,' she said simply, although Nesta realised the girl was very near to tears. 'I'm an outcast in my own home, my own village.' She lifted her head. 'I have to think of the child, and so I accept Mr Caradog's offer.' She glanced around. 'Let everyone here witness that.'

Meurig stepped forward immediately, and hesitantly took Mary's hand. 'Miss Rafferty – Mary, I solemnly swear I'll treat you well and with respect, and will provide for you and your child all your lives.' He patted her hand, looking pleased. 'We must make plans,' he said.

It was too much for Nesta in the depths of her own misery, and she stood up abruptly. 'It can't be,' she blurted out. 'Mary is only fifteen, below the legal age of consent.'

'That is true!' Mr Ellis said quickly, an expression of relief on his face. 'Even if Mary's mother were to agree, the marriage would not be legal at fifteen.'

'But this is absurd,' Meurig blustered.

'It's the law!' Mr Ellis affirmed. 'To flout it would mean prison.'

Nesta felt ashamed suddenly. Her envy had scotched Mary's chances.

'I'm sorry, Mary,' she said uncomfortably, yet she could not prevent the thought coming into her head that she would make a much more suitable wife for Meurig Caradog, even though he was a year or two younger than she was.

'Mary, when is your sixteenth birthday?' Meurig asked interrupting Nesta's contemplation.

'Next February.'

'And when is your baby due?'

Mary bit her lip. 'January next.'

Meurig rubbed his thumb along his jaw line pensively. 'I had hoped the child would be born in wedlock,' he said. 'With my name on the birth certificate as the father.'

'But that would be a falsity,' Mr Ellis exclaimed.

'I'm willing to risk it,' Meurig went on in a determined tone. 'We'll marry in February, immediately after Mary's birthday,' Meurig said determinedly. 'It can't be helped that the child will be near enough one month old at that time. People will soon forget.'

Mr Ellis shook his greying head but said nothing.

'There's one more thing, sir,' Meurig said turning to him.

'I think it right and proper that Mary's younger brother Billy, who is no more than the boot-boy in your employ, should come into my business, and I propose to take him on as an apprentice baker as soon as you can release him.'

'Now that is a sensible suggestion,' Mr Ellis agreed. 'I have no quarrel with that. And it's well that you must wait to marry. Hopefully you will come to your senses before the new year.'

'Are you refusing to perform the ceremony, sir?' Meurig asked, his lips thinning.

The clergyman hesitated and then he sighed. 'No, I'm not refusing. But I beg you to reconsider.'

Meurig retrieved his hat from the floor and held it against his chest. 'No one will persuade me against it,' he said firmly. 'May I have your permission, sir, to call here at the vicarage to see Mary from time to time?'

Mr Ellis raised his brows. 'I have no objection, I suppose, as long as the meetings are properly supervised by Nesta. I want no gossip about this in the village. I have my parishioners to think of.'

'I wish to see Mary's mother, and get her formal agreement to the marriage,' Meurig went on. 'I'll do nothing behind her back.'

Sheila Rafferty will be more than eager for such a fine match, Nesta thought bitterly. Mary's future was assured, but there was no gallant man waiting to relieve Nesta's humiliation and she felt sick at the thought of what would happen to her when her own baby was born in December.

Meurig was taking his leave, and Nesta watched with envy as he and Mary lingered at the door in conversation, the girl still obviously shy, and her stance showed her unease in her future groom's presence.

Nesta turned away from the sight of them together, tears welling in her eyes. She had been as helpless a victim of Algwyn Caradog's lust as Mary had, but was condemned to bear her shame all alone. If only she could tell her parents, but she dared not; she couldn't risk losing her father's love and respect. All she could do was pray that a miracle would happen to save her from public condemnation and the life of an outcast.

As Nesta surmised Sheila Rafferty was overjoyed at the fortunate turn of events, but was still distressed that the child would be born out of wedlock and wanted the ceremony performed immediately. When Mr Ellis explained the law would not allow it, Sheila was outraged, saying it was a plot against them because they were Catholics. Nesta decided the woman did not know when she was well off.

It was the following Wednesday when Nesta was taking Mr Ellis's boots to the cobbler's cottage just below the Marquis Arms public house that she spied Big Jim Jenkins standing on the door step of one of the neighbouring cottages. He was coatless and hatless and she realised that he was standing at his own threshold.

He touched his forelock respectfully as she came by and smiled.

'Good morning, Nesta,' he said and stepped out onto the dirt road to intercept her. 'We've not passed the time of day for some time, but I must say you're looking lovely, even blooming.'

Nesta felt her cheeks flush up. People would soon begin to detect changes in her. 'Good morning, Jim,' she replied awkwardly. 'I'm surprised to find you home midweek.'

'Ben gave me the day off,' Big Jim said. 'He wants me to work on Sunday instead.'

'Sunday?' Nesta gave a sniff. 'Ben Talbot has no respect for the Sabbath.'

'The land and the animals need the farmer's attention all days of the week. The better the day the better the deed.' He half turned towards his front door and raised a hand. 'Do you have time to inspect my fine property? I'd value your opinion of all the work I've done to it.'

Nesta hesitated. 'I'm on my way to Jones the Boot,' she said. 'And haven't the time today.'

She made to move on but Big Jim caught at her arm.

'Nesta, I know you consider me beneath you, a mere farm labourer, but we needn't be at odds, surely?'

'We're not at odds, Jim,' Nesta answered quickly, feeling sorry to hurt him. He did not deserve that.

She stared up at him. He was a tall strongly built man, with rugged good looks which the prize-ring had not yet corrupted, but, although he appeared steadier of late, she doubted he would ever change his rumbustious ways. The lure of the prize-ring would always be with him, and that meant he would continue to associate with dangerous men like Jebediah Crabbe.

'I bear you no grudge,' she went on. 'And I don't think you beneath me.' She thought about Algwyn Caradog. 'I know you for a trustworthy and decent-living man, Jim. It's just that I have responsibilities to my child and need security in marriage.'

'Nesta, I'd do anything for you, you know that,' Big Jim said quickly and she heard sincerity in his voice. What a pity he would never make anything of himself, she thought with regret, for in all other ways he would make a good husband.

'My threshold is always open to you.' He smiled at her. 'And so is my heart.'

'Very prettily said,' Nesta answered, and smiled in return. 'You're a good man with a good heart, Jim. But now I must say good day to you. I must be about my employer's business.'

Nesta walked on swiftly to Jones the Boot who lived five or six cottages beyond Jim's. The cobbler's door stood open and Nesta went in. There were one or two customers waiting, sitting on some bentwood chairs standing on a sawdust-strewn floor.

An elderly man rose at Nesta's entrance and offered her his seat. She accepted with a grateful smile. Vigorous hammering could be heard from the back room at the cottage, while everyone waited.

Nesta thought of her encounter with Jim Jenkins. It was galling to realise that he was the only man in the village who had offered marriage. There were other eligible young bachelors, such as Ben Talbot and Bleddyn Williams, farm labourers, too, and utterly respectable, as far as she knew, but they had shown no interest in her.

'There you are, Mr Crackthorn.' Jones the Boot came out from the back carrying a pair of much worn boots and handed them to the old man. 'Soled and heeled and right for another two months. After that mind . . .' He clicked his tongue. 'You'll be needing a new pair made, I reckon.'

The old man paid. Jones pocketed the money and looked about the small room. 'Who's next?'

The stout woman sitting next to Nesta rose hurriedly. 'A broken heel, Mr Jones,' she said. 'What can you do?'

Jones the Boot inclined his head, examining the shoe she handed him, while Nesta went back to her thoughts of marriage, a subject that preoccupied her night and day of late.

She could guess why Ben and Bleddyn shied away from her. It was Bronwen. No man wanted to take on the responsibility of another man's child. Only Big Jim Jenkins was foolhardy enough to do that, which was in keeping with his big-heartedness and generosity, yet might also point to his old irresponsibility. She could not ignore that.

Although, Nesta thought in fairness, at least he'd had the sense to make good use of his winnings in the ring by buying that cottage. Was he really changing for the better? A good wife might be able to make all the difference to him; encourage him to make something of himself.

'It'll take some time, Mrs Price,' Jones the Boot said to the stout woman, his cheerful tones breaking into Nesta's thoughts. 'Come back in a couple of days, right.'

With a sigh, the stout lady left and Jones glanced at Nesta. 'What can I do for you, Mrs Crow? The vicar's new boots won't be ready until next week.'

Nesta handed him Mr Ellis's old boots. 'Soled and heeled. Mr Jones, please,' she said. 'And the vicar says, mind you use the best leather.'

Jones nodded, smiling. 'A couple of days, Mrs Crow. Business is brisk.'

Nesta went outside and began to walk slowly back the way she had come. The terrible truth was that in four months' time her baby would be born, and she could not let the child be born out of wedlock. She must save face if she could, perhaps anyway she could.

She had to accept the reality of her situation, and shelve her ideas of making a good marriage. Her foolishness in letting Jebediah Crabbe trick her had put paid to that. Now any marriage would be better than no marriage at all.

She paused outside Jim's cottage. There was no sign of him now, although she could hear the tones of a man's baritone voice floating through the open door singing some ditty.

Nesta looked at the doorstep, scrubbed clean, and at lace curtains at the tiny windows. Could this really be the home of Big Jim Jenkins, wild man and incorrigible prize-fighter? Jim said he would do anything for her, but would he, when the crunch came? And could she trust him?

Without thinking about it further Nesta tapped at the door. Within a moment Big Jim appeared, looking surprised to see her.

'Nesta! Come in, come in!'

Nesta stepped into a room much larger than she had expected which looked clean and well-kept, and she was impressed despite herself. Even in August a fire was lit in the large black-leaded range, and a black iron kettle was busy steaming on the hob. A well-scrubbed table stood at the centre of the room, and an old-fashioned wooden armchair was placed at the side of the range.

Big Jim ushered her towards this and invited her to sit.

'I can't stay, she said hurriedly, but sat just the same. She did not know why she had called now. 'The vicar is expecting his lunch.'

Big Jim stood over her, beaming like a child with a toffee apple.

'Mr Ellis has gone to Llanelly to see an old friend,' he said cheerfully. 'And won't be back until tomorrow.'

'How do you know his business?' Nesta asked, startled.

'Dilys Griffiths loves to talk,' Big Jim said. 'I bumped into her outside Tucker's the butchers earlier.'

Nesta tightened her lips. 'She was on an errand for me. Mr Ellis doesn't pay her to stand around the village flirting with every man she meets. She's a disgrace.'

'So I've heard,' Big Jim said with a grin.

Nesta rose, put out by Dilys's indiscretion. 'I must go,' she said.

'No, no please,' Big Jim exclaimed. 'You can stay a few minutes. Look, the kettle's boiling. Have a cup of tea. You're the first lady visitor I've received in my humble home.'

Nesta was undecided. She could not afford to be so sensitive she reminded herself with her entire future at stake, so she sat down again, and took firm grasp of her courage.

'A cup of tea would be nice,' she said affably.

She was curious to see how he would conduct the matter, and was surprised how quickly the tea was provided in a thin china cup with saucer and poured from a sturdy brown earthen teapot.

'You're well settled in, I see,' she remarked. 'I'm pleasantly surprised.'

He sat on a stool opposite her, awkwardly balancing his bulk while holding the cup and sauce in his great hands. He looked so incongruous that she had to smile at him. He smiled back.

'You can see that I'm now a man of property,' he said eagerly. 'And a landowner, too.'

'Land?'

He shifted uncomfortably on the stool. 'Well, the land my cottage stands on.' There was pride in his voice. 'A small parcel, it's true, but mine. And no man can take it from me.'

'All you lack is a wife,' Nesta said boldly.

The china rattled in his hands and he stared at her in astonishment. 'You're right, Nesta,' he said softly. 'But there's only one woman I want for my wife, and that's you.'

Nesta looked away quickly at the intense gleam in his eyes and felt uncomfortable. She put the cup and saucer down on the hearth, and fidgeted with her gloves and reticule.

'I shouldn't be here,' she said hurriedly. 'We're alone and people will talk. I should go.'

'The door stands open,' Big Jim pointed out. 'We've known each other many years. I see no harm.'

Nesta felt wretched suddenly. What was she trying to do anyway? Trap him? He did not deserve that. Had she really fallen that low?

She rose. 'I must go.'

Big Jim rose too. 'You've not said what you think of my home,' he said. 'Ben and Bleddyn helped me build an extra room on the back with stones from the quarry. I'd like your opinion.'

Nesta looked up at his eager and earnest face. 'Another time perhaps. I really must get back now.'

He was so proud of what he had achieved, and her heart softened towards him. All he lacked was the guidance of a good woman. She knew that with the slightest encouragement he would ask for her hand again.

'Perhaps I can call on you another day,' she said tentatively. 'And bring my daughter Bronwen with me.'

'Oh, Nesta! I'd be honoured.'

She was being imprudent, her common sense told her. It would not do for her to be seen going in and out of Jim Jenkins' cottage. It would be much less conspicuous if he came to the house.

'Better still,' Nesta went on thoughtfully. 'You could call on me at the vicarage next Sunday afternoon. Come to tea.'

Jim beamed his delight, and Nesta took her leave.

As she walked back to the vicarage her head buzzed with guilty thoughts. She had no doubts that Jim Jenkins genuinely loved her. It would be so easy to manoeuvre him into a proposal, but it would be impossible to deceive him for long. He would realise soon enough that she was with child.

She must trust him to a certain extent before marriage; but she could not tell him the whole truth, merely a version of it. It would be a test of his love for her, if he believed her. She needed his name now, needed him to accept her as she was, but he would be shocked by her revelations. It was up to her to make her story as heartrending as possible to gain his sympathy.

Nesta's step faltered as she realised Jim could turn from her in disgust, see her as damaged goods, and wash his hands of her, even betray her to the people of the village.

No, Jim would not do that. She had seen something in him today which she had not realised was there. Beneath that boisterous hell-for-leather exterior were a warm heart and a good nature. Perhaps, in spite of all her high-flown ideals, that was all a woman needed in a husband.

Jim Jenkins called on Sunday afternoon. He had the good sense to knock on the back door, and Nesta invited him into the housekeeper's sitting-room, next door to the kitchen. She had the back of the house to herself. Mr Ellis was taking a nap, while

Dilys had the afternoon off, and Mary and her mother had accepted Meurig's invitation to tea in his house at the top of Ravenhill Road.

Jim's height and broad shoulders seemed to fill the room, and Nesta was glad when he sat down. Now the time had come to put his love to the test, she felt uneasy and not a little frightened. No one knew her secret, but here she was about to reveal all to the least likely confident. Was his heart as true as he had led her to believe?

Little Bronwen made friends with him immediately, scrambling up onto his lap without asking permission first, and began chatting to him in her quaint way.

'I like ginger-bread men,' she told him, and offered him one from her sticky fingers.

Nesta was ready to scold her, but Big Jim laughed. 'No, no!' he said. 'Let her be. She's a beautiful child, and does you credit, Nesta.'

Nesta poured the tea, and handed him a choice of cakes she had made, and then sat back while he and Bronwen conducted an amiable discussion about the merits and drawbacks of eating fairy cakes with or without cherries. He had an easy way about him, she observed, and was not the least condescending to the child.

'How are things at Ystrad Farm?' Nesta asked, more for something to say than anything else.

Big Jim gave her a sidelong glance. 'You've heard stories, then?'

Nesta shook her head puzzled. 'No. I was just making conversation.'

'Well, you must be the only one in the village not to have heard,' Big Jim said and looked embarrassed for a moment. 'It's common knowledge that Algwyn Caradog visited Mrs Probert regularly, particularly when her husband was away,' he went on. 'And I'm certain Geraint knew of it.'

Nesta quickly turned her head away and lifted a linen handkerchief to her mouth, giving a little sob.

'Mammy cry,' Bronwen said, and scrambled off the sofa to come to her knee, looking up into her face. 'Mammy?'

Nesta gathered the child up onto her lap as Big Jim rose quickly to his feet also and came to her.

'Nesta, what is it?' he asked, his voice full of concern. 'If something's wrong you must tell me.'

Nesta trembled with apprehension. She was about to reveal a shameful secret to a man she had previously dismissed cruelly when she had first returned to Cwmrhyddin Cross.

Now she realised what a good man he was and hated the deception she must use against him to get a husband at any cost.

His remarks about Algwyn's disgraceful behaviour with Dorah Probert had been a shock, but it had also given her the opening she had been waiting for. She had no doubt that Jim loved her, but was that love strong enough to withstand the disgrace of what she had to tell him? She had no option but to trust that love.

'Oh, Jim, I've been so foolish,' she cried out, and the anguish in her voice was genuine. She swallowed hard as the lie she was about to utter stuck in her throat. 'I believed Algwyn when he said he loved me and wanted to marry me.'

Immediately Jim took a step back from her. Her heart skipped a beat as her apprehension grew. She ventured a glance up at him. The skin on his face had paled beneath its weather-burnished hue, and he was staring at her as though at a stranger.

The tears that welled in Nesta's eyes were not false. 'I believed him,' she went on hurriedly. 'I had no idea the kind of man he really was until that terrible Sunday when he attacked poor Mary Rafferty.'

'You and Algwyn Caradog?' Big Jim's voice was as hard as granite, and Nesta's heart sank. 'Did you love him?'

'No!' Nesta's voice faltered realising how calculating that must sound and she clutched Bronwen more tightly. 'Yes! Oh, what I mean is I was flattered by his attention.' She peered up at him. 'What woman of my class wouldn't be, Jim? Algwyn's family are prominent in Cwmrhyddin Cross. I thought to make a good match.'

He turned away abruptly and strode to the window to take a stance; his broad shoulders hunched with anger, his stalwart legs, encased in hide leggings, wide apart. She had not seen him in anger before.

'How many times did I ask you to be my wife, Nesta?' he said his voice heavy and ominous. 'And always you turned me away without giving me a chance to show my love. I wasn't good enough for you.'

Nesta was silent as she stared at his turned back. It was a just rebuke. She deserved his censure; she did not deserve his love. Nesta lifted a hand to her compressed lips to subdue another sob at the knowledge.

He swung around to glare at her. 'I warned you about him!' he said wrathfully. 'You can't say you weren't told.'

'I'm just a poor weak widow-woman!' She had no excuse but that. Dare she risk telling him the truth of her full shame? There was no sense in holding back now, and by the look in his eyes he had already guessed. 'I'm in trouble, Jim,' she went on, wetting her lips nervously. 'Shameful trouble, and there's no escape from it except death.'

'Nesta!'

She shook her head miserably. 'I can't face the condemnation that must be heaped on me when the truth is known in the village. I might as well be dead!'

He looked her straight in the eye. 'So, you are . . .' He hesitated, his mouth trembling and he shook his head as though unable to say the words.

Nesta made it easier for him. 'Yes, I'm with child, Algwyn's child. I have no excuses except that I'm a foolish woman.' She glanced up at him pleadingly. 'But I'm not a wanton woman, Jim. You must believe that.'

'Must I? And is this why you asked me here today?' he rasped. 'To let me think you feel as I do, stir my sympathy, make me your support and benefactor?'

'There's no one else I can turn to, Jim,' Nesta said plaintively.

'Huh!' He pushed his great hands in the pockets of his breeches, and stared out of the window again, while Nesta waited. 'What about your parents?' he asked at last.

Nesta could not hold back a bitter laugh. 'It would break my father's heart, and my mother would turn me out of the house in an instant,' she said. 'I have Bronwen to think of, too. She mustn't suffer for what I've done.'

She stood up and placed Bronwen on the chair and then faced him.

'I understand if you never wish to speak to me again, Jim,' she said in a low voice. 'I don't know what I expected in telling you this. Yes, I do. I tried to take advantage of you and I'm ashamed.'

She stood with bowed head and waited. She did not deserve his mercy or his love for she had tried to trick him, and been clumsy at it too.

'How soon?'

Nesta kept her head lowered. It was difficult to look at him now and see the dismay and disappointment in his eyes. 'My baby is due in December. I'll leave Cwmrhyddin Cross before then. I couldn't bear . . .'

'Where will you go?'

Nesta pressed her lips tightly together, and shook her head, not trusting herself to speak without bursting into tears.

'You have nowhere to go, have you?'

'No, except to the river Tawe in Swansea. I wouldn't be the first woman to take refuge in the waters there.'

Big Jim uttered an oath. 'There'll be no more talk of that, woman!' he said loudly, and Bronwen began to grizzle at his harsh tones.

Nesta lifted her into her arms immediately and cuddled her close. 'It's all right, Bron, *cariad*,' she murmured. 'Uncle Jim is not angry with you.'

'It's best the child calls me Da from now on,' Big Jim said slowly. 'If we're to be a family.'

Nesta looked up at him quickly, her heart fluttering in her breast at the new tone in his voice, one of resignation perhaps.

'Do you really mean it, Jim?'

'I'm a man of my word.' He gave a deep sigh, gazing at her closely. 'I know you're not wanton, Nesta, just a little head-strong,' he said frankly. 'With silly ideas above your station.'

Nesta was silent because what he said was true. This was how she had acquired her terrible secret, and why she could never let Bronwen want for anything, why she would gladly die to protect her.

'I'll get a special licence,' he went on. 'And we'll be married as soon as possible.' His smile came through at last. Perhaps he had not yet forgiven her, but she felt that might come in time.

'I've always loved you, Nesta,' he went on. 'Long before you left to go gallivanting to Cardiff to seek your fortune. A man doesn't stop loving a woman because she's made a mistake.'

'Oh, Jim!' Nesta gazed up at his, her whole being flooded with gratitude and even fondness towards him she realised. 'God bless you!'

He reached out and took Bronwen from her, and held the child against his broad chest, wiping a stray tear from her cheek with gentle fingers.

'One thing I must insist on, Nesta,' he said. 'I don't want it said that I've taken on another man's leavings, so I'll claim your unborn child is mine and my name must appear on the birth certificate as the father. Do you agree?'

Nesta clasped her hands against her breast. 'Oh, yes! Thank you, Jim.'

'It's not going to be easy,' he warned. 'There'll be gossip about us, but since we'll be married before the birth it may silence more vicious tongues.' He paused to study her. 'Will my humble cottage satisfy you after the grandeur of the vicarage, because that'll be your home for life when you're my wife, Nesta?'

'I'll make it a warm loving home, Jim, I promise. You'll never regret this, I swear.'

20

'Nesta, be sensible for once,' Meg Lewis said irritably. 'You
need another week of lying-in. It was a terrible hard birthing. I
was telling Mrs Penry of Iorworth Street. She said it was
surprising seeing as it was your second.'

Gritting her teeth, Nesta stood up from the bed and pulled
the strings of her stays tighter. 'Mother, I wish you wouldn't
discuss matters of my confinement with complete strangers.'

Grateful as she was for her mother's help during her confinement, Meg seemed to be spending most of her waking day
fussing around Jim's cottage, and it was beginning to get on
Nesta's nerves.

'Mrs Penry isn't a stranger,' Meg retorted. 'She's had ten of
her own. I've known her for years.'

'But I haven't!' returned Nesta sharply, pulling her petticoats over her head. 'I don't want to be gossiped about.'

'Oh!' Meg drew back, putting a hand to her throat drama-
tically. 'To accuse your own mother of spreading gossip is
utterly ungrateful after all I've done for you and Jim these last
months.'

'I'm grateful, Mother. I couldn't have managed without
you.'

'Tuh!'

'I do mean it, Mother. And Jim is grateful, too.'

Nesta shrugged into her dark blue housekeeper's gown and

quickly did up the buttons, thinking it was lucky it still fitted reasonably well after the arduous battle her body had been through. Her new baby daughter little Ceridwen Jenkins had fought hard and long to come into the world. One might imagine she *was* Jim's child.

'Why are you putting on that gown?' her mother asked in sharp tones. 'Surely you don't intend to go back to work at the vicarage?'

'Oh, don't you begin on me, too,' Nesta exclaimed crossly. 'I get enough of that from Jim. We need the money now there's another mouth to feed.'

Meg sniffed loudly, folding her arms across her chest. 'Well, you should've thought of that before you gave into your animal instincts before marriage,' she said pithily. 'We reap what we sow.'

'There's no stigma, Mother. I'm not the first girl to be caught out,' Nesta retorted sharply. 'Jim did the honourable thing and married me. He's a good man. I'm lucky to be his wife.'

The thought was heartfelt. She was lucky. Jim had been stalwart in his care of her since they had wed. She could have found no better man. She would be true and grateful to him all her life, and was determined to make him happy. Her feeling for him was growing day by day, and she knew her declared love for him was all he ever wanted to hear, yet she struggled to tell him of what was blossoming in her heart.

'Yes, well! Nothing like that went on in my day,' Meg declared with a superior air. 'Young women today have no moral sense. Look at Mary Rafferty . . .'

Nesta was just twisting her long hair into a bun at the nape of her neck, but swung around to face her mother, furious.

'Don't you say a word against Mary,' she burst out. 'Algwyn Caradog was an evil scoundrel who forced himself on her. And I for one am glad he's dead!'

'Nesta! May God forgive you!'

God would forgive her, Nesta was sure, after the way Algwyn had used her, humiliated her, and it would have gone on for years perhaps if he had not made the bad mistake of ravishing Mary and died for it.

She hated and despised Algwyn so much she had been afraid that she would feel the same about his child, and dreaded it being born. But now that little Ceridwen was here, and she had held her child in her arms, Nesta was filled with an overwhelming love for her daughter. Jim's daughter now. He would be the only father she would ever know.

'I'm off to see Mr Ellis,' Nesta said firmly. 'And look in on Mary. Her time is drawing near and she'll need support.'

'She has plenty of that from Meurig Caradog, so I'm told, and Sheila Rafferty is never away from the vicarage these days,' Meg said grumpily. 'And her a Catholic, too.'

'Tsk!' Nesta put on her hat and pushed the long hatpin through her thick hair. 'Mother, you make me impatient with your foolish ideas.'

She put on her old woollen three-quarter coat, and did up the buttons against the cold outdoors. It would be the first day abroad after giving birth ten days ago. She did feel shaky still, but was determined to make sure her job was safe. They did need the money despite what Jim said.

'Now, please mind Bronwen and Ceridwen while I'm gone. I shan't be long. Ceridwen will need another feed soon.'

Nesta was gone no more than an hour before she returned, feeling pleased that Mr Ellis was eager for her return to duties as his housekeeper the following Monday.

Nesta was not surprised. The vicarage was awry. Mary, in her condition, could do little of the chores that were necessary, while Billy, her brother, who had been so reliable and a great help to Nesta in the past, was now learning his trade with Meurig Caradog. Dilys Griffiths was a lazy good-for-nothing girl, letting the vicar and his house go to the Devil for want of a firm hand.

'I return Monday,' Nesta told Meg happily, as her mother handed her a hot cup of tea to ward off the cold outside. They might have a white Christmas yet. 'The poor man was quite desperate for my return.'

'That's as maybe,' Meg snapped. 'But what's to be done with your children while you work? Don't look to me! I'll not be tied down because you're greedy for money. Your father needs looking after too.'

'Oh, don't worry, Mother,' Nesta retorted. 'I expect nothing from you. The children will come with me daily to the vicarage. I can easily tend to their needs there.'

'What will Jim have to say about that?'

Nesta tightened her lips. Jim would probably have plenty to say. Wives should remain at home, he had insisted. For her to work would reflect badly on him.

Jim was a good husband, and she was beginning to respect him more and more, and yes, even love perhaps, yet she was determined to have her way in this. To give up the wage the vicar was prepared to pay her would set them next door to penury, like her parents. She was determined that would not happen.

Snow was thick on the ground one crisp morning the following January, and Nesta found it hard work climbing up the steep incline of Ravenhill Road to Meurig Caradog's fine house. The soles of her boots needed tapping; she could feel coldness of the snow seeping through the seams, but they must last another month. She was putting something of her wage away each week, hidden in a leather pouch in the outhouse. One day an opportunity might arise for Jim and she was determined to be ready to take advantage of it.

Nesta went to the back door of the house which was opened

by Sheila Rafferty. 'Good morning, Nesta,' Sheila greeted her. 'Cold one.'

'Yes.' Nesta shivered involuntarily, and then gasped at the warmth of the kitchen, kept well heated by the large range. 'How are Mary and the babe?'

'Doing very well, so Dr Powell tells us,' Sheila answered cheerfully. 'Take off your coat. Sit by the fire. Have a cup of tea before you go up to see her.'

Sheila had every right to be cheerful, Nesta reflected. It was good of Meurig to insist that Mary Rafferty and her family leave their hovel and move into his house. Sheila was now acting as his housekeeper, and sporting a gown of fine-quality twill.

Good sometimes came out of evil, Nesta thought. On the face of it the Raffertys certainly had risen in the world already, and next month Mary would wed Meurig.

'I miss Mary these last few weeks at the vicarage,' Nesta said wistfully. 'She's a good worker, with plenty of common sense.' She shook her head. 'More than can be said for that Dilys Griffiths.'

'Meurig thought it wouldn't be right, his future wife working as a kitchen maid,' Sheila said, not without some haughtiness, Nesta noted. 'And there was the child to think of, too.'

'Of course, he's right,' Nesta conceded. 'I'll not find another like Mary,' she went on gloomily. 'Mr Ellis has persuaded Dilys to live in, so that he'll have a servant there at all times.' She shook her head. 'I dread to think of the goings on when his back is turned.'

In a while Sheila took Nesta upstairs to see Mary and her baby son, named Lucas after Meurig's late father. Nesta was gladdened to see the happiness now in Mary's young face as she nursed her baby boy, a child with lusty lungs by the sound of him.

'He's hungry,' Mary said shyly. 'I must feed him.'

Nesta departed, feeling a heavy depression settle on her shoulders. Meurig Caradog's house was as fine a property as one could find in the village of Cwmrhyddin Cross and poor little Mary Rafferty, once looked down on and even despised, would be mistress of it within weeks; married and respectable and wanting for nothing for the rest of her life.

Nesta felt her throat close as tears threatened as she trudged downhill through the snow, back to her two-up-two-down cottage, with its unpredictable range that sometimes sent billows of suffocating smoke into the room.

Perhaps it was God's punishment for the terrible thing she had done against Sir Tecwyn and Bronwen, she reflected guiltily, her heart filling with bitter remorse. Bronwen, too, would have lived a privileged life, but for Nesta's interference. What could the future hold for the child except drudgery and poverty and even an early and violent death perhaps if Jebediah Crabbe, by some quirk of fate, ever discovered her whereabouts?

21

Nesta lay back against the pillows still feeling exhausted, and watched Big Jim Jenkins standing near the bedroom window, cradling his day-old son in his sun-browned brawny arms.

She watched him with mixed emotions. Deep love had grown in her heart for this big strong husband of hers, yet sometimes she could not help being impatient with him. He worked hard for the Proberts at Ystrad Farm but would never amount to more than a labourer. She thought of the little nest-egg she had hidden away in the outhouse. Jim knew nothing of it, and she intended he never should unless an opportunity for betterment came their way. Then she would surprise him with her thriftiness.

'What shall we call him,' said Jim with wonder in his voice. 'What name will we give my son?'

'He must take his father's name, of course,' Nesta replied tiredly, covering her mouth to yawn. 'He'll grow up big and burly and break every girl's heart in the village.'

Big Jim glanced across at her and grinned. 'He might grow up as ugly as a duck, like me.'

'Fishing for compliments, Jim?' Nesta answered with a warm smile, and lifted her arms. 'Bring our son, Little Jim, to me for his feed,' she said. 'And I'm parched for a cup of tea.'

Big Jim handed her the precious bundle, and then bent closer and kissed her forehead. 'Thank you from the bottom of my heart, Nesta, for this wonderful gift you've given me, my own son,' he said. 'I'm so grateful.'

Nesta grasped his arm, looking up into his face. 'I'm the grateful one, Jim,' she said softly. 'You saved me, and now we can share this child of ours, and be happy. And I love you for it.'

She meant those words wholeheartedly. They might be poor, but she and her children had love and security under the protection of Big Jim Jenkins. And who knew what opportunities the future might hold?

Big Jim kissed her again and then left the room, while Nesta got on with the delightful duty of feeding her son, feeling love for him spread throughout her body. But she loved all her children equally and would give her life for any one of them.

Big Jim came back quite soon with a tray of tea things, and she saw there was more than one cup.

'You've got a visitor,' Big Jim said as he laid the tray down near the bed. 'Mary Caradog is here to see you.' He paused near the door. 'By the way your mother insists she has to go now to see to your father's needs.'

Nesta sighed heavily. 'My mother can be very trying. Let Mary come up, and bring the children up here, too.'

Bronwen burst into the room and immediately jumped onto the bed, gazing at her new brother with adoration. 'Oh, Mammy, he's so tiny. Was I ever so small?'

'Smaller,' Nesta said with a smile. Bronwen was astonishingly pretty at five years old, and Nesta was very proud of her. Most of the time she forgot Bronwen was not the child of her body, and only remembered in times of depression and anxiety.

'Me too!' Ceridwen toddled forward too, and tried to scramble up onto the bed like her big sister, but could not, her small face puckering as she started to cry. Dutifully, and without being prompted, Bronwen helped her younger sister to mount the bed, too, and the sisters cooed and chortled over the new arrival to their family.

Mary Caradog came into the bedroom a few minutes later, carrying her son two-year-old Lucas. While she and Mary saw a great deal of each other, being firm friends, Nesta never ceased to be amazed at the change two years of marriage to Meurig had wrought in her.

Mary was poised, calm and always well-dressed; today wearing a cream sprig muslin gown, with a close-fitting blue velvet coatee over it. A matching hat was set at a smart angle on her fashionably coiffured hair.

'How are you, Nesta dear,' Mary asked. She set her son down on the bed, too, and then bent and kissed Nesta on the cheek.

'I'll live,' Nesta said with a smile. 'And how are you, Mary? You look blooming, I must say.'

To Nesta's surprise Mary blushed scarlet. 'I'm expecting a happy event myself next February,' she said. 'Meurig is over the moon with delight.'

'Oh, Mary, my dear girl! Congratulations!' Nesta answered, happy for her friend that everything had turned out for the best.

While Mary had blossomed since marriage, there were those in the village, like Meg Lewis, who still looked on Mary as that Rafferty girl, and would not accept her new status, which was so unfair.

They chatted for while, about their children, their lives and the future. Laughing and giggling, Ceridwen and Lucas tumbled about at the foot of the bed, their tender little faces animated with excitement.

Watching them, Mary smiled. 'Aren't they a picture to-gether?' she said. 'Who knows, one day they might be sweethearts and marry, and then you and I will be related, Nesta.'

Nesta felt an acute pain of anguish in her breast and could only smile back stiffly. One day soon she would have to tell

Mary the truth about Ceridwen's father. She dreaded the thought of it, but it would be a disaster if the children, half brother and sister, should ever fall in love.

She was reminded then of Ethel Thomas, and Algwyn's cruel attempt to make her love him, knowing she was his sister. She was so sorry for Ethel now, left all alone since her mother had died last year. It wasn't right that she was struggling to make a living, when she had a connection to a monied family who might help her.

Nesta made a resolve. At the soonest opportunity, she must tell Meurig about his half-sister, if he did not know already. And if he did, she would jog his conscience. Something should be done. But how would her friend take this?

Mary seemed very happy Nesta thought despite her difficulty in being accepted. Nesta decided she was happy herself, as happy as she could expect to be with a warm home and a loving husband. Hopefully the terrible crime she had committed was safely buried in the past, and nothing except a fluke of fate could harm her now.

After Mary and Lucas had left, Big Jim came back up to the bedroom, and stood looking out of the window, arms folded across his broad chest. There was a suppressed air of excitement about him which made Nesta uneasy.

'What're you brewing, Jim?'

He turned to her, his eyes dancing. 'Now, don't be cross,' he began. 'Remember you're still weak.'

'Jim?' asked Nesta in a warning tone. 'What have you done?'

'Nothing, woman!' He grinned at her. 'It's what I'll do. I've a chance to make some money, real money.'

Nesta sat forward in the bed, ready to push back the covers and get out. Big Jim moved swiftly to stop her and sat on the bed, holding her hands.

'Nesta, *cariad*, listen to me,' he said earnestly. 'Ben Talbot has had a word in secret from a friend in Swansea. There's to be a big fight in Cardiff in two weeks' time. The current champion is to defend his title against some American contender. The Fancy from all over the country will be there to witness it and have a gamble.'

'No! No, Jim!'

Nesta had a sudden vision of Jebediah Crabbe and his crony Mangler Harris. Cardiff was their stamping ground. Suppose they were to meet up with Jim and he unwittingly gave her whereabouts away? He was so affable and talkative, especially in drink, ready to tell his business to anyone who would listen.

Jebediah was wily, and he probably had spies everywhere. One mention of her name to the wrong people, and both her life and the life of Bronwen would be in jeopardy.

'Jim, you mustn't think to go.'

'Listen, will you,' he insisted. 'There'll be lesser fights, too, with good purse money for each one. I could win us a couple of hundred pounds, perhaps. Think what we could do with that, Nesta.'

'Jim, I forbid it!'

He stood up abruptly, his face tight. 'You forbid it, Nesta? A man's wife doesn't forbid him to do anything he wishes.'

'I'm afraid! Afraid for you. Afraid for us.'

He sat down again. 'There's no need to be afraid, my dear,' he said soothingly, his anger gone as swiftly as it rose. 'There's this young fighter by the name of Slasher Tonkin. A giant by all accounts but green to the gills at the game, although it seems he thinks a lot of his chances. I know I can beat him hands down.'

'Jim.' Nesta grasped his arm desperately. 'Jim, the people who promote the sport these days are no more then villains, criminals and worse – murderers,' she said fearfully. 'Have nothing to do with it, I beg you. We don't need blood money.'

Big Jim laughed. 'Nesta, my good girl, you know nothing of it. How could you? You mustn't go by gossip. There's nothing to fear. Ben is going to see the sport and so is Bleddyn. What can happen? I'll come home with a few bruises and a pocket full of money.'

Nesta swallowed hard, wondering how she could dissuade him without giving away her desperate fear. 'You promised me you wouldn't fight ever again, Jim.'

He raised his eyebrows. 'I don't remember that.' He patted her hand. 'It'll cost us next to nothing to journey to Cardiff. Ben will borrow a trap from Geraint Probert.'

Nesta shook her head vehemently. 'Suppose you were badly hurt and couldn't work afterwards? It's not worth it, Jim. It's too risky.'

'Risky for Slasher Tonkin, no doubt.' Big Jim grinned widely. He stood up and flexed his shoulder muscles and danced a few steps, shadow boxing, as light on his feet as a feather. 'It's a long time since I was in a good scrap. My blood is calling for the fight ring.'

'Jim, I don't want you to go,' Nesta said in a serious voice. 'I'm asking you not to get involved with it.'

He stopped prancing to stare at her. 'Nesta, I don't understand you. What is it really you're afraid of?'

'I . . . I'm afraid I'll lose you, my husband,' she said lamely. 'Men have died in such fights.' She shook her head. 'Don't bring disaster on us, Jim.'

'Tsk! What nonsense,' he exclaimed, jigging about again, and lunging at the air. 'It's the chance of a lifetime, Nesta. Don't you understand? The whole country will be there to see it. I could make a name for myself.'

'A name? It's a bit late for that,' Nesta blurted angrily. 'Bare-fist fighting is a young man's game. You're twenty-six, and with a family. You have no business to go putting yourself at risk.'

'Why must you be disagreeable, Nesta?' Big Jim asked tetchily, sitting on the bed again. 'I don't hope for much in life, except your love and good health. But I do like a scrap especially when there's a good purse to be had.'

Nesta sat bolt upright in the bed, and lifted her chin defiantly, looking straight ahead. It was time to play her trump card, yet she hated doing it.

'If you insist on contending, Jim, I can't stop you, but I tell you this, if you do go to Cardiff, you'll never again be welcome in my bed.'

'What?'

She gave him a challenging glance. 'I mean it, Jim. If you do this, then it's over between us. I'll take my children and go and live at the vicarage again. Mr Ellis would be delighted to have me back.'

'Like hell you will! You'll take my son nowhere,' he thundered, rising to his feet. 'Damnation, woman! What's got into you? You've never opposed me in such a way before.'

'You've never steered us towards danger before,' Nesta shouted back. 'My children's welfare, their lives, their future were never at risk before.'

'Danger?' He looked puzzled and was about to say more, but Nesta forestalled him.

'And another thing,' she said fiercely. 'Prize-fighting is not respectable, quite the opposite in fact, and with good reason. It taints all who associate themselves with it. People will look down on us, and on our children.' She tossed her head. 'I won't have it, Jim.'

'You're being unreasonable!' He stared at her for a long moment. 'And you don't mean it about bed,' he went on, his tone tender.

She remained silent but stared back at him, holding his glance defiantly and fearlessly, her expression impassive.

After another moment he rose and turning, snatched a small ornament from the mantelpiece, to throw it against one wall, where it broke into many pieces to fall on the floorboards.

'Oh! Hell's Flames and the Devil's Damnation!' he exploded. 'Was ever a man so sorely tried?'

22

Geraint Probert of Ystrad Farm had a good send-off. It must be the biggest funeral ever seen in Cwmrhyddin Cross, Nesta speculated.

Holding Little Jim in her arms, she stood among other villagers on the grassy verge in Church Lane, the dirt track leading to St Mark's on the Hill, watching the cortège go slowly past; the coffin borne in a black draped carriage with two high-stepping black horses. Trust Dorah to make a spectacle, Nesta thought. More money than sense, that one.

The carriage was followed by a long procession of mourners walking sombrely behind, many prosperous looking, wearing top-hats, but there were others, too, local tradesmen and labourers, her Jim being among them.

Nesta spotted Ethel Thomas on the verge, standing apart from a group nearby. Here was someone who could use an extra shilling, Nesta thought with pity. Ethel was two years younger, still a spinster, yet seemed to have aged more quickly. She was thin beneath her red plaid Welsh wool shawl, which, Nesta noted, had one too many darns in it.

Nesta felt guilty. She should have told Meurig years ago the secret his brother had revealed to her. She had meant to, time and time again, but the opportunity had never presented itself. Now, seeing Ethel looking so wan, alone and in need, she knew she must.

'He must've been a very important man,' Bronwen remarked as they watched the last of the cortège disappear up the hill towards the church. 'I've never seen so many mourners.'

Nesta had to smile. Bronwen was very self-possessed at eight years old, and showed cleverness beyond her social status. High breeding will out, Nesta thought guiltily. 'Well, he had plenty of money,' she replied. 'But that may not be the same thing.'

'Not as important as my da,' Ceridwen piped up, pride in her voice. 'I bet old Mr Probert couldn't lift a tree trunk off the ground like Da can.'

'Mr Probert wasn't old,' Nesta said thoughtfully. Forty-five was no age at all really.

'But he died,' Ceridwen insisted. 'So he must have been. Only old people die.'

'Come on,' Nesta went on, turning away. 'Let's go and see Granddad and Grandma.'

The children dutifully kiss their grandparents, and Meg, obviously feeling benevolent today, provided each with a glass of milk and a fresh Welsh cake.

'Your Aunt Sarah was here earlier,' Meg said to Nesta. 'Showing me the new fine black woollen coat Dorah bought for her.' She clicked her tongue. 'Very gratifying it must be to receive gifts from your generous daughter.'

'A well-off daughter,' Nesta reminded her quickly. 'The money Dorah must've spent on the funeral is nobody's business. She was always a showy piece.'

Meg raised her eyebrows. 'Well, you're not wrong there. And the more you have the more you get, so it seems. Sarah tells me Dorah is selling Ystrad Farm.'

'Oh!' Nesta was startled. She had not considered this as a possibility. 'Who will she sell to and what will happen to Jim's job? Will the new owner keep him on?'

Meg shrugged. 'Who can tell? I hope you've been saving your pennies, Nesta. There may be even leaner times ahead.'

Nesta bit at her thumb nail. This was an added worry to plague her and disturb her sleep.

Nesta hurried the children back to their cottage to await Jim's return from the funeral. She needed to discuss the possible sale of Ystrad Farm with him, find out what he knew and what it might mean for them. It galled her to realise that her own cousin had the power to send them all into penury, and Dorah would do it without a second's thought, just as long as it suited her.

As they passed through the cross roads she saw Meurig Caradog on foot, dressed in mourning clothes, hurrying homeward. He stopped and raised his top hat.

'Good morning, Nesta. These March winds are treacherous, aren't they? Mary and our boys are remaining indoors. It's Thomas's second birthday tomorrow. I don't want him catching a chill.'

Nesta clutched Little Jim closer, feeling that Meurig was somehow implying that she was neglectful of her children. She thought of Ethel Thomas and her much darned shawl. There was neglect for you!

'Meurig, could you spare me a few moments of your time?' she asked. 'There's something I feel you should know; something Algwyn told me about your family.'

He looked perplexed. 'Something about Mary?'

'No, no. It's about your father,' Nesta went on hurriedly. 'Will you come to our cottage for a moment out of this sharp breeze?'

Meurig accompanied her, looking mystified.

'Did you see my Jim at the funeral?' she asked as she open the cottage door.

'I believe he went along with other mourners to the farm for the funeral spread.'

'But you declined.'

She put Little Jim down on his feet and then pulled the hood of her cloak from her head, slipping the heavy garment from her shoulders, thankful for the worth of the fire in the range grate.

Meurig smiled. 'I'm not one for the drink, and I prefer the company of my wife and children.'

'Would you like some tea,' Nesta asked as the children, free of their outer garments, scampered away to their own amusements.

Meurig took out his pocket watch. 'Thank you but I can't stay long, Nesta.'

'Please sit though,' she invited. She was nervous now wondering how to broach the subject.

'I should've mentioned it a long time ago,' she began when he was seated. 'It's a delicate subject and I didn't know how to begin.' She swallowed. 'Some years ago, well it was seven years ago, Algwyn told me something, a secret concerning your father.' She paused, looking at him keenly. 'Perhaps you know already?'

Meurig smiled uncertainly and shook his head. 'I've no idea what you're talking about, Nesta.'

She swallowed hard again and wetted her lips. 'It concerns the dressmaker, Ethel Thomas and her mother.' She stopped again searching his face, but his puzzled expression convinced her he knew nothing.

'Algwyn told me that Ethel Thomas is the natural child of your father.'

'What?' He stared at her in astonishment and there was a touch of anger too in his eyes. 'Algwyn told you this?' he asked. 'Why would my brother reveal something so private and personal about my family to you, Nesta, someone no more to him than a mere acquaintance?'

Nesta did not like the dismissive tone in his voice as though he thought she was lying. 'I don't know,' she said evasively.

But she did know. Algwyn liked to taunt her with his power, believing she could never repeat anything he said without revealing her own shame.

'He made a joke of it,' she blurted. 'It amused him to lead poor Ethel on, making her love him when all the time he knew she was his half sister, and there was no hope for her. It . . . it's despicable!'

His face whitened. 'Nesta, why are you telling me this now? What do you hope to gain by it?'

'I?' Nesta bridled, lifting a hand to her breast. 'I gain nothing nor wish to. Ethel Thomas is having a thin time making ends meet, especially since her mother died. She's your half-sister, Meurig. Her mother was betrayed by your father like . . . ' She stopped abruptly realising she had almost said too much, almost giving herself away.

'Like Mary was betrayed, you mean?' he asked angrily. 'I believe I have made it up to her.'

Nesta shook her head. 'No I don't mean Mary. She has nothing to do with it. This is about your half-sister, Ethel Thomas. I thought you might find it in your heart to help her . . . financially.'

She wondered briefly why she was interfering. The memory of Algwyn's abominable treatment of her all those years ago still burned like hot coals in her heart, and her mind was never free of the shame of it. But she had no quarrel with Meurig, the husband of her best friend. It was pity for Ethel, also a victim of Algwyn's vileness that had made her speak out, and Meurig had a right to know.

Meurig seemed not to think so, for his features stiffened. 'You have brought this matter to my attention, Nesta, but you needn't concern yourself further. I ask you not to speak of it again, to anyone.'

'I wouldn't dream of it!' Seeing the distant expression on his face she was uncertain. 'I hope I've done right.'

'I must leave,' he said curtly. 'My family await my return.'

Big Jim was late returning. Although he rarely if ever partook these days, being always careful of his physical prowess as a fighter, Nesta could smell the drink on him now, but he was far from drunk.

She hardly gave him a minute to take off his hat, muffler and coat before broaching the subject of Ystrad Farm.

'Has Dorah Probert said anything to the farmhands about her intention to sell up?' she blurted. It irked her to think he was keeping important matters from her.

He sat on the chair before the range and took off his boots. 'Not directly,' he said, too easily. 'Although there's plenty of talk.'

'Talk?' Nesta spluttered. 'Why haven't you told me?'

He shrugged. 'What's there to say, Nesta? It doesn't affect us. I can work for another master as well as I worked for Geraint Probert.'

She was angry. 'You take your children's livelihood very lightly, Jim Jenkins,' he said. 'Have we no more to look forward to than the workhouse if you lose your employment?'

'You exaggerate, woman!' he retorted. 'You make too much of it.'

'Too much!' Nesta was furious at his equanimity. 'Dorah could sell to anyone, an outsider, a master who already has his own labourers. It's happened before.'

'It'll not happen now,' Big Jim insisted, not without some irritation. 'The new owner of Ystrad Farm isn't an outsider, and he's certainly not a farmer. He'll need experienced men; he'll need me.'

Nesta stared at him, her mouth open. 'You know who it is, then?'

'It's Meurig Caradog,' he answered. 'Apparently, so rumour

has it at the wake today, the sale was signed and sealed yesterday.'

'Meurig?' Nesta could hardly believe it. 'And before the funeral!'

She turned to gaze out of the window. Meurig had been in her house only a few hours ago and had said nothing. But then, why should he? She was no more than a poor farm labourer's wife.

'But he knows nothing of the land.' She was surprised at this turn of events.

'It's an investment, apparently. It's said he looks for a tenant for the farm, but wants a year's rent in advance.'

Nesta whirled to face her husband. 'Jim, this is our opportunity!' she exclaimed excitedly. 'You must apply to Meurig for the tenancy. Go now. He is at home, I know it.'

Big Jim shook his head. 'Would you make a fool of me, woman?' he asked sharply. 'Where would I get a year's rent?'

Nesta thought of her nest-egg. She had been saving diligently over the years since she as first married. Surely there would be enough to secure the tenancy for Jim?

'How much is the rent?'

'I don't know! Beyond our means, I've no doubt.' He paused. 'But Ben Talbot says he has the money to hand and intends to apply.' He shrugged again. 'I reckon he'll get it, too. He's been at Ystrad Farm longer than me.'

'Only a year!' Nesta cried. 'And you're the better man.'

'And only money counts,' he said bitterly. 'If I hadn't bought this cottage . . .'

'You regret it?'

He stood up and held her forearms gently, drawing her closer to him. 'I regret nothing, Nesta,' he said softly. 'I have you and three bonny children. What more can any man want?'

'A great deal,' Nesta retorted. 'Meurig is certainly out to get all he can. A landowner now he is. I didn't realise how shrewd he'd become. Ystrad Farm is a good solid investment, judging by the way my cousin Dorah spends money.'

'Well, we needn't fear,' Big Jim said with confidence. 'Ben has promised me that my job is safe when he takes over.'

Nest said nothing further. It was not yet time to tell Jim about the money she had put by. She was determined to see Meurig at the earlier opportunity and bid for the tenancy. After all, she was Mary's best friend. Nesta had stuck by the girl when all else was against her. That friendship must count for something.

Nesta rose at four thirty the next morning, the same time as Jim, and after seeing to the children and packing Bronwen off on the long walk to the Bethal Chapel school at Cadle Mill, Nesta, with Ceridwen and Little Jim, set off for Meurig's house on Ravenhill road.

She took the precaution of going to the back door, not to presume on friendship. It was answered by Sheila Rafferty, already up and about in the kitchen. Sheila looked astonished to see her.

'You're an early caller, Nesta,' she remarked. 'Mary isn't up yet and can't receive callers.'

Nesta's glance at her was scornful. 'Mary never failed to be up at five when she worked at the vicarage.'

Sheila's face stiffened. 'Yes, well, that was a long time ago. Mary is a lady of leisure now. Meurig won't have it any other way.'

Nesta set Little Jim down and removed her gloves. 'It's not Mary I've come to see,' she said shortly. 'I've called early to catch Meurig before he leaves for business.'

'He's in the dining room finishing off his breakfast,' Sheila said doubtfully. 'I'll need to ask whether he has time to see you.' She paused regarding Nesta with curiosity in her eyes. 'What's it about?'

'It's private,' Nesta said pointedly. 'I won't keep him long.'

After a few minutes Nesta was called to Meurig's study. Leaving the children in Sheila's care, Nesta stepped through the door to see Meurig standing before the mantelpiece.

'Good morning, Nesta.' She thought his greeting was not as warm as usual, and suddenly she regretted telling him about Ethel Thomas. 'What can I do for you at this early hour?' he went on coolly.

Nesta lifted her head high and wetted her lips. 'It's about Ystrad Farm,' she began. 'And the tenancy.'

He looked surprised. 'Word spreads like wildfire in this village.' He looked keenly at her. 'What about the farm?' His tone suggested it was none of her business.

'I'd be pleased, that's to say, Jim would be pleased if you'd consider him as your tenant.'

'I see.'

'I know what you're thinking, Meurig,' she rushed on. 'But Jim has saved enough for the year's rent. How much is it?'

He seemed reluctant to answer. 'Why didn't Jim come himself?'

'Jim's a good reliable worker,' Nesta answered evasively. 'Geraint Probert's most reliable man and he has a good relationship with the other men. He'd make a good fair master. Your investment would be safe in his hands.'

'I should talk to Jim about it.'

Nesta put her hand to her throat nervously. 'He doesn't know I'm here,' she said. 'Look, I have the money.'

She rummaged in her reticule and took out the little leather pouch which contained their future and held it out to him. He made no move to take it from her.

'There are almost twelve pounds here,' Nesta said eagerly. 'I've been saving for the last six years. I knew an opportunity would come for Jim some day.'

He said nothing but moved to his desk before the window. 'It's not enough, Nesta.'

'What?'

'The rent I'm asking is twenty-five pounds per annum.'

Nesta's jaw dropped. 'But that's a fortune! No mere labourer has that much money.'

'Ben Talbot does, as least his father has it,' Meurig said stiffly. 'I've more or less promised the tenancy to him.'

'But Meurig, we've known each other for years, since we were children. Your wife is my best friend. Doesn't that count for something?'

'Friendship and business don't mix,' he said. 'I've not built up my thriving bakery by being sentimental.'

Nest stared at him. 'You sound like Algwyn,' she said pithily. 'And I thought you were different from him or your father.'

His expression became strained. 'I don't take kindly to insults about my family, Nesta.'

Nesta nodded her head, suddenly understanding his attitude. 'Oh, I see! I had the temerity to tell you of your father's indiscretion, and asked for aid for his natural daughter, Ethel Thomas. Now Jim is to be punished for my interference.'

Meurig looked angry. 'It may interest you to know that yesterday evening I went to see Miss Thomas,' he said heavily. 'To offer my protection and help, as her half-brother.'

'That was good of you . . .' she began.

He held up a hand to silence her and stepped away from the desk and came towards her, his face thunderous.

'Let me tell you, Nesta,' he went on tensely. 'She was mortified that I should speak of it, and bitterly and vehemently denied it all. She ordered me out of her home. I was made to look a complete fool.'

Nesta put a trembling hand to her mouth. 'I only did what I thought best.'

'As you're doing this morning, no doubt, although by your own admission your husband knows nothing of your visit here. Are you prepared to humiliate him too?'

Nesta glared at him, her own anger rising. 'I never took you for a man given to pettiness,' she blurted. 'Because of your anger with me you deny Jim his chance.'

'It has nothing to do with you,' he said. 'Jim Jenkins is a good worker as far as it goes, but he has a long reputation for wildness and irresponsibility. His talk is always of the prize-ring and wagering. I need a good steady man as tenant, and Ben Talbot fits that bill exactly.'

'But that's unfair!' Nesta blurted. 'Jim hasn't been involved in the sport for years.'

'That's all I have to say on the matter, Nesta. Now, good day to you.'

23

DECEMBER 1847

The vicarage was filled with people, clergymen from the surrounding towns and villages, even the Bishop himself, rubbing shoulders with local men of standing and a number of important dignitaries from the nearby town of Swansea. All had come to pay their respects and mourn the passing of the well-loved Reverend Ellis.

It riled Nesta to see one of Jim's cronies Bleddyn Williams among the throng in his Sunday best. He had recently obtained the licence at the Marquis Arms, and as landlord of the biggest public house in the area, had assumed status of important personage. He was grinning and looking very smug, pleased to be included in such an influential gathering. Nesta simmered. Everyone was getting on in life except Jim.

Nesta and Dilys had been working since the early hours preparing the funeral supper, and now she was worn out, not only from the work and responsibility but also from worry about her position. It was rumoured that a new vicar was about to take possession of the vicarage, but so far no one had spoken officially to her, and she was unsure of her future.

Men stood around talking in all the downstairs reception rooms, drinking Mr Ellis's fine port and sherry, and partaking of the repast Nesta had provided. She was moving discreetly among them gathering glasses and plates when a young churchman touched her arm.

'Mrs Jenkins, I believe?'

Nesta curtsied. 'Yes, sir.'

'I'm Reverend Isaiah Pugh, the new incumbent at St Mark's on the Hill,' he said. 'Have you been told of my arrival?'

Nesta swallowed and shook her head. 'No, sir.'

He was young, perhaps younger than her, Nesta judged; very tall and narrow of shoulder, with a long tapered head that appeared too heavy for his neck, for it lolled forward slightly, as though he expected always to stoop. The most prominent feature of his clean-shaven face was a large hooked nose. His mouth was small, but his blue eyes were kind.

'I'm sorry to take you by surprise then,' he said pleasantly. 'And let me congratulate you on the spread you've provided today.'

'Thank you, sir,' Nest said. 'Mr Ellis left good provision for it. He was very much respected and loved by his parishioners.'

'I don't doubt it,' Isaiah Pugh said genially. 'At present I've a room at the Marquis Arms, but I'd like to move into the vicarage at the earliest moment.' He cleared his throat. 'Would tomorrow be too soon for you, Mrs Jenkins?'

'Why, no sir,' Nesta said taken by surprise at the haste. 'But I wonder, sir, do you have staff of your own or will you still require me to remain in the position of housekeeper?'

He raised a hand. 'Oh, please, by all means,' he said quickly. 'You must remain and serve me as you did my predecessor.'

'What of your own furniture, sir? Will we need to make room for your . . . bed for example?'

He put his hand to his mouth and looked at her under his lashes. Nesta thought she saw a twinkle there and was confused.

'Mrs Jenkins, you see before you a poor cleric,' he said frankly. 'St. Marks is my first ministry. I have little to my name, not even a bed, I regret to say. Since Mr Ellis left everything he owned to the Church, I've been given to understand I may use whatever furniture and effects that are here.'

'Yes, sir.' Nesta smiled at him. 'Mr Ellis slept in the master bedroom at the front of the house. I'll see that it's cleaned and prepared for you by tomorrow.'

'What other servants did Mr Ellis keep?'

'Apart from myself, sir, there's the maid, Dilys, who lives in. Mr Ellis was elderly and required someone here at night.'

'I see.' He wetted his lips. 'I'll require no one at night,' he said firmly. 'In fact, I doubt I'll need more than a housekeeper. Perhaps you'll explain to the maid Dilys that her services are no longer required.'

Startled, Nesta stared at him astonished and concerned. 'Beg pardon, sir, but that will be an awful shock for her.'

'Yes, I'm sorry for her plight,' Isaiah Pugh said, and there was regret in his voice. 'But the fact is I have no fortune behind me and can't afford more than one servant. You understand?'

Nesta closed her mouth. She understood him all right. If Dilys did not go then she would have to.

'I'll see to it directly, Mr Pugh, sir,' Nesta assured him. 'And I'll be in the kitchen or in the housekeeper's sitting room should you require anything further.'

'The key to Mr Ellis's fine cellar,' he said quickly. 'I believe you have it.' He held out his hand. 'I think you may leave it in my keeping from now on.'

'Yes, sir.' Nesta lifted the ring of house keys which she wore on a chain at her waist and took the cellar key from it and handed it to him.

'Good!' he said with a smile. 'And also, of course, Mr Ellis's own key to the main entrance. I shall need that.'

'That together with his keys to the desk and all else will be in his bedroom, sir, on the table next to his . . . your bed.'

He smiled an easy smile. 'Thank you, Mrs Jenkins. I believe we'll get along famously. Oh, by the way, I'm a plain man, and shall require only the plainest of food. We needn't go to extravagance.'

Nesta wetted her lips. 'Mr Ellis entertained quite often,' she ventured to remark. 'Hence the full cellar and larder.'

He pursed his lips. 'Alas, I don't have the means as I said . . . as yet.' He smiled again and held out his hand. 'Thank you, Mrs Jenkins.'

Nesta stared at his extended hand, Wondering what he intended and was nonplussed. It was unthinkable that a master, especially a cleric, a man of high position in society, should shake hands with his servants.

'Please,' he said, obviously recognising her confusion. 'Let there be respect on both sides.'

Nesta grasped his hand, her cheeks suffusing with heat. The Reverend Isaiah Pugh was a strange one indeed. The pious air that had always been present in Mr Ellis was somehow missing in Mr Pugh. But his clasp of her hand seemed strong and honest, and Nesta found herself liking him. But something told her things would never be the same again at the vicarage.

Dilys was sitting close to the range fire, her stocking-feet on the fender enjoying the warmth on this cold day.

'They're scoffing the food as though they never eat from one week to another,' she said grumpily as Nesta entered the kitchen. 'There'll be no pickings for us.'

'You can have anything that's left,' Nesta replied as she piled dirty crockery into the stone sink. She steeled herself for what must be said. Dilys was not easy to like, but just the same, it was a shame she must be dismissed.

'You're getting very generous all of a sudden,' Dilys remarked, suspicion in her voice.

Nesta carried a large iron pot from the range and emptied the heated water into a tin bowl, adding a handful of soda crystals.

'Now that Mr Ellis is gone there'll be changes,' she began. 'The new vicar is a bachelor and not a rich man.'

Dilys tossed her head. 'How do *you* know that?'

Nesta hesitating a moment before answering. 'He's among the mourners here today and has just made himself known to me.'

'What's he like?' Dilys jumped up immediately and slipping into her shoes hurried forward. 'Young? Handsome?'

Nesta inclined her head unsure how to answer. 'Mr Pugh is young, certainly,' she agreed at last. 'And pleasant enough.'

'A Mr Pugh eh?' Dilys twitched the blonde curls at her forehead. 'I wouldn't mind being a vicar's wife,' she said as she lolled against the draining board. 'Almost gentry, that is.' She giggled. 'And me sleeping here as well. I'll have him trussed up like a goose in no time.'

'You won't be sleeping here any longer,' Nesta said quickly. She turned to the girl giving her a frank look. 'In fact Mr Pugh says he's unable to keep a maid at all. I'm sorry, Dilys, but he's instructed me to let you go.'

Dilys straightened. 'What?'

'I'm sorry.'

Dilys's face tightened with anger. 'You're not a bit sorry, and I don't believe the new vicar said anything of the sort. You've been looking for an excuse to get rid of me for years. Jealousy, that's what it is.'

'That's not true,' Nesta insisted. 'Look here, Dilys, we've not got on, I agree, but I'm sorry you're losing your position here.'

'Liar!' Dilys stamped her foot. 'I won't have it!' she stormed. 'I'm going to see Mr Pugh this minute.'

She rushed towards the door leading to the front part of the house. Nesta dashed after her, catching her in the passage and grabbed at her arm.

'Don't be a silly fool, Dilys. You don't even know what Mr

Pugh looks like. You'll shame yourself and him and that'll spoil your chances of getting another position.'

'This is your doing,' Dilys shouted, pulling her arm from Nesta's grasp.

'No it isn't!'

'It is! You're jealous of me.' Dilys glared at her in rage for a moment. 'I want what money is coming to me immediately,' she went on before turning back towards the kitchen. 'Oh! Hell's Flames! Now I'll have to go back and live with my mother.'

Nesta followed her into the kitchen. She would not apologise again. It was not her doing after all.

'I'll ask Mr Pugh for your money tomorrow when he moves in,' she said evenly. There was no point in quarrelling with the girl. It was understandable that she was upset. 'I'm sure you can remain here tonight.'

'No fear!' Dilys tore off her apron. 'I'll not give you or him another minute of my time,' she shouted. 'I'm packing my bag now. I'm off!'

'The dirty crockery . . .' Nesta exclaimed.

'Do it yourself,' Dilys snapped giving her a sneering smile. 'I don't skivvy by here any more.' She marched to the foot of the servants' stair case in the corner of the room and then turned and stared balefully at Nesta. 'I'll not forget this dirty trick, Nesta Jenkins. And I'll see that everyone else knows about it, too.'

At the end of the month Nesta was surprised when Isaiah Pugh informed her that he would not need her to cook dinner on Christmas Day or Boxing Day as she had always done for Mr Ellis.

'I've been invited to spend Christmas with Mr Baxter and his family,' he explained. 'Very civil of him, very kind.'

'Yes, sir,' Nesta agreed, and smiled as she turned to leave the study. Kind indeed! Mr Baxter had two unmarried daughters and the new vicar was already causing a stir in the village as an eligible bachelor.

As usual Meg Lewis knew every last detail about his background. Isaiah Pugh was the youngest son of Lord Tresedar-Pugh of Carmarthen; an excellent pedigree, indeed, but Isaiah had no hope of the title, not with five older brothers all with children of their own.

'It was either the army or the church for him,' Meg said. 'And it looks like he chose the easiest path.' She sniffed. 'Poor as a barn owl, he is, and will remain, unless he marries money. Not much of a catch, with no looks to speak of.' She sniffed again. 'Of course, some people will scramble for the family connection.'

Nesta had to agree. And now it seemed Mr Baxter was trying to snare the young vicar for one of his daughters. Nesta was pleased at the turn of events. For the first time in years she could spend all the Christmas holiday with her own family.

Nesta was not so pleased on Christmas Eve to discover she was two days short in her week's wages and no Christmas box either.

'Is there a mistake, Mr Pugh?' she asked, the coinage in her hand.

He looked up from papers on his desk, mild surprise on his long face. 'You'll remember, Mrs Jenkins that you have two days off over Christmas. Doesn't it suit you?'

Nesta smiled weakly. His tone was mild yet she felt there was some kind of a threat in his words. 'I understand, sir,' she said meekly. 'Thank you and Merry Christmas to you.'

The New Year was well in, and Nesta was slowly coming to understand the ways of her new employer. Whereas Mr Ellis had lived high off the hog, Mr Pugh insisted she purchase the cheapest cuts of meat, the smallest amount of other provisions, and doled out just enough to cover the bills. She was beginning to feel very sorry for him.

At the end of January Nesta answered the front door to a morning visitor, and was surprised to see her cousin, Dorah Probert standing there, in a splendid fur cape and hat of the best quality.

'Why, good morning, Dorah,' Nesta said pleasantly enough, although there was no love lost between them.

Dorah lifted her chin and looked down her nose. 'Mrs Probert to you, and don't you forget it. I'm never on familiar terms with mere servants.'

'What?'

Dorah pushed past and marched into the hall. 'Kindly do your duty and inform the dear vicar that I've come to call on him.'

Nesta was furious. 'Don't you get on your high horse with me, Dorah Probert. I know too much about you.'

'And I'll not bandy words with you, Nesta Jenkins.'

With a toss of her head, Dorah eased the collar of the cape onto her shoulders and away from her face to reveal more of her even features, which Nesta conceded might be termed pretty by some, but today was marred by too much rouge. She was four years older than Nesta, and soft living had made her plumber. As Meg always said, Dorah looks the perfect lady until she opens her mouth.

'Now,' Dorah went on icily. 'Must I announce myself and tell Isaiah you're lacking in your duties, or will you do what you're paid for.'

'Geraint's money has gone to your silly head,' Nesta snapped. 'Poor man! I wonder if he knew about you and Algwyn Caradog.'

Dorah's gaze snapped with open hostility, although she was silent for a moment, her mouth puckering in a prune shape.

'It seems you may've known Algwyn better than I,' she said at last. 'How's your daughter Ceridwen these days?'

Nesta gasped, taking a step back, then realised, too late, that Dorah was shooting in the dark and could not possibly know the truth.

'You're talking rubbish,' she said quickly trying to cover her mistake.

She felt nervous suddenly. What did Dorah know? Algwyn had never known of the existence of his child, but he knew about Bronwen's origins. Had he betrayed her after all?

Dorah laughed, a high discordant sound that jangled on Nesta's nerve ends. 'I thought as much. Algwyn told me all about his sport with you.'

Nesta felt her mouth go dry with fear. Had Algwyn told Dorah everything? Even about Bronwen? With bated breath she waited for her cousin to reveal her knowledge, but Dorah laughed again.

'You were never very clever with men, Nesta,' she said disparagingly. 'You let him walk all over you and he finally got you with child, didn't he?'

'Ceridwen is Jim's child.'

'I don't think so,' Dorah smirked. 'Jim was just handy to take the blame. Mind you, I wasn't the least surprised you had to settle for a mere labourer to save face.'

'How dare you?'

'You listen to me, Nesta Jenkins,' Dorah hissed. 'I understand men better than you. I'm setting my cap at Isaiah Pugh, and I'll get him, mark my words. I warn you, Nesta, don't get in my way.'

'Geraint hasn't been dead two years yet,' Nesta said derisively.

'I've been a widow too long already,' Dorah exclaimed. 'I need a husband, and Isaiah is ideal.'

'Your haste for a new bed-mate is disgusting,' Nesta sneered. 'Besides, he has no money.'

'*I* have the money,' Dorah retorted. 'While Isaiah has the connections to the aristocracy. The son of a peer of the realm no less! Ah! It'll be a very fine match.'

'I think Mr Pugh has more sense,' Nesta said nastily. 'As young as he is he'll spot tarnished goods quick enough.'

Dorah's mouth was tight with anger. 'The day I walk into this house as Isaiah's bride,' she said at last, 'that's the day you lose your position here as housekeeper. You'll not get another post as cosy as this one has been all these years. You'll be scratching in the dirt to find an extra farthing to put a potato in the pot.'

'Empty threats,' Nesta retorted, but suddenly she was fearful.

'You know nothing,' Dorah said, her lip curling in disdain. 'I'll have Isaiah eating out of my hand before the year is out. He'll worship all right; he'll worship the ground I walk on, or my name isn't Dorah Probert.'

Nesta was silent.

'Now!' Dorah went on, obviously gloating at her cousin's discomfort. 'Announce me, and then be about your business while you still can.'

24

Nesta felt she could not move about the kitchen at the vicarage without tripping over one of the new maids Dorah had engaged to help with the wedding reception. Not that any were to serve at table, of course. Dorah felt that a sit down meal was far too outmoded, so everything was to be informal. Trust her to be different!

Nesta was exasperated at the extra work when Dorah insisted that all the partition doors of the lower floor sitting-rooms be folded back so that guests could move about at will, partaking of the large variety of foods laid out on numerous tables. There was wine, whisky, sherry, port, but most of all there was champagne.

It was the most extravagant spread Nesta had ever seen. It was unbelievable. Not even Sir Tecwyn had entertained to such lavish scale.

Walking through the rooms to make sure everything was in order, Nesta could only wonder at the cost of it all. Dorah must have spent a fortune already.

Isaiah Pugh had already left for St Marks on the Hill to await his bride and his fate, and since preparations seemed to be complete, Nesta went back to the kitchen to make a pot of tea.

The three new maids, not local girls, were clustered together at the far end of the kitchen laughing and talking loudly. Ignoring their giggles, Nesta pushed the heavy iron kettle over the fire. No sooner had she done so than the latch of the back door opened and she was surprised to see her mother step in furtively.

'Mother? What are you doing here?' Meg rarely if ever visited her at the vicarage. 'Is Father ill?'

'No, no. Curiosity, it is, like,' Meg said frankly, puffing a little. 'Been up the church, I have, to watch the blushing bride arrive and what a palaver!'

'Why? What happened?'

With a smirk Meg came forward and put her parasol on the table. Nesta could see her mother was bursting with news. 'Dorah rolled up in an open carriage festooned with white ribbons, drawn by two white horses.' Meg nodded at Nesta's astonished look. 'I tell you!' she went on. 'I thought the circus had come to town.'

'Poor Mr Pugh!' Nesta shook her head sadly. 'He doesn't know what he's taken on; a flighty wife and her two spoiled brats. Berwyn Probert's just fourteen but he's an arrogant little coxcomb already.'

'And that young Cassie is a pert madam,' Meg said. 'She was in the bakery last week fingering the sticky buns as though she owned the place. I'd have her across my knee if she were mine.' Meg looked at the kettle beginning to steam. 'Any chance of a cup of tea?'

'I expect so,' Nesta said, longing to hear more. 'Sit down.'

Meg glanced across at the twittering girls. 'Who're they?'

'Dorah took them on to help out at the reception,' Nesta said impatiently. 'A lot of good they are too.' She laid out two cups and saucers. 'Were there many people at the church?'

Meg lifted her hands. 'Scores! And mostly toffs by the looks of their carriages. Dorah must've invited half the county.'

Isaiah Pugh's lineage had gone to her cousin's head, Nesta thought scornfully as she poured out the tea.

'Dorah's selling her house in Ravenhill so your aunt Sarah

tells me,' Meg went on. 'More money to throw around. She'll turn the vicarage upside down, see if she doesn't.'

'This is church property, so she can't do much,' Nesta said, but felt a little quiver of anxiety. She hadn't forgotten her cousin's threat eighteen months ago to throw her out of her position as housekeeper, but she hoped Dorah had forgotten. Now that she had married Isaiah Pugh Dorah might be more charitable.

'What's her dress like?' she went on to take her mind off the worry.

'Tsk!' Meg sniffed. 'Ecru lace and white satin, mind; all frills and flounces, with a bustle an elephant could sit on,' she said disparagingly. 'Slighted Ethel Thomas, she has, see, by having her wedding gown made by some courtier in Cardiff. Ethel is very upset.'

'Couturier, Mother,' Nesta corrected absently, her mind still concerned with losing her job. What on earth would she do if Dorah carried out the threat? She was determined not to demean herself by taking another position less than house-keeper.

'That's what I said!' Meg sniffed. 'Oh, riding for a fall our Dorah is, mark my words. Too big for her pigskin pumps.'

Nesta said nothing. Dorah wasn't the type to come to grief. Quite the reverse. Her cousin would walk on the bones of others to satisfy her vanity and greed.

Distracted, she glanced at the clock on the wall. The cere-mony would be coming to an end about now and the guests would start to arrive soon. Nesta didn't want Meg under her feet then.

'You'd better go now, Mother,' she said firmly. 'We'll be run off our feet in a minute.'

Meg looked annoyed but picked up her parasol. 'There're bound to be leftovers,' she said sourly. 'You won't forget your poor parents, will you?'

When her mother had gone Nesta glanced across at the three maids.

'You should look lively, you girls,' she said in a commanding tone. 'Guests will be arriving.'

None of them moved but stared at her sullenly.

'Didn't you hear me?'

The tallest of the three looked down her nose at Nesta. 'We don't take orders from you,' she said nastily.

Nesta's jaw dropped open. 'I beg you pardon!'

'We don't do nothing until Mrs Parks gets here.'

'Who?'

At that moment the door latch rattled again and a tall, big-boned woman stepped into the kitchen. She was in her mid-fifties, Nesta judged, and dressed from head to foot in black bombazine, as though in mourning. Her sour expression completed the impression.

The three girls immediately jumped to attention, lining up in a row pulling their aprons and caps straight. The woman's critical gaze surveyed the maids and then lighted on Nesta.

'Why are you all standing around idle?' she demanded in a harsh tone. 'I won't stand for it when there's work to do.'

'Who're you?' Nesta asked.

'I'm Mrs Parks, madam's housekeeper. And who might you be?'

'Mrs Jenkins, I am,' Nesta said firmly. 'Mr Pugh's house-keeper.'

Mrs Parks sniffed. 'Not any more. I take precedence.'

'Now look here!' Nesta began, but Mrs Parks ignored her. She put her black reticule on the table, removed her gloves and directed a stern gaze at the girls.

'Now then, let me see your hands,' Mrs Parks said and stalked forward to inspect them. 'Passable, passable. Cleanliness is next to godliness, and young girls today certainly need some of that, the loose way they carry on.'

'Yes, Mrs Parks,' they chorused.

'Excuse me!' Nesta said with irritation. 'This is *my* kitchen, and you've no right to waltz in here give orders to my staff. Besides which, all the hard work has been done. Everything is ready.'

'I'll decide that,' Mrs Parks said imperiously. 'Madam relies on me entirely and I have high standards.' She gave Nesta an enveloping stare, her mouth turned down at the corners with disdain. 'And this kitchen falls far below them, I must say.'

'Oh!' Nesta was affronted. 'You can't come in here and take over, just that that,' she shouted. 'I'm employed by Mr Pugh, and I'm going to speak to him about it this minute.'

Mrs Parks looked disdainful. 'Wasting your time, you are,' she said in a dry tone. 'Madam is mistress of this house now, and I rule the kitchen.'

'This is disgraceful,' Nesta retorted at the top of her voice.

She turned to leave intending to find Isaiah Pugh, but the green baize door leading to the front of the house was flung open and the new Mrs Pugh sailed in. Dorah had changed from her bridal wear and now wore a magnificent afternoon gown of blue velvet. Her yellow hair, piled on her head in the manner of a lady of fashion was decorated with interwoven blue velvet ribbons.

Dorah was all of thirty-five, and Nesta could not help smirking to see her cousin got up like a girl half her age.

'What's all this shouting about?' Dorah demanded to know, glaring at Nesta. 'You sound like a lot of fishwives.'

'Dorah, tell this woman to leave my kitchen immediately,' Nesta demanded angrily, indicating Mrs Parks. 'She seems to think she has some authority here.'

Dorah's eyes flashed as she stared at Nesta. 'I've warned you before not to be familiar when you address me,' she said airily. 'I'm Mrs Pugh to you. And as for Mrs Parks, she has replaced you in this household.'

'But you can't do that,' Nesta cried. 'Mr Pugh is my employer.'

Dorah smiled thinly. 'My dear husband has left all household matters in my hands, as it should be. Mrs Parks is now housekeeper at the vicarage as of this hour.' She gazed at Nesta, a supercilious expression on her face. 'Of course, Nesta, I wouldn't want you to starve, so you may take the position of scrub woman, doing the rough work, at a lower wage, of course.'

'Rough work?' Nesta was flabbergasted for a moment and then opened her mouth wide to give her cousin a piece of her mind, but she was forestalled by Mrs Parks.

'Beg pardon, madam,' she said to Dorah. 'But I don't want this woman in the house. Mrs Jenkins is a born troublemaker. I know for a fact that she had Dilys Griffiths sacked out of spite. Dilys told me that herself.' She gave Nesta a withering glance. 'There's no place for the likes of her here.'

Dorah smirked. 'Well, I trust your judgement implicitly, Mrs Parks. And I insist we maintain a high tone in our servants as befits my husband's background and social position – a churchman and the son of a peer of the realm, don't you know.'

'Dorah! I'm your cousin,' Nesta exclaimed. 'Our mothers are sisters, close in their affection. How can you treat your family so shabbily?'

'Dregs of the family,' Dorah sneered. 'A candle-maker's daughter. I'm ashamed of the connection. After all, my husband is a son of a lord.'

There were titters from the three serving girls, and Nesta felt her face flame with humiliation.

'Why, you scheming Jezebel!' she shouted back at her cousin. 'You're not better than me and never were. You're no more than a jumped up milkmaid with the morals of an ally cat.'

Mrs Parks took in a hard sharp breath as though Nesta had

insulted her personally and Dorah's rouged cheeks paled slightly.

'Careful, Nesta,' she warned through gritted teeth. 'Don't utter words you'll regret. After all, no one is without *something* to be ashamed of.'

Suddenly afraid, Nesta closed her lips tightly. Dorah stared at her in triumph for a moment, and then glanced at the new housekeeper.

'Mrs Parks, I believe you have something for Mrs Jenkins.'

The woman in black took up her reticule, pulling out a small leather purse. She opened it and let some coins fall in to her palm and then handed them to Nesta.

'Here's your wages to date,' the woman said in a harsh tone. 'Take it and be thankful to Madam for her generosity.'

'You have your money, Nesta,' Dorah added imperiously. 'Now, get out!'

Nesta's cheeks burned as she left the vicarage. Dorah had not only sacked her in front of witnesses, she had humiliated her into the bargain. Mrs Parks had damned her as a trouble-maker and every word that had been said in the kitchen this day would be around the village in no time. Dorah had not only taken her livelihood she had taken her good name as well. How would she find a decent position now?

'Any luck?' Meg asked as she pushed the iron kettle over the hob as Nesta came into the small living room behind the shop, to slump onto a wooden chair, feeling fatigue throughout her whole body.

'Nothing,' she said dejectedly. 'Oh, Mother, it's so hopeless. Two months out of work and no one will take me on. I'm sure Dorah is still spreading lies about me.'

'Maybe and maybe not,' Meg said. 'It's partly your own fault.'

'What?'

Meg shook her head, an expression of irritation on her face.

'You won't settle for less, that's the trouble with you, my girl. Fancy ideas have been your downfall.'

Nesta glanced up sharply. Her mother did not know how true that was. 'I've got standards,' she said defensively. 'Why should I settle for less?'

'You will if you want to live. You should be thinking of your children, not your pride.'

'That's unfair!'

'Tell that to your husband and children when they have empty bellies. Jim's wage doesn't go far, I know that. Something must be done. You've got to come to your senses.'

Nesta sat silent, brooding, watching her mother make a pot of tea. It cut her to the quick to think that she must take menial work after having so much pride in being a housekeeper, and for the vicar, too, the personage with the highest social standing in the community.

'I was talking to Mrs Mainwaring in the ironmonger's this morning,' Meg said casually. 'She tells me old Dr Powell is looking to take someone on.'

Nesta sat forward with a jolt. 'As housekeeper?'

'Tsk! No,' Meg snapped. 'His housekeeper is looking for a woman to do rough work . . .'

'Don't say another word, Mother!' Nesta exclaimed angrily. 'I'll not demean myself.'

'You're an unnatural mother!' Meg hooted, thrusting a cup and saucer at Nesta. 'Conceited and selfish. When will you learn?'

Meg pulled up a chair and sat opposite her daughter, leaning forward. 'Now you listen to me, Nesta,' she said firmly. 'It's your Christian duty to find work, and there's work going begging with Dr Powell. Walk down to the doctor's house at Cadle Mill this minute. Ask to see his housekeeper, Mrs Pope.'

Damn Dorah and her spiteful nature! She would never forgive her cousin for this.

But her mother was right. There was little choice left. Things were tight and Jim was beginning to look at her reproachfully. She must lower herself and take this menial work for her children's sake. Hadn't she already sworn to herself that Bronwen would never suffer because of the crime Nesta had committed? She would go at once to Dr Powell's house, and beg Mrs Pope to take her on, if need be.

'It's not fair!' Ceridwen shouted on Christmas afternoon 1852. 'I should have two gifts, one for my birthday and one for Christmas. Bron and Jimmy always get birthday gifts. Why not me?'

'She's right you know,' Big Jim said reasonably to Nesta from his chair before the fire. 'It's not fair.'

'We can't afford two gifts for her at this time of year,' Nesta said, flopping into a chair opposite him, feeling tired out. She had been up at five o'clock to walk two miles through heavy snow to Dr Powell's house in Cadle Mill, working like a Trojan all morning, then had hurried back to cook the goose for their own Christmas dinner.

'Then we'll have to pick a date in the summertime for her birthday,' Big Jim insisted. He gave her a steady look. 'We mustn't treat one different from the others.'

'Jim!' Nesta was hurt. 'I'd never do such a thing.'

'I want colouring chalks and a slate,' Ceridwen piped up, quick to take advantage of her mother being in the wrong. 'To make pictures at school like the other pupils.'

'You go to school to learn your bible, not to make pictures,' Nesta said irritated. At thirteen, Ceridwen was becoming wilful and obstinate.

'My teacher, Mr Simpson says that loving the beauty of nature is the same as loving God.'

'Ooh!' Nesta was outraged. 'That's paganism, that is! I've good mind to report him to the school governors.'

'Come now, Nesta, don't be so hard on the child.' Big Jim leaned forward to pat her arm cajolingly. 'Mrs Pope has worn you out, hasn't she?'

Nesta ran her fingers across her aching forehead. 'She gets the money's worth and more,' she said tiredly. 'Now Dr Powell has taken on a partner, a young doctor from Haverfordwest, Nathaniel Bowen.'

'I'm not surprised,' Big Jim said nodding sagely. 'Dr Powell is getting very shaky.'

'Dr Bowen will be living in, making even more work for me. More laundry, more scuttles of coal to lug in, more floors to scrub.' Nesta yawned widely before going on. 'Mrs Pope is a slave driver and I don't know how much longer I can stand it.'

But stand it she would, for she had no other choice. Her children and husband must not go in need.

Nesta called in on her parents on returning from Dr Powell's on New Year's Day 1853.

'A good new year to you, Father,' Nesta greeted warmly, kissing his cheek.

'And to you, my good girl, and many more of them,' Enoch said, giving her a warm hug. 'Sit down. You're looking tired, *cariad.*'

'It's the snow,' Nesta said, taking a seat. 'It always makes me out of sorts. Where's Mother?'

'Gone to Tucker's for half a pound of best pork sausage,' he said and grinned. 'We're having a treat today. I've just been paid for a big order of fancy candles from the vicarage. It seems your cousin Dorah is giving a grand dinner party.'

'Huh!' Nesta was dismissive.

Meg Lewis came in then, her high button boots tracking in snow on the kitchen flagstones. 'I'm glad you've called in, Nesta,' she said, putting her wicker basket on the table. She pulled off her bonnet and slipped the shawl from her shoulders.

'I've got some good news for you. I've found work for Bronwen.'

'Our Bronwen work?' Nesta exclaimed and shook her head. 'I don't think so, Mother. She's barely turned fifteen; too young.'

'Nonsense!' Meg snorted. 'She's not the daughter of gentry, you know. She should've found employment after her thirteenth birthday.'

'Where is this work anyway?'

Meg hesitated, fussing with the contents of the basket.

'Mother?'

'Now don't get excited,' Meg exclaimed impatiently, turning to her, eyes sparking defiance. 'I asked your Aunt Sarah to persuaded Dorah to take Bronwen on as kitchen maid at the vicarage, and she's agreed, starting straight away. She's to live in.'

'What?' Nesta jumped to her feet. 'Over my dead body! Dorah has agreed to this just to humiliate me.'

'Be sensible, Nesta,' Meg said. 'The girl should be earning her keep. I don't know why you're so protective of her.'

'It's out of the question,' Nesta shrilled. 'I'll not have Dorah bullying Bronwen and turning her into a skivvy. The child will be miserable away from her family.'

'Bronwen's growing up fast,' Meg said. 'And a proper little firebrand, like her mother.'

'What?' Nesta felt a little quiver in the pit of her stomach.

'Your child has turned into a beautiful girl, Nesta,' Meg insisted impatiently. 'And even if you can't see it, others do. Already the village youths are clustering around her.'

Nesta was appalled. 'Then they'd better not let Jim catch them!' she warned.

'Bronwen can take care of herself. She has plenty of common sense,' Meg said sagely. 'Why, only yesterday I saw her at the crossroads when that young buck Lloyd Treharn approached her. I don't know what he said, but he had a sharp slap across his chops for his trouble.'

'Oh, Mother!' Nesta put up a hand to her mouth. 'Nothing bad must happen to Bronwen. I owe it to her . . .'

'What do you mean? How can you owe your own child anything but your love?'

Nesta shook her head, averting her gaze. 'You wouldn't understand,' she said quietly.

'No, I don't!' Meg snapped. 'You're talking poppycock. And you must let Bronwen decide for herself. It's only right.'

To Nesta's surprise and concern Bronwen was excited at the prospect of earning a living. 'Oh, Mam! When can I start?'

'Bron, it's not going to be easy, living in, at everyone's beck and call,' Nesta warned nervously. 'You know my cousin Dorah and me are . . . well, enemies. I don't want her taking advantage of you.'

'You mustn't worry about me, Mam,' Bronwen said quickly. 'I can look after myself.'

Nesta blinked and stepped back to look at the child she had stolen from its father all those years ago. For the first time she saw a lovely young woman, tall and comely, with raven black hair that fell in curls and waves over her shoulders and almost to her waist; laughing blue eyes, and skin with the translucence of alabaster.

Tenderness overtook her, and stepping closer, Nesta lifted a hand to touch the glossy black hair. 'Bron, my dear child,' she said, feeling her throat close up with emotion. 'I've sworn to protect you, and I must.'

'Mam, I love you too,' Bronwen declared, putting her arms around Nesta and hugging her close. 'But Grandma's right. It's time I earned my bread and cheese.'

Nesta swallowed down the lump that was constricting her throat, and held Bronwen away from her, looking earnestly into her face. 'God bless you, Bron. And may the angels watch over you.'

'Mam, it's only the vicarage, mind,' she said laughing. 'I'm not going to the ends of the earth.'

'You'll be spending your nights under another roof,' Nesta said earnestly. 'A young girl needs to protect herself. There are dangers . . .'

Bronwen flushed. 'If you mean Berwyn Probert, have no fear, Mam. Berwyn's aware I have a sweetheart, and Lloyd Treharn can get very jealous. Berwyn couldn't match Lloyd if it came to a fight and he knows it.'

Nesta stared at the girl aghast. 'Fight? You're talking like your father.' She realised suddenly that she had been blind these last few years. 'You have a sweetheart? Lloyd Treharn, the blacksmith's son? Bronwen, what're you saying? You haven't done anything . . . foolish with Lloyd, have you?'

Bronwen stared at her in consternation. 'Mam! How could you think such a thing of me? I've more self-respect.'

'I'm sorry, Bron, I'm sorry.' Nesta quickly apologised. 'I'm so worried for you.'

'Then don't be, Mam,' Bronwen said gently. 'The chick is leaving the nest, and not before time, either.'

Nesta clasped both her hands to her breast and shook her head. 'I don't know what your father will say when he comes home. He'll blame me.'

25

'Take your filthy hands off me,' Bronwen screeched in fury, dropping the empty coal scuttles she was holding, and whirled to face her assailant. 'Stand back, Berwyn, or I'll scratch your eyes out, you pig!'

In the outhouse where the household coal was stored Berwyn Probert stepped hastily away from her, his face reddening with fury. 'Don't you dare speak to me like that,' he snarled. 'You're no more than a kitchen drab, anyway. I'll have my mother dismiss you immediately for insolence.'

Bronwen elevated her chin and looked at him with disdain. At eighteen Dorah's cherished son, Berwyn, thought himself a gentleman with his fancy clothes and money to burn, but his narrow shoulders and slack mouth told of weakness, and Bronwen despised him.

'Have me dismissed then,' she said scornfully. 'And I'll have Lloyd Treharn beat you to a pulp.' She curled her lip at him. 'Mammy's boy!'

His face flushed scarlet. 'You bitch!' His glare raked her figure. 'I don't want Treharn's leavings, anyway,' he went on spitefully. 'Used goods, that's what you are.'

Furious, Bronwen leapt forward and struck him with her open hand across his left cheek. He howled and took a few more steps back, his hand to his reddening face.

'That's for the insult.' She glowered at him. 'Keep away from me in future,' she said angrily. 'If my father knew what you are trying to do he'd stake you out at the crossroads for the crows to peck at you.'

With a pathetic attempt at a growl he turned and marched away. Bronwen stood for a moment, panting with relief. Someone had tried to get into her room in the attic last night, and she was certain it had been Berwyn. There was no lock on her door, but she had taken the precaution of wedging the back of a wooden chair under the doorknob.

She had been very conscious of his lustful eyes on her ever since she moved into the vicarage, and knew she must be extra wary of him in future, for he'd molest her again if he could catch her unaware. It was obvious Berwyn Probert thought he had the God-given right to do as he pleased since his mother had so much money. But if he laid hands on her again, Bronwen vowed, she would mark him for life.

Retrieving the coal scuttles she filled them and lugged them back to the house. Mrs Parks glanced up as Bronwen struggled in through the back door with the heavy load.

'Heavens above!' the housekeeper exclaimed. 'Look at the state of your apron, miss!'

'I couldn't help it.'

'Don't answer back,' Mrs Parks snapped. 'I told you to wear a sacking apron for the dirty work. Are you deaf as well as stupid, girl? Go and change immediately.'

Bronwen bit down heavily on her lower lip to prevent a sharp retort. Crossing Berwyn was one thing, getting on the wrong side of Mrs Parks was another.

'I'll take the scuttles to the sitting rooms first.'

'You'll do no such thing!' Mrs Parks exclaimed. 'I'll not have you parading through the house in a dirty apron. Good heavens above, girl! Have you no sense of what's proper in a servant?'

'No, I'm only a kitchen drab,' Bronwen said under her breath.

'What's that?'

'I said I'll go and change straight away,' Bronwen said loudly, moving towards the servants' staircase in the corner of the kitchen.

Bronwen ran up the bare staircase which led up to the attic rooms. Jane, the other maid who lived in, had the room next to hers. Jane was older and stout and had no worries about attracting Berwyn's unwanted attentions.

As Bronwen approached her door she saw it was standing ajar when she knew she had closed it firmly when leaving her room that morning. There was the sound of someone moving about inside.

Bronwen clenched her teeth in fury. Berwyn was lying in wait for her. Well, she would teach him a lesson he would never forget. Jane's chamber pot was standing outside her door. Bronwen had emptied both hers and the other maid's that morning, and had left Jane's outside her door with clean water in it.

She picked it up now and crept to the door pushing it open quietly. There was flurry of movement as someone tried to scurry away, and with a cry of triumph Bronwen threw the contents of the chamber pot at the fleeing figure. There was a female scream of rage and Bronwen stopped and stared in astonishment and then anger.

'Cassie Probert! What're you doing in my room?' Bronwen stormed. 'What're you looking for?'

Dorah's daughter Cassie was the same age as Bronwen. Unlike her brother she had striking looks, with a mass of golden hair like her mother's, done up in velvet bows and ringlets, but she looked a fright now, with water dripping from her nose and chin, and her blonde hair straggly, her ribbons limp, her figured brocade morning dress clinging damply to her shoulders.

'Look what you've done,' Cassie wailed. 'I'm soaked to the skin.'

'You deserve it,' Bronwen shouted wrathfully. 'You've no right here in my room.'

'This is my mother's house,' Cassie retorted archly. 'I go where I please and do as I please.'

'This house belongs to the church,' Bronwen corrected her. 'Your step-father merely rents it, so don't get hoity-toity with me, Cassie Probert.'

With a glare of rage Cassie tried to sidestep to escape, but Bronwen barred her way out. 'You were looking for money, weren't you,' she accused the other girl. 'Have you spent your month's allowance on fripperies at Baxter's already? Won't your dear mother give you any more?'

'I hate you, Bronwen Jenkins,' Cassie spat out the words. 'Lloyd Treharn is too good for the likes of you. I'm going to steal him from you, and there's nothing you can do about it.'

Startled, Bronwen's jaw dropped open. 'What?'

Cassie tossed her head, her wet hair sticking to her face. 'Lloyd can do better than a prize-fighter's daughter. My mother says Big Jim Jenkins is the lowest of the low. Bare-knuckle fighting is against the law and he should be in prison.'

'You spiteful little cat,' Bronwen shrilled. 'You don't know what you're talking about.'

She made a dash at the other girl and grabbed handfuls of wet curls with both hands, tugging at them vigorously. 'My father is the best man in the world,' she yelled. 'Don't you say a word against him.'

'Ouch! Ouch! Let go!' Cassie squealed. 'Let go! I'll have you sacked.'

Coming to her senses Bronwen let go, and stepped back. 'You'd better not say any more bad things about my father,' she panted. 'Because I'll scrag you if you do, sack or no sack.'

Cassie's lip curled and she looked at Bronwen with deep disdain. 'You're so common and low-born, Bronwen Jenkins. No wonder Lloyd prefers me.'

'Lloyd is *my* sweetheart,' Bronwen asserted hotly. 'He won't look twice at you. You're too full of airs and graces to suit him.'

'Huh! That's all you know!' Cassie retorted. She lifted her chin arrogantly. 'Lloyd bought me a red silk ribbon at Baxter's last week. And he kissed me, too, so there!'

'You're lying!' Bronwen declared loudly. 'I don't believe a word of it.'

Suddenly there were heavy footsteps on the stairs outside, startling both of them. Both girls rushed to get through the doorway only to be confronted by a surprised Jane. She stared at Cassie's dishevelment and Bronwen's thunderous expression.

'Mrs Parks says, get a move on, Bron,' she said grinning. 'What's going on?'

'Mind your own business!' Cassie shouted furiously, and dashed down the staircase to the floor below, where a door led to the main part of the house.

Jane continued to look at Bronwen questioningly. 'What happened to her?'

'She got what she deserved,' Bronwen answered tightly. 'Cassie was searching my room.'

'The nosey little brat!' Jane said. 'Did she take anything? You ought to report her to Mrs Parks. The old girl is strict but she is fair, mind.'

Bronwen looked earnestly at the other maid. 'Jane, please say nothing of this to anyone, especially Mrs Parks. Dorah Pugh is my mother's cousin, and they don't get on. She would just love an excuse to get rid of me.'

Jane shrugged. 'Well, if you say so, Bron. I think Cassie ought to be taught a lesson in manners. But then, what can you expect from a jumped up milkmaid's daughter, eh?'

Isaiah Pugh dipped the nib in the inkpot several times then let the pen hover over the sheet of writing paper, but no suitable pious thoughts came into his mind. Damnation! He had no head for words and was thoroughly bored with the need to compose an original sermon each week. Why had he chosen the church anyway? He should have gone into the army like his brothers. At least they were free to carouse without having to keep up this awful pretence.

With another oath Isaiah threw the pen onto the blotter, and then put his elbows on the desk and rested his head in his hands in despair. Sermons were the least of his worries. His gambling debts were mounting, and one particular creditor was getting edgy. His gaze fell on the letter he had received that morning, and with a deep sigh picked up to read it once again. There was no mistaking the implicit threat it contained.

Isaiah rubbed his hand over his jaw nervously. These were dangerous men he was dealing with. How had he got in so deep of late? He must write to his father again and ask what the delay in settling these matters was.

He brought his fist down onto the desk with a crash. Hell's Flames! As Dorah's husband he had eagerly taken charge of her income as was his right by marriage, and was angry and disconcerted to realise, too late, that she had fooled him; letting him think she had more wealth than she really did. It was more than enough to live on comfortably, but a mere pittance when it came to satisfying his extreme appetite for wagering on the turn of a card, or the heady sports of prize-fighting and the turf.

Isaiah rose and strode to the mantelpiece, to gaze down into the burning coals. There was that notable prize-fight in Chester next week, not to mention an enticing race meeting at Cheltenham. He was determined to attend both, and had already fobbed Dorah off with a story about yet another summons from the Bishop as an excuse to be away from home. Dare he go, though, risking more debts with this threat hanging over him?

A sharp tap at the study door interrupted his melancholy thoughts, and then the maid Jane entered, curtsying. 'Beg pardon, sir,' she said. 'There's a gentleman called to see you.'

Isaiah had an impulse to swear at her and demand the caller

be turned away, but controlled himself. Another damned parishioner, no doubt, pleading for his help and assistance. He needed help himself!

'Who is it, Jane? I'm very busy at the moment.'

'A Mr Jebediah Crabbe, sir, come all the way from Cardiff.'

'What?' Isaiah leapt away from the fireplace as though burned. 'Who did you say?'

'A Mr Crabbe, sir.' She hesitated. 'Shall I tell him you're not at home?'

'Yes. No.' Isaiah swallowed hard, his thoughts in turmoil. 'Is he alone?'

'Yes, sir.'

Relieved to hear that, Isaiah walked shakily to his desk and sat. There was no alternative but to receive his caller, but he could not control a tremble of apprehension at having to face him.

Isaiah cleared his throat in an effort to sound normal. 'Have Mr Crabbe come in, Jane,' he said. 'I'll ring if we need refreshments.'

Jane curtsied and disappeared only to reappear a moment later in the company of a tall, well built fashionably dressed man, who strode into the room exuding power and confidence, his hat and gloves still in his hand, his cane under his arm.

'Ah! My dear Reverend Pugh. How relieved I am to find you at home, sir.'

Isaiah waited until the door had closed behind Jane. 'What the devil are you doing here, Crabbe?' he asked heavily. 'How dare you come here? I told you I'd pay up when I could.'

Jebediah Crabbe took a seat without being asked. 'I know you did,' he said evenly. 'But I'm afraid Sir Fletcher Watkins is not a patient man. I assume you received the letter from him?' He smiled. 'Sir Fletcher wants his money, Mr Pugh, and I'm here to see that he gets it.'

'I don't have it.'

'Dear me! How unfortunate.' Jebediah gazed around the room. 'You live well by the looks of your furniture and fittings.'

'All church property, as is the house,' Isaiah said hastily.

Jebediah smiled again, a smile Isaiah did not like. 'I met your wife briefly a moment ago,' Jebediah said and tilted his head, his eyes keen and watchful. 'Older than you by several years I think, and not nearly of your class, Mr Pugh. I assume therefore that you married her for money, which by law is at your disposal, so, what is your difficulty?'

'My debt to Sir Fletcher is more than I can raise at present,' Isaiah said edgily. 'I need more time. Besides, my father, Lord Treseder-Pugh is my guarantor. He'll settle my debts as in the past, and no quibble.'

'His lordship has already been approached,' Jebediah said. 'He's refused to honour the obligation.'

'What?' Isaiah was stunned.

Jebediah shrugged. 'His sentiments are that now you have a rich wife, you need no longer look to him to stand surety.'

Isaiah sat down heavily, thoroughly shaken. 'There must be some error,' he said weakly. 'I can't believe my father would desert me.'

'The error is on your part, Mr Pugh,' Jebediah said. 'You must admit you have cost your father a pretty penny in the past.'

Isaiah rallied. 'That's hardly your concern, Crabbe,' he said sharply.

'Well, Mr Pugh, the debt is my concern, and the money must be got somehow,' Jebediah said almost genially. 'If not, your obligation must be paid off some other way. Do you own land hereabouts?'

'No.'

'Pity. That might have served. This is an area of rich farmland, which might have turned a tidy profit.' Jebediah's gaze was cold as it bore down on Isaiah. 'What do you have of value?'

'All I have is the money I acquired on marriage,' Isaiah said wretchedly. He knew Crabbe's reputation and was afraid. 'And not enough of that, that I can settle this debt without my wife discovering my situation and without ruining myself in the parish. I'm a sixth son. I have nothing of my own.'

'Sir Fletcher won't like this news,' Jebediah said, shaking his head sadly. 'He's a man of uneven temper and little patience, as I said, unlike myself. I have a kindly nature and would grant you extra time willingly.'

'Couldn't you use your influence, Mr Crabbe?' Isaiah looked at his dangerous companion hopefully.

Jebediah shook his head again. 'Alas, I'm a mere underling, Mr Pugh, and have no sway with Sir Fletcher.'

'What . . . what will happen now?' Isaiah held his breath dreading the answer.

'We must put our heads together over the next few days, Mr Pugh,' Jebediah said pleasantly. 'And find a solution to your predicament. I strongly wish no harm to come to you or your family.'

Isaiah's heart sank further. 'You don't return to Cardiff today, then?'

'Hardly, Mr Pugh,' Jebediah said. 'This heavy snow has made the journey from Cardiff very arduous. I've been on the road three days. I'm a man of robust physique yet, as you can see, I'm worn out.'

'Do you stay at the Marquis Arms tonight?' Isaiah asked in a low tone, all hope of being rid of his unwelcome visitor gone.

'I'm sure you can provide bed and board at the vicarage, Mr Pugh,' Jebediah said. 'I've a fancy to see the village of Cwmrhyddin Cross and environs, and you must escort me. Who knows, we might strike upon an answer to your problem.'

Isaiah smiled weakly, willing his hands not to shake as they rested on the desk. 'I'll be delighted,' he said without enthusiasm.

How could he explain this man's presence to Dorah? For all

his outward appearance, it would be evident even to his empty-headed wife that Jebediah Crabbe was no gentleman.

Jebediah stood. 'Perhaps you'll arrange for me see my room now and my bags taken up. I wish to rest before enjoying the hospitality of you and your good wife at a hearty family dinner.'

Isaiah rose and walked on stiffened legs to the bell-pull to summon the maid. 'Of course, Mr Crabbe. You must make yourself comfortable during your stay.'

Berwyn Probert entered the study abruptly without knocking to stand before the desk with an arrogant slouch to his shoulders. Isaiah took one look at his stepson's rebellious face and sighed heavily.

'Sit down, Berwyn. I need to talk to you,' Isaiah said quietly, putting down his pen.

'What do you want?' Berwyn asked rudely. 'I don't appreciate being summoned like this. If my mother knew, she wouldn't like it.'

'Do sit down.'

'I'd rather stand.'

'Very well.' Isaiah rested his elbows on the desk and gave the young man a studied look. 'I hear from Mrs Parks that you're abusing your position as the young master of the household; forcing your attentions on Bronwen Jenkins, one of the kitchen maids.'

Berwyn looked furious. 'Has the common little bitch complained?'

Isaiah chose to ignore the crude remark. It was his own fault for marrying beneath him, he reflected. It was one more punishment for his sins.

'The girl has said nothing,' Isaiah said. 'But Mrs Parks is no fool, and she's concerned. I'm sure your mother wouldn't approve of your low behaviour.'

'I do as I please,' Berwyn shouted. 'I'm of age after all.'

'I can persuade your mother to cut your allowance.' Isaiah rearranged several objects on the desk. He was on thin ground here, for Dorah believed the sun shone from her son's eyes. 'I think you'd find that inconvenient.'

Berwyn stared at him silently for a moment and then to Isaiah's surprise, laughed. He turned to a chair nearby and sat, languidly throwing his legs over one of the polished wood arms.

'Isaiah, you can't pull the wool over my eyes as you do with Mother,' Berwyn said haughtily. 'I know what's going on. I know how deep you are in.'

'I'd prefer you called me Papa.' Isaiah said, trying to gain time to think. He felt a deepening unease at the triumphant gleam in the boy's eyes.

'Damned if I will,' Berwyn rasped. 'You're not my father. I've been watching you. I've also been keeping check on the household accounts.'

'You can't have,' Isaiah retorted quickly. 'They're under lock and key.'

'Oh! I have a key,' Berwyn told him. 'I suggested it to Mother just after you were married. I've never trusted you, you see.'

'I'm insulted,' Isaiah said. 'I insist you stop this now, before you say something you'll regret.'

Abruptly Berwyn put his feet to the floor and sat forward. 'Oh no. We'll have this out now. I've been waiting for an opportunity to challenge you.'

Isaiah stood up, attempting to look commanding, but felt afraid. 'This is outrageous!'

'I was right about you,' Berwyn said. 'You've steadily swindled Mother out of hundreds, maybe thousands of pounds since she married you.'

'By laws of marriage your mother's money is mine to do with as I think fit,' Isaiah countered in a strangled voice, placing both hands palm down on the desk to disguise their trembling. 'I have done nothing wrong in the eyes of the law.'

'You've gambled away the best part of my inheritance,' Berwyn accused. 'And this man who has come here to see you today, this man Crabbe; anyone with half an eye can see what he is.'

'You're mistaken!'

'No,' Berwyn snapped. 'When Crabbe alighted from the coach at the Marquis Arms earlier today, Bleddyn Williams, the landlord spotted him; recognised him as a prominent prize-fight promoter from Cardiff.' Berwyn smiled unpleasantly. 'And lo and behold! He comes straight to you!'

Isaiah swallowed hard and sat down heavily. 'It's not what you think.'

'My mother may be stupid, but I'm not,' Berwyn rasped, rising to his feet.

Isaiah looked up pleadingly. 'You must say nothing of this to anyone, least of all your mother. I'll be ruined.'

Berwyn looked at him for a moment, a cunning smile on his face. 'I'll say nothing at all just so long as you pay me well, *Papa*.'

'I can hardly pay my debts,' Isaiah said in a strangled voice. 'How can I pay you as well?'

'That's for you to manage,' Berwyn said harshly. 'I'll get my monthly allowance from Mother in the usual way. And you'll pay me an equal amount as well.'

'It can't be done, I tell you!'

'They say Jebediah Crabbe has a reputation for slitting the throat of any man who jibs paying him. I wouldn't hurt a hair of your head, Papa, but I'll make you the laughingstock of the county.'

Berwyn strode to the door.

'Your first payment to me is overdue. I expect it tomorrow – or else.'

26

Jebediah's inner clock woke him at six the next morning, his normal time of rising. He felt pleased with himself, having slept well after the delightful meal of the evening before.

He got up, lit the lamp and put on his dressing gown. Embers still burned warmly in the grate. He added a few nuggets of coal, lifted the glowing cinders carefully with the poker to encourage new flames, and then sat down before the reviving fire.

It was a pity the house belonged to the church, he reflected. It would have been more than adequate to repay the fool parson's enormous debt. There were some good properties and businesses in the village, and resale might have fetched a tidy sum. Or he might have kept it for himself, for who knew when he might need a secure and secret rural bolt hole.

His musings were interrupted by a tap at the door and a young girl came into the room wearing a sacking apron and carrying two steaming china pitchers.

'I've brought hot water for washing and shaving, sir,' she said, curtsying, and moving gracefully towards the washstand.

Despite smudges of coal dust on her cheek, there was no disguising her beauty, a beauty almost regal, Jebediah thought with admiration.

'Thank you, my girl. What's your name?'

'Bronwen, sir.'

'Bronwen, indeed,' Jebediah smiled. 'A name hardly befitting a wench with hair the colour of a raven's wing,' he remarked.

He had noted previously that country girls had a beauty all their own, but this one was exceptional; tall, slender and that abundant black hair, falling almost to her waist, was indeed a crowning glory.

'And who is your father, my girl?'

'My father is Jim Jenkins,' she said with a proud toss of her head. 'Big Jim Jenkins.'

'The devil you say!' Jebediah sat forward. He had been wondering why the name of the village had been so familiar. 'Of course! I've heard of him,' he said. 'Your father is a prize-fighter of some note, if I'm not mistaken, or at least he used to be.'

'He no longer has dealings with the sport,' Bronwen said. 'He works for Mr Talbot at Ystrad Farm.'

'What a waste,' Jebediah remarked. Memories were coming back of a young fighter with much promise. He had seen Big Jim Jenkins fight more than once, and he had proved himself a courageous man in the ring. Whatever had become of that promise? 'And why does he no longer appear in the ring, may I ask? Has his health failed?'

'No. My mother forbids it,' the girl declared.

Jebediah heard this with some astonishment. 'If your father has little spirit enough to let a mere woman tell him what to do, he'd better stay out of the ring, I think.'

He was amused to see the girl instantly bridle at his words, her lovely face flushing with anger. 'My father is a brave man and an honourable one,' she exclaimed hotly. 'He puts love of his family before baser instincts.'

Jebediah bowed his head to her. 'Well said, young woman. I'm chastised.' He waved a hand at her dismissively. 'You're dismissed, but we may talk again.'

She was about to close the door. 'Wait a moment,' he called, and rose swiftly to walk to the night stand near the bed, fingering the coins there and selected half a sovereign. He admired courage and spirit even in a female, and believed it should be rewarded.

'Here!' He tossed the coin in her direction and she caught it skilfully. 'Buy yourself some pretty fripperies to tantalise the lads hereabouts.'

With another quick curtsy the girl was gone.

That evening Isaiah and Jebediah were in the dining room each with a glass of fine port after an excellent dinner.

'A good life you have here, Mr Pugh,' Jebediah remarked pithily. 'A pity for it all to come to nought.' He watched the clergyman's face turn pale. 'I'd help you if I could, of course, but I dare not cross Sir Fletcher. He's a man to be feared.'

It amused him to paint Fletcher Watkins as black-hearted as possible, and to appear to be the sympathetic lackey. It put many people off their guard, and he suspected the cleric might be one. There was no doubt by the pallor of his skin Pugh was a frightened man, and he had reason to be. He, Jebediah Crabbe, would allow debtors no quarter, no mercy, especially those lacking spirit like Pugh. Such men must be made an example to persuade others to comply.

But what was he to do with this quivering parson? To have him pay the ultimate price would not be sensible. Death would mean the debt must be written off, and Jebediah was unwilling for such a loss.

'But how can I repay when I have nothing?' Isaiah asked miserably.

'You have money to live well enough.' Jebediah thoughtfully watched the cleric wipe sweat from his brow. An idea had occurred to him earlier as they had toured the village, albeit a limited tour because of banks of drifted snow, but he had been quick to see the possibilities in the surrounding farm lands.

'I think there may be a way you can work off the debt,' Jebediah said.

'Work?' Isaiah looked startled. 'The church will not let me undertake other employment whilst an incumbent.' He hesitated, looking nervous. 'And certainly not of an unsavoury nature.'

'Unsavoury?' Jebediah grunted with derision. 'Is it not unsavoury for a cleric to be brought to his knees by a weakness for gambling? If the Bishop were to learn of your predilection, you'd be unfrocked and disgraced, sir.'

Isaiah half rose from his seat, his lower lip quivering. 'I beg you, Mr Crabbe, don't force me to break the law.'

'My dear Mr Pugh, what choice do you have?' Jebediah said coldly. 'Besides, all must be done in secret. If you're clever enough no one will know you're involved.'

Isaiah sank back, his shoulder drooping. 'What must I do?'

Jebediah took a sip of port before answering, watching his companion carefully. The fool parson was weak and would do as he was told.

'Being a follower of the sport of the prize-ring you must know how difficult it is to secure a safe venue for fights to take place out of sight of magistrates and the police,' Jebediah said. 'This is particularly true when the combatants are of high notoriety, for instance when the championship is to be won.'

Isaiah nodded his large narrow head.

'Cwmrhyddin Cross is a village suitably out of the way,' Jebediah went on. 'And yet is accessible from all parts of the country.'

Isaiah rose from his seat. 'My parish to be the venue of a championship prize-fight and my reputation put at risk?' he quavered. 'Oh no, Mr Crabbe, it's not possible.'

'It must be!' Jebediah retorted loudly. 'Or your wife will be wearing widow's weeds before the year ends.'

Isaiah sank down. 'Oh, my God! I can't do it.'

'You must,' Jebediah shouted. 'There's a fortune to be made in such an event, and I'll not be denied it.'

Isaiah put his head in his hands and was silent, while Jebediah paused to collect his temper. He watched the clergymen through narrowed eyes, despising what he saw: a man of so-called gentle birth, a weakling whose own father had thrown him off. Was it wise to leave the arrangements of so important an event in his hands?

'Rouse yourself and take heart if you wish to live!' Jebediah exclaimed in a harsh tone. 'You've more than enough time to make arrangements.'

'How long?

'Almost eighteen months,' Jebediah said. 'In August of next year Sir Fletcher intends to hold a contest for the championship between Daniel Pitney of Llanelly, known as The Turk, and Samuel the Crusher Sullivan of County Down. This fight will draw many hundreds of spectators and speculators to Cwmrhyddin Cross, possibly thousands, as such events did in the old days.'

'Such an assembly of thieves and cutthroats in my parish!' Isaiah bleated. 'The church will forbid it.'

'Neither the church nor the authorities must get wind of it beforehand, understand?' Jebediah growled. 'Not if you value your life, Mr Pugh.'

'But I've no idea how to go about organizing it,' Isaiah whined. 'Let alone keep it secret. How can I, as a virtuous cleric?'

'I'll send a man down who will assist.' Jebediah smiled thinly. 'And keep an eye on you at the same time. He'll be your constant companion.'

Isaiah swallowed hard. 'Not the Mangler!'

Jebediah smiled at the man's obvious terror. 'No, a lesser known figure, one by the name of Pedro Arnez, a Mexican by race and a promising young fighter, who is devoted to me,' he said. 'You'll take him into your household, as a valet perhaps.'

Isaiah wrung his hands. 'How will I explain the presence of

such a man to my wife? She'll think it very odd that I employ a foreigner, as will my parishioners.'

Jebediah thought he saw tears glistening in the man's frightened eyes and felt his temper rise again.

'Damn it, man!' he exploded. 'These family matters are of piffling concern to me.'

He checked himself. There was far too much profit at stake here to let his temper get the better of him.

'You'll bear the total expense of organising the event,' he went on more soberly. 'Including the prize purses, fees for the use of land, Pedro's wages, and any other costs, thus working off your debt. At the same time all proceeds will go to Sir Fletcher. Is that understood?'

'I'm undone!'

'Nonsense, man!' Jebediah exclaimed irritably. 'See this as an extension of time to pay. I've given you almost eighteen months to clear your debt. Consider yourself lucky.'

'But how will I spread word if everything is to be kept secret?' Isaiah protested.

'Leave that to me,' Jebediah said confidently. 'Sir Fletcher is a member of The Pugilistic Club and I belong to the Daffy Club. Between us every man jack in the country with an itch to gamble will be made aware. The Fancy will arrive in their hundreds with money jingling in their pockets, burning to be wagered. I tell you, there's a princely fortune to be made!'

Isaiah sat with his head lowered, his long fingers entwined in the stem of his glass. Jebediah wondered if he were praying. He thought not. Isaiah Pugh was the least pious cleric he had ever chanced upon.

'Console yourself, Mr Pugh,' he said mockingly. 'Afterwards, you will be free of debt and the tradesmen of Cwmrhyddin Cross will be that much richer. I bring you prosperity.'

*   *   *

The vicar's generous visitor left without Bronwen meeting him again, and it was well into January before Mrs Parks allowed Bronwen time off to visit her parents. Even then the house-keeper insisted she took a Sunday afternoon when life at the vicarage was less hectic.

Snow was still thick on the ground, piled up against walls and hedges, and the heavy sky promised more to come. Bronwen found it hard work trudging along the icy dirt track from the vicarage to the crossroads at the centre of the village. She pulled her shawl closer around her shoulders as the cold wind whipped mercilessly about her, piercing the fabric of her clothing.

But Bronwen's thoughts were on other things than the coldness of the day. Cassie Probert's taunts about Lloyd Treharn still rankled in her mind and heart and she could not rid herself of suspicion. Yet, she could hardly believe Cassie's boast was true.

Bronwen's troubled thoughts went back to last October when on her fifteenth birthday she and Lloyd had exchanged tokens, and had pledged themselves to each other. She had been so sure of him that she even allowed him to kiss her.

This year she would be sixteen, old enough to be promised in marriage, if her father allowed it. Da thought well of Lloyd, so there'd be no objection. But, if what Cassie said was true, then Lloyd was not the faithful sweetheart she believed him to be.

Reaching the main road through the village Bronwen turned her steps towards the blacksmith's and stables owned by Ruben Treharn. Lloyd was often to be found here this time on a Sunday cleaning the harnesses ready for business the following day. She was determined to confront him about Cassie's allegation.

The door of the stables was partly open and Bronwen edged her way through. Lloyd was sitting on a low stool besides a bench rubbing away at a brass decorated bridle, his dark curly hair flopping over his eyes. Even sitting he seemed tall, the muscles of his well-built shoulders straining at the material of his flannel shirt.

He was so handsome. Bronwen's heart jolted as a shaft of jealousy pierced it. 'Lloyd!'

He glanced around and then stood up swiftly. 'Bronwen! Oh, there's lovely to see you, *cariad*. I've missed you so much mun.'

'Have you?' Bronwen asked petulantly, tossing her head. 'Perhaps you'd rather see Cassie Probert standing by here instead, offering her kisses?'

She hadn't meant to speak of it so soon, but it was all she could think of for the moment. She needed his reassurance that Cassie lied, but knew she was going about it the wrong way.

'Sweetheart, what's the matter?' Lloyd dropped the bridle and came towards her. 'Are you ill? Are they working you too hard at the vicarage?'

'Am I your sweetheart, Lloyd?' she asked, feeling like the child her mother always insisted she still was. 'Or have you taken up with Cassie? Her mother *is* very rich, of course.'

'How can you ask me such a thing, *cariad*?' he asked, reaching out to touch her, but Bronwen shrank away. 'We're pledged to each other, remember?'

Bronwen stared up into his face, suddenly wanting so much to feel his arms around her, holding her the way she loved, although she permitted no other liberties. She allowed a kiss sometimes when the longing for him grew too much to bear. Perhaps Cassie was more accommodating with her favours.

'I don't know what you mean, love,' he said when she didn't speak, and looked perplexed. 'What's she been saying to you?'

Bronwen felt foolish for a moment. She might be playing right into Cassie's hands by picking a quarrel with Lloyd. Perhaps Cassie was trying to drive a wedge between them with her lies.

'She said you bought her a red ribbon for her hair, and . . . kissed her.'

Lloyd's gaze flickered for a brief moment. 'She's lying Bron,' he said forcefully. He reached out again and this time clasped her arm in his strong hand. 'She's jealous because I won't even look in her direction. You're my sweetheart, Bron. Only you.'

She wanted so much to believe him. 'You swear it, Lloyd?'

'I swear. Look!' He pulled aside the edge of the sleeveless leather jerkin he wore. A blue ribbon was pinned to his flannel shirt, the token she had pledged to him. 'How could I be untrue wearing this?'

She put her hand against his chest, leaning towards him. 'I'm so sorry for doubting you, Lloyd, dearest. What must you think of me? I'm ashamed.'

He held her close then and she snuggled against the warmth of his chest, and didn't object when he pressed his lips to her temple.

'I think you're the most wonderful girl in the world, Bron, *cariad*,' he whispered. 'No other man shall have you but me. I long for us to be married.'

With a happy laugh Bronwen pushed herself out of his caress, gazing up at him. 'You haven't asked me yet, not properly on bended knee,' she said. 'And I haven't said yes.'

'But you will,' Lloyd said huskily. 'You will be mine.'

With another peel of laughter, Bronwen dodged his arms as he tried to clasp her to him again, and ran to the stable door. There she paused to look back at him teasingly.

'Maybe I will and maybe I won't,' she said gaily and blew him a kiss before darting outside, and hurried along the road towards her father's cottage.

Lloyd Treharn stood for a moment deep in thought after Bronwen had disappeared through the stable doors. She was wonderful and beautiful. She would make the best and most faithful wife any man could wish for. He did love her and wouldn't he be the fool of fools to do anything that would cause him to lose her?

Damn Cassie Probert with her easy ways and wayward tongue! With another oath, Lloyd turned abruptly and strode back to the work bench, and in a fit of pique swiped at the harnesses and cleaning clothes, sending everything tumbling to the sawdust strewn floor.

Cassie was a minx! He'd known that from the start. He should never have weakened, but what red-blooded man could resist her wiles, refrain from taking what was so openly offered?

Cassie had sworn she would keep their meetings a secret. He should have known she couldn't be trusted. For the moment Bronwen believed him, but Cassie wouldn't let it rest. There was more trouble ahead.

The stable door opened and Lloyd started, whirling around thinking Bronwen had returned. Instead his father, Ruben stood there, glowering at the tangled mess of harnesses on the floor.

'What's this, boyo?' he bellowed. 'You should've been finished half an hour ago, but it looks like you haven't even started yet.'

'An accident, I had, Father. Work through until supper, I will.'

'Huh! You'll get no damned supper, boyo,' Ruben roared. 'Not until I can see my face in those brasses and the leather is gleaming. Put your back into it mun.' He raised his massive arms above his head as though appealing to heaven. 'God help the business when I'm gone!'

Cold nipped at her cheeks and the icy wind tugged at her shawl, but Bronwen felt no discomfort. The happy glow around her heart was warming her through and through. Cassie had lied in her teeth out of sheer spite, and Bronwen knew she would rest peacefully in her bed at night knowing Lloyd was as true as the day was long. She should never have doubted him for a minute.

She hugged herself gleefully, her boots slithering about on the icy track as she made her hurried way to her father's cottage. Lloyd loved her and that was all that mattered in her life.

The half sovereign the gentleman had given her was safely in her pocket as she lifted the latch of the cottage and walked in. They were all sitting down to a meal of cold mutton, and were glad to see her.

'Sit down, my good girl, and take a bite of food with us,' Big Jim invited quickly. 'We see you so rarely now. I wish you lived at home.'

Bronwen heard tenderness and sadness in his voice, and knew she was missed. 'I believe I will have a bite, Da, and thank you.'

'That Mrs Parks keeps you busy and hungry, too, I expect,' Nesta said, dishing out a portion of mutton and potatoes, a tone of anger in her voice.

'She's not so bad, Mam. Strict but fair,' Bronwen answered. 'And Mr Pugh has taken on a valet by the name of Pedro. Strange man he is too,' she said.

She did not mention in front of her father that she found the powerfully built man rather frightening with his sullen expression and brooding watchful eyes. He seemed to be the vicar's constant companion.

'A foreigner is he?' Big Jim nodded. 'Noticed him I did going into the Marquis Arms the other evening.' He paused in the act of forking meat into his mouth, and frowned. 'A servant? He looks more like a prize-fighter to me. Only what would the vicar be doing employing a prize-fighter?'

'Of course he wouldn't have anything to do with such riff-raff,' Nesta scoffed. 'Why only last Sunday Mr Pugh preached an impressive sermon on the sin of gambling.' She glanced pointedly at Big Jim. 'He especially mentioned the terrible sport of bare-knuckle fighting. Scourge of the earth, he said it was. A barbarous practice enjoyed by thieves and cutthroats. No respectable person should have anything to do with it.'

Big Jim sniffed and mumbled something under his breath.

'What's that?' Nesta snapped, eyeing her husband suspiciously.

Fearing a family row might ensue Bronwen quickly took the half sovereign from her pocket. 'Here you are, Mam,' she said cheerfully. 'That's for you towards housekeeping.'

Nesta stared, as she took the coin. 'Where did you get that?'

'A gentleman gave it to me.'

'What?' Big Jim jolted upright, his fork clattering onto his plate. He looked sternly at her. 'Who is this man? Have his eyes, I will, for taking liberties with my daughter.'

'It's all right, Da,' Bronwen smiled at him as she cut into her piece of mutton. 'He did me no harm and was very polite. A visitor from Cardiff he was, staying at the vicarage. I took his hot water up one morning and he gave me the half sovereign then.' Bronwen forked meat into her mouth. 'Very gentlemanly, I thought.'

'And what's this generous gentleman's name?' Nesta asked with curiosity.

Bronwen put down her knife and fork thoughtfully. 'I don't know, Mam. I only saw him the once.' She shrugged. 'I'll probably never see him again.'

27

Bronwen wiped the back of her hand across her sweating brow, as she lugged the last bucket of coal into the kitchen from the yard. Yesterday the heat was blistering and it looked like today would be just as hot. It was not yet half past five, the sun barely risen but already she could feel her calico dress clinging to her body. The kitchen would be unbearable later when Mrs Parks began cooking.

Bronwen built the fire in the range, carefully positioning sticks, paper and coal until a respectable blaze was going. She pushed the poker between the coals gently lifting, so that air could get at the heart of the fire.

Satisfied, she stood upright and then heard the stealthy tread of a man's boots on the flagstone floor behind her. Whirling she brandished the poker.

'Keep back, Berwyn,' she yelled. 'I'll use this on your stupid head, I promise you.'

But the swarthy-faced man standing there unflinching at her threat, watching her through narrowed eyes was not Berwyn Probert, but the vicar's strange manservant, Pedro.

'Oh!' Bronwen exclaimed. 'I thought . . . I'm sorry, Pedro. I expected someone else.'

She still held the poker raised above her shoulder, but slowly lowered it and leaned it against the wall. Pedro's foreign appearance and the way he moved so silently about his duties, always made her uneasy. Yet he had never made himself unpleasant towards her, and in fact, had never spoken a word to her but seemed to hold her in contempt if his superior stare was anything to go by.

'Mr Arnez to you, girl,' he said in broken accents. 'Remember that.'

His teeth were stained yellow and were crooked or broken, and there was an unfamiliar pungent smell about him. She remembered that her father had likened him to a prize-fighter. He was big and burly enough. She wondered if he had come down looking for food.

'Mrs Parks won't be up for another hour yet,' Bronwen said nervously. 'No one else is allowed to prepare food in her kitchen, but there are the remains of yesterday's veal and ham pie in the larder.'

She dared not take a slice, but Pedro Arnez was beyond the housekeeper's control, as had been proved more than once over the last six months, much to Mrs Parks' indignation.

He remained silent. His dark eyes glittering as he looked at her. Jane, who made it her business to collect as much gossip as possible, had told her Pedro was from Mexico, and therefore must be a heathen. Bronwen had no idea where Mexico was, but weren't heathens to be found in the depths of the African jungles, where they ate poor missionaries, sent to save their souls? Her mind suddenly filled with terrible images, Bronwen began to sidle away.

Pedro lifted a hand to detain her. 'Wait, you girl,' he said. 'I've not finished with you.'

'What do you want with me?' Bronwen asked nervously, wishing she still had the poker in her hand.

'Your father is Big Jim Jenkins, is he not?'

Taken by surprise at the question, Bronwen nodded uncertainly.

'You will take a message to him,' Pedro said. He paused a

moment, tilting his dark head as though listening intently.

'What can you want with my father?' Bronwen exclaimed.

'Speak quietly!' he hissed. 'I wish no one to know if this.'

'Why?'

His lips thinned. 'You will not question me, kitchen wench,' he said arrogantly. 'I'm descended from a long line of great warrior emperors.'

Bronwen stared, thinking it very unlikely.

'Your father is a man of the prize ring,' Pedro went on. 'Once as a youth, recently brought to this country, I saw him fight. He was courageous.' He hesitated again to listen, before going on. 'Tell Big Jim to meet with me at the crossroads at midnight.'

'I won't have my half day off until next Sunday,' she explained patiently. 'I'm not allowed to leave the house otherwise.'

Pedro's glance showed exasperation. 'I care nothing for that,' he snapped. 'You'll take the message to your father this morning. Go now while it's still early, before you're missed.'

'I can't, I tell you,' Bronwen insisted. 'I've chores to do. Mrs Parks will be furious if I neglect them. She'll demand to know where I've been. Besides Da has already had left for work, I expect. He'll be on his way to Ystrad Farm.'

Pedro's eyes gleamed at her fiercely. 'You'll go and find him now, girl,' he hissed. 'If you value your life.'

'What?' Bronwen was startled at the sudden change in his demeanour and was frightened. Was her father in danger from this strange man? Perhaps she should warn him.

'Tell Big Jim that I must talk to him on behalf of Jeb Crabbe,' Pedro went on. 'He'll understand.'

'Jeb Crabbe? Who's he? What has he to do with my father?' Bronwen stepped back, fright making her voice rise. 'How do I know you and this Jeb Crabbe aren't planning to harm Da? I'll tell the constable . . .'

He growled words in a strange tongue and abruptly

reached forward to grasp her arm, his fingers digging into the soft flesh.

'You will tell the constable nothing. Speak the name of Jeb Crabbe to anyone but Big Jim,' he growled, 'and I'll slit your throat and eat your gizzard.'

Staring up wide-eyed into his savage expression Bronwen was speechless with fear. He swung her around and pushed her towards the back door.

'Be on your way, girl, now.'

Bronwen hesitated no longer, but rushed to obey. She had to warn her da that some devilry was afoot.

The fields and meadows of Ystrad Farm were some way beyond the boundaries of vicarage land, the countryside in between a warren of lanes and pathways. Bronwen ran along one such pathway that led to the farm's cow sheds and the farmhouse itself about half a mile away.

The morning's milking was still in progress, and she saw Ben Talbot near the sheds.

'Mr Talbot!' Bronwen shouted as she ran. 'Where's my da?'

He swung around at the sound of her voice. 'That's what I'd like to know,' he called irritably. 'He hasn't turned up this morning and hasn't sent word either. Left me shorthanded, he has, damn it!'

Bronwen pulled up short, a chill suddenly running up her spine. Her father had never missed a day's work in his life. Something was wrong. Without another word, she whirled away taking the track that led to the top meadow behind the Marquis Arms.

'Bronwen!' Ben Talbot shouted after her. 'What's going on? Where's Jim?'

She didn't stop to answer, but sped on. She was out of breath as she raced up the steep track that led to the main road and her father's cottage.

Only something very serious could keep Big Jim Jenkins

away from his employment. An accident at home or illness, perhaps? Was her Mam all right? Bronwen felt a shaft of guilt pierce her. She should not have taken work that kept her away from home. Her mother needed her. Nesta Jenkins worked far too hard for their bread.

Bronwen's heart was in her mouth as she lifted the latch of the cottage door and went inside. Her eleven year old brother, Jimmy, was sitting at the table, head resting on his arms. He looked up as she came in, and she could see his face was stained with tears.

'Where's Mam?' Bronwen asked in panic.

'I'm hungry, Bron,' he said miserably. 'I've had no breakfast.'

'Where *is* Mam and Da?'

'Upstairs with Ceridwen. She's poorly.'

Bronwen dashed toward the staircase, but Jimmy let out a wail. 'I'm hungry, Bron!'

'All right!' Bronwen glanced around. The breadboard and a home made loaf stood on the table. 'What's the matter with Ceridwen, then?'

'Dunno,' he said thickly. 'She's been sick all over the bed. It smells!'

Bronwen hastily cut a thick wedge and spread it with butter.

'There you are,' she said handing it to her brother. 'Make do with that for now.'

She raced up the stairs and into the little back bedroom that she had shared with her brother and sister. The bed linen had obviously been changed but the hot air of the room still held the pungent smell of vomit. Her parents both looked extremely weary and upset. Big Jim stood near the open window looking on helpless and worried, while Nesta was bending over Ceridwen, sponging her face with water, and calling her name over and over.

'What's wrong with our Ceridwen, Mam?' Bronwen asked, coming forward to the bed.

'Oh, Bron, love,' Nesta exclaimed in agitation, looking up. 'How did you know she was bad?'

Bronwen could only shake her head as she gazed at Ceridwen's flushed face. 'Have you called the doctor to her?' she asked shakily.

The doctor would have to be paid, but Bronwen knew the fee could be found in an emergency. Although Nesta was unaware that she knew, Bronwen had found the cache of money hidden in the outhouse some time ago but of course had left it untouched.

'Your father is just going down to call on Dr Powell,' Nesta said. 'But it's a bit early. He may not have risen yet.'

'We mustn't wait, Mam,' Bronwen urged. 'How long has she been like this?'

'Well, she was sick in the night and I noticed the rash then,' Nesta said. 'She was crying that her neck was hurting and I rubbed some goose grease in it, thinking it would help.'

'You did your best, Mam.'

Nesta's face crumbled. 'She was very poorly, burning up with fever.' She sobbed and put a hand to her mouth. 'She didn't know us Bron, her own parents, and now she just lies there suffering, and I can nothing for her. I'm so frightened.'

'Da must go for Dr Powell straight away,' Bronwen insisted. 'The doctor is used to coming out at all times.'

Big Jim took a worried look at Ceridwen and hurried away. Bronwen put her arm around Nesta. 'Mam, you go have a cup of tea or lie down a minute, at last until the doctor comes. I'll bathe Ceridwen's head.'

'Oh Bron,' Nesta wailed. 'It's my wickedness that's done this. God is punishing me for my sins.'

'And making our Ceridwen suffer for them, too, I suppose?' Bronwen scoffed gently. 'Don't be silly, Mam. And what sins could you possibly have? No, sickness comes to good and bad alike. Now rest a moment.'

Bronwen was thankful when she heard her father's deep tones again and knew he had brought the doctor. But it wasn't Dr Powell who came into the bedroom, but his partner, Dr Nathaniel Bowen, a youngish man of medium height but wide of shoulder. Except for vivid blue eyes, and a thick mane of hair the colour of ripe corn, his facial features were unremarkable.

Nesta was right behind him as he came in. 'Where's Dr Powell?' she asked in a loud worried voice. 'He always comes to us.'

Dr Bowen shrugged out of his jacket, and came quickly to the bedside.

'Dr Powell is ill himself,' the doctor said. 'Extremely ill and weak. I doubt he'll ever be well enough to see his patients again.'

'You're very young for a doctor,' Nesta insisted in a tone that verged on hysterical, Bronwen thought. 'I would prefer a man of more learning to attend my child.'

Ignoring her Nathaniel Bowen ran his capable-looking hands over Ceridwen's head, neck and thin young body as the child twisted and turned in the bed.

'Raging fever. Her neck is stiff and painful, you say, and she has been vomiting?' he asked and then grunted when he saw the rash. He stood back a moment, his hand cupping his chin thoughtfully.

'I have to tell you this is serious, Mrs Jenkins, very serious indeed I'm afraid,' he said giving her an appraising look. 'How long as she had this rash?'

'I noticed it last night,' Nesta said, standing by with her hands pressed against her breast. 'Can't you give me some ointment for it?'

He shook his head and sighed heavily. 'I fear it'll do no good,' he said solemnly. 'I've seen this group of symptoms before. This child has the brain fever. I must warn you younger suffers rarely recover, and I fear your daughter is in the last stages.'

'Oh my God!' Nesta almost collapsed. Bronwen put her arms around her and eased her into a chair nearby, where Nesta started to weep and groan, swaying to and fro.

Bronwen gave the doctor an angry glance, furious with him for his off-hand manner in delivering his calamitous news.

'Surely you can do something?' she exclaimed brusquely. 'You call yourself a doctor. Do you propose to just stand by and watch her die?'

He looked at her and something like anger flashed in his vivid eyes for a brief moment. 'Young woman,' he said tightly. 'There are some ills no doctor can cure, no matter how clever and learned they are. Brain fever is one of them.' He wetted his lips. 'We might try leeches. Bleeding her might reduce her temperature. All we can do otherwise is to make her as comfortable as possible . . . and pray.'

'It's my fault!' Nesta cried out. 'I should've called Dr Powell last night.'

'I doubt anything could be done. As I've told you there is no cure for brain fever, Mrs Jenkins,' Nathaniel Bowen said. 'The onset is quick and then it's over within a day, if not mere hours.' He paused as Nesta began to sob. 'This is terrible to face I know,' he went on. 'But there's no point in giving you false hope.'

He glanced at Bronwen. 'Have your other children been in close proximity, Mrs Jenkins? Do they show the same signs?'

'Oh, *Duw annwyl!*' Nesta wailed. 'Not my son, too!'

Nesta was swaying on her feet and Bronwen clasped her close to support her. 'I don't live at home,' she told him. 'But my brother is with my father downstairs. Please look at Jimmy, for pity sake, to put my mother's mind at rest.'

Dr Bowen glanced at Ceridwen restless in the bed. 'I'll do what I can to ease her suffering,' he said. 'Laudanum may deaden any pain she's in. Meanwhile, I'll examine the boy.'

He left the bedroom and Nesta sank onto the edge of the bed weeping uncontrollably. Bronwen sat with her, holding her tight, feeling the vibrations of her sobbing. Tears were streaming from her eyes, too, tears of grief and also disbelief. She couldn't believe that Ceridwen would not recover. What would they all do without her? She held Nesta closer. Losing her daughter must seem like the end of the world for her mother. How helpless they were.

Dr Bowen returned to the bedroom after a while. He came and put a hand on Nesta's shoulder. 'The boy is free of symptoms, for the moment,' he said. 'I suggest he be lodged elsewhere for the time being.'

'He can stay with my grandparents,' Bronwen said quickly. It was obvious she must take charge, as Nesta looked completely stupefied and bewildered. 'My father can take Jimmy there immediately. I'll stay here with my parents and nurse my sister until . . .'

'You're young yourself,' Nathaniel Bowen said. 'You run a risk.'

'I'll stay,' Bronwen said firmly.

After a long doubtful glance at her the doctor went to his bag and took out a vial filled with liquid. He poured water from a jug into a glass and carefully allowed a few drops of the colourless liquid from the vial into it. He gently lifted Ceridwen into a sitting position and put the glass to her mouth.

'Give her a few drops of the laudanum in water when it's obvious she's in pain, but not too often, mind. Be very careful that she doesn't choke on it,' he said.

Giving Ceridwen the water was a slow process. When he had finished Dr Bowen put on his coat.

'I'll return immediately with the leeches and put them in place. Later this evening I'll call in again to see how she is.' He looked at Nesta. 'All you can do, Mrs Jenkins, is to make her as comfortable as possible.'

With that he turned and left the bedroom. Bron followed him downstairs quickly. Big Jim was just leaving with Jimmy.

'Dr Bowen, you can't leave now,' Bronwen said in agitation, as her father closed the cottage door behind him.

'I've other patients to see, and I can do nothing more for your sister.'

'You won't you mean,' Bronwen burst out angrily. 'Ceridwen is just a farm labourer's daughter so of no consequence. But we have money to pay you. You'll get your fee, don't you worry.'

His mouth tightened. 'If you weren't so young and foolish I'd be offended,' he said. 'But I know you're upset over your sister.'

'Don't you patronise me, doctor!' Bronwen exclaimed, furious. 'As Mam said, you look too young to know much about doctoring. Dr Powell wouldn't let our Ceridwen die.'

'You're hysterical,' Nathaniel Bowen said tightly. 'I'm just a man. I can't work miracles. I can only do my best.'

With heavy heart Bronwen watched him go, and then turned to retrace her steps back to the bedroom. All they could do was pray fervently that a miracle would happen and Ceridwen would be spared.

Ceridwen died at seven o'clock that evening while Nathaniel Bowen was present. Bronwen was relieved that Jimmy was not at the cottage when the end came, for Nesta was inconsolable and Bronwen could see that her father, too, was fighting not to give into grief. She herself felt numbed except for a pain around her heart which she knew to be deep sorrow and grief.

'I'm sorry for your loss, Mr and Mrs Jenkins,' Nathaniel Bowen said just as he was taking his leave. 'It's so hard to lose a child so young.'

'So you should be sorry!' Nesta burst out, suddenly coming to life. 'If Dr Powell had been here my child wouldn't have died.'

'Please, Mrs Jenkins, I beg you . . .'

'You're no doctor!' Nesta howled like a banshee, and Bronwen could see her mother was demented in her grief, and didn't know what she was saying. 'You're a quack, that's what you are. A quack! You should be hounded out of Cwmrhyddin Cross as a charlatan.'

'Nesta, *cariad*!' Big Jim began. 'Don't carry on so, mun. The doctor did his best.'

'You don't know what you're saying, Mrs Jenkins,' Nathaniel Bowen said, his face whitening. 'Medical science doesn't yet have an answer for the brain fever. It's a scourge.'

'Get out!' Nesta screamed hysterically, and Bronwen ran to hold her lest she fall, for her mother was shaking uncontrollably from head to foot.

'Mam! Are you all right?'

'Get out, you quack!' Nesta raged at the doctor. 'I'll never forgive you for my Ceridwen's death, never.'

Nesta collapsed then in a flood of tears and Big Jim dashed forward. He lifted his wife up in his arms and carried her towards the stairs. 'I'm sorry, doctor, and I bid you good night,' he said raggedly over his shoulder. 'Leave us to our grief, please.'

Nathaniel Bowen stood like a statue, his hand on the latch of the door. 'I could give your mother something to help her sleep if I'm allowed to.'

'What's the matter?' Bronwen exclaimed heatedly, glaring at him. He was very young, and perhaps her mother was right that he lacked the knowledge to save Ceridwen. 'Waiting for your fee, are you? You'll get it, don't worry.'

Nathaniel stared at her for a moment, his jaw working as though he was struggling not to speak out. Then he opened the door and was gone.

Bronwen sank onto a nearby chair and stared around at the silent kitchen usually alive with the sound of children's chatter. Home would never be the same again without Ceridwen, and her mother would never be the same.

She resolved that moment to give up her job at the vicarage. She was needed here to help Nesta recover from the unbearable loss. They all needed to be close to each other now and draw strength from each other. And God help them in bearing their grief.

Two days before Ceridwen's funeral when Nesta was a little calmer, Bronwen took the opportunity to call at the vicarage to give in her notice and receive any wages due to her. Out of politeness she knocked at the back door and waited. It was opened by the maid, Jane. Her eyes widened in surprise when she saw Bronwen.

'Oh, it's you, is it?' she exclaimed. 'You're for it, mind. The mistress is livid with you for waltzing off without so much as a by your leave.'

Bronwen was nettled. 'Well, surely Mrs Pugh must know what's happened?' she retorted sharply. 'The whole village knows of our terrible bereavement?'

Jane shrugged but did not move aside.

'Well, can I come in?' Bronwen asked tartly. 'I want to see Mrs Parks.'

'I dunno, mun,' Jane said dubiously. 'The mistress told Mrs Parks to sack you if you turned up again.'

'Sack me?' Bronwen tossed back her hair angrily. 'I'm here to give notice,' she said.

'You'd better come in then.'

Mrs Parks was just coming into the kitchen from the larder as Bronwen walked in, and stared sternly at her. 'Oh, so you've turned up at last, have you?'

'I couldn't come before,' Bronwen said. 'My mother's been beside herself with grief for days, and I had to be with her. She can't accept that our Ceridwen has gone.' Bronwen felt a lump in her throat and swallowed hard. 'I can't believe it myself sometimes.'

Mrs Parks blinked. 'And I'm sorry for your sad loss, Bronwen, but you should've got word to the mistress somehow, if only to save your job.'

'Got word?' Bronwen snapped. 'There's been a steady stream of callers to our cottage, offering condolences, even from people we hardly know, but my aunt Dorah hasn't even sent a message to her own cousin let alone call.'

'That's as may be, and none of our business,' Mrs Parks said. 'I'm sorry, Bronwen, there's no place for you here now. The mistress has made her decision.'

'I don't want a place,' Bronwen retorted. 'My place is with my mother. I'm here to give notice, and receive whatever wages are due to me.'

'The mistress has left nothing for you,' Mrs Parks said. 'And there's nothing more to say.'

'What?' Bronwen shouted furiously. 'I worked a week in hand, for a start. She owes me that, and I had already worked the best part of a week before . . . before the tragedy happened to my family.'

The kitchen door was flung open suddenly and Dorah Pugh stood there regally in a blue silk gown, with blue ribbons braided in her blonde hair piled high. 'What's all this unseemly shouting?' she demanded to know sourly. 'Who has turned my kitchen in a Bedlam? Her glance fell on Bronwen, and immediately a dull red flush infused her cheeks. 'What's this girl doing here? I gave strict instructions she was to be sacked.'

'I give notice,' Bronwen exclaimed defiantly. 'And I want the wages due to me, Aunt Dorah.'

Dorah's mouth fell open, and she looked infuriated. 'How dare you speak to me in such familiar manner?' she spluttered. 'A lowly kitchen drudge. You'd better learn to show respect to your superiors.'

'I don't work for you any longer, do I?' Bronwen snapped

angrily. 'And I certainly don't intend to bow and scrape to my mother's cousin.'

'Get out! Get out, you little ill-bred wretch.' Dorah was almost frothing at the mouth.

'I'm not leaving until I get my wages,' Bronwen announced stubbornly. She heard Mrs Parks gasp and Jane giggled. 'What kind of a woman are you?' she went on to demand. 'Our Ceridwen has just died but you haven't uttered one word of sympathy for our loss. You're as hard as nails.'

'Oh! You minx, you!' Dorah exclaimed in fury. 'How dare you insult me in front of my servants? Leave this house immediately.' ·

'Not without my wages,' Bronwen said. 'Funerals are costly. My mother needs all the money she can scrape together to cover the cost.'

Dorah seethed in silence for a moment and then a look of scorn settled on her face.

'Let Nesta ask the Caradogs for money, then. That would be fitting under the circumstances.'

Bronwen frowned, utterly puzzled. 'What do you mean by that?'

She stared at Dorah's face, bright now with malice. What did Ceridwen's funeral expenses have to do with Meurig and Mary Caradog? At one time they had been very friendly with her mother, but in the last year or two the friendship had cooled.

'I demand to know what you mean, Aunt Dorah,' Bronwen said.

'Ask your mother,' her aunt snapped back. 'Although I doubt she'll have the courage to tell you the truth. Too ashamed.'

With that Dorah turned on her blue satin-heeled pumps and swished out of the kitchen, slamming the door behind her.

Bronwen stood blinking for a moment, until she became aware of the silence of Mrs Parks and Jane.

'You'd better go, my girl,' Mrs Parks said, although not unkindly. 'You won't get a penny out of her now.'

With one last glance at the closed kitchen door, Bronwen left. What Dorah had said made no sense at all, and she would certainly not repeat one word of it to her mother. Nesta was just one step away from the total madness that can come with inconsolable grief, and Bronwen had no intention of making things worse for her.

Bronwen kept silent about Dorah's remarks about the Caradogs, but it gave her an idea about finding another job. A month after Ceridwen's funeral, while buying a small piece of mutton at the butcher's shop, Bronwen saw Mary Caradog coming out of the haberdasher's and hurried to speak to her. Mrs Caradog was wealthy and influential in the village, and Bronwen was careful to be polite and not presume on her previous friendship with Nesta.

'Mrs Caradog, may I speak with you briefly?'

Mary Caradog turned and on seeing Bronwen smiled kindly.

'Bronwen, my dear girl. How is your poor mother these days?'

Bronwen shook her head. 'The pain is easing, I think,' she said. 'Although there are days when she does nothing buy cry.'

Mary Caradog shook her head sorrowfully. 'I feel for her. I know if I lost one of my own . . .' She shivered and then patted Bronwen's arm. 'You, too, my dear, must miss your sister.'

'We all do.'

Mary's kindness and understanding touched Bronwen's heart and she felt hopeful for what she wanted to ask. 'Mrs Caradog, I wonder if you could help me,' she started quickly before she lost courage. 'I lost my job at the vicarage.' Bronwen compressed her lips. 'My aunt Dorah was less than sympathetic. I wondered if there might be a job for me in the bakery. I'm a hard worker and very strong.'

Mary looked bemused. 'I never presume to interfere in my husband's business matters.'

'I just thought,' Bronwen went on. 'That since you were once my mother's friend you could have a word with Mr Caradog on my behalf.'

'I hope I'm still Nesta's friend,' Mary said and then smiled uncertainly. 'Very well, I'll try Bronwen, but I can't promise anything. I'll speak to Meurig this evening. Call at the bakery tomorrow morning early and he'll probably let you have his decision.'

'Oh! Thank you so much, Mrs Caradog.' Bronwen clapped her hands with joy. 'I'm so grateful.'

'Now, now!' Mary cautioned. 'No promises, mind.'

The following morning Meurig Caradog regarded Bronwen solemnly. It wasn't yet five o'clock, but she felt bright and alert and watched him eagerly.

'A bakery seems hardly the place for a girl,' he said. 'It's hard, heavy going, and we are always at work long before dawn, as you can see.' He pursed his lips doubtfully. 'You're just a slip of a thing.'

'I'm strong, Mr Caradog,' Bronwen assured him eagerly. 'At the vicarage I carried coal scuttles up the stairs full to the brim with coal every morning. I chopped wood. I can do anything a man can do.'

Meurig Caradog smiled. 'Well, you seem very willing, I must say.' He pursed his lips again. 'All right, I'll give you a trial. Be here at four-thirty tomorrow morning, and I'll see how you go.'

Bronwen beamed at him. 'You won't regret it, Mr Caradog, I promise.'

'Let's hope not!'

28

'You've killed him!' Bronwen screamed, pointing an accusing finger at Slasher Tonkin now sitting in his corner of the prize ring. 'You've killed my da! You butcher! You'll hang for this.'

'Bronwen, come away!' Meurig Caradog was at her side, pulling at her. 'You've no business to be here, girl. You've done more damage than you know.'

Bronwen whirled on him. 'Call yourself a friend to my Mam, do you?' she blurted. 'You're no friend. How could you let this happen to my da?'

The dense throng of men around the ring was getting restless. There were jeering catcalls and demands that the injured fighter be taken down, so that the next bout could begin.

'Ghouls! Fiends!' Bronwen screamed at them, shaking her fist. Her father was dead or dying and they didn't care. 'Mindless brutes!'

There was laughter at her insult and one man threw a coin into the ring to land at her feet. 'Give us a dance, wench,' he called. 'Show us your petticoats and an ankle.'

'Bronwen, leave now quietly,' Meurig urged. 'Before real trouble begins.' He glanced nervously at the hundreds of men surrounding them. 'They've paid to see the championship bout which is on next, and they could turn very ugly if we keep them waiting.'

Bronwen glowered defiantly at the mob. 'I'm going to fetch
the magistrate from Cadle Mill,' she shouted, shrugging out of
Meurig's grasp. 'He'll put a stop to this.'

'You had better not do that, wench,' a new guttural voice
warned. 'Or your father will not be the only one to die this day.'

Bronwen glanced up, recognising the foreign accent of
Pedro Arnez. The vicar's strange and sinister manservant
was standing at the edge of the ring. The menacing gaze of
his glittering dark eyes sent shivers up her spine, and she
remember his dire threat to slit her throat if she betrayed him.

'You're responsible for this,' she accused, despite her fear.
'You led him to break his promise.'

'Take her down,' Pedro Arnez instructed harshly. 'And see
that she goes nowhere.'

Lloyd suddenly appeared at her side. 'I'll see to her,' he said
quickly to the Mexican. 'I'll take her home. She's upset. She
doesn't know what she's saying. I'll see she goes nowhere.'

He put a protective arm around Bronwen.

'It's all right, Bron,' he murmured in her ear. 'Big Jim isn't
dead, but he is badly hurt. Nate Bowen is doctoring him.'

'No!' Bronwen whirled out of his grasp and ran to where her
father was being lifted down from the ring. Nathaniel Bowen
was with him, supervising the manoeuvre.

'No!' Bron shouted again at the doctor. 'Get away from my
da, you quack. You let my sister die.'

'Bronwen! For God's sake,' Ben Talbot bellowed. 'Big Jim is
badly hurt. Oh! Bugger it, mun! The last thing your father
needs is a hysterical girl.' He jerked his head at Lloyd. 'Get her
away from here.'

Without more ado, Lloyd grasped hold of her and slinging
her unceremoniously over his shoulder like sack of potatoes,
jumped down from the ring amid gales of laughter from the
mob. Bronwen felt she would die of shame and screamed in
rage as she hung upside down, and continued to scream,

beating at Lloyd's broad back with her fists, but her blows seemed to have no effect on him.

The crowds made passage for the injured man and his seconds, the doctor leading the way, while Lloyd carrying Bronwen, followed behind. When they were clear of the clustering mob, the doctor's group, carrying the injured man between them, went on up the lane toward Big Jim's cottage.

Lloyd set Bronwen down on her feet on the turf. She glanced after her father, longing to run after him to see for herself how he was. But first she was determined to deal with Lloyd for the cruel unfeeling way he had humiliated her.

'How dare you handle me like that in front of that riff-raff?' she flared. 'You're no gentleman, Lloyd Treharn.'

'It was for your own good, Bron,' he began reasonably. 'Getting dangerous it was, mun. You should've had more sense than to come here.'

Bronwen scowled up at him, and then swinging her arm with all her might struck out at him with her clenched fist, aiming at his nose. She missed the target completely as he stepped nimbly away untouched, and she staggered, almost falling.

'I hate you, Lloyd Treharn,' she panted as she regained her balance. 'You're no sweetheart of mine any longer. You betrayed me and my mam by helping that foreigner heathen to snare Da into this.'

'I did no such thing,' Lloyd retorted angrily. 'Big Jim knew what he was doing. He was eager for the fight.'

A great roar went up from the crowds, and Lloyd looked longingly towards the ring.

'The championship is about to start,' he said wistfully. 'Samuel Crusher Sullivan is defending his title against Daniel The Turk Pitney of Llanelly.' He shook his head. 'We'll never see the like of this spectacle again in Cwmrhyddin Cross, Bron, and I'm missing it because of you.'

'You make me sick!'

'If The Turk takes the title it'll be a great thing for Wales.'

'A great scandalous shame, you mean,' Bronwen snapped. 'It's brutal, never mind being unlawful.'

Lloyd's glance at her was defiant. 'I'm thinking of taking up the sport myself, Bron. Pedro says I show promise.'

'Pedro sees you for a gullible fool,' Bronwen retorted. 'You saw what happened to my father.'

'Well, Cassie thinks the prize-ring is a fine thing for a man.'

'Cassie Probert?' Bronwen stepped back staring at him in consternation, hardly believing her own ears. 'Since when is Cassie's opinion of importance to you?' she glared at him. 'You've been seeing her behind my back. You lied to me!' She whirled away from him, clapping a hand to her brow. 'Oh, what a fool I've been!'

'Bronwen, please! Cassie means nothing to me, I swear. We're just friends, that's all. There's no need for you to take on.'

Bronwen looked at him through narrowed eyelids. 'Cassie Probert wouldn't know how to be friends with any man. She's like her mother – a rich trollop!'

'That's not fair!' Lloyd's face flushed angrily.

'Don't talk to me about fair,' Bronwen exclaimed.

Bronwen spun around quickly attempting to dash away after her father, but Lloyd grasped her arm, holding her back.

'Listen, will you, Bron,' he said. 'It was just foolishness with Cassie. She's, well, persistent, clinging like, wants her own way all the time. I couldn't help it.'

'Oh, you couldn't help it!' Bronwen mimicked in a mocking tone. 'Poor you!' She pulled her arm from his grasp. 'Let me go, you pathetic philanderer!' she shouted with contempt. 'Get out of my sight.'

The crowd was roaring again, and Lloyd took a step towards the throng.

'Go on,' Bronwen urged scathingly, jerking her head towards the crowds. 'Get back to the blood bath. Cassie Probert can have you, and welcome.'

She turned and ran for the lane. A moment later she glanced over her shoulder, hoping he was following her after all, but instead she saw him running like a hare towards the ring.

Tears clouded her vision as she hurried on towards home. She loved Lloyd and his betrayal with Cassie Probert cut her deep. But now she had her father to think of. He needed her, and she had to protect him against that charlatan of a doctor.

As the coach from Llanelly rolled into the outskirts of the village of Cwmrhyddin Cross Nesta stared through the windows in bewilderment. So many strangers on the road, mostly men, but some women and children, too. Some were roughly dressed but others were finely clothed.

She alighted from the coach in the yard at the back of the Marquis Arms, carrying her light bag, gazing around at luggage piled up here and there. What was happening?

Nesta had written to say her Aunt Sarah's health was much improved and she was coming home today. She expected Jim to meet her. Their cottage was only a stone's throw away, but still, it would have been nice to see a familiar face. The sight of strangers made her nervous.

Nesta walked from the yard out onto the road and was astonished to see a ragged and filthy beggar man squatting at the base of the wall of the archway. He held out a tin cup to her, muttering incomprehensibly. Such a sight had never been seen in Cwmrhyddin Cross in her memory, and suddenly she was frightened.

She hurried to their cottage nearby and let herself in thankfully, and then paused inside the door, disturbed by the silence. None of her family were at home. The tragic loss of Ceridwen was still a great pain in her heart, and the silence that met her now was terrifying.

Nesta flung her bag down and turning left the cottage. Perhaps they were all at her mother's. In any case if anyone knew what was happening in the village it would be Meg Lewis.

It was disconcerting to be jostled and badgered at the road's edge by strangers, peddlers, tinkers and roving traders, and she was relieved to reach her father's home. Her parents were sitting down to a light meal, and she was delighted to see young Jimmy with them. He jumped up excitedly at the sight of her.

'Mam!' The boy rushed forward to fling himself into her arms. 'Oh, Mam, I'm glad you're back. I've missed you.'

Nesta hugged and kissed him. 'And I've missed you every minute, my lovely boy,' she said, feeling tears sting her eyes.

'Sit down, my girl,' Enoch Lewis invited. 'Have a bite with us and some tea.'

'Yes,' Meg said. 'And tell us, how is my sister, Sarah?' She sniffed. 'It's too bad, Dorah, her own daughter is too grand now to look after her ailing mother.'

'Aunt Sarah is much better,' Nesta said quickly. 'Although she's getting frail. I must have a word with Dorah about her. She should bring her mother to the vicarage to live, I think.'

'Huh!' Meg exclaimed. 'Not much chance of that. She's too posh now to have a plain countrywoman in her grand home. The minx!'

'What's happening in the village?' Nesta asked, bursting to know. 'All these people. What do they want here?'

'Well, the Roxston Fair has come to Cwmrhyddin Cross,' Meg said. 'Ben Talbot has rented out two meadows to them. The lower field is full of tents and stalls selling all kinds of things. Entertainments for children as well, like swings. Mrs Cooper, housekeeper at the Manse tells me there's a fortune-teller's booth as well.'

'A fortune-teller!' Nesta blinked.

For some reason an old memory surfaced in Nesta's mind concerning Ma Rafferty and her strange prophecy. And today the streets were teaming with strangers from all over the country. Anxiety rose in her breast. 'How long will the fair be here?'

'Most of the week, so they say,' Enoch said. 'The top meadow is given over to the prize-fighting booth. Hundreds of men gathered down there to watch, apparently, hundreds.' He shook his head in wonder. 'Never seen the like in Cwmrhyddin Cross before, I haven't.'

'Prize-fighting?' Nesta felt her blood run cold.

'There'll be prize-fights all week,' Enoch said nodding. 'But today is the big day. The championship is being fought.'

Suddenly cold with fear, her chilled blood seemed to run throughout her body, making her hands and feet icy and numbed. She checked her rising panic. There was no reason to suppose Jebediah Crabbe was here in Cwmrhyddin Cross, yet would he stay away from such an important occasion?

Another frightening thought struck her. 'Where's my Jim?'

Meg stood up suddenly to collect the crockery, and Enoch's glance slid away from Nesta's frantic stare.

'Now don't get upset, my girl,' Enoch said soothingly. 'Jim is taking part in a fight.' He shook his head. 'I advised him against it, but the purse is high, and Jim wouldn't listen to me.'

'Oh, my God! He's thirty-eight years old, for heaven's sake,' Nesta wailed. 'Strong as he is, he can't stand up to that punishment.' She put both hands to her mouth in despair. 'I should never have gone to Llanelly. If anything has happened to him I'll never forgive myself.'

'That's not all,' Meg said suddenly, worry plain in her voice. 'Bronwen went to the top meadow to try to stop the fight. I told her to keep away, but she wouldn't listen. It's no place for a woman.' Meg put her fingers to her mouth, looking apprehensive. 'A young girl amongst all those men. Frightened for her I am.'

Nesta leaped to her feet. 'You should've told me straight away!' she exclaimed. 'I must go and find my husband and daughter.'

She turned to leave and Jimmy followed her, but she held up her hand. 'No, Jimmy, *cariad,* you stay here safe with Grandma. I'll come back for you soon.'

Outside she jostled her way past hawkers and peddlers. A fashionably dressed couple arrogantly refused to give way to her at the road's edge, and she had to step out of their way, only narrowly escaping being knocked down by a passing carriage and a cart which were raising clouds of dust on the dry dirt road.

Panting with fright, Ma Rafferty's prophecy was suddenly complete and crystal clear in her thoughts.

And be warned. When the streets of Cwmrhyddin Cross be teaming with paupers and peers of the realm, fine carriage and carts, the evil one will walk amongst them. He searched for you, with murder in his heart.

The awful words echoing in her head, Nesta was filled with a new terror as she searched the faces of those passing by. Jebediah Crabbe stalked the roads and lanes hereabouts. She could feel his evil presence in her bone-marrow, and fear's clawed hand clutched at her heart anew.

Nesta quickened her step homeward. She and Bronwen must leave Cwmrhyddin Cross immediately, at least until the fair had moved on. It would be too dangerous to remain. At any time she might come face to face with Jebediah and she would not give a farthing for her life then or Bronwen's either.

When she reached the cottage she shared with Big Jim she found her home filled with neighbours, among them Ben Talbot and Tucker the Butcher, too, and most disturbing of all, Nathaniel Bowen.

'Leave my home immediately, you quack,' she shouted at him. The sight of him always reminded her of Ceridwen's death, bringing on waves of renewed grief, and she could not bear the pain of reliving those dreadful hours. 'You're never to set foot inside this cottage again.'

'Whisht, woman!' Bobby Tucker said harshly. 'Your man has been injured and the doctor is tending him.'

'Jim!' Nesta glanced around frantically. 'Where's Jim? *Duw annwyl!* I knew he'd be hurt.'

'Jim's upstairs in his bed,' Nate Bowen said calmly to her. 'He's been badly beaten, Mrs Jenkins. He may lose an eye yet.'

'What?' Nesta put both hands to her head in misery. 'Oh, it's a punishment on me for my sins.' She glanced up at the men. 'Where's my daughter. Where's Bronwen?'

'I'm here, Mam,' Bronwen said, coming down the narrow stairs. 'Da's in a bad way.' The girl look dishevelled and Nesta could see she had been crying. 'It was criminal, Mam, criminal the way he was beaten,' Bronwen went on with a sob. 'And Lloyd Treharn had a hand in it. I'll never forgive him.'

Nesta rushed towards the staircase. 'I must see my husband.'

'I wouldn't do that just now, if I were you,' Nate Bowen said gently. 'He's in a bit of a mess. I'm just going back to my surgery for bandages and the like.'

'Lucky Nate was there,' Ben Talbot put in.

'It wasn't luck, though, was it?' Bronwen said scathingly. 'Our so-called doctor is as blood-thirsty as the rest of you.' She glared at Nate. 'You were there to enjoy the spectacle. Don't deny it.'

'You're wrong, Bronwen,' Nate answered. 'I was there in case someone got hurt. And I was right, wasn't I?'

'Huh!' Bronwen turned away from him to go into the scullery.

As she did so Nesta caught a strange expression on Nathaniel Bowen's face as he gazed after the girl. She recognised the look as desire and was outraged.

'You keep away from her, do you hear me?' she hissed into his face. 'Don't you dare even look at her.'

'Mrs Jenkins, I assure you . . .'

'Nesta!' Ben Talbot exclaimed loudly in exasperation. 'You're being unreasonable, woman. You must let Nate see to Jim's injuries. They're bad and there's no one else able to help him.'

'Mrs Jenkins, it looks bad for Jim,' Nate said quickly. He glanced at Ben Talbot. 'It'll be some time before he can return to his work.'

Ben Talbot looked concerned. 'When can he return? I can't afford to be shorthanded on the farm. I'll have to replace him.'

Nate looked thoughtful. 'Perhaps he'll never work again,' he said solemnly. 'I detect an irregularity in his heart. He over-exerted himself in that fight. It wasn't only his head that took a battering. There may be damage to other organs.'

'Oh, no! My poor beloved Jim,' Nesta exclaimed. He was their main breadwinner. How would they live if he could no longer work?

She sent a challenging stare at Nate Bowen. Guilt hung heavy in her heart for her own wrongdoings in the past, and if she once let herself suppose that Ceridwen's death was a punishment on her for her sins then she would go mad. No! She must blame someone else and believe that this young doctor was responsible instead. It *must* be true!

'How can I be sure you know what you're talking about?' she went on. 'You let my child die after all.'

Nate's face whitened at her words and no one spoke. Nesta glanced around at the men and then without another word dashed up the narrow staircase to the front bedroom. She almost screamed in anguish when she saw Jim lying on the bed. His face was covered in blood and was so swollen she hardly recognised him.

'Jim!' she ran to the bedside, overcome with compassion and

love for him. 'Jim? Why did you do it? Why did you break your promise to me? How could I ever have borne it if you had been killed in the ring?'

The thought sent shivers down her spine. Seeing him helpless like this she realised she loved him more than she had known, more than she had ever been able to express, and could not quell the sobs that rose in her throat.

'I couldn't have gone on living without you, Jim,' she murmured shakily. 'It would have been the end of me.'

'Nesta, *cariad*, I'm sorry.'

His voice was just a hoarse whisper and she could see it was agony for him to move his bloated lips. She realised then that she could not run away and leave him in this state. Perhaps she was imagining danger when there was none. She had no proof Jebediah Crabbe was anywhere in the area.

'Don't try to speak or move,' she said hurriedly as he attempted to lift his head from the pillow. 'Just listen.' She hesitated. 'It's bad, Jim. Nathaniel Bowen says you may never be able to work again.'

Making sounds of protest Jim tried to struggle up but Nesta forced him back onto the bed.

'We'll manage somehow,' she assured and tried to smile but failed. She shook her head. 'You're too old for the prize-ring, you old duffer,' she said tenderly. 'Oh, Jim, dear, why did you take such a chance?'

He grasped at her arm with a hand that was bleeding and bruised.

'It was the purse, *cariad*,' he managed to say. 'A handsome sum. Put us right for life it would've if I'd won.' He swallowed with difficulty. 'Last year I was contacted by the owner of the boxing booth that travels with the fair, the top man himself, mind, Jeb Crabbe. I couldn't refuse the chance of a purse like that.'

Nesta drew back with a jerk, snatching her arm away.

'You've had dealings with Jebediah Crabbe? Oh, my God, Jim! You've killed us, Bron and me!'

'Nesta, what is it? What are you talking about?'

'Jim, you don't know what you've done,' she said in terror. 'Bronwen and I must leave Cwmrhyddin Cross immediately.'

'Why?'

'Our lives are in danger from Jebediah Crabbe.' She held up a hand as he started to speak again. 'I can't explain now, my dear. I'm sorry to leave you in such a state, but Bronwen must not stay here a minute longer. Both of us are in fear of our lives.'

Heavy footsteps sounded on the staircase.

'Say nothing about my plans, Jim, please,' she whispered urgently. 'No one must know where we are.'

At that moment Nate Bowen came into the room with his bag.

'Perhaps you'll excuse us now, Mrs Jenkins,' he said stiffly. 'I must tend to Jim.'

Nesta went back down stairs without a word. Ben Talbot and Bobby Tucker were just taking their leave of Bronwen. When they had gone, Nesta called Bronwen to her.

'Listen to me, Bron,' Nesta began earnestly. 'Something's happened, something very dangerous. You and I must leave Cwmrhyddin Cross immediately. We'll go to Aunt Sarah in Llanelly, at least until the fair has left the village. Only then can we return.'

Nesta was aware of Bronwen's concerned stare. 'Mam, what're you talking about? Are you unwell?

'I'm frightened, that's what I am,' Nesta said hastily. 'And you would be too, if you understood.'

Bronwen put her arm lovingly around Nesta's shoulder. 'Da getting so badly hurt has been a terrible shock for you, I know,' she said kindly. 'Now you must rest yourself. I'll see to everything for him.'

'Bron, you don't realise what's going on,' Nesta said desperately. 'Our very lives are in danger, girl, every minute we stay here.'

'You've got a touch of the vapours, Mam,' Bronwen said confidently. 'It's not surprising after all you've been through these last years. But you mustn't worry. I'll give up my job at the bakery to look after Da.' She shook her head. 'I won't work for Meurig Caradog again anyway, not after what he did, allowing Da to get hurt.'

Nesta grabbed Bronwen by the shoulders and shook her.

'Now look here, my girl!' she exclaimed angrily. 'I'm not going out of my mind and I'm not having the vapours. This is real.' She hesitated, reluctant to reveal her crime. 'It's about something terrible I did years ago. Retribution is staring me in the face, but worst of all, your life is in danger, too. Someone wants us both dead.'

Bronwen pull away from her grasp. 'I've never heard such nonsense! Who in Cwmrhyddin Cross would want to harm us? You're ill, Mam, I can see that now. Of course we're not going to leave Da here all alone. How could you even suggest such a thing?'

'But Bron, *bach* . . .'

'No, Mam!' Bronwen said determinedly. 'You can go to Aunt Sarah's if it makes you feel better. Perhaps it would be a good idea, after all for you to get away for a while. I'll stay here and see to Da and Jimmy.'

'Jimmy!' Nesta was jolted. She had forgotten her son! How could she? 'Jimmy must stay with Grandma,' she said quickly. 'He'll be safe there. Your Da will have to manage as best he can.' She was sorry to leave Jim in such a plight but Bronwen's life depended on it. 'The neighbours will help him.'

'I'm not leaving him!' Bronwen shouted. 'And that's that!'

She stalked away to the scullery, and Nesta flopped onto a chair near the range, her head in her hands. What was she to do to save them? If only the fair would leave the village, taking the boxing booth with it, but apparently it was to remain several more days. It wasn't right! It was disgraceful!

Nesta thought of her previous employer, the Reverend Isaiah Pugh. The vicar was always preaching against the sins of drink and gambling. As the incumbent at St Marks on the Hill, he was the most important and influential man in the village. Perhaps Mr Pugh could use his good office to force the fair and all its trappings to move on?

Nesta went to the scullery door where Bronwen was busy.

'I'm going around to the vicarage,' she said quietly. 'I'm not mad, Bron, and I wish I could explain. One day, perhaps I will, although you may think the lesser of me for it.'

'You must do what you think right, Mam,' Bronwen answered. 'And I'll do the same.'

Nesta pressed her lips together, holding back tears. Her family was being destroyed. First Ceridwen lost, Jim crippled for life perhaps, and now Bronwen was turning against her. She hesitated no longer and taking up her reticule set off to see Isaiah Pugh.

She was so wrought up by the time she reached the vicarage that she didn't even stop to knock at the door but flung it open wide and walked straight into the kitchen. Mrs Parks was at the table rolling out pastry, while a maid was at the sink washing pots. Both turned to stare at her abrupt entrance.

'I must see Mr Pugh straight away,' she announced loudly to the astonished pair. 'It's urgent.'

'I beg your pardon,' Mrs Parks said in a flustered tone, grabbing a cloth to wipe her floured hands. 'How dare you barge into my kitchen without so much as a by your leave? Get out!'

'I must see the vicar, I tell you,' Nesta shouted. 'Are you deaf as well as stupid?'

Couldn't the woman see it was vitally important, she thought impatiently, and strode toward the door that led to the front of the house without another word.

'He'll be in his study this time of day,' Nesta said confidently. 'I'll go straight through.'

Mrs Parks moved swiftly to bar her way. 'Oh, no you don't!' she said stridently. 'I know your game, Nesta Jenkins. You're trying to get your old job back.'

'Get out of my way,' Nesta bellowed, almost beside herself with fear and worry. 'This has nothing to do with your position here. You're welcome to it.'

She pushed Mrs Parks aside roughly, and the woman gave a loud scream. 'Oh! You mad woman! You hussy, unhand me. Oh! I'm assaulted.'

Before Nesta could lift the latch of the door that led to the front hall, it was unceremoniously thrown open and Dorah Pugh marched in, wearing a handsome gown in dark red figured brocade.

Her expression furious. 'What's the meaning of this unseemly din, Mrs Parks?' Dorah asked imperiously. 'You can be heard throughout the house. Have you forgotten we have visitors? Oh!'

Her gaze fell on Nesta, and for a moment she looked astonished and perhaps a little guilty, Nesta thought, but her cousin recovered quickly. 'What do you want here, Nesta, may I ask?'

'Here to see your husband, I am,' Nesta said quickly. 'He must put a stop to this Roxston Fair. He must drive them out of the village.'

'What're you talking about?' Dorah looked down her nose at Nesta. 'The fair has nothing to do with Isaiah.'

'As a clergyman, the vicar of this parish, he's the most influential man in Cwmrhyddin Cross,' Nesta replied. 'He has the power to do it.'

Dorah idly brushed a lock of hair from her forehead, her

expression condescending. 'Well, that's true of course,' she said importantly. 'Isaiah is much sought after by the aristocracy.'

She took a few steps into the centre of the kitchen, flicking her skirts about as she went, as though on parade to be admired.

'His father is a peer of the realm, did you know,' she went on theatrically to no one in particular. She leaned back her head and glanced haughtily at Nesta. 'Why, even as we speak he is in deep conference with a baronet, no less. Yes, Isaiah, my husband, is a man of immense influence.'

'Oh! Stop strutting about like a silly peacock!' Nesta said angrily. 'No one's impressed, especially your own staff.'

'How dare you!' Dorah looked completely deflated and glanced suspiciously at Mrs Parks and the maid to catch their reaction. 'You take liberties, Nesta Jenkins. I won't have it.'

With her own nerves frazzled by recent events, Nesta was not about to let her bumptious cousin off so easy.

'It's a pity you don't take as much interest in your own mother as you do in polite society,' she snapped. 'I notice you haven't even asked me how Aunt Sarah is. You remember, of course, that I've been nursing your mother for the last three weeks.'

Dorah's face was stony. 'I don't discuss family matters in the kitchen,' she said severely. She glanced at the housekeeper. 'Mrs Parks I'll use your sitting-room to interview Mrs Jenkins on a private matter. Kindly see that we're not disturbed.'

'I haven't time for that,' Nesta said. 'I came here to see Mr Pugh. I demand as a parishioner to see him immediately.'

'I tell you he's in conference,' Dorah said firmly. 'Come to Mrs Parks' sitting-room. If and when Isaiah is free and is willing to see you, you will be told.'

Nesta had no choice but to follow Dorah through the passage to the sitting room that used to be hers. It looked the same as always, and she was reminded unpleasantly of Algwyn Caradog.

Dorah left the door ajar. Nesta knew from past experience that with the baize door that led into the hall open as it was today, as soon as the vicar's visitors took their leave from the study she would hear their going. She was determined nothing would stop her seeing him then.

Dorah took a seat herself but did not ask Nesta to sit. 'Now then,' she said coldly as if to a servant. 'How is my mother?'

'Aunt Sarah has recovered from her bout of influenza, although it might easily have developed into pneumonia,' Nesta answered, her ears cocked for any sound from the front hall. 'She's frail, Dorah. Can't you find it in your heart to bring her here to the vicarage where she can be looked after properly? It's only right and fitting.'

'How dare you presume to tell me what's right and fitting,' Dorah exclaimed archly. 'You, no more than a farm labourer's wife.'

'I was good enough to nurse your mother, wasn't I,' Nesta retorted scathingly. 'Saved you from getting your dainty hands dirty.'

At that moment men's voices could be heard in the hall. Dorah spluttering in fury, did not hear them, but Nesta whirled around and bolted. She ran down the passage and through the baize door into the hall.

'Mr Pugh, sir,' she began loudly, hurriedly stepping towards him. 'Mr Pugh, sir, I must speak with you. It's about the Roxston Fair, sir, you must . . .'

The words died on her dry lips as the vicar's two visitors turned at her abrupt entry to stare at her. Both men were tall and fashionably dressed. One was grossly fat with a bloated face, and she did not recognise him. But other man had hardly changed at all over the years, and she knew him instantly. Jebediah Crabbe!

And he knew her. 'By all that's just!' he exclaimed, his eyes glittering as he looked at her. 'We meet again. I knew we would one day.'

Nesta was frozen to the spot, but suddenly as his evil gaze pierced her very soul, she whirled on her heels and ran for her life, through the baize door, down the passage, through the kitchen, not stopping to look left or right, out into the fresh air. She swallowed it in great gulps as she ran. Escape! Escape! It was the only thought her frenzied mind was capable of at that moment.

29

Startled at seeing that familiar face, Jebediah's gaze was fastened on Nesta as she disappeared at speed through the baize door at the back of the hall.

'Wait! Sir Fletcher – Mr Crabbe.' Isaiah Pugh scurried out of the study, eyes staring in his long lean face. 'I beg you both to reconsider,' he cried. 'You promised that my . . .' He glanced apprehensively at his wife who had come to stand by his side. 'My . . . obligation to you would be settled after my efforts on your behalf. I've incurred tremendous expense and I'm being blackmailed by . . .' Isaiah licked his lips, glancing again at his wife. 'My position is now untenable,' he went on weakly.

'Who is that woman?' Jebediah took a few steps towards the baize door, ignoring the cleric's plea. 'What's her name?'

'Woman?' Isaiah Pugh hesitated, looking bewildered, and Jebediah was annoyed when the cleric's ridiculous wife stepped forward fussily, smiling in an inane manner, trying to take his arm.

'She's no one of importance, Mr Crabbe, I assure you,' she said, shaking her head and laughing lightly. 'Just a low-class woman who is allowed to do rough household work when anyone takes pity on her.' With a wide smile she turned to the other visitor. 'I do apologise, Sir Fletcher, for her ignorant interruption. A peasant woman, you understand. She knows no better.'

Jebediah removed Dorah Pugh's hand from his arm none too gently and spoke to her husband. 'I want to know that woman's name, Pugh,' he said harshly. 'And where she can be found.'

Isaiah's bewildered expression remained, as well it might, Jebediah thought. He could hardly believe it himself. Nesta Lewis! Alive and well after all these years. Somehow he had always known she had survived, and so the child must also be alive. That was a serious matter for himself and Fletcher Watkins. Nesta Lewis could still hang them if she had a mind to it.

'She's beneath your notice, sirs,' Dorah persisted. 'Really.'

'Be silent, woman!' Jebediah snarled at her. 'Leave us and be about your own business.'

'Oh!'

'I'm waiting, Pugh!'

'Mrs Nesta Jenkins,' Isaiah said distractedly. 'She lives in the first cottage just below the Marquis Arms.' He shook his head. 'But Mr Crabbe, what am I to do? The Bishop is bound to hear of this now. I've no answer for him. I'm ruined, sirs, ruined.'

There was a cry of alarm from his wife. 'Ruined? Isaiah, what does this mean?'

Without a word in reply, Jebediah strode towards the front door impatient to be gone, his stout companion hard on his heels.

He and Fletcher Watkins had done very well over the past sixteen years after gaining control of Sir Tecwyn's title, wealth and properties. Each had increased his own power and personal fortune threefold, and they had become complacent in their success. But Nesta was still alive and that changed things entirely. There was much to think about and plan if they were to remain free men.

Outside the vicarage gates, Jebediah paused and turned to Fletcher Watkins. 'I take it you didn't recognise the woman in the hallway?' he said impatiently to his companion.

'Hardly worth a second glance, I think,' Fletcher answered in an off-hand manner. 'Let us get back to the tavern. This heat is giving me a chronic thirst. There'll be time for wenching later.'

'You blind fool!' Jebediah snarled. 'Didn't you see it was the nursemaid, Nesta Lewis? She lives! And so must the child.'

'Child?'

'Your niece, man!' Jebediah bellowed, and then checked himself, glancing about lest they had been overheard. 'Blanche Watkins, the rightful heir to your brother's wealth,' he hissed. 'The child that could send us to the gallows.'

Fletcher's bloated features whitened. 'But you assured me she was dead,' he exclaimed loudly, seizing the lapels of Jebediah's jacket in a frantic grip. 'You swore to me, Crabbe, damn you!'

Jebediah threw off the other's hands. 'Lower your voice, you fat fool,' he harshly. 'Or you'll undo us.'

Fletcher swayed on his feet. 'Oh my God! What are we to do?'

'We must secure them both and deal with them,' Jebediah said with more confidence than he felt. 'This time making certain that they die.'

He and Mangler had searched Llanelly and its environs for months all those years ago without catching even a whiff of their quarry. Now fate had thrown her in their path again.

It was a good omen he told himself, yet felt some nervousness. They must take action as soon as possible. Nesta had proved cunning prey in the past and would try to get away again. He must not fail to silence her this time.

'We'll settle with the nursemaid first,' he said thoughtfully.

It seemed unlikely to him that Nesta Lewis had revealed the extent of her crime to Blanche Watkins over the intervening years. 'I wager the child is still with her and doesn't know her true origins. She'll be off guard, and can be taken at our leisure once the woman is dead.'

'This is a small village,' Fletcher said nervously. He was sweating profusely. 'A slit throat or two will not go unnoticed, I think. We should leave it for now, and come back in secret in a week or two.'

'No!' Jebediah was adamant. 'She recognised us, and will take action of some kind, either betray us or flee. This is the ideal time.'

'Nevertheless, it's dangerous.'

Jebediah looked at his companion with dislike and mistrust.

'Look about you, man,' he said with irritation. 'While the Roxston Fair remains in Cwmrhyddin Cross the roads and lanes hereabouts will team with the dregs of the towns and villages for miles around. We'll hardly be suspected among such riff-raff. Besides, you forget, we have the local magistrate in our pocket; the cleric has seen to that.'

'Nevertheless, I believe I should leave at once,' Fletcher croaked nervously. 'You and Mangler can deal with her without my assistance.'

Jebediah was further angered by his whining. 'You stay,' he rasped. 'We're in this together, Watkins. Besides, there's no profit without danger.'

'But two deaths, seemingly related,' Fletcher argued. 'It'll cause too much commotion, Crabbe. This isn't Cardiff where we do as we please without question.'

Jebediah had to concede that his companion had a point.

'All right. We won't kill the child here,' he agreed thoughtfully. 'We'll take her by closed carriage to Brynhyfryd House at Roath.' He nodded in satisfaction at his own suggestion, feeling it was fitting that the child would die where she was born. 'We'll bury her in the grounds there. Her body will never be found.'

'And I'll be there to make sure she is dead,' Fletcher said. 'I was a fool to trust you, Crabbe.'

'You'd have rotted in debtors' prison long ago were it not for me, remember that,' Jebediah snarled a reminder. 'I've trebled your fortune these last sixteen years. Do you think the lovely Mrs Vansier would have remained with you without all that wealth?'

Fletcher took a step forward scowling. 'I don't want to hear Alexis's name on your foul lips, Crabbe.'

'To quarrel now would be madness,' Jebediah opined. 'We must act. Hurry! Find Mangler and Pedro. The cottage must be watched at all times. We must be ready for an opportunity to take the nursemaid.' He touched his cane lovingly. 'Betsy here has work to do this night.'

Nesta almost fell through the cottage doorway, slamming it after her. If there had been a bolt she would have shot it. She was shaking from head to foot. The evil one – yes, she knew his face only too well. And now he had found her.

'Bronwen!' Near hysteria, Nesta shouted up the staircase as she flung off her bonnet. 'Bronwen!'

No time must be lost. No matter what Bronwen said, they must leave immediately. She glanced at the old timepiece on the mantel. The afternoon was drawing towards early evening. The mail coach from London always changed horses and drivers at the Marquis Arms about seven o'clock and then continued post haste on its journey west, travelling through the night. They rarely took passengers, but Nesta was confident there would be room for two. The leather pouch hidden in the outhouse held more than enough money to provide the fare, and sustenance until it was safe to return.

Bronwen came quickly down the stairs. 'Mam, I'm glad you're back. I've just given Da some warm sop, but he's asking for you.'

'Bronwen, love, there's no time,' Nesta said hastily, the image of Jebediah Crabbe's face was etched in her mind's eye, and she could think of nothing else. It wouldn't take him long to find out where they were. 'Pack a few things in a canvas bag. We must be ready to catch the mail coach to Llanelly this evening.'

'What're you talking about?'

'We're in terrible danger, Bron,' Nesta insisted in a tight voice, trying not to scream hysterically. 'We must run for our lives.'

Bronwen stood still staring, and Nesta could see from her expression that she thought her mother had gone completely mad. 'Mam, you must rest,' Bronwen said gently. 'You're exhausted after looking after Aunt Sarah and now this. It's all been too much for you.'

'Stop that, will you, Bron!' Nesta shouted. 'I'm afraid for both our lives, and you would be too, if you knew the truth.'

'What truth?' Bronwen shook her head in puzzlement. 'What's got into you, Mam?'

Nesta hesitated, her lips trembling. She could not say the words, could not confess her terrible crime against Sir Tecwyn and against Bronwen herself. Her adopted daughter might well hate her if she knew what had been done all those years ago.

'Bron, love, you must trust me,' Nesta said earnestly, trying to take Bronwen's hand. 'It was something that happened years ago, when I was young, foolish and vain. Now the reckoning has come for me . . . for us. We can't stay in Cwmrhyddin Cross any longer, my girl.'

Bronwen snatched her hand from Nesta's grasp. 'Leave Da when he needs us the most?' She shook her head. 'I can't believe you really mean it, Mam.'

'Jim will manage,' Nesta said tightly, her tone verging on hysteria. 'And Jimmy can stay with Grandma. They're not in any danger.' She hoped that was true.

'Mam, that's the first uncaring thing I've ever heard you say. I'm not leaving here and neither are you,' Bronwen said forcefully. 'This is just a lot of nonsense. Worry has made you lose your wits. Now sit down and I'll get you a strong cup of tea.'

'You foolish, foolish girl!' Nesta shrilled. 'If you won't come with me then I must go alone.' She paused. Yes, that was it! Jebediah Crabbe knew her on sight, but he had no idea what Bronwen looked like now. 'You may be safer here. After all, they don't know who Blanche really is. I can draw them away from you, my dearest girl.'

'Who's Blanche?' Bronwen shook her head, obviously bewildered. 'What has she to do with us?'

Nesta swallowed. 'Blanche was a child I used to take care of, but betrayed,' she said shakily. 'They want her dead.'

'They? Who are they?' Bronwen asked impatiently. 'Mam, listen to your own words. You're not making any sense. You're wandering in your mind.'

Nesta wrung her hands helplessly. What was the best thing to do to protect Bronwen? Should the girl stay or should she run? Nesta decided to give it one more try. 'Will you come with me, Bron? Please, please, I beg you.'

'No, Mam!' Bronwen said firmly, shaking her head vehemently. 'I'm not going anywhere. Da needs me. Don't you love him any more?'

'Of course I love him!' Nesta exploded. 'But I don't want us to be murdered either. It would kill your da if that happened.'

Nesta saw Bronwen's lips tighten stubbornly and knew it was no good pleading any longer. 'Very well, Bron,' she said deflated. She had done all she could, and perhaps it was fate. 'Stay, but I want you to remain indoors with your father. Beware of any strangers, no matter how gentlemanly they may look, and take no chances, promise me that.'

Bronwen did not answer.

Nesta felt as though her heart would break. 'I'm leaving now,' she said miserably.

'Well, go if you must,' Bronwen retorted. 'Perhaps it's just as well that you do go! Perhaps you'll come to your senses in Llanelly.'

Nesta took one final look at the girl's angry face, and turned to run upstairs. She would say no more.

She went to the bedroom she shared with Jim. He glanced eagerly in her direction as she came in, but she could see he was unable to raise his head from the pillow.

'Nesta, *cariad*, are you still angry with me?'

'No, Jim, it's gone past that,' she answered, opening the drawers of the chest and taking out underclothing, to stuff hastily into her old canvas bag. 'I'm sorry Jim, but I have to leave. I can't tell you where I'm going, but don't worry.'

'You're leaving me! *Duw annwyl!* You can't mean it, Nesta, not after all these years.' He gave a little sob. 'I've broken your heart, is that it?'

'No!' Nesta went to the bedside and gently grasped his poor damaged hands. 'I don't leave you willingly, Jim. I love you dearly but I have to go. It's . . . it's a matter of life and death.'

'Nesta, wait!' Big Jim cried out. 'I need you. You can't leave me alone.'

'You've got Bronwen,' she pointed out. 'And the neighbours will help, you'll see.' She put the bulging bag over her arm. 'Goodbye, Jim, love. You'll see me again, quite soon, I hope.'

'Nesta! Don't go, *cariad*! Don't go!'

Feeling she was being torn apart, Nesta left the room as tears began to burn her eyes. To think her life had come to this, after all the pain and humiliation she had been through with Algwyn Caradog. And it was all because of vanity and weakness in her younger years; her determination to better herself and find a wealthy husband. She had ruined her life and Bronwen's too.

Downstairs, Nesta took her shawl from behind the back door before going into the outhouse to retrieve the leather money pouch. When she returned to the kitchen, Bronwen was waiting.

'You're determined to go, then, Mam?'

'I've got no choice, love, I told you.'

Bronwen shook her head. 'Mam, I won't forgive you for deserting Da, like this,' she said, and Nesta could see she was on the verge of tears. 'I only hope you don't regret it.'

'Oh, you don't know how much I regret,' Nesta answered sadly. 'You can't know how much remorse I feel.' She hesitated. 'Try not to hate me, Bron, love. When this is over perhaps I'll find the courage to explain it all to you.'

Bronwen turned her back and remained silent. With one last look at her beloved adopted daughter, Nesta went to the front door and out onto the dirt road.

People were still about, all strangers, but none seemed particularly interested in her as she hurried to the coach yard at the back of the inn. She peered anxiously through the archway leading to the yard. It was deserted, except for a private carriage piled high with luggage outside the back door of the tavern, but there was no driver to be seen.

Relieved, Nesta stepped cautiously forward. She would keep well out of sight until the mail coach arrived and would then take her chance to ask the driver to let her ride along. She had no doubt a half-sovereign would soon persuade him.

Nesta clutched her reticule nervously. Luck was with her. She had outwitted Jebediah Crabbe once again.

Jebediah carefully lifted the edge of the blind over the carriage window and peeked out into the yard.

'There she is!' he muttered urgently. 'No! Wait until she comes closer,' he went on as Mangler moved to open the carriage door. 'She must be given no time to raise the alarm. There must be no commotion to draw attention or we're done for.'

Jebediah turned from the window to glance at the men with him in the carriage, Mangler Harris, Fletcher Watkins and Pedro Arnez.

'Pedro, you go outside and wait your chance to grab her,' he instructed curtly. 'She'll be less suspicious of you perhaps, but stay out of sight until the last minute. Quietly now!'

Pedro stepped out of the carriage, but left the door open, and Jebediah looked through the window again.

Looking about her like a frightened rabbit wary of the stoat, Nesta was making her way cautiously towards the inn's back door. A fly to the spider's web, Jebediah thought with satisfaction. She would not escape this time.

'Good evening to you, Mrs Jenkins,' Pedro's voice came suddenly from outside. 'How is my friend Big Jim faring after the fight?'

Nesta was at the side of the carriage now out of Jebediah's sight but he heard her startled gasp and there was a moment of silence.

'He's badly injured,' she said finally in a breathless voice, her words clear to Jebediah's ears. 'He may lose an eye.'

'That's not good, missus,' Pedro answered sympathetically. 'I owe him a sovereign.'

'A sovereign!'

Jebediah smiled to himself. The Mexican had brains as well as brawn.

'Here! Take it,' Pedro's deep tones urged.

There was a stifled cry and the next moment Pedro bundled the woman bodily into the carriage, remaining outside himself to slam the door shut. Mangler seized her immediately, placing her roughly on the vacant seat next to him, his arm around her neck and his hand over her mouth.

'I have you at last!' Jebediah said triumphantly, gazing across into the woman's staring eyes. 'I have you, and soon I'll have the child, too.'

He put his head out of the window to call to Pedro who had climbed up into the driver's seat. 'Leave the village. Go westward,' he instructed. 'To open country.'

It amused Jebediah to see the woman struggle, but Mangler's grip was beyond her strength.

'You've been clever, my dear Nesta. And you've caused us much trouble.' He signalled Mangler to release the woman's mouth and then leaned forward suddenly. 'Where's the child Blanche Watkins?' he grated. 'You had better speak, or I'll leave you to Mangler's mercies.'

He expected her to scream but instead she shook her head and said nothing, staring at him with hatred in her frightened eyes. But stubbornness glinted there, too, and it made him impatient.

'You'll tell me before the night is out,' Jebediah said harshly. 'Before you die.'

'Mangler must beat it out of her,' snarled Fletcher Watkins.

'All in good time,' Jebediah said confidently. 'All in good time.'

He had never admitted, even to himself, that Nesta's disappearance all those years ago had unnerved him; not knowing whether she were alive or safely dead, not knowing when the hand of the law might fall on his shoulder. Now the uncertainty was over. He had her.

After a while the carriage slowed and stopped. Fletcher Watkins lifted the blind on his side and looked out. 'We appear to be in some woods,' he said.

'Very good,' Jebediah said. 'Take her outside.'

Mangler dragged the struggling woman from the carriage and now she began to whimper and plead. Following, Jebediah heard her pleas and was gratified. Soon he would know everything.

'Where is this place?' he asked Pedro.

'The woods are two or three miles from the village. This is common ground,' the Mexican answered. 'Few have business here, so her cries will not be heard.'

'Nevertheless, the evening is still very bright,' Jebediah said. 'Take her further in, where the trees are denser, with less chance of being seen.'

They all moved forward, Mangler half carrying, half dragging the woman with him.

'This will do,' Jebediah said at last.

They stood in a half circle, the woman in front of them, her arms secured behind her back by Mangler.

'Now,' Jebediah began. 'I want to know all. Who helped you escape? Was it Fat Lil? Answer me!'

'No,' Nesta whispered. 'It was Jack Crow.'

'Black Jack! I might have known it.'

'I should've finished him off when I had the chance,' Mangler snarled.

'You'll never find him,' Nesta spoke up. 'He took sail to the New World.'

'I'm glad you're being sensible in talking, Nesta, my dear,' Jebediah said. 'It will cause you a lot less pain in the end.'

'You can't kill me now,' Nesta gasped. 'You'll never get away with it.'

'Enough of this chitchat,' Fletcher exploded. 'Make her tell us where Blanche is or I'll beat it out of her myself.'

He stepped forward suddenly and struck Nesta across the face with his open hand. She staggered and would have fallen had Mangler not had a firm grip on her.

'You fat fool!' Jebediah stormed, dragging him back roughly. 'You'll kill her before she can reveal anything.'

'Blanche Watkins is dead,' Nesta said, lifting her head. 'I renamed her Ceridwen, so you would never find her. She died of the brain fever years ago. If you don't believe me, look for her grave in the churchyard at St Marks on the Hill.'

'You lie!' Jebediah said.

'I'm not lying.' Nesta shook her head vehemently. 'The child is dead. I was trying to escape when you caught me. Do you think I would've left without her? Blanche Watkins is dead, I tell you.'

Jebediah stared at her. That glint of stubbornness was still in her gaze. He didn't like it one bit and had the urge to strike her himself.

'I don't trust you, dear Nesta,' he said tensely. 'I think she still lives. How many children do you have?'

He saw a spasm of fear flick across her face. 'I've a son only. You will not touch him. He's just an innocent child.'

'She lies. She has a daughter, about sixteen years or so,' Pedro volunteered. 'Tall, with hair the colour of a blackbird's wing. I know her. She is called Bronwen. She was in the ring earlier when Big Jim was beaten.'

'That sound about right!' Fletcher Watkins said triumphantly.

'No! You've got it wrong,' Nesta cried out. 'Bronwen is Jim's daughter.' She struggled violently. 'Leave her be! I swear Blanche is dead.'

'I think you protest too much, dear Nesta,' Jebediah said much pleased at her reaction. He nodded at the Mexican. 'Good work, Pedro.'

He glanced jubilantly at their captive. 'You've betrayed yourself with foolish dissembling,' he said. 'I've no further use for you.'

'Damn you to hell, Jebediah Crabbe,' Nesta screeched. 'You'll not get my Bronwen. I'll see you dangle from a rope first even if I dangle with you myself!'

Nesta kicked back suddenly catching Mangler in his shinbone. He howled and his grip slackened. She was out of his grasp in a moment and running through the trees.

'After her, you careless fool,' Fletcher Watkins shouted in fury.

Jebediah charged after her, Pedro and Mangler running through the trees at his side. Fletcher was left behind, too fat to keep up with them.

Pedro was the first to catch her. He grabbed at her hair, yanking it back. Nesta almost fell but managed to stay on her feet. The Mexican pinioned her arms and then swung her around to face the others.

Jebediah was beside himself with rage. He reached forward and struck her across the face. 'You die now, this minute, Nesta. You'll not make a fool of me again.'

'Jack Crow made a fool of you,' Nesta gasped. 'Crippled as he is, he's a better man than you, Jebediah Crabbe.' She glanced around scornfully at all of them. 'A better man than any of you.' Her gaze went to Fletcher. 'I despise you most of all, Sir Fletcher,' she said. 'You plotted the death of your own kin for greed. Your soul is damned.'

'Silence, woman!' Fletcher spluttered.

'I'll not be silent!'

'You will be silent,' Jebediah grimly took his cane and withdrew the rapier. 'As silent as the grave.'

Terror flared in Nesta's eyes as she looked at the blade. 'No! Have mercy! Oh my God! Save me!'

'You're wise to appeal to your maker, Nesta,' Jebediah said harshly. 'For you'll meet Him very soon.'

Without hesitating further he stepped towards her and raising the short rapier above his shoulder struck down at her with it, plunging the thin blade into her throat. Without another sound, Nesta sank to the ground and did not move again.

'It's done,' Fletcher Watkins said with satisfaction as the woman's canvas bag was thrown down on the ground beside her. He kicked at the lifeless body. 'We're safe.'

'It's half done,' Jebediah reminded him. He wiped the length of the blade with his handkerchief and returned it to the cane scabbard. 'Now we must find the girl and dispose of her. Only then will we be safe.'

'Let us go and find her now,' Fletcher Watkins suggested.

'No,' Jebediah said curtly. 'We must bide our time.'

His fat companion was too reckless. Jebediah had not forgotten Chippie Tonkin's murder. That hasty act had cost him a fine ransom. Now his neck was at stake.

'We'll go to the cleric's house and stay there the night,' he said. He took one last look at the body at his feet. 'We must plan

carefully; find out all we can about the girl first. Leave nothing
to chance. A mistake now could cost us dear.'

Later that evening Jebediah pushed past the stout young maid
who answered the door of the vicarage.

'Tell your master that he has three guests for the night,' he
commanded. 'Prepare our rooms immediately.'

The flustered maid took their coats and then hurried away
towards the study, and Jebediah strode into the over-furnished
sitting-room.

Dorah Pugh was there, with a pretty fair-haired young
girl and a young man of about eighteen or nineteen. The
three jumped up as Jebediah and Fletcher entered unan-
nounced.

'Why! Sir Fletcher, Mr Crabbe, This is indeed an honour,'
Dorah Pugh gushed, her face flushing. 'We were not expecting
you. I'm afraid dinner is long finished.'

Fletcher threw himself onto a sofa. 'Stop gabbing and get me
some food, woman,' he commanded arrogantly. 'Be quick
about it. I've not eaten since mid-day.'

Dorah looked startled at Fletcher's harsh tone. Her son
stepped forward, his face darkening. 'How dare you speak
to my mother in that outrageous way?'

'Hold your tongue, boy,' Jebediah commanded. 'Stay out of
our way or you'll be very sorry.'

'It's all right, Berwyn, dear,' Dorah said, but her face had
whitened in shock. 'Go tell Mrs Parks to prepare some trays for
the gentleman, cold cuts perhaps and some ale.'

As Berwyn left the room, Isaiah appeared. It seemed to
Jebediah that the tall cleric's frame was bent in supplication as
he hurried forward. 'Sirs, this visit is a surprise. I had thought
we'd seen the last of you.'

Jebediah gave a bitter laugh. 'So you hoped! However, we
still have some business to conduct, and may remain here a day

or two. Either way, we'll leave without a moment's notice, if it serves our purpose.'

'You're welcome,' Isaiah said, but Jebediah could tell from his expression that he wished them in hell.

'Tell me,' Jebediah went on, taking a seat also. 'How is our friend Big Jim Jenkins? He made a good display in the ring. It was a pity he was outmatched.'

'Doing poorly, so I understand,' Isaiah replied in an offhand tone. He seemed relieved at a change of subject.

'But he has family to support him?' Jebediah persisted. 'To provide a weekly crust if he can no longer work?'

'He has a wife and daughter, both employed.'

'Where exactly?'

'I've no idea, sirs.' It was obvious that the cleric was puzzled by these questions. The man was weak but he was no fool.

'I ask,' Jebediah went on quickly, 'because if the man is destitute I'll leave him a small purse for his trouble in the ring.'

Dorah Pugh coughed politely. 'Have no fear, sir,' she said to Jebediah. 'The man is well provided for. His wife does rough work at the Manse, and the girl works at the bakery.' Dorah gave a shudder. 'Low and vulgar she is too. She attacked my poor Cassie for no reason. Ill-bred, sir, ill-bred.'

Jebediah was glad of the information, but he had had enough of the cleric and his wife. 'You may leave us now,' he told them loftily. 'Sir Fletcher and I wish to talk in private.'

'Hurry that food!' Fletcher snarled.

'We leave with our quarry first thing in the morning,' Jebediah said when he and Fletcher were alone. 'I've no doubt she'll be away to her work near dawn. With no one about we can snare her on the road.'

Fletcher shifted uneasily in his seat. 'I'll not sleep well again until the child is in her grave.'

30

Bronwen woke before dawn after spending a fitful night, and reluctantly swung her legs from the bed she had once shared with her sister Ceridwen. Her body ached as though she had toiled for hours. It was no wonder with all that had happened the day before.

And then she remembered Nesta had left home, deserting them all, and pain filled her heart. She could hardy believe it to be true. Her mother must be sick in her head, she decided, for she could not understand any other reason for her strange behaviour and for running away.

Bronwen paused a moment, saying a little prayer that Nesta would return soon. She felt reassured after that, and lit a candle and prepared to go down to make breakfast.

At least little Jimmy was safe with his grandparents, she reflected. She hated the idea of leaving her father alone at the cottage during the day, but she must go to her work. Even though she had sworn not to return to Meurig's employ it was more important than ever that she keep her job at the bakery. With Mam away and Da laid up, she as now the main breadwinner.

She made some porridge and then went up to her father's bedroom. She was loath to wake him so early, but the sun would be up soon, and she must leave. Meurig always frowned if she were even a minute late.

'Da, are you awake?' She put her head around the door, lifting the candle high, to see him stretched out on the bed, bare-chested and still in the breeches he had worn the day before. 'I've brought you some food.'

'I'm awake, my lovely girl,' he said softly. 'I've been lying here all night without sleep.'

'Are you in pain, Da?' Bronwen was anxious for him. He probably needed a doctor, but she was reluctant to call Nathaniel Bowen. Her mother was so set against him, and Lloyd had lately told her gossip about the doctor's other failures. 'Shall I go and wake the apothecary for a powder?'

'No, *cariad,* not now,' he said tiredly. 'I'm worried about your mother. Nesta wouldn't go off like that without good reason. Something's amiss and here I am, helpless in my bed.'

'She's sick in her head, Da, I'm certain,' Bronwen said. 'We mustn't blame her – or blame ourselves.'

'I do blame myself though,' Big Jim said. 'I've let her down, Bron. I should be horsewhipped.'

'Oh, Da! Don't talk like that, mun.' Bronwen took the dish of porridge to him, and gingerly helping him into a sitting position, spooned the food into his mouth.

'Look at me,' he said in despair, a sob in his throat. 'I have to be spoon-fed like a child. I'm a wreck, Bron. No good to any woman, man or beast.'

'You'll recover, Da.' Bronwen hesitated. 'Perhaps you won't be able to do heavy work at the farm, but Ben Talbot won't turn you off. After all, he's as much to blame as anyone for this, I'm sure.'

'You said we must blame no one,' Big Jim said. 'And I don't, except myself. I knew what I was doing.'

Dawn was already lightening the room and Bronwen blew out the candle. 'Shall I help you bathe before I leave for work, Da?'

'No! That would be the last straw, Bron!' Big Jim said in a stronger voice. 'Leave me be as I am. Nesta will come home soon, I know it. She won't stay away for long.'

'I hope so, Da.' Bronwen paused, knowing how proud her father was. 'I've asked the neighbours to come in from time to time to see to your wants. I'll be home as soon as I can, Da. In fact, I intend to ask Meurig to let me off early.'

Her employer could hardly refuse, could he, after being party to the terrible spectacle the day before? She would remind him of it.

'You're a good daughter, Bron, but I don't want to be a burden to you,' He put his damaged hand lightly on hers. 'You mustn't worry about me. I'll manage. I feel stronger today. I'll probably get up and have a swill at the sink later.'

The sun would break through soon and she should be at her work.

'I'll go now, then,' she said. 'Take care of yourself, Da.'

It would be hours before the shops and businesses opened for trade, so the road through the village was deserted. As Bronwen made her way towards the bakery, close by her grandfather's shop, she was surprised at the sound of carriage wheels rapidly approaching from behind. As it drew level with her the horses were abruptly reined, and the carriage halted. Immediately two men jumped out to confront her.

Bronwen stared at them. She instantly recognised one as Pedro Arnez. The other man, big, burly with an ugly shaven head, was a complete stranger. Bronwen screamed in terror as they seized hold of her and dragged her toward the carriage.

'Let go!' she yelled, the sound echoing in the empty street. 'Take your hands off me, you animals! What do you want?'

'Silence, or I will knock you senseless,' Pedro snarled at her. 'Come with us quietly or else it will be the worse for you.'

'No, I won't.' Bronwen struggled wildly, frightened and confused. What was the meaning of this attack? 'You have no right to do this. I will not get into that carriage.'

She kicked out, catching Pedro on the shin. He bellowed, and muttered in a strange language what sounded like an oath.

The other man struck viciously at her face. For a moment she was dazed by the force of the blow; her legs buckled and she sank down painfully onto her knees on the sun-hardened road, only to be dragged upright again.

'Jeb said not to mark her.'

'Does it matter? She'll be dead soon.'

'Crabbe is not a man to be crossed, Mangler,' Pedro warned. 'Let us waste no more time.'

The bald-headed man grabbed her by the nape of the neck; his other arm held her tightly around the waist, lifting her bodily, while Pedro grasped at her skirts and ankles. Bronwen resisted feebly, still half-stunned by the blow.

'No! No!' She tried to struggle in their grasp but their combined strength was too much for her.

They had her partially in the carriage when there was a new commotion alongside them; men shouting and cursing. Suddenly her captors' grip was released, and Bronwen fell heavily onto the road, knocking her face against the step of the carriage.

Heaving herself upright, she stood shakily, gazing about her in utter bewilderment. Had villagers come to her rescue? No. The five men attacking Pedro and the bald-headed man were all complete strangers to her. They milled about at the roadside, throwing punches, wild kicks, wrestling her two captors into submission. Finally Pedro and the bald man lay sprawled on the ground apparently unconscious, but they might have been dead for all Bronwen knew.

More frightened than she had ever been in her life, Bronwen began edging her way along the carriage, hoping to make a run for it, but one of the newcomers turned towards her, a big evil-looking bearded man with a broken nose and a misshapen ear.

'You come along with us, wench,' he said to her.

Bronwen shook her head. 'No! No! Leave me alone. Get away! I'll set the constable on you.'

'You come quietly, missy, or I'll sling you over my shoulder.' He laughed heartily at his own joke. 'Like a sack of potatoes.'

'What about these two?' another man asked him.

'Throw 'em into the carriage. Let 'em sleep it off.'

Before Bronwen could escape, she was seized by the bearded man, and was unceremoniously marched off towards the crossroads, the other men closing ranks around them.

There were no other vehicles in sight and Bronwen, stumbling along with her new captors, wondered in terror where she was being taken and for what purpose. To her surprise they paused outside the Marquis Arms which stood at the crossroads. The door was opened immediately by the landlord Bleddyn Williams who stepped aside to let them come in. Bronwen was relieved to see him.

'Mr Williams!' she cried out desperately. 'Help me!'

'It's all right, Bron,' he said calmly. 'You're safe now.'

'No! These men have abducted me. Call the constable.'

'It's all right, my girl,' he repeated unconcerned. He led the way down a passage, through the back parlour and into what seemed to be a private room.

The early morning sunlight streamed in through the window overlooking the fields beyond the inn. Bronwen blinked in the brightness and then was aware of a figure standing before the fireplace.

He was a big man, heavily built, and at first she thought he stooped, but then realised that his body was horribly warped; his large head was awry and sunk onto his chest, so that he must look at her sideways from under his lids.

'Welcome, Miss Blanche,' the man said, taking an uneven step towards her which showed his legs, too, were out of kilter. 'We meet again.'

For all his fashionable clothes his whole appearance was grotesque, and Bronwen was filled with revulsion and fear. She stepped back quickly, ready to make an escape.

'I don't know you. Who are you?' she asked fearfully. 'What do you want with me?'

The man's twisted gaze was keen as he looked at her and the expression on his dusky face became concerned. 'Fetch the doctor immediately,' he instructed Bleddyn in masterful tones. He waved a hand displaying many gold rings, gems glinting in the sunlight. 'The child be hurt, bleeding.'

'Right away, Mr Crow,' Bleddyn said respectfully, touching his forelock before hurrying from the room.

'I don't want a doctor,' Bronwen exclaimed loudly as in trepidation she watched the landlord leave. Now she was alone with this gargoyle of a man. 'I want to go home. You've no right to bring me here.'

'I'm afraid you can't go home,' the man said evenly. 'Your life be in mortal danger.'

'What nonsense is this . . .?' But suddenly she was reminded of Nesta's strange words before she left home, and was even more alarmed.

'Sit down, child,' the man said. 'I've much to tell you.'

'I demand you set me free immediately,' Bronwen cried in distress. 'When my da gets to know of this you'll be sorry.'

'Sit!'

Frightened, Bronwen sat, trembling now from head to foot. His bizarre appearance was so disturbing she tried to avoid looking at him directly.

'I be a man with scores to settle,' he said grimly. 'And settled they will be.'

'But not with me,' Bronwen exclaimed in dread. 'I've done you no harm. I don't even know you.'

'But I know you.' The man strained his twisted head to look at her, a smile on his face. 'When we first met you were no more than a mewling babe with an insatiable appetite for warm milk.'

'You're mistaken, mister.'

'My name is Jack Crow. They call me Black Jack,' he told her. 'And I make no mistakes. Where be Miss Nesta, your nursemaid?'

Bronwen shook her head. 'I've no nursemaid. You're mad!'

Perhaps her mother wasn't crazy after all. She could make no sense of what was happening, but there was danger here all right. One look at this strange man told her so.

'Where be Nesta? You must tell me.'

'I won't tell you anything,' Bronwen yelled stubbornly. 'You can torture me if you will, but I'll never tell.'

Black Jack chuckled. 'There be a good fighting spirit here, I think,' he said as though to himself. 'Calm yourself,' he went on to Bronwen. 'Miss Nesta be a friend of mine. I fear for her safety. I want to make sure she's also protected.'

At that moment the door opened and Nathaniel Bowen came into the room, followed by Bleddyn Williams. The doctor pulled up short when he saw her.

'Bronwen! What's happened to you?' He turned furious glances at Bleddyn and Black Jack. 'Her arms and face are covered in scratches! Who's been ill-treating her?'

'Not us, Nate!' Bleddyn exclaimed hurriedly.

'An attempt was made to abduct her,' Black Jack explained. 'Fortunately, I anticipated such a move and my men thwarted it.'

'Abducted?' Nate stared, his expression even more furious. 'What's going on?'

Black Jack waved a hand. 'Later, doctor. Get on with treating her.'

Bronwen could see no revulsion in Nate Bowen's face as he gazed at the misshapen man, but there was a look of interest and curiosity, which Black Jack obviously recognised.

'There be your patient, doctor,' Black Jack said pointing at Bronwen. He gave a slow smile. 'Nothing can be done for me. My injuries are decades old.'

Nate nodded and advanced towards Bronwen. She drew back.

'Keep him away from me,' she cried. 'He's no more than a quack. He killed my sister Ceridwen with his quackery!'

Black Jack gave a startled look towards Bleddyn Williams, who shook his head and smiled. 'The child Ceridwen died of the brain fever. No one could have saved her.'

'That's not what my mother says. Ask her!' She remembered then that her mother had deserted them, and tears filled her eyes. 'I want to go home to Da! Let me out!'

'Dang-ding it, child! Be silent!' Black Jack exclaimed impatiently. 'Doctor, do your duty and you'll be well paid. We be waiting outside. But she must not leave. Her life depends on her remaining here under my protection.'

Bleddyn and Black Jack left the room and Bronwen resentfully allowed Nate Bowen to bathe her cuts and bruises with alcohol, crying out when it stung. 'You butcher!'

'Why do you hate me so much, Bronwen?' he asked. 'I'm just a country doctor trying to care for his patients as best I can.'

'You're a fraud! Lloyd Treharn told me all about you,' Bronwen declared glowering up at him. 'You were hounded out of Haverfordwest when your quackery killed your patients.'

'That's a confounded lie!' Nate stormed, his face reddening. 'Young Treharn is jealous. He's guessed my feelings for you, true feelings, and he's afraid you'll reciprocate when you discover his deceit.'

Bronwen frowned at him. 'Feelings? What do you mean?'

Nate looked shaken, and stepped away from her. 'You're now my patient,' he said quietly. He gazed at her, a muscle in his jaw working as though he were under strain. 'I can say no more.'

At that moment the door opened and Black Jack came into the room, the bearded man and Bleddyn in his wake. Black

Jack made a signal and the bearded man took a small leather pouch from his jacket pocket.

'Here's your payment, doctor,' Black Jack said.

Nate shook his head. 'There's no fee, sir.' He took one last look at Bronwen. 'I'll call in later today to see how she is.'

'Don't bother,' Bronwen snapped. 'I won't be here.'

A spasm of emotion passed across Nate's face, and then he turned and left the room.

'A good man that, I think,' Black Jack said, looking at her keenly.

'You know nothing of him and his history.' Bronwen's tone was scornful. 'But I know him for a charlatan.'

'You're young,' Black Jack said. 'Youth can be cruel and harsh, and often very blind.'

'I'm tired of this,' she shouted. 'I want to go home to my father.'

'Your father is dead, child.'

'What?' Bronwen leapt to her feet. 'No! That's impossible. I left him not half hour since.' She took a step towards Black Jack. 'What have you done to my da?'

'Big Jim Jenkins is not your father,' the crippled man said gently. 'Your father was Sir Tecwyn Watkins of Brynhyfryd House, Roath.'

'What balderdash!' Bronwen shook her head at this absurdity. 'You mistake me for someone else,' she said obstinately. 'Or else you're a lunatic. I'm Bronwen Jenkins. I've lived in Cwmrhyddin Cross all my life. Ask anyone in the village.'

'No, Bron,' Bleddyn spoke up. 'Nesta brought you here as a baby. You were more than a year old when she married Big Jim.' He gave Black Jack a curious glance. 'She called herself the Widow Crow in them days.'

Black Jack chuckled. 'She took my advice. Miss Nesta be a woman of quick wit.'

'You speak as if you know her,' Bronwen said uncertainly.

'I knew her briefly,' Black Jack agreed. 'I came here to repay her kindness to me all those years ago.'

Bronwen shook her head. The more she heard the less she understood. Her mother had been afraid of something. Did this man have anything to do with Nesta running away? She must find out more.

'Her kindness?'

'The lot of a coloured man be poor in the New World, especially a free coloured man,' Black Jack said in explanation. 'But the money Miss Nesta so generously shared with me was my salvation. I used it well and now I be a very wealthy man. I seek revenge on those who made me the cripple you see before you. They will dangle from a rope. I've sworn it!'

'Nesta Jenkins is my mother. Why did you call her my nursemaid?'

'That's what she once was.' Black Jack waved a hand impatiently as Bronwen tried to protest. 'I've made it my business to delve into your family history,' he declared quickly. 'Your real mother was Lady Sarah Watkins. 'She died as you were born.'

This was too much!

'I don't believe a word of it!' Bronwen exclaimed heatedly. 'You're mad, completely mad!'

'Listen, child. You be in mortal danger,' he insisted. 'I and my party arrived here very late last night to find that the men I seek, your uncle Sir Fletcher Watkins and Jebediah Crabbe, had already left the inn some hours before, bag and baggage.'

Bronwen shook her head. 'I know of no such uncle.'

'You'll be quiet and listen,' Jack Crow said sternly. 'I suspected they had taken themselves off to the vicarage. I've discovered the parson is their unwilling ally.'

Bronwen opened her mouth to interrupt again, but he lifted a hand in warning, and she sank back in her seat, her gaze measuring the distance to the door. It was too far, and with the other men present there was no hope of eluding her captors yet. She was anxious for Da, and Meurig would be angry that she had not turned up for work.

'Crabbe and Watkins now know you're alive and a threat to them,' Black Jack went on. 'They'll do all they can to see you dead, and Miss Nesta too. I guessed they'd make an attempt to take you both this morning.' He paused and looked at her earnestly. 'Where be Miss Nesta? We must find her before they do.'

Bronwen shook her head stubbornly. 'I don't trust you. I'll never tell.' She shook her head in disbelief. 'Why would these men possibly want to harm me or Mam, anyway?'

'You're a threat not only to their wealth but also their lives; you could send them both to the gallows.'

'But I don't even know them.'

'Your very existence is enough.' Jack Crow insisted and then paused. 'You see, Bronwen, you outlived your father, Sir Tecwyn, and are still his rightful heir. A vast fortune is at stake as I understand it, and it belongs to you, child.'

Bronwen folded her arms across her chest, her lips in a tight stubborn line. This was all beyond her and nothing made sense. The sooner she got away the better.

'Well, that be enough for now,' Black Jack said after giving her a thoughtful look. 'You be upset from all that has happened. Our good landlord here will give you a room to rest. There you'll remain until I find the guilty ones and secure them for the authorities. Don't fear for Big Jim. I'll see that he is attended.'

'Come along, Bron, *bach*,' Bleddyn said. 'Do as Mr Crow orders.'

She allowed herself to be led away without protest. While there was no hope of eluding her captors at the moment, when left alone there might be an opportunity. And escape she would!

★   ★   ★

Jack Crow strained his neck to watch the girl being led away, thankful that he had been in time to save her, but it troubled him that Nesta Jenkins was not in the village. Had she managed to get away from Jebediah a second time?

He found it ominous that Crabbe and Watkins had left the inn so abruptly and had taken refuge in the house of a prominent member of the community, as though they feared to be observed in public. At the vicarage they could come and go as they pleased, and no one would be the wiser – except Black Jack Crow.

He glanced towards the bearded man, awaiting his next command.

'Tom, take some men and look for the Mexican Jackal in or around the village and also Mangler Harris. Bring them here to me,' he said curtly. 'I want to question them. I fear we're too late to save the mursemaid.'

'Right away, Mr Crow.' He grinned. 'Can we paste them a bit?'

'I want them conscious and able to talk, otherwise do as you will, but quietly.'

Bronwen glanced around the bedroom usually used by overnight travellers, and wondered what to do next. She heard Bleddyn turn the key in the lock and it made her blood boil to be treated in such a highhanded way. She pounded on the door with clenched fists.

'Let me out! You'll pay for this Bleddyn Williams, when Da gets hold of you.'

She pounded and shouted for some time but no one came near. Well, she wouldn't give in. There must be some other way of escaping. Going to the window she looked out on trees, at sheep and cattle grazing in the meadows behind the inn, and in the distance the smoking chimneys of Ystrad Farmhouse. If she could climb out somehow, she could make her way home to Da unseen by the tracks between the meadows. But dare she try?

The room was on the third floor, but just below the window and to her left there was a sloping gabled roof. Just beyond that was an old oak tree, some of its stout branches overhanging the building. That was her way of escape if she had the heart for it.

Bronwen pulled back the catch, lifted the lower sash and put her head out of the window. She swallowed hard seeing how high up she was. If she missed her footing on that roof it would be a long fall to the cobbled yard, and certain injury if not death.

She glanced back into the bedroom undecided. Black Jack Crow and his men had not hurt her so far, but who knew what he really had in mind for her. She would not wait about to find out.

Gathering her courage, Bronwen scrambled out onto the wide stone windowsill, fixing her eyes on the gabled roof just off to her left. It was far too risky to simply leap for it, but if she lowered herself down by clinging to the sill by her fingertips, it might just be possible.

She slid gingerly over the edge, letting her legs dangle, and then lowered her upper body, hanging from the rough stone sill by her fingers. The sudden pull on her arm muscles as her body swung free made her want to cry out with pain, but she bit down on her lower lip, determined that she would master it.

Edging painfully inch by inch she worked her way along the sill, and then trying to stay calm, glanced down. It was frightening to see her feet swinging in mid air, her skirts billowing out in the light morning breeze.

People moved about in the yard below. She recognised the inn's ostler, Old Billy Bain as he ambled across the cobbles towards the coach sheds. She could not help gasping on seeing Lloyd Treharn, emerging from the stables a moment later, leading a horse harnessed to a smart gig. Usually at this time of the morning he was to be found at his father's blacksmith's shop. She wondered vaguely why he was here, and was tempted to shout to him, but it was too dangerous. Unknowingly, he would alert everyone inside, and she would be captured again. This was her only chance, and she must do it alone.

Bronwen eyed the sloping roof some feet below her, and tried not to think what would happen if she misjudged it. Although it brought agony anew to her arm muscles, she started to swing her body from side to side, until she achieved a good momentum, and then when she believed the timing was right, flung herself toward the roof.

The sensation of falling was sickening, and she hit the roof with such force that the breath was knocked from her lungs. Her boots could not get a purchase on the lichen-covered slates, and she began to slide down towards the flimsy guttering and certain death.

Flinging an arm up desperately, she felt the crest of the roof beneath her hand; the sharp edges of the decorative tile cutting into her fingers, but she clung on with both hands for dear life, panting with near exhaustion.

She stayed like that for a moment more, one cheek against the slates, trying to ignore the weakening of her arms. When she had got some breath in her lungs, she began to edge steadily along the crest, her boots finding crevices between the slates to support her weight.

Finally she was on the edge of the gabled end, and the tree branches were within reach. As she groped out towards the nearest one she prayed that it wasn't rotten and that it would bear her weight.

Taking a firm grasp of the branch, she found the courage to let go of the roof crest, and bet her life in the strength of the tree. It did not fail her, and praying thankfully, she scramble to safety among its abundant leaves. It was a relatively easy climb down for she had been climbing trees all her life.

The tree grew outside the grounds of the inn, and so it was easy enough to slip away in the undergrowth, and head across common ground towards the lower meadows of Ystrad Farm. It was only when she lifted a hand to wipe sweat from her face that she noticed her hands and fingers were cut and bleeding, and were beginning to stiffen up.

In the lower lane that ran past the farmhouse, she bathed both hands in the cool water of the horse trough, and after wiping them on her skirts, hurried on.

Exhausted and still frightened, she took little heed of the clip of horses' hooves on hard ground or the rattle of wheels in the lane behind her. All she knew was that she must get home to Da and tell him what had happened. Perhaps he had an explanation for it all.

As she stumbled on, the vehicle was suddenly right behind her and alarmed, she threw herself against the hedge out of its way. She stared in panic as a small gig drew along side her, and then cried out in relief to see the driver was Lloyd Treharn.

'Oh! Thank the Lord!'

'Bron!' He was equally astonished to see her, and reined the horse immediately. 'What're you doing here? Your face is filthy and your skirts are torn. What's happened to you?'

Bronwen scrambled into the gig beside him. 'Lloyd, I'm in desperate trouble,' she said breathlessly. 'I was abducted and held prisoner at the Marquis Arms. Wait until my da hears about this!'

Lloyd stared for a moment and then laughed. 'Bronwen, I've never heard anything so crazy. What're you up to?'

'It's true, I tell you,' she exclaimed angrily. 'And anyway why aren't you at your father's shop? And who does this gig belong to?'

The corners of his mouth drooped, and Bronwen recognised that as a sure sign that he was about to lie. 'It belongs to a customer,' he said flatly and looked away.

She didn't believe him, but there was no time to ponder on his dissembling. 'Take me to my father's cottage, Lloyd,' she begged. 'I'm worried about him. He still hasn't recovered fully from the fight yesterday.' That was another bone she wanted to pick with him but it would have to wait.

Without a word he flicked at the reins, and the horse moved forward. She had not forgiven him for his part in her father's downfall, but her quarrel with him could wait until another time.

The gig rounded a bend where two tracks converged, and Lloyd had to rein in the horse again suddenly, for blocking their way in the lane was a large enclosed carriage, and two men stood at the horses' heads.

Bronwen recognised them both immediately. One had attacked her that very morning; the bald-headed man Pedro had called Mangler, his features swollen and cut about from the hiding he had received from Black Jack's men earlier. The other man was the fighter who had beaten her father so cruelly the day before.

Bronwen clutched at Lloyd's arm in terror. 'Don't let them take me, Lloyd.'

'That's Slasher Tonkin,' Lloyd said nervously. 'Bron, what's going on?'

'I don't know.'

Mangler and Slasher approached the gig cautiously. 'Get down,' Mangler said to Bronwen. 'And you!' He pointed a finger at Lloyd. 'You'll make yourself scarce if you know what's good or you.'

'Do something, Lloyd!' Bronwen cried out.

'What do you want?' he asked of the two men, as Mangler took hold of their horse's bridle. 'Stand back or I'll run you down!'

Bronwen gasped in fright as Mangler produced a pistol from his jacket pocket and pointed it at Lloyd, and she felt his muscles tense.

'You won't argue with a shot in your gut, I think,' Mangler snarled. 'Now dismount, and leave here.'

Lloyd turned his head and looked at Bronwen. She saw stark fear in his eyes. 'This in none of my business, Bron,' he said, a quiver in his voice. 'I can do nothing.'

'Don't leave me, Lloyd!' Bronwen shrieked, clutching at his arm as he was about to dismount from the gig, but he pulled away roughly, and quickly got out. 'Lloyd! You can't leave me to my fate. You said you loved me.'

Lloyd took one last look at her and then at the pistol and turning, began to run back the way they had come without another word or glance.

'Lloyd!' Clinging to the sides of the gig, Bronwen turned to watch him run away full pelt, yet unable to believe he had deserted her. Lloyd Treharn, the man she thought of as her sweetheart, was a coward.

Mangler gave a scornful laugh and waved the pistol at her. 'I've a mind to finish you where you sit,' he grated. 'In payment for the punishment I got earlier.'

'You deserved it!' Bronwen yelled, shaking with fear, but trying not to show it. 'I wish they'd killed you!'

Mangler uttered a coarse oath and raised the pistol.

'Mangler!' Slasher Tonkin barked at him. 'A shot will echo in this wooded valley. We'll have the whole village down on us. Besides, Mr Crabbe said to bring her back unharmed.'

Mangler's lips twisted and he glowered at her under his eyelids.

'I can wait,' he said. 'It'll give me great pleasure to kill you with my bare hands, wench, for the trouble you've caused Jeb and me.'

'You'll pay for this, you blackguard!'

'Shut the gab!' He grabbed at her wrist and wrenched her from the gig, putting the barrel of the pistol against her head. 'Now keep still and do as you're told.'

Bronwen watched as Slasher Tonkin removed the horse for the shafts of the gig. When it was free he struck at its flanks, sending it galloping away, nostrils flaring in terror. The gig was heaved to one side, so that there was room for the larger vehicle to pass.

'Now get into the carriage,' Mangler instructed her harshly, pushing her roughly toward the opened door. 'And no tricks or I'll put a shot into your brain and to hell with Jeb Crabbe.'

Shaking so much she could hardly put one foot in front of another, Bronwen did as she was told. Mangler followed her into the carriage, while Slasher Tonkin clambered up into the driver's seat.

'Back to the vicarage,' Mangler shouted up him. 'Jeb and Sir Fletcher are waiting, and we've wasted enough time.'

'What about her?' Slasher asked uncertainly. 'She could easily raise the alarm when we get into the village.'

Mangler grinned across at Bronwen, as she sat crouched against the further seat. 'No she won't.'

Without warning he lunged forward, striking at her with his balled fist. Bronwen felt an agonising pain in the side of her face for a split second before senselessness engulfed her and she knew no more.

31

'Take some of that mutton stew up to Miss Blanche,' Jack Crow instructed Bleddyn Williams at midday. 'She'll be hungry by now.'

The landlord signalled to a serving girl, but the bearded man rose from his seat in the kitchen.

'I'll take it up,' he offered. 'She's a lively one all right, and could easily overcome a wench if she has a mind to run off.'

'Very well, Tom,' his employer agreed, shuffling along the passage to the parlour which he had made his headquarters. 'Make sure she be comfortable. I regret restraining her, but there be no other way.'

'She's a pretty little thing, too.'

'Damn you, Tom Barrett!' Jack Crow barked. 'I'll have your eyes if you show her any disrespect! Miss Blanche be quality, high born, and don't you forget it.'

'I meant no harm, boss.'

Jack, already in a dark mood, growled but said no more as the bearded man went about his task. His plan to render Jeb Crabbe helpless by capturing his cronies was not going well. The Mexican Jackal was safely imprisoned in the inn's cellars, but Mangler Harris had escaped their net.

Perhaps it be just as well, Jack reflected philosophically, as he sat down awkwardly to sample the stew himself. His hatred of Mangler was so great, his need for revenge so bitter, that he might be tempted to do the man a serious injury and that would not serve his ultimate purpose. Retribution would only be complete when he witnessed Mangler and Crabbe swinging from the gallows.

'Boss!' Tom Barrett came dashing into the parlour. 'She's gone! Escaped by the window by the looks of it.'

Alarmed, Jack struggled painfully to his feet, clumsily bumping into the table and knocking over his dish of stew. 'Damnation!' he shouted. 'How can this be?' He shuffled forward. 'Gather the men. They must search the village and the surrounding area. There's no time to be lost!'

Jack cursed the fact that he was unable to sit a horse and join in the search, but had to wait at the inn for news. It was mid-afternoon when Tom Barrett returned.

'A body has been found, boss,' he said, eyeing his employer warily. 'But it's not the girl,' he went on hastily. 'They say it's her mother.'

'Miss Nesta!' Jack's head sank even lower onto his chest. He had failed her, his benefactress. And it looked as though he had failed the child also. He felt a great swell of hatred rise in his chest, and struggled to keep control of his feelings. 'No sign of the girl, then?'

Tom Barrett shook his head. 'No, boss. But something strange happened earlier today. A horse and gig belonging to the vicar's wife, lately kept here at the inn's stables was taken.' He shook his head. 'By whom no one knows. The loosened horse returned later. Our men have just found the gig abandoned in a lane alongside a nearby farm. There were spots of blood on the seat.'

Blood! Jack felt a spasm of rage in his throat. 'I see Jeb Crabbe's hand in this.' His mood darkened even more. 'How was Miss Nesta killed?' He could not hide the tremor in his voice.

'Weapon like a stiletto thrust through the throat,' Tom Barrett told him flatly. 'The local doctor says it probably happened sometime last evening.'

Jack clenched his fists. A thin blade. Jeb Crabbe's signature without doubt. 'Has Big Jim been told?'

'Aye!' Tom sounded scornful. 'I never thought to see a strong man blubber like a baby.'

Jack twisted his neck to look up at the man. 'Your scorn is misplaced, Tom. Where there are no tears, there are no feelings,' he said in a caustic tone. 'No tears, no happiness. You'd do well to remember that.'

'Aye, boss.'

Jack's fist crashed onto the table suddenly. 'By God!' he shouted, overwhelmed with remorse and fury. 'Jeb Crabbe will answer to me for this before he answers to his Maker.'

He slumped back in his seat, feeling spent and useless. 'They have her, Tom,' he said in a hollow tone. 'They have her.'

'Looks like it, boss.' Tom hesitated. 'She's been missing hours; probably already dead in a ditch someplace.'

'I'll not accept it until I see her corpse,' Jack exclaimed staunchly. 'Bring the Mexican up here,' he went on grimly. 'He knows something and he'll talk, or else suffer the consequences.'

Jack studied the man brought before him, assessing his physique, so typical of the fighter. He was relatively young with many more years of the prize-ring in him, and he probably lived for the sport. This was the man's strength and also his weakness.

'What plans does Jeb Crabbe have for the girl?' Jack asked suddenly in a thunderous voice. 'Where have they taken her? To the vicarage?' He felt it unlikely, but nothing must be overlooked. 'Answer, damn you!'

Pedro was silent, his swarthy face inscrutable; his gaze unflinching.

Jack was very conscious of the passage of time. Every moment might be the girl's last. 'A woman's body has been found, Pedro. Did you have a hand in her death?'

Pedro remained silent, but Jack caught the almost imperceptible flicker in his dark eyes, and was satisfied that the Mexican had witnessed Miss Nesta's death at least, and was in Jeb Crabbe's confidence. They would not beat it out of him. The threat had to be more subtle.

'I hear tell you have a future in the ring, Pedro,' Jack said in a milder tone. 'They say you have it in you to be champion one day.'

Pedro's lips twisted in pride, but he said nothing.

'To be champion, a man has to have good hands,' Jack went on. 'Without good hands, he be nothing.' He signalled to the men holding Pedro. 'Bring him forward. Make him kneel, and place his hands on this table top.'

'*Dios!* What is this?' Pedro spoke at last, struggling in the men's grasp. 'What do you intend to do to me?'

'I be making sure you never fight again, Pedro,' Jack said grimly. He brought a heavy hammer from beneath the table. 'You'll never fight, you'll never work. You'll be good for nothing.' He laughed grimly. 'You won't even be able to button your own flies. Are you ready to sacrifice all for Jeb Crabbe?'

'*Que barbaridad!* You will not do this, I think!' Pedro exclaimed, and Jack was pleased to hear fear in his voice. 'It's against the law.'

Tom and the other men laughed.

'Murder be against the law,' Jack pointed out harshly. 'The cruel murder of a helpless woman.'

'I swear I did not know they meant to kill her,' Pedro cried out, struggling to free his wrists from the grip of his captors.

'Where have they taken the girl?'

'I know nothing!'

Jack suddenly smashed the hammer down on the table inches from Pedro's trembling fingers, the wood splitting with the force of it. Pedro screeched in terror.

'You be not hurt,' Jack snarled in disdain. 'But when the hammer falls again you will be. Now tell me everything!'

'I'm not in Jeb Crabbe's confidence,' Pedro protested stubbornly.

'But you know all,' Jack snorted. 'You be that kind of a man.' He lifted the hammer again. 'Talk! Or I'll finish you.'

'Wait!' Pedro's eyes were fixed on the hovering hammer. 'I overheard them talking at the vicarage last night. They spoke of Sir Fletcher's house at Roath.'

'Ah, yes!' Jack said with satisfaction. 'Brynhyfryd House. Of course!' He looked at Pedro. 'Your hands be saved, but I can't vouch for your neck.'

There was a plaintive cry from Pedro. 'You'll let me go now.'

'Take him to the cellars,' Jack instructed curtly. 'Bind him securely. We'll let the authorities deal with him when we have Crabbe in our grasp.'

Pedro was dragged away, and Jack sat for a moment, thinking.

'Tom, gather the men,' he said at last. 'We travel to Roath within the hour. See if any of the villagers wish to accompany us. The more the better. Every man will be armed. We pursue dangerous quarry.'

Within a short time a band of men had gathered at the inn, ready to ride. Among them were the landlord, Bleddyn Williams and the local farmer Ben Talbot. Jack was surprised when the doctor, Nate Bowen arrived with another man, obviously a fighter by the looks of his battered face.

'This is Bronwen's father, Big Jim Jenkins,' Nate told him. 'He's still weak but insists on travelling with us. I agreed for the sake of his peace of mind.'

'I want to get my hands around the throat of the man who killed my Nesta,' Big Jim said harshly. 'And I must save my daughter if I can.'

Jack rose awkwardly from his chair. 'I grieve for your loss,' he said earnestly, straining to look up at Big Jim. 'Miss Nesta was a woman of generosity, strength and courage.'

'I don't understand why this has happened to her,' Big Jim said in bewilderment. 'And why has Bronwen been taken? Who are these men? What do they want with us?'

Jack looked up at the big man with difficulty. 'As you can see I'm unable to sit a horse, and you're hardly fit enough yet. You'll ride with me in my carriage, and I'll tell you all I know.'

Most of the volunteer vigilantes had mounts. For those who did not Bleddyn Williams provided horses from the inn's stables. When they were all gathered in the inn's yard, a dozen or so grim-faced men on horseback, Jack spoke to them.

'We be after dangerous men,' he warned. 'The murderers of Nesta Jenkins and others, men who will stop at nothing to evade capture. Any man among you who fears for his life may step down now and not be thought the less for it.' Jack waited but no one dismounted. 'Very well, then,' he said triumphantly. 'Let's be after them!'

The violent rolling and rocking of the carriage brought her back to vague consciousness. At first she was aware only of her sore, aching body and a nagging pain in her face as she lay huddled in the corner of the carriage. She longed to stretch and move her limbs, but some instinct warned her to remain as still as death.

'Do you think the body has been discovered yet?' someone asked.

Body? Whose body were they speaking of? The voice was very familiar, and suddenly Bronwen recognised it as the man called Mangler. All at once she remembered being seized and struck in the face by him, and her blood chilled in terror. How foolish and rash she had been in spurning Black Jack's protection. Now she was in very real danger of losing her life and had no one to blame but herself.

'We should've buried it, like I said.' Another man spoke, a voice she did not know.

'There was no time,' a third man said impatiently. 'We had to move quickly.'

'Pedro disappearing without explanation. I don't like it.'

'Damn you! Fletch, I'm sick of your belly-aching! We have the girl. She'll be dead and buried soon. We'll be in the clear.'

'He has a point, though, Jeb,' Mangler opined, uneasiness in his tone. 'Pedro wouldn't have gone off without getting his money first, not him! Somebody's taken him, same ones as beat us earlier, I reckon. And now they're after us, and it's not the peelers.'

'I'll do the thinking, Mangler,' the man called Jeb snarled. 'You just take orders as usual.'

There was an uneasy silence after that and the carriage rolled on. Bronwen could not gauge how long it was before the pace slowed and they stopped.

'Slasher! What's the hold-up? I've not ordered a stop.'

'It's the horses, Mr Crabbe,' another man said from outside the carriage window. 'They can't keep up this pace. We'll need to change them. There's a coaching inn about half a mile up the road. We can change them there.'

'It's not safe to stop, Jeb,' Mangler cautioned. 'They could be right behind us.'

'There's no one behind us, you fool!' Jeb Crabbe stormed. 'Slasher's right. We can't take a chance on lame horses. Sir Fletcher and I will stretch our legs. Mangler, you remain with the girl. She might wake and bolt.'

Mangler chuckled. 'I've tied her wrists and ankles. She's not going anywhere.'

The carriage moved on for a time and then came to another stop. Someone grabbed a handful of her hair and lifted her face. Bronwen kept her neck limp and her eyes shut. Someone grunted with satisfaction and released her.

The carriage tilted slightly as two of the men stepped down, and after a while a third left, which she guessed was Mangler. Only then did she open her eyes. It was dark but she could see moonlight through the carriage window although little else. The rumble of men's voices came to her at a distance and the occasional laugh of a woman, and she realised the carriage stood outside an inn. If only she could raise the alarm. She stretched her legs experimentally and tried to rise up but rough ropes restricted movement. She was helpless.

Should she call out, cry for help? She could hear the jingle of harness, and horses' hooves clattering on the cobbles and knew the fourth man was nearby. Struggling not to give way to weakness, Bronwen decided she must bear the pain and discomfort; wait it out until an opportunity arose. The ropes must be removed at some time.

The men returned eventually. As they sat in the carriage with her, Bronwen could smell the aroma of food on their clothes, like onions and lamb stew, and suddenly, surprisingly, she felt hungry.

Then the carriage was on the move again. Amid the rattle of the wheels on the hard rutted surface of the road and steady murmur of men's voices, Bronwen, exhausted by all that had befallen her, dozed off into a fitful sleep.

She was woken when a man's hand gripped her shoulder roughly to shake her. For a moment she did not know where she was, only that she hurt in every fibre of her being.

'Come on! Get out,' Mangler snapped harshly.

'I'm ill!'

He laughed. 'Have patience. You'll soon feel nothing.'

The ropes were taken from her ankles but her wrists remained tied. Mangler dragged her unceremoniously from the carriage. Her legs were stiff and weakened, and she almost fell onto ground covered in gravel, but Mangler pulled her upright.

'No tricks or you'll get another cuffing.'

Dawn was breaking, the new light revealing a large house of handsome proportions, surrounded by lawns and trees. Mangler marched her towards the entrance.

Two other men joined them and Bronwen immediately recognised one as the visitor at the vicarage the year before who had given her half a sovereign. He was not a man easily forgotten.

'Where is this place?' she asked him in a trembling voice. 'Who lives here?'

'I own this mansion.' The other man spoke with obvious satisfaction. He was tall, fashionably dressed, but the effect was marred by his large paunch and his face which was bloated and mottled by drink and high living. 'Amongst other properties.'

'Who are you?' she asked him plaintively. 'Why have you abducted me?'

'I'm Sir Fletcher Watkins,' he said. 'Your uncle.' He laughed then as though it were a great joke, and gave a mocking bow. 'Welcome to Brynhyfryd House.'

'Did you say Brynhyfryd House?' Slasher Tonkin spoke up behind them, a strange wary pitch to his voice.

Jeb Crabbe rounded on him impatiently. 'Slasher, take the carriage and horse to the stables,' he said sharply. 'And then join us inside. We have an urgent undertaking.'

Slasher hesitated, staring from one man to the other.

'What're you waiting for, you dolt?' Jeb Crabbe shouted at him.

Slasher moved off slowly, leading the horse, but his backward glances at them were dark and moody. Bronwen watched him go with little hope. She desperately needed an ally, but the man who had beaten Big Jim so mercilessly would hardly be sympathetic to her plight.

Sir Fletcher took a large key from his coat pocket and opened the oak double doors and walked in followed by Jeb Crabbe, while Mangler pushed her forward in their wake.

'The servants?' Jeb Crabbe asked.

'The entire staff are at my house in Cardiff,' Sir Fletcher answered. 'With Alexis. I've dismissed the gardener here. We're completely alone.'

Inside Crabbe held her tightly by the shoulder while Mangler lit the wall-mounted gas mantles. Bronwen saw they were in a large well-appointed hall with a high domed ceiling. An enormous fireplace stood at one side, tall enough for a man to stand upright inside.

Above the mantelpiece was a portrait. As the gas light flared even brighter, she saw the painting represented the head and shoulders of a woman. She stared at it and gaped; for the woman bore remarkable resemblance to herself. It was like looking into a mirror. Had Jack Crow spoken the truth?

'Who is she?' Bronwen asked tentatively.

'That is Lady Sarah Watkins, my late sister-in-law and your mother,' Sir Fletcher said scornfully. 'You were born in this house.' He paused, guffawing loudly as though at some secret joke. 'And this is where you'll die.'

'But why?' Bronwen cried out. 'What have I ever done to you?'

Sir Fletcher scowled at her. 'Your father intended to deprive me of my inheritance, bring me to penury, and he paid for that slight with his life.'

'Have a care, Fletch,' Jeb Crabbe warned.

Sir Fletcher looked smug. 'She'll tell no one, Jeb.' He turned his glance on Bronwen. 'She'll never leave this house alive.'

'I don't believe a word of this,' Bronwen cried out. 'My mother is Nesta Jenkins.'

'She was your nursemaid,' Sir Fletcher said. 'Not many months after you were born she stole you away for ransom.'

'Silence!' Jeb Crabbe snarled. 'You have a dangerous mouth, you fat fool.'

'It doesn't matter, I tell you,' Sir Fletcher answered wrathfully. 'She dies within the hour. Indeed, why do we wait? The deed must be done now.'

'You're in such a hurry, Fletch,' Jeb Crabbe observed contemptuously. 'Perhaps you'd like to do the killing yourself? It's time you felt the power when thrusting the blade deep into warm living flesh.'

Sir Fletcher uttered a guttural sound of revulsion and his bloated face whitened. He turned and marched through a nearby doorway, muttering under his breath.

Crabbe followed him. 'She dies when I say so,' he said harshly. 'All of us must be present, all culpable, including Slasher. Then none of us can betray the others without betraying himself. That is our safeguard.'

With Mangler's hard fingers gripping her shoulder, Bronwen had no choice but to follow them and found herself in a large comfortable sitting room. She had never been in such a beautiful room, but she had no time to appreciate her opulent surroundings. The ropes were chafing her wrists painfully and she longed to sit and rest, but was made to stand near the fireplace. Desperately, her gaze darted about her looking for a way out, but escape was impossible under the gaze her three captors.

Sir Fletcher went immediately to a sideboard, opened the cupboard and took out a crystal decanter to pour himself a drink.

'A little early in the morning for that, isn't it, Fletch?' Jeb Crabbe taunted as he took a seat on a nearby sofa. 'Or are you searching for courage in the bottom of a glass as usual.'

'Damn you, Jeb. I take too much from you. You forget who I am.'

'And you forget who made you what you are,' Crabbe

barked back. He gave Sir Fletcher a hard look. 'Don't become a liability, Fletch, like your niece here. My Betsy takes no heed of class.' He paused, smiling narrowly. 'There could be two graves in the orchard by nightfall.'

Sir Fletcher looked startled and opened his mouth but before he could speak, Slasher Tonkin strode into the room. He stood in the doorway legs apart, a mountain of a man whose presence seemed to make the room smaller. He gazed at each man in turn, the dark expression still on his face.

'Is there another house by the same name in these parts?' he asked unexpectedly.

'You waste our time, you dim-witted cur,' Sir Fletcher bawled at him, rallying. 'Now stand there and wait like a dog while we discuss how this disposal shall be done.'

'What do you suggest, my fat friend?' Jeb Crabbe's tone was deceptively serene, but Bronwen saw an expression of anger in his hard face.

'I'm tired of your insults, Crabbe,' Sir Fletcher rasped. 'Especially before inferiors. I demand respect.'

'Then earn it!' Jeb Crabbe said. 'Know this! I tolerate you only because of your name and the money it attracts. Don't outlive your usefulness, Fletch.'

Mangler gave a mocking chuckle while Sir Fletcher spluttered incoherently, his slack mouth trembling, and Bronwen realised he was afraid of his companions.

Suddenly she knew a faint hope. If they quarrelled between themselves she might yet find a way to elude them. Perhaps she could sow doubt in their minds, set them against each other. But how?

'It's time,' Jeb Crabbe said. 'Bring the girl into the kitchen.'

Mangler yanked her forward, while Bronwen struggled to hold back.

'You won't get away with killing me,' she wailed in terror.

Sir Fletcher poured more liquor into his glass and threw it

into the back of his throat. 'It must not be done in the house,' he declared heavily. 'Killing my brother here was too risky.'

'You'd better let me go and run for your lives,' Bronwen cried out desperately. 'Black Jack Crow is after your blood.'

'Black Jack!' Jeb Crabbe leapt to his feet while Sir Fletcher was so startled he spilled his next drink. 'What's this girl?' Crabbe shouted. 'Black Jack? The cripple is long dead, he must be.'

'He was at Cwmrhyddin Cross with a band of men yester-day,' she said triumphantly. 'He spoke to me at the Marquis Arms.' She could tell by their faces she had stirred up appre-hension. 'He knows everything. He's out for revenge for what was done to him at your hands.'

'I warned you we might be followed,' Mangler snarled at Crabbe. 'Pedro's disappearance was no accident. Black Jack has him. He'll talk.'

'My God!' the cry came from Sir Fletcher. 'We must dispose of the girl immediately, and get back to our own haunts at Cardiff. No one can reach us there, not even the police.'

'You're right for once.' Jeb Crabbe nodded, his face thought-ful.

'Take her into the scrub ground beyond the gardens,' Sir Fletcher exclaimed hastily. 'Quickly! We have no time for burial. There's a deep ditch a mile or so along the road to Cardiff. She'll never be found there.'

'Is that where my brother's corpse lies?' Slasher exclaimed suddenly.

Unnoticed he had taken a stance before the doorway, looking speculatively from one man to another, while they stood in an electrifying silence. Jeb Crabbe was the first to recover.

'Slasher, what tomfoolery is this?' he asked harshly. 'We've no time to lose, man. The peelers may be on their way here.'

'Brynhyfryd House,' Slasher nodded. He seemed not to hear the words of warning. 'It all comes back to me now. My brother

Chippie visited this house some sixteen years ago and was never seen again, dead or alive.' He took a threatening step forward. 'What happened to my brother? One of you must know.'

Mangler released her shoulder to step closer to Jeb Crabbe, and Bronwen took the opportunity to edge away from the fireplace. She put her back against the wall and watched. A subtle change had come over the men and the atmosphere of the room, and her senses were alert for any advantage.

'Chippie was never here,' Crabbe said soothingly. 'You're mistaken.'

Slasher jabbed a finger at him. 'You're lying!' He looked around at them fiercely. 'Chippie told me why he was coming to Brynhyfryd House that night, but never mentioned the name of the man who sent him.'

'Then you have no quarrel with any of us, Slasher,' Crabbe said mildly.

Slasher turned blazing eyes on him. 'Don't take me for a lamebrain, Crabbe! Chippie told me he didn't trust the cove and wanted me to go along too, but I refused. May God forgive me!' The muscles in his bull-like neck began to swell as he took a step towards Jebediah. 'I never knew who to take my revenge on until this very morning when I heard the name Brynhyfryd House from your own lips, Crabbe. He must have been on *your* business so which one of your lackeys killed him?'

'None of us know what you're talking about,' Jeb Crabbe said harshly. 'Have you taken leave of your senses, man? Perhaps you've fought your last fight.'

Slasher's expression turned ugly and more menacing. 'I'll have the truth at last, damn me if I don't. No one leaves this house, peelers or no peelers, until I know what happened to Chippie.'

'But we can't stay here much longer,' Sir Fletcher exclaimed in a frightened voice. 'It was Tecwyn Watkins who killed your brother, the night he came for the ransom. Tecwyn told me so himself!'

Mangler guffawed, nervously, Bronwen thought, and Slasher must have thought the same for with an angry growl, he took a step towards him.

'This is no laughing matter, Mangler,' he snarled. 'I'll have my mitts on the man who killed Chippie now, or I'll take you all on and smash you. Now, which one of you is it?'

Mangler's gaze flickered towards Sir Fletcher, who whimpered and took a step back. Slasher was on him in a moment.

'It was you, you drunken swine,' Slasher bellowed, lunging forward to take him by the throat. 'I'll kill you!'

Sir Fletcher, making choking, gurgling sounds, fell backwards onto a sofa, his legs thrashing about, with Slasher on top of him, yelling wildly. Jeb Crabbe and Mangler dashed forward attempting to pull the fighter off, but in his rage, the man appeared to have the strength of ten.

No one was paying attention to her in the uproar. As quickly as her stiff legs would allow, Bronwen moved to the corner of the room nearest the door, struggling to loosen the rope around her wrists, but they were bound too tight.

'Hold your hand, Slasher,' Jeb Crabbe shouted urgently. 'Don't kill the golden goose, yet. We must keep him alive or his lawyer will betray us.' Bronwen thought she heard a touch of panic in his voice. 'Besides,' he went on coaxingly, 'there's more money to be had, and you can have your brother's share.'

'What do I care about that?' Slasher bellowed. 'He took my brother's life. I'll take his!'

She eyed the struggling men warily to see if they had noticed her movement, but they were too busy attempting to restrain a maddened Slasher Tonkin.

This was her chance. With her heart thumping in her breast, Bronwen darted through the open door into the hall. Hesitating only a moment she ran to the front door, and awkwardly grasped the knob with her tied hands, pulling desperately, but the door was locked.

Sounds of the struggle were still heard in the sitting room, but within seconds Jeb Crabbe or Mangler must notice she was gone. She glanced up the wide sweeping staircase. It was no good hiding in the house; she would be found almost instantly. She must get out into the open if she would avoid them.

Panic and dread almost choking her, she ran to the back of the hall, through a door and down a long dark passage. All at once she found herself in a huge kitchen, and stared around wildly, conscious of the precious seconds ticking away.

Running to the back door, she almost cried out in relief to see the key was in the lock. It was difficult to turn it with bound wrists and hands that trembled almost uncontrollably, but she managed it and suddenly was outside.

A wide cobbled yard surrounded by a high stone wall was before her, with outhouses and stables, but they held no sanctuary. She ran the length of the yard and saw a gate standing open. She was through it in a moment and lurched along a stone path through a shrubbery, soon to find herself in a garden with wide lawns, flower beds and low hedges.

Bronwen stood for a moment, staring around her desperately. The sun had risen above the horizon and was sending beams of sunlight through tall trees on her left.

Where there was a line of trees, she reasoned, there might be a track or lane, and so she ran towards them, dashing across lawns and flowerbeds unheedingly. As she reached the trees she heard them behind her; men's voices, raised in fury. They were after her! Her time had run out!

Bronwen stumbled through the closely-planted trees, sobbing in terror, not knowing which way to turn. There was no lane, no track, just open scrubland and undergrowth. She plunged on, skirts catching and tearing on the brambles, barely able to keep her balance with her hands tied.

The shouts and curses grew ever nearer. She could not outrun them in the circumstances. She must hide. Bronwen looked around frantically. Ahead of her was a thick gorse bush with clumps of ragged grass at its base. Enduring scratches to face and arms, Bronwen scrambled underneath, and lay still, holding her breath.

She had not been a moment too soon in seeking shelter for almost immediately the men were crashing around her, shouting to each other, cursing and thrashing about the undergrowth. Bronwen closed her eyes tightly and prayed.

Abruptly, the men were silent, and she held her breath afraid to hope that they had moved away. And then to her dismay and terror she felt a man's hand grasp her upper arm, and straight away she was roughly dragged out from under the bush.

'Here she is!' Mangler shouted triumphantly, holding her tightly by both shoulders, to swing her around to face Jeb Crabbe and Slasher Tonkin. She wondered vaguely whether Sir Fletcher was dead, but then he came panting to join them, red in the face and sweating profusely.

'Kill her now!' he croaked, staggering to Crabbe's side. 'Before she escapes again, the cunning little jade.'

'I had hoped you were dead yourself, Uncle!' Bronwen shrieked at him. 'You murderer!'

'Silence!' Jeb Crabbe's face was livid with rage as he looked at her. 'You've led us a pretty dance and no mistake,' he said grimly. 'But that's over.' He stared at her, his lip curling in callous humour. 'How convenient to find you here where a human foot rarely steps. This'll be your eternal resting place, my beauty.'

'Less talk!' Sir Fletcher cried out hysterically. 'Kill her!'

Jeb Crabbe lifted his cane and withdrew the rapier from its scabbard.

'Bring her nearer to me, Mangler,' he said, a cold smile stretching his mouth. 'Betsy here is eager for her soft neck.'

With a laugh Mangler dragged her closer, and Jeb Crabbe raised the rapier above his shoulder.

Sunlight glinted along the length of the steel blade aimed at her throat, and Bronwen could not take her mesmerised gaze from it. All coherent thought was wiped from her mind at that instant. Nothing else existed but that blade, and as it descended towards her, she opened her mouth and let out a scream of sheer terror.

32

The sun broke clear of the horizon as Jack Crow's carriage rattled and jolted along the dry rutted track and he hung on to the side for dear life, his twisted, rheumy body wracked with pain. But he bore no heed of it, his mind intent on what must be done.

'I pray to God that we're in time,' he muttered to his companion, Big Jim Jenkins, hardly in better health than himself after the horrendous journey they had endured from Cwmrhyddin Cross. 'If anything happens to the child I'll never forgive myself.'

'And I'll kill any man who harms my daughter,' Big Jim said grimly. 'Bronwen is not of my blood, but I'm her father all right.'

'Hey, the carriage!' the cry came from outside, and Tom Barrett came alongside on horseback keeping pace with them, bending down in the saddle to speak through the carriage window. 'The gates to the Watkins estate are just ahead, Mr Crow,' he shouted. 'What are your instructions?'

'Ride straight through,' Jack shouted back. 'Let the front riders gain entry to the house if possible, by any means. Each man to keep his weapon at the ready. But hasten!'

Tom Barrett rode off at speed to take his place as leader of the band of vigilantes.

'Is she still alive, Mr Crow?' Big Jim's voice quivered as he spoke. 'As God is in his heaven, I'll die myself if they've murdered my daughter, too.'

Jack did not answer. He dared not, for reason suggested that Jeb Crabbe would not wait too long to bury his guilty secret.

The girl might be dead, indeed, but he felt sure they would still be in time to capture Crabbe and his men. He would see them all swing yet.

Then the carriage was being driven at full speed through the stone gates of Brynhyfryd House and up the long drive to the house about a quarter of a mile distant. When they reached the front entrance, Jack Crow climbed down with difficulty onto the gravel driveway. His men were already dismounted, some attempting to force the stout oak doors, others trying to open windows.

'Have they gone?' Big Jim asked in a voice full of dread. 'Are we too late?'

Tom Barrett came running up as they stood helplessly outside the doors. 'At the back, Mr Crabbe, quickly!' he called, beckoning them. 'Towards the stables. I heard men's voices. They're somewhere in the grounds.'

'Don't wait for me,' Jack urged. 'All of you get after them! But quietly. We must take them by surprise.'

A dozen or so men ran towards the side of the house following in Tom Barrett's steps, Nate Bowen and Big Jim with them, while Jack had to go at a slower pace, hampered by his crooked legs.

He hobbled across the stable yard as fast as he could, while his men raced ahead through shrubbery and the gardens beyond. Reaching that point, he took a pause for a moment to catch his breath. Then the sound of men's voices raised in anger came to him from a small copse in the far left. His men heard it too, for they swerved in that direction. Far ahead of the others, Tom Barrett with Ben Talbot at his side was already running through the trees.

Suddenly, a blood-curdling scream rang out on the still morning air, and stopped in his tracks at the terror in it, Jack almost fell to his knees. He was too late.

*   *   *

Screaming in mindless terror at the sight of the descending blade, Bronwen was suddenly aware of another sound ringing in her ears, a short sharp report of a firearm being discharged. The deadly blade was suddenly hurled from Jeb Crabbe's grasp, and he staggered back, shrieking and clutching at his bloodied hand.

Relief draining her body of strength, Bronwen collapsed onto her knees amid the thistles and coarse grasses. Around her new voices were shouting and more warning shots were fired. Men were scuffling about, cursing and shouting. Oh Thank Heavens! Da and Lloyd had come to save her.

'Bronwen!' Someone called her name anxiously. 'Bronwen, my darling! Are you all right. Have they hurt you?'

Someone's hands helped her to her feet, released her wrists from the ropes, and strong arms enclosed her in a protecting grasp. Dazed, she gazed up into the face of Nate Bowen, feeling astonished and bewildered. Why wasn't Lloyd, her sweetheart, here holding her instead of Nate Bowen?

The next moment Da was reaching out for her, and releasing herself from Nate's embrace, she turned thankfully to be clasped in her father's arms.

'Oh, Da! I'm so glad to see you,' she cried hugging him, pressing her face against his broad chest. 'I thought I'd never see you and Mam again.'

'Bronwen, *cariad*, thank God you're alive,' Big Jim said, with a sob.

At that moment, from the corner of her eye, Bronwen saw Mangler Harris rush towards them, about to strike at Big Jim's head with a wooden club. Before she could cry out a warning, Mangler himself was knocked off his feet and Bronwen saw Slasher Tonkin standing over him, kicking him as he crouched on the ground.

'You killed my brother, you scurvy dog!' Slasher shouted in fury, waving his great fists. 'I'll kill you with my bare hands.'

'No!' Mangler screamed, trying to protect himself from Slasher's boots. 'It was him!' He pointed at Sir Fletcher now cowering back as Jack Crow and his men surrounded him and Jeb Crabbe, laying hands on them.

Before anyone could stop him Slasher lunged at Sir Fletcher, grasping him by the throat, attempting to throttle him at he stood. It took several men to haul him off.

'Don't dirty your hands further,' Black Jack said to Slasher disdainfully. 'It's the rope for him and you.'

'I'll gladly swing for him,' Slasher growled. 'But I've killed no one else, mister.'

'You helped abduct the girl, and you'll answer for that,' Jack Crow told him harshly.

Jeb Crabbe, cursing and shouting, was restrained with ropes to his wrists, as was Sir Fletcher, now whimpering like a child. Mangler was hauled to his feet, his hands tied behind his back like the others.

'He tried to kill me, Da,' Bronwen cried out, pointing her shaking finger at her tormentor.

'You're safe,' Nate said gently, standing nearby. 'There's nothing to fear now, my dear.'

'It's not over yet,' Jeb Crabbe snarled struggling savagely in his bonds, and Bronwen drew back a step behind her father's shoulder, still afraid of Jeb Crabbe. 'You're all trespassing on private property,' he roared. 'Sir Fletcher will have the law on you all.'

'Silence, you murdering cur!' Black Jack Crow shouted at him and went to stand before him. 'You and Watkins are finished, Crabbe, one way or another,' he said menacingly. 'We could string you up here and now and no one would be the wiser. It's what you deserve.'

Mangler merely grunted at the threat, but Sir Fletcher began to moan in terror. Jeb Crabbe glowered in silence, yet Bronwen saw real fear in his eyes at that moment.

'But I be no fool,' Jack Crow went on. 'I be a wealthy man thanks to Miss Nesta, and don't intend to throttle for the likes of you, Jeb Crabbe.'

Jeb Crabbe turned his head and spat on the ground. 'You can prove nothing against me, Crow.'

'I won't need to prove anything,' Jack Crow said. 'Your cronies would gladly betray you to save their own necks from the rope.'

Jeb Crabbe turned apprehensive glances on his fellow prisoners, and said nothing more.

'I've waited sixteen years for this day,' Jack Crow went on. 'Do you remember Fat Lil and the beating you gave her? She died shortly after. You killed her as sure as if you had plunged that rapier into her heart. You killed Miss Nesta, too. You'll pay for these deaths, Crabbe, and I'm pleased to be the one to bring you to justice. My men will take you all to the magistrates in Cardiff immediately.'

Bronwen clutched at Big Jim's arm. 'What does he mean, Da? Where's my Mam? What's happened to her.'

'Oh, Bron, *cariad*,' Big Jim sobbed. 'You must be brave. Your Mam is dead.'

'No!' Bronwen screamed. 'It can't be true. There's been a mistake. Mam's in Llanelly.'

'No, *bach*.' Big Jim shook his head sorrowfully. 'Her body was found in Penllegaer Woods the day before yesterday.'

'How did she die?' Bronwen trembled to ask, for in her heart she knew. The image of that blade sweeping through the morning air, aimed at her throat was still vivid in her mind's eye. She would never forget it. 'Did *he* kill Mam as he would have killed me?'

Big Jim's face crumpled and it was obvious he was too distraught to speak.

'Oh, Da!' Bronwen cried out in despair. 'How will we live without Mam? I can't bear it!' She felt her knees weaken in shock and almost sank to the ground again, but Big Jim clasped her to him, supporting her.

'It must have been very quick, Bronwen,' Nate Bowen said gently. 'She didn't suffer, my dear.'

Bronwen was hardly aware of him or what was happening around her. Her beloved Mam was dead! She couldn't take it in. She stared across at Jeb Crabbe now being led away. That evil man and his cohorts had destroyed her warm comfortable familiar existence and almost destroyed her family. She prayed his soul would burn in Hell for eternity.

In tears, she clung to Big Jim. 'I want to go home, Da.'

Jack Crow drew near. 'Not yet, my child. Take her to the house, doctor,' he instructed. 'Although we've caught the murdering swines, there be much to discuss. Miss Blanche must know her proper place.'

Someone lifted her up into his arms and started carrying her back to the house. Bronwen was in a stupor, hardly aware of her companions or surroundings.

'Da?'

'No, it's Nate, Bronwen. Don't fret. I'll take care of you.'

'Da? Where's my Da?' Suddenly she was fearful of losing her father, too.

'It's all right, Bron, *cariad*. I'm here too.'

Nate Bowen carried her into the sitting-room from which she had so recently escaped and placed her on a sofa. Someone put a glass to her lips and Bronwen almost choked on the brandy it contained.

'That's enough,' she heard Nate Bowen say.

A bowl of water was brought and he bathed the cuts and scratches on her face and arms. After the cool water on her face, she felt calmer and began to take an interest in what was happening.

She saw with dismay that her skirts were filthy and in tatters and her hair a tangled mess. Bemused, she looked around at her rescuers. Ben Talbot, her father's employer, stood near the mantelpiece talking to Bleddyn Williams.

'Where's Lloyd?' she asked. 'Was it he who raised the alarm?'

In the silence that followed her question she was aware of a worried expression on Big Jim's features, and saw a dull flush suffuse Nate Bowen's face and neck. And then Ben Talbot gave a cough of embarrassment.

'Just before we rode after you we heard the young fool had run off with Cassie Probert,' he said, looking at her warily. 'Gone to Gretna Green, according to the note she left for her mother. I'm sorry, Bron.'

Bleddyn Williams gave a scornful laugh. 'Not that it'll do him any good. Dorah's money is gone; wagered away by that fool husband of hers. He'll be defrocked for certain and then Dorah will be homeless.' He gave another guffaw. 'It's true what they say – pride goeth before a fall.'

Bronwen hardly heard him, her mind elsewhere. Lloyd had betrayed her yet again. After all that she had been through in the last twenty-four hours, his duplicity seemed trivial. She realised then that he meant nothing to her.

'Lloyd knew I'd been taken,' she told them all. 'But he ran away like a coward. He's not the man I thought he was. He and Cassie deserve each other. She'll be the bane of his life.'

She looked at Nate Bowen, noting the worry and concern for her in his blue eyes, and realised she was seeing him properly for the very first time. Her eyes opened wide as she saw something else there, something that made her heart beat faster. She looked away, flushing.

'Well, Miss Blanche Sarah Watkins,' Jack Crow interrupted her confusion. 'You're returned to your home and fortune at long last.' He was sitting on a sofa opposite her, watching her with keen interest. 'You must engage a lawyer straight away.'

'What for?'

Jack Crow waved a hand around. 'This be your property, Miss Blanche, this and much more. The inheritance left to you by your father, Sir Tecwyn Watkins, which your uncle stole, must be placed into your hands at the earliest time.' He chuckled. 'You be a very wealthy young woman.'

Bronwen stared at him bemused. 'I'm rich?'

'Indeed you are, Miss Blanche.'

Nate Bowen rose silently from where he had been kneeling at her side while attending her, and moved away. Bronwen glanced at him in surprise as he went to stand at the mantelpiece, his back turned to her. There was stiffness in his shoulders as though he were angry, and she felt a stab of disappointment.

'My name is Bronwen Jenkins,' she said firmly. 'I don't want the money. It has blood on it.'

'No, no.' Jack Crow peered up at her from under his brows. 'Your father, Sir Tecwyn, was a mine owner, a worthy and decent man. His wealth was honestly got. There be no shame attached to it.'

Bronwen pressed her hands to her breasts. 'Mr Crow, I know you mean well, and I thank you for helping to save my life, but the man of whom you speak, Sir Tecwyn, means nothing to me.' She shook her head. 'I don't remember him, not even as a shadow.'

She reached out a hand to Big Jim and he came forward eagerly to grasp it. 'Here's my one and only father,' she said, a sob in her throat as she looked at his battered face. 'Big Jim Jenkins, the courageous prize-fighter, and I'm not ashamed of him.'

'Oh, Bron, *bach*!'

'I love you, Da, and no one can take your place.' Bronwen brushed at a tear as it ran down her cheek. 'And my beloved mother was Nesta Jenkins and no one else.' She shook her head as she gazed at Jack Crow. 'My home and family at Cwmrhyddin Cross are all I want.'

'I understand, child,' Jack Crow said softly. 'But think of the good you could do with the wealth.' He twisted his head to glance at Big Jim. 'Do you want your father to spend the rest of his life wanting for a crust, because the doctor here says Big Jim may never work again? And what of other members of your family?'

'My family?'

Bronwen was suddenly sorrowful, thinking of Nesta who had worked so hard for them all her life, and now when she might have helped her it was too late; her beloved mother was gone.

She thought of her grandparents and what they were going through at this moment; the grief they must feel at the loss of their daughter. Enoch and Meg Lewis had known poverty all their lives. She could bring them comfort in their latter years.

And Jimmy, her brother. A gentleman's education would stand him in good stead later in life. Perhaps Jimmy would be a lawyer or even a doctor.

And there was Da, her beloved Da.

She glanced across at Nate Bowen. He was looking at her with pain and sorrow in his eyes. She guessed the reason. She was now rich and therefore beyond his reach. He was a good man too, and seeing him in this situation, she knew he was a man of integrity, and she could trust him.

'I'm wondering,' she began. 'After I help my family, would there be enough to provide a hospice for the poor and sick?' The idea appealed to her greatly all of a sudden. 'I could build it in Swansea,' she went on eagerly, giving Nate a tentative smile. 'Perhaps Dr Bowen – Nate, could help me with it?'

He came forward. 'Bronwen, I'll do anything for you. Just name it.'

She held out her hand to him and he took it into his own. 'I want you to be my adviser, Nate,' she said shyly. 'If you will.'

'Gladly!'

She looked around at each of her rescuers in turn. 'Simple thanks for my life doesn't seem enough,' she said. 'But I can do some good now for many people, and I will.' She smiled up at Big Jim. 'I'll build a hospice in memory of my beloved mother, Nesta Jenkins. Good can come out of evil.'

She looked at Nate, still holding her hand. He met her gaze and smiled. Amid the great grief in her heart for Nesta, something else was suddenly born, something new and wonderful. She saw a reflection of it in Nate's eyes and knew beyond a shadow of a doubt that true happiness lay ahead for them both.